Butterflies

Sally Oldman

Contents

Chapter One

—'As a writer you try to listen to what others aren't saying...and write about the silence.'~ N.R Hart ~ ——

Family Reunion ~~ Isabelle

"Izzy!" I jump backwards a step and stumble over my feet, groaning as my luggage follows me towards the floor. My butt stings for a few seconds after the initial fall making my nose scrunch up towards my forehead in discomfort. "Oh my gosh I didn't mean to scare you." My mom laughs, extending her arm out to help me. After letting my butt recover, I take it.

She pulls me into a hug instantly. "How was your flight?" She mumbles against our hug. "Boring." I was sat in between a dad and a mom while they kept switching their baby back and forth over me. I decided not to be picky with my seating, speaking for the fact that I have no money and the last of it was on my flight. Even though my parents offered to pay for it, I would never let them do that.

Once we pull away from our hug, my mom's arm wraps around my shoulder as we begin our journey towards the exit door to the airport. To be honest I slept most of the flight and was only conscious the one time that their baby 'spit up' and I finally just switched seats with the dad.

I can be a projectile vomiter at times.

The minute we step out of the airport, the hot muggy Florida air hits me in the face, making me blink violently against the sun. At the same time though it gives me waves of nostalgia.

Sadly though, my shorts and sweatshirt are doing nothing to prevent sweat to drip down my skin instantly. "Right over here." I make a strangled noise when I see the same car that my parents apparently still own.

"No." I moan in pain. There's no way this thing still runs. This car doesn't even have air conditioning.

My mom laughs at what she thinks is me joking. This is not a joke. Abort mission. My brains screams for help don't register my body's movement because I'm still following my mom's arm towards her car. Her blue Volkswagen.

"How is this thing even still running?" I ask, actually curious of the answer. She stops mid movement, spinning around on the heels of her feet. Her eyes narrow when she sees my serious face. "This is my favorite car. You will not be mean to her." She pats the windshield with her palm, before circling the front and getting into the drivers seat. I laugh quietly to myself while filling my luggage into her tiny trunk.

To be honest this car is pretty cool. Over my dead body would I ever admit that to her.

I hop into the passenger seat beside her, the windows down, and she takes off towards the house.

I get nervous, like a jittery feeling bouncing in my stomach, fluttering through my toes and fingers. I let my head hang out the window as I feel the salty humid air against my hair, and smell the beach. This is definitely home.

Wow I'm home. I make a squealing sound, and don't even acknowledge my mom's confused look. I just can't get this stupid happy smile off my face. I feel the wind slow as we pull into our driveway, making me disappointed the ride is over, but thrilled that I'm at my home now.

"Isabelle!!" I'm bombarded by my dad as soon as I step foot outside of the car, knocking the wind out of me. I put my arms around his neck and squeeze the life out of him. "Gosh I missed you dad. FaceTime is just not the same." I groan, causing him to chuckle.

He pulls away and takes a good look at me. "Look at you getting old." He shakes his head, and scratches his slight beard. Which for the record is definitely gray. "I'm 17 dad," I laugh mocking his stance. "Your the one with the gray hair." He touches his hand to his head and gasps. "Don't criticize my hair." I lean over laughing at my dads playful tone. I think I missed my dad more than anything. "Seriously though, I'm really glad you're back." He smiles, creating wrinkles below his eyes.

"Oh my gosh, you have wrinkles." His smile drops and his finger lifts in the air to point at me. "Be carful what you say Izzy." He warns causing me to smile. "I love you dad." He softens, and pulls me back into a hug. "I love you too honey." We share a meaningful moment before my mom bust it. "You need to get your stuff Isabelle." I pull apart from my dad. "Uh oh, she used your full name. You didn't insult her car by chance did you?" He winces when I nod slowly.

"I can hear you guys!" My mom screams. We both burst out laughing, walking towards her trunk to grab my stuff. "We're just kidding mom!" I yell back to her. She stands in the doorway, with her hands on her hips.

"Hey, where's Luna?" I ask my dad, grabbing my suitcase as he grabs another one. Luna's my sister that's 12 years old, and a spitting image of me. We never really got to bond before I left at the ripe age of 15. She was only 9 at the time. I was hitting puberty, and she was into coloring books.

Then everything went down, and suddenly I was gone. What a change of events. My dad hesitated before answering my question making me even more curious for the answer. "She didn't want to see you." He mutters lowly. My smile falters as does my stepping. "Why?" I whisper back sadly. He sighs, and rubs his forehead to smooth out the crease that's formed.

"She was only 9 when you left, and she looked up to you. You were her roll model. She'll just take some time to get used to you being back. Don't worry sweetie, she'll come around eventually." He smiles, but I can tell it's through a lie. He's just trying to make me feel better. Good thing I'm the most determined person you will find to make things right with people.

I sigh when I feel the cool AC hit my face lightly, making me stand in place to enjoy it. My dad continues up the stairs, I'm guessing to place my stuff in my room. After I cool off, I follow after him and walk into my room. It looks exactly the same as it did when I was here before.

"You guys literally changed nothing." I gasp. My walls are still light green, there are still Harry Styles, and Taylor Swift posters on my walls. I still have stickers around my mirror, and my candles that I was obsessed with on my desk.

I do notice new stuff too. There are plants now in front of my big open window. There's sun beaming in to keep the plants living too. I have a new comforter on a queen bed instead of a twin that sits against the right wall in the middle of my room. My desk is across from my bed, and then my dresser is in my closet which is to the left of my desk.

My bathroom is to my left on the same wall as the door, and straight ahead of me I see my huge window that has always been my favorite. "Me and your mom upgraded it a little bit, but what do you think?" He bounces on his feet waiting for my response. "Dad, I love it. You guys did a wonderful job." I gush, wanting to cry at how perfect it is.

"I'm glad you like it. Now do what you need. Shower, sleep, whatever but I'm gonna start making dinner downstairs." I nod still staring at my room, as he passes me in the doorframe and walks down the stairs. I have hardwood in my room, but the new fluffy carpet they have in here is freaking worth it.

Most of my bags--3 to be exact--are sitting on my bed, and my one big suitcase is laying on the floor at the foot of my bed. I have a decently sized room, and everything fits perfectly in it. My cheeks start to hurt from how hard I've been smiling all day.

I close my bathroom door and strip out of my clothes to take a shower. I need to get the baby stench off of me from the plane and all of this straight sweat that is sticking to me. I turn the shower on, and don't wait for it to heat up before I step in and sigh into the water.

I don't take long to wash my hair or body, and once my amazing shower comes to an end I switch the water off, and wrap a fluffy white towel around my body. I trudge back into my room, feeling wind brush my wet hair out of my face. When I look over at my window I see it cracked open.

I sit on the edge of my bed, and swing my legs letting my feet hover over the ground. My comforter is soft and fluffy, making me want to just sink into it, and forget about all bodily problems ever.

Like the problem that I've shoved into the back of my head. The tiny tiny bit of information my parents gave me about Milo still being next door. I don't know why I was surprised to hear this news. It's not like I was gone for an eternity, although it sure feels like I was.

My old best friend that 3 years ago I couldn't imagine going a day without seeing. I know this problem of seeing him is going to resurface sooner or later.

What will happen when I see him? Will be act like nothing every changed between us? Will he hate me for leaving without a goodbye? Will be not even acknowledge my existence? So many unanswered questions that I can definitely keep in the back of my head for now.

At this very moment in time, my only worry is how I'm going to sleep with all these bags on my bed.

——

I hear thunderous footsteps pounding up the stairs, waking me up from my nap. Rolling over onto my other side, I glance at the door to see it cracked open. Well it's cracked open for a second before it's being slammed open, and two bodies are jumping on me.

I make a sound that's between a huff of air leaving me, and a groan. "Your finally here!" A voice says. A voice I recognize to be Lottie. "Oh my gosh, we are going to have so much fun this summer!" The other one, Violet, grips my face and squeezes it while I begin to yawn.

"This is super welcoming." I say sarcastically. Throughout the years all 3 of us have FaceTimed multiple times just like I did with everyone else, but even then it's just so nice to be able to see them besides through a screen.

"Can you guys move now?" They both roll off of me to my side, letting me get more air into my body. That was a brutal thing to wake up too. "We can't start talking about anything until the guys get here, they should be coming soon." Violet says, looking over at me.

Once we're all sitting up, we finally share a nice, warming hug. One where I'm not suffocating and I'm smiling like an idiot. Again.

"Lottie has big news." She grins pulling apart, and I follow. If Lotties got big news, it's big. "It's not that big." She whispers while a blush creeps up her neck. Oh, this is gonna be good. "Her and Henry are finally dating."

Violet squeals, throwing her hands in the air. "Like I said, it's not that big of a deal." Lottie is now in a full blown blush.

"Aw, no way! I've been waiting forever! You guys couldn't wait a little longer until I got back?" I joke. She smiles sheepishly and shrugs. "I'm kidding Lottie, this is awesome. I'm really happy for you." She smiles and thanks me softly. Violet on the other hand is typing away at her phone.

They both look almost the exact same as before I left except for the fact that Lottie no longer has glasses and Violet no longer has braces. Violet has dark brown hair that's super long, reaching her belly button with eyes that are hazel. She's also got a taller, more model like boy frame.

Lottie on the other hand has a smaller more petite figure that still fits her body beautifully. She has long braids that cascade down her back like thread, with dark brown eyes that complete her light brown skin very nicely. All in all they are both gorgeous queens.

"They said they're on their way now." Violet explains, setting her phone down on my bed. I had moved all my bags to the ground with my suitcase so I could sleep. Who knows when I'm going to put all of that away. "So how has it been without me?" I ask with a grin.

"So boring." Violet jokes back. "Honestly though, it really was. None of us really talked that much when you were gone." Lottie says seriously. It makes me feel kinda bad that I ruined it all. We all fell apart because of me. I laugh along with them awkwardly though. Then I hear more footsteps coming up the stairs.

"Not again." I moan leaning my head back. The minute my door burst open two more bodies are thrown onto me. I huff out the air that they push out of me and pat their backs. "Hey guys, can't breath." They scramble off of me and stand at the foot of my bed.

"I want a hug first." Noah calls out opening his arms out to me. I laugh and get off the bed to meet him half way. He lifts me in the air and twirls me around prompting me to squeal. When he releases me I finally get a good look at him, and lets just say time did both of them well.

Noah still has his blonde hair that used to sag on his head but now it's fluffy and kinda looks like a cloud. I can't even tell what color his eyes are but they look to be a mix of blue and green. There actually really pretty. Then he has round Harry Potter glasses."It's really nice to see you again." Is all I get to say before Henry bombards me with a hug.

He still has the exact same look except for his more defined jaw. He has dark brown fluffy hair that reaches his ears and blue eyes. They look just like mine actually.

By the time I pull apart I'm already ready to ask the question. "Where's Milo?" They all go silent making me a little worried. Then they all start talking at once trying to make up an excuse for him. "Guys? You don't need to do that." The girls sigh while the guys just look around awkwardly.

"He's just not exactly ready to see you yet." Violet says giving me sad eyes, as does Lottie. They are the only ones besides my parents that know what really happened, and the real reason why I left in the first place. All our parents are close, so it was more or less inevitable. Of course they still gave me the choice of who I wanted to tell, I just felt more comfortable telling them. "That's ok." I smile and plop myself back onto my bed where everyone else follows.

"There's a beach party tonight. You guys wanna do that?" Lottie suggest changing the subject. Henry sits besides her and interlocks their fingers. "Sure why not." Violet says. The guys nod along, already on board with it. "Uh, I'm not sure." I finally say. "Look Izzy, you don't have to if you don't wanna, but I promise it's gonna be fun. We can just stay in and have one of our amazing sleepovers if that's what you want." I smile and nod my head.

"We can go to the party." Seeing their faces light up at my words makes my heart beat faster. I love making my friends happy. "You're sure?" Lottie asks. I nod my head. "Guys! Pizzas done!" My mom yells from downstairs. "Your dad made pizza?" Noah ask in disbelief. I shrug, about to say 'I guess' when everyone burst through my door and races down stairs.

My dad does make really good pizza.

~~~~~~~~~~~~~~~~~~~~~~~~~~~~~~~~

AN:First chapter done!
~~~~~~~~~~~~~~~~~~~~~~~~~~~~~~~~

Chapter Two

—'The villains will always be the villain if the hero tells the story.'~ K ~ ——

Beach Party~~Isabelle

We are all sitting down at the table eating pizza when I finally decide to ask my dad about the party. "So dad, there's this beach party tonight and I was wondering if I could go." I look up at him in question.

"Absolutely not."

"Of course." My parents say at the same time. My dad being the one who said yes. I look back and forth between them, very confused. My mom was never like this before. "Let us just have a minute." My mom holds up her finger, and shoves my dad into the other room.

The girls look at me confused, while the guys continue to scarf down their pizzas. "God Izzy, your dad makes the best pizzas." Noah groans, with a mouth full of food. I grimace, and shut my eyes. "Noah, talk after swallowing." I say, regretting my words the second they're out of my mouth.

"That's what she said." Violet burst, laughing like a 13 year old. "Hey, that's what I was gonna say." Henry whines, disappointed but also with a mouth full of food. I place my elbows on the table, and stuff my face into my hands shaking my head.

Lotties giggling from across the table, stuffing a napkin over Henry's mouth like that is going to get the image of his chewed up pizza out of my head. "Ok." My parents come walking back in, pausing for a second trying to figure out what's going on.

After a couple of seconds, they continue walking in and stand in front of the table. "Do I even want to know?" dad asks. I shake my head, and urge him to continue. "You can go." My dad says, and shrugs his shoulders like it's no big deal.

"But," My mom starts. "I want you home by 11, and if you need anything call me." She gives me a stern look, the mom look, and when I nod she nods and then she walks away. "11:30." My dad whispers, and follows behind her.

"Your dad is so chill." Noah says, as if he's daydreaming about my dad. "He just knows I'll do the right thing if needed." I say because it's the truth. I don't wanna do anything illegal, or that could get me in trouble. My dad trust me, and I trust him. It goes both ways.

"Ok well, what are we waiting for?" Violet gently throws her plate in the sink, then collects our plates and puts them away. She stands all jittery at the bottom of the stairs waiting for us. I roll my eyes, and start getting up with Lottie to follow. "Guys, wait in the car. Girls, upstairs." Is the last thing Violet says before she disappears up the stairs.

"That girl is crazy." I whisper to Lottie. She nods her head, and whispers back, "Imagine what the last 3 years were like for me." Let's all take a moment to pray for past Lottie. All jokes aside though, I really do love them both.

Lottie playfully lips the words 'traumatizing' as we enter my room, where Violet is going through my stuff. "What are you doing?" I know what she's doing, she's throwing my clothes everywhere which isn't even from my closet. She's going through my suitcase.

"Hey, no. I still have to put that away." I snatch the clothes she throws midair and try to shove them back in the suitcase but it's no use. "We gotta find you something to wear." She stresses and looks over at Lottie for help. "Is what I'm wearing right now not fine?" They both glance up at me slowly.

I'm wearing shorts and a t-shirt. "No." They say in unison. I look down at my fit and huff when I find nothing to say back. "Here, how about this?" Lottie ask nicely, pulling out one of my favorite crop tops. It's cute and doesn't show to much so I'm comfortable in it. It is skin tight though and I don't know how I feel about that at the moment.

I need to get used to the people here before I know what I can wear. As stupid as that sounds, it makes me feel better. "Um, ok, I'll wear this over it to." I smile, and pull out my favorite cardigan that I own. I take the clothes and walk into the bathroom, changing quickly and walking back out afterward.

"Damn Isabelle." Violet mutters and stands up from her knees. She has folded all my clothes in a pile on my floor. "Aw, you didn't have to do that." I gush. Then she blushes and waves me off. That reminds me that Violet blushes at attention and I laugh. God, she likes to act like she's all tuff and she is, but she has a total soft spot in the end.

"Ok, we ready? Henry's texted me about a million times." Lottie says, typing away at her phone. I nod my head, and so we're off. My parents are watching tv as I leave, and my mom doesn't fail to drill 11:00 into my brain. My dad on the other hand just waves me goodbye and gives me his farewells.

What a pair.

Us 3 girls squeeze into the back while the guys start to drive away from my home. "You guys took for-freaking-ever." Noah says, emphasizing the words 'for' and 'ever'. I roll my eyes and lean from the middle seat on my knees. "It was no longer than 10 minutes." I mutter, twirling a piece of my hair.

It's a habit I gained after I left Florida. A lot of stupid stuff happened after I left, stuff that I did not have any control over. We pull into a quiet parking lot, as the low drum of music reaches my ears. We must be parking further away, so that we're in a less crowded area.

We hop out, and the minute we do I can see lights shinning from the beach. My anxiety levels reach threw the ruff when we begin walking over towards it. People are supposed to run away from this stuff, not towards it. It's ok Isabelle, we're going to have fun. Right, fun.

A couple deep breaths later, and I feel exactly the same if not worse. We're still decently far when we hit the sand, but now I can see post buried in the ground that have pretty fairy lights connecting all of them. Beside each post is a cooler and keg. Where the heck do a bunch of teenagers get kegs?

"Come on, I'll introduce you to a couple more people." Violet smiles, and interlocks our fingers. I see Lottie and Henry slow down but I've lost complete sight of Noah. I'm not surprised when I see him chugging a solo cup of liquid.

"This is Jake, I'm sure your remember him." Jake is Lotties twin brother. "Oh my gosh Isabelle? You've grown up." I'm engulfed in a pair of chocolate arms that belong to Jake. At gatherings he would always hang out with all of us. I was never close to him like the others, but I still consider him a good friend.

"So have you. Your tall now." Tall is an understatement. I'm not very sure what genes he got, because he's gotta be the tallest in his family now. He pulls away from our hug and flexes his muscles. Very big muscles might I add. "And I got these baby's." I giggle when Violet hits him upside the head in a disapproving manner. She is such a mama bear.

"This is Anna, my girlfriend." Jake introduces, wrapping his arm around her shoulder and laying a big kiss on her cheek. "Hi Anna, it's nice to meet you." I respond with. She nods her head, and repeats the same back. I'm glad Jake found somebody. He always seemed so lonely when we were younger.

I stand awkwardly watching everyone talk when Violet taps on my shoulder. "I'm gonna go get myself a drink. You want anything?" I shake my head no politely, and so she walks away. Ok, now this is definitely embarrassing. "Ya know everyone talked about you." I turn around seeing Anna smiling at me.

She has gorgeous red hair, I notice, that only meets her collar bones. I bet it would be really bright in the sunlight. She has brown eyes though, which surprisingly complement her hair nicely. "Sorry, what?" I ask confused with an awkward smile. "I mean everyone missed you. Like I swear I know you so well through all the stories, but now your here. I'm happy to finally put a face to the name."

I know that she only meant that in a good way, but I can't help feeling guild wrap around my bones and tug. All I want to do is pretend that I never left, and I still know everyone but I don't, and that's not what happened. "Oh, I'm glad too then." I say with a smile.

"Anywho, I've got to get going." She looks down at her watch, and waves me goodbye as she begins to walk away. I wave back, but as soon as she's out of my vision I grow a little more anxious. I look around the crowd to try and see if I recognize anyone, but I come up with nothing.

Ok, well, this is fun. Rubbing the palms of my hands together I suck in a breath through my mouth and release a tense one. I spin around in circles, seeing all unknown faces everywhere. Maybe I shouldn't have come here. My breath grows unsteady as people pass me, heat radiating off their bodies. I think I might throw up.

I bee line for the way that we came from, trying to get out of the big crowd. Once I'm out of the line of fire, and walk down the road we parked on, I come upon the car.

My breathing is still erratic, so I place my head in between my knees and breathe what my therapist had taught me when the anxiety was bad. Once I feel as normal as I'll ever feel, I lean my head back on the Jeep, and stare straight into the stars. There's so many, and it's so beautiful. It calms me even more actually.

I startle when I hear shuffling. Getting to my feet, I brush my hands on the back of my cardigan, and turn to the car where the sound is coming from. There's thumping, and then a loud bang. Ok, what the heck is going on. I turn around from the back of the car and stand in front of the passenger door.

A screech leaves my lips as I immediately turn around, and cover my eyes. What the heck man. My first day back and I have to see that? There's a small yelp from the car, and then a girl half wearing a shirt comes stumbling out of the car. "I am so sorry, Milo said that no one would be coming all the way over here."

I feel bile rise in my throat when the man comes stumbling out. Milo Wesley was just banging a girl in the car I have to drive back home in. A strangled cry leaves my lips, and then I feel bad for embarrassing this poor girl so I clamp a hand over my mouth. "It's....fine. My friends just drove me here in this car." I say quietly, almost wishing that Milo couldn't hear me.

Milo stared at me through the darkness and it was obvious he had already put two and two together, but I didn't wanna believe it. I didn't wanna believe I just saw...gah, it's in my brain forever now. "Oh, um. You must know Milo. What's your name? I'm Ava." This girl, who seems to be sweet, and this guy, who I didn't know at all, were standing before me staring at me.

Milo looks mad, and this poor girl that I now know as Vic looks so embarrassed. Are they dating? Nope, no, this is not any of my business. "I'm," I gulp, dashing a glance towards Milo, then back to Ava

"I'm Isabelle."

——

I couldn't sleep at all last night. I lay in bed, and forced myself not to think about the night that had just occurred. That horrific event that I had to witness in the back seat of my friend's car. I could've totally avoided that If I just didn't freak out, and run away. Ugh, and now I'm cranky with things to do.

It's ok though, being negative will only make it worse. The first thing I do is get out of bed and crawl into the shower. The minute the water touches my hair, and my arms, I already feel better. I needed to wash my hair anyway, so I got that out of the way and then made sure to wash my face as well.

Once I was out of my shower, I slid a knee length dress over my body, and covered my legs in my vanilla lotion. When I checked the time on my phone it was 7:30, and when I looked outside there was a pretty sunrise expanding the sky.

My hair was still damp when I ran my fingers through it, and brushed out all of the nots. I made my way downstairs, just in time to see Luna sitting at the table with a bowl of cereal. She was scrolling through something on her phone peacefully, which made me feel bad that I might disturb her time at peace.

I took a deep breath, and began walking into the kitchen. My first question was why she was even up right now, because it's before 8am and she's 12. I guess she's an early bird like me.

I haven't seen her yet since I got in, and I start getting antsy when she doesn't look up at me. I clear my throat, and stand in front of the table she's sitting at. A big window behind her, and our pretty backyard in view.

She looks up at me, and her mouth falls open. "Hi." I say politely with a wave, and grab my own bowl, pouring lucky charms into it with the milk after. She keeps staring at me, no expression on her face. I sit down in front of her, and start eating my cereal. "So, it's been a while." I say, smiling. She doesn't smile back, making my confidence falter slightly.

"Um, well. How was school? 6th grade? I mean it was your first year of middle school, must have been–" She cuts me off by looking over my shoulder and speaking. "Mom, can you drive me to the beach? Milo's giving me lessons again this morning." She says. I choke on my cereal, spiraling myself into a coughing fit.

"Chew your food for christ sake Izz." My mom stresses from the kitchen. After my last cough, I clear my throat, and look up at Luna. She has a small grin on her face when I look at her, making me happy that I was dying for a couple seconds. "I don't think I'll have time honey. Why doesn't Isabelle drive you?" Now I smile wider, and Luna's drops.

"But why can't you just–" My mom scolds her, and she quiets. "So what is Milo teaching you?" I ask, swinging my legs under the table, and leaning my shoulders on the top while taking another bite of cereal. "To surf." She answers, not looking at me. I choke and sputter again. "Isabelle Mona!" My mom screams. "Sorry, mom. Big cereal chunks." I cough, then compose myself.

I look back up at Luna, and she has the same small grin on her face. "He's teaching you to surf?" I ask, trying to sound happy but feeling irritation peak in me. "Yeah. Why, jealous." She asks tauntingly, and sticks her tongue out at me. "No, why would I be jealous?" I say, now eating a full bite of cereal, making sure to chew slowly.

"Dunno, just a thought." She murmurs, typing something on her phone. I'm suddenly worried about what she's typing. Is she texting Milo? Is she warning him I'll be there? Ok, why would she be warning him. Wait, oh lordy what if she's telling him to hide so I don't see him. You're overthinking this. Of course, right.

I take a deep breath, and pour the rest of my milk into the sink, then wash my dish and put it on the drying rack. "Ok, so when do you wanna go?" I ask, leaning my hands on the sink, and facing her.

She shrugs, and gets up to only leave her bowl on the counter. I frown, and grab her bowl to wash. I stay in the kitchen for about 10 minutes after just doing dishes, and putting them away. I mean it's the least I can do. "Ok, let's go." She mutters walking out the door. If it weren't for the patted footsteps of hers I wouldn't have known she came down stairs. I grab the keys from the bowl at the front door, and follow her out to the Volkswagen parked in the driveway. My dad's truck is in the garage.

We began our short journey to the beach with all the windows down because it will get extremely hot if not. It's quiet, no music playing and extremely awkward. "So, do you have any friends?" I ask, trying to start a conversation. She huffs, and crosses her arms. "Of course I have friends." Ok, bad thing to ask. "I mean I know that. I didn't mean it in—"

"Then why'd you ask?" She says in a snarky tone. "Ok, well um, what do you guys do?" I try again. I think I am only making her more mad, but I'm really trying here. "Stuff." Is her answer. You'd think with non one word answered questions, you wouldn't be able to answer with one word. "What type of stuff?" I ask.

I try driving as slow as possible to prolong the car ride, so that maybe, just maybe I can get to know who she is now. "Look could you stop driving like a grandma now so we can hurry up. I don't want to keep Milo waiting." She says, looking over at me with a glare.

I nod my head, shooting her a smile and picking up the pace. We get to the beach within 5 minutes, and she's hopping out like I'm poison. "Call me when you want to be picked up!" I scream after her. She doesn't even turn around when she says, "Milo will drive me home." Of course Milo will.

I roll up the window, and watch her walk up to him. He smiles, actually smiles and I swear I can see a small sign of his dimples, but it's hard to see from here. They do a handshake, and then start walking over to where the surfboards are. My ex-best friend and ex-sister are now besties. What the heck am I supposed to do to win them both back? By the looks of it last night Milo didn't like me, and for sure did not want my presence.

He didn't smile, only glared at me the whole time, and that was if he looked at me. Then I went back home, and stared at my ceiling. This is going to be a lot harder than I thought.

Chapter Three

—'The trouble with fiction is that it makes to much sense. Reality never makes sense.'~ Unknown ~——

Mama Hazel's~~Isabelle

The next day started like the rest, and so the only thing I could do was move along and try not to think about my sister's new best friend.

It's Friday now, which doesn't really change anything, because I still have things to do after being in a slump mode yesterday and not wanting to do anything. I was also going to try and find some sorta summer job that will keep me occupied, and also because I'm broke, like broke broke and I need money.

So I've decided to fill my day with tasks for myself to keep my mind off of other things. I dress myself in a plain crop top with a long skirt, followed by my flat converse. My hair is down in it's natural style when I walk down stairs to leave.

My parents already said I could use their car, so I just said a quick bye to my dad and headed out. Both my parents work, it just so happens that my dad works from home so I get to see him more often. Even if he's just on work calls, it's nice to have his presence around.

He waves back to me, and so I grab the keys to the Wagon, and make my way outside. It's 8am, and yet the sun is warming my face to the max already. The wind's dead, and the nudity is livid. So much for coming here at the end of May.

The engine starts with a buffer, but nonetheless turns on. It's scorching inside, so I just decided to let it cool down, by keeping the windows down. I lean my butt on the door, and cross my arms over my chest as I take in my neighbors home. AKA Milo's house.

It's a light shade of yellow, like it always has been. Although it looks a little faded now that I really see it. I look at the side where there's still a mark across the window from when my shoe came off during a cartwheel and hit his house. I can't believe he never washed it.

A part of me wants him to walk out, just so I can see him again. I saw him for the first time the other night in years and he didn't even smile. I haven't been able to see his deep green eyes, or his black hair in the sun. I've only seen him from a distance, and it's sorta upsetting.

I want to get to know this new him. I want to know why he doesn't smile at anyone. I want to know what's going on in his brain like I used to. Wow Isabelle, real back to reality. I shake my head, and climb into the car, ignoring the burning seats.

I drive out of the driveway to the slow hum of the air passing by the window. I see kids walking dogs, kids playing, kids eating ice cream. Adults running, and walking. Everyone in their own individual world of bliss. The drive is short, but I soon make it to the local beach shop that has pear access, and a small cafe inside.

Well at least I hope it still does. I pull into the closet parking lot, and shut the car off. Sending a small wish that it will turn back on when I come back out. I clear my head of all the bad thoughts swarming it, and walk into the building.

The AC slaps me in the face, making me moan in happiness. It's too hot here, and I am loathing getting used to it. Let me just say, the Western weather is so much better than Florida. "Isabelle Everest?" My eyes open, wondering who in the world is calling my name when I see her.

Mama Hazel standing in the flesh. She doesn't look a day over 70. "Is it really you?" She moves her glasses to the top of her head and squints, forming wrinkles around her eyes. I nod my head, and she engulfs me in a hug. "I've missed you Mama Hazel." Her face softens as she pulls me into a hug, and I get her scent that I've never smelt anywhere else up my nose.

"So you're really back huh?" She quirks her eyebrow, chewing on a piece of gum. "Only for the summer." She seems to be disappointed by that, but doesn't say anything. "So, what brings you into the shop today?" She walks back around the counter, and drums her fingers on the table. "Uh, well I was kinda looking for a job." I laugh nervously, but all I notice is her face lighting up.

"Oh my, please work here! With that boy always in a grumpy mood, having you here will—" I don't mean to be rude and cut her off, but now I'm interested in who this guy is. "Wait, who else works here?" She waves her hand in the air, and scrunches up her face as if she's thinking really hard.

"Gosh, that boy never speaks, barely works either. It's on the tip of my tongue. M...Miso?" Oh lord help me please. "Milo?" I suggest. She looks over at me, her eyes holding questions. "Yeah, yeah that's it." She looks off out the front window and then back at me. "That man needs some light in his life." What if I'm the one that took it away though?

"I don't know...what would I do?" If Mama Hazel asks me one more time I might just give in. She can be a hard head, and stern when it comes to certain things, but she's also the sweetest old woman in the town of Hastings.

'Serve ice cream, take orders, make coffees. Whatever you want. Just please, or I'll call your mom." Even with her threat, I still hesitate. Do I really want to work with him, I mean I'll probably just make it worse. Then again, it would be a great way to spend time with him and get to know him. At least the new him. Another plus, it would be a way for me to try and get closer to Luna.

There are a lot of benefits for me here. "Ok, sure. When will I start?" Her eyes light up like fireworks at my words. "How about tomorrow? Morning?" I nod, slowly, still trying to wrap my head around the fact that I'll be working with Milo.

"So, what can I get for you today?" She says, now seeming so much happier now that I'm working for her. "How about whatever you consider your best pastry." She nods her head, and walks into the back room behind the swinging doors.

I take my time admiring Mama Hazel's work, all her desserts and sandwiches in the display box. It's all so pretty. I almost forgot how wonderful this place used to be. "Alright, here you go. Will that be all?" I grab the bag and start to grab my card out when her hand stops me. "Oh no, consider it a welcome back present."

"Oh, Mama Hazel, you don't have to do that." She shakes her head telling me she's not going to give in. Stubborn women. "So, how did you know Milo?" By the mischievous look in her eyes, it seems like she might know the answer to her question. I gulp. This lady can and always has been able to read me like an open book.

"We're neighbors." I say, shrugging. She nods her head slowly, jutting her chin outward. "Ok...well. It was nice to see you. Is there anything else in particular you need help with?" I think for a second. I do need new bikinis. "Do you know a place that sells good bikinis? She smiles, and rounds the corner.

I follow her to the back of the store where a door opens up, leading to the peer where there are multiple more stores. "See 2 shops down next to the ice cream place." I nod. "There." She pats my back and pushes me out the door. "See you later Mama Hazel." I waved goodbye to her, and began my next journey. "See you soon hun." I continue my walk, with a happy content smile on my face.

This day has totally flipped around to the good side.

———

I take it back, I take it back. Please let me take it back. I've walked a total of 10 steps, and I see a walking brunette, smiling at her phone. She's got a bag in her hand, and the exact same eye color as the girl from the other night.

Ava, she looks like Ava. I pause, begin the pivot on my feet when she looks up from her phone, and spots me. Oh no. She waves at me. Jesus help me. I wave back, and give her a polite smile. I take it back. My brain whines for help when she starts walking over to me.

Ok, I got this. She was nice, nothing to be scared about. Except she knows Milo and you don't. Oh shush. I meet her half way, now standing awkwardly in front of her. 'Hey, what are you doing here?" She says. "Shopping, how about you?" I ask in return. She shrugs and holds up a bag. "Just walking around."

"Isabelle right? Sorry my brains a little...foggy from the other night." Her face brightens in color slightly, and now I feel a little bad. "Yes. It's Ava right?" She nods her head, releasing a relieved breath. I know I remembered her name, but she doesn't need to know that. How could I forget the name of the woman who slept with my neighbor?

"Are you new in town? If so, I could help show you around." I cringe, and clear my throat. "No, I'm not new. I just moved back a couple days ago." She nods her head, a look of slight curiosity in her eyes, but she doesn't question anything. "Anyways, I better get going, but it was good to see you." I say, starting to walk past her when she stops me by the arm.

I shake her off politely, not liking the physical touch, but still turn towards her with a smile. "I'm sorry. It's clear you don't like me very much," She pauses, and laughs. "But I lied, I knew who you were—know who you are. I know you used to live here, and I just kinda freaked out a little when you got back here, because everyone always talked about you and Milo being...something—" I get the gist of what she's saying and stop her.

"Ava, There's nothing going on between me and Milo." I pause, fishing for the right words I should use next. "I don't not like you, It's just been a stressful move since I got back, but you really have nothing to worry about." She visibly softens, and breathes deeply.

"Is there, um, something going on between you and Milo?" I ask, immediately regretting it. I did not need to know this. She flusters in color, and stutters through her words. "Well, no, but I really like him." She finally says. So Milo's single? Shut up Isabelle, you are not helping right now. "Ok, well I wish you the best of luck." She thanks me, and we finally part ways.

I try to ignore the pounding in my heart, and the relief I felt when she said she wasn't anything with Milo. All I'm trying to do is get my best friend back, not try and find a boyfriend. No, Milo would never like a girl like me like that. A girl that's dirty. He wouldn't want me.

I enter the store that Mama Hazel told me about and see bathing suits on the first rack, buy one get one free. I also see dresses, and cute shirts the further back I walk. This might be bad. I have no control when it comes to clothes. Especially cute clothes.

I stick to the bathing suits, and find one that has underwire and pretty pretty flowers all over it. The background is just white making them look so pretty. Plus the bottoms aren't too showy either. I grab it off the rack, and keep looking around. The next one I come across is a light blue background with darker colored strips that look to be blurry.

I picked that one up too.

After shopping for a total of 30 minutes, which I find impressive, I walk up to the cash register to pay. "Hiya, how's your day going!" The nice lady asked. I smile, and start pulling out my money.

"Good, how about yours?" I ask back politely. "Great thanks for asking." She continues to ring up my stuff in a comfortable silence before she has it all bagged, and I pay. "Have a nice day,: I say with a wave. She returns the jester and starts ringing up the next people. I'm to busy looking behind me that I don't see what's in front of me when I walk out of the store.

With a huff I bounce off a chest, and immediately snap my head to the front. "Sorry, I wasn't paying attention." I laugh nervously, until my smile die's down seeing who's in front of me. I don't know him, but he looks so familiar. "All good, no worries." He smiles, giving me a bad feeling in my stomach.

Where the heck do I know this guy from? "I'm...you look so familiar, have we met?" He takes a once over on me making my skin crawl before shaking his head no. "My name's Blake though." He extends his hand to shake, and I do so hesitantly. Blake, Blake, Blake. Where have I heard that name from? I don't give him my name, but smile before walking away.

I don't glance behind me as I continue walking back towards the Voltz, feeling as if I'm being watched now. I'm definitely being paranoid. People look alike, I'm sure I just have seen someone before in Portland that looked like him. Then why did he give me such a bad feeling? This town is small, there is a chance I could've gone to school with him before I left, maybe seen him in the hallway once or twice, maybe we had a class together.

I slide into the car and turn it on without even thinking about the burning hot seats under my thighs. This shirt does nothing to prevent the heat from seeping through. Without another thought about Blake, I step on the gas and take off into the streets. It's quiet, and not very busy for the odd time on a Friday afternoon, which I'm happy about.

When I look out to my right, I can see the sand and a hint of the ocean when there's no trees blocking it. There are parts of this town that are a solid 10 minute drive from the beach, but from where we are, and all the shops are, you can see it all. I personally love it.

I pull into my house, firstly noticing the lack of cars in Milo's driveway meaning that he and Luna are still out. I sigh, and grab my bag while stepping out of the car. Making my way inside, I see my dad at the counter with his reading glasses on, and a computer in front of him.

I place my bag at the bottom of the stairs, before walking in to grab a glass of lemonade. "Hey dad." He looks up at my presence and slides his glasses onto his head. "Hey sweety, how was your little trip?" He gives him full attention to me, as I pour the sweet yellow liquid over ice in my cup.

"It was good. I saw Mama Hazel, and got a job at her place." He smiles, before grimacing. "That woman's still beating the bushes," I laugh, and take a sip of my drink. "She's sweet, I like her." I say. My dad shrugs, looking off in thought for a second before turning back to me. "Hey, doesn't Milo work there?" I almost choke on my drink, key work almost. I compose myself and swallow, while responding with a simple, "Yeah." He gives me a look, as if he's reading right through me before disming the subject and starting a new one.

"I'm having a barbecue. We throw them a lot here but I was thinking about it being more for your welcome back." I smile, and nod my head. "Sure. Although I gotta work some in the morning tomorrow." He nods his head, and smiles in Aw. "I'm really glad you're getting back into things."

"Me too dad, me too."

~~~~~~~~~~~~~~~~~~~~~~~~~~~~~~~~

AN:I promise we will be getting more Milo next chapter;)
~~~~~~~~~~~~~~~~~~~~~~~~~~~~~~~~

Chapter Four

——'The question isn't who is going to let me; it's who is going to stop me.'~ Howard Roark ~——

Beef Patties ~~Isabelle

I'm up at the crack of dawn on Saturday morning, my alarm blaring at me from my nightstand at 5am. Mama Hazel's opens up at 6:30 for all the early birds who need their coffees before going to work. I think it's a smart idea. Though I also thought it would be nice for me to not be in a rush to get there.

Just take is nice, and slow–

Out of nowhere a shriek is heard; that shriek coming out of my mouth when I turn the corner of our house after the stairs, and almost smash right into a broad chest that has a black cotton shirt over it

Why is Milo Wesley standing in my house? I grip my chest as my dad comes running around the corner to aid the situation, looking like he literally flew out of bed. "Why did you scream?" He asks in confusion, only seeing Milo.

He was probably expecting some murder to be killing me or something. Well dad, by the look of irritation on Milo's face I think he is the murder, and he is about to kill me.

I look over my shoulder and answer my dad. "Nothing, he just scared me." My dad yawns, and saunters off somewhere else. I wanna scream out for him to stay, and save me from the murder.

"What are you doing here?" I ask quietly. I don't know why I whisper but I do. His eyes narrow out of nowhere, and he pushes past me. "Rude." I mumble, walking out to the kitchen.

"Goodmorning." I say happily to my mom, who's sitting at the counter eating breakfast. She's working earlier today so she can get off by noon. She smiles at me and mutters a goodmorning as well.

I smile as I begin boiling some water for my tea—I've never liked coffee—and wait for it to heat up. "Mom," She looks up at me. "Why is Milo here?" I ask. She looks over my shoulder, so I do so as well and see Milo standing there as well. "Your father said that it would be better if you guys drive together to Mama Hazel's because of everything that's going on today." Wait what's going on today? Barbecue. Oh, I forgot about that.

Milo glares at me again, and I realize his anger is sprouting from the fact that I'm now working with him. "I'm sorry, Mama Hazel wouldn't let it go until I agreed to work there. I swear—" He cuts me off with a rude, "I don't care." One that my mom apparently doesn't hear.

I breathe deeply, and pour the water into a mug once it boils. "What time are we leaving?" I ask Milo. He's just standing here, leaning up against the wall with his arms crossed. A black shirt, and denim jeans. A ball cap on top of his head. He looks effortlessly beautiful. I blush when I realize I've been caught staring, and focus on my tea bag.

"When I say so." Is the response I get. Well then, I guess this really might be a little harder than I thought. My mom stands up, and kisses me goodbye on the check. "Bye Hun," She says to Milo, and he politely waves back, no longer glaring. He doesn't smile though. I have a feeling that's just something he doesn't do. Or maybe it's just reserved for the view of Luna.

I take a seat at our table next to the big window, and smile as I drink my nice green tea. Milo doesn't move, and the air between us is thick as ever. I try not to glance up at him, but it's getting really difficult so I just turn towards the window and stare into the dark abyss of early morning. The sun still asleep.

I hear heavy footsteps, and try but fail to not look up. Milo sits his large, tall, body down into the chair across from me, but he refuses to look anywhere near me. "So, maybe you can help me learn how to do everything at Mama Hazel's." There's silence, and when he looks up at me I shiver.

Those freaking green eyes. His jet black hair is almost covering them up. These things could hypnotize someone. I gulp down a sip of tea, and continue to stare back at him. His lips are tugged down in a frown, and he has a crease between his eyebrows from glaring I assume. It makes me want to smooth it out, and fix whatever is making him conflicted. It's you dummy. Argh.

"Let me make this clear because I'm only saying it once," His voice is deep, a lot deeper than it used to be. Before I left he was going through the stage when his voice was constantly cracking. Now it's just like molten lava seeping through my veins. Oh boy.

"I am in no way shape or form trying to spend time with you. I don't want to spend time with you. I am doing his because your parents asked." His face shows nothing. His words make me flinch. What happened to the boy that couldn't stop smiling. Couldn't look at me without laughing. Watched the sunrise, and stars with me?

Did my leaving hurt him this bad? There is no way. There is definitely something else going on. I'm missing something, and I am going to find it out. Something must've happened when I was gone. Even though it doesn't seem like something Milo would say and mean, he doesn't break eye contact, and as much as I try to stop it his words break through my skin.

They peel away at my heart, and pick at my confidence. They make me a little mad. I don't get mad often, and I can usually contain myself if I do, but for some reason his words hurt. He stands up from the table, and right before I hear the front door shut he says, "Be in the car in 30 minutes." Then it shuts, not hardly, most likely because my dads still sleeping, but I can feel the anger in his footsteps.

I don't let myself cry as I finish up my tea. I don't let a single tear fill my eyes when I slip into one of my soft light blue dresses. One that is bell sleeved from the elbow down, and has small buttons on my chest. I suck up my feelings as I put on my converse, and walk out the door in the 30 minute time limit he gave me.

He's parked in my driveway with his car, staring down at his phone. He doesn't even look up at my presence when I get into the car. It's a black 4-runner. Perfectly suits him. He takes off down the street in what I would call tension, but he seems completely relaxed.

Well, ever so often his hands flex on the wheel, but I can't tell if he's purely just stretching them, or if he's still irritated. I'd bet on the latter. If he didn't want to spend so much time with me, why the heck would he agree? Why couldn't he just simply say no.

My thoughts run wild on our short drive to the cafe. Things to say, jokes, reasons for what is going on. It's like I'm building a puzzle, but half of the pieces are gone, and within those half it's scattered across the picture. So now I have a weird looking thing, and I have no idea what it's supposed to be. Does that make sense?

As soon as he parks, he jumps out of the car and I follow suit. Putting on a smile when he walks in, still no sun yet risen, I see Mama Hazel reading a book on a sofa. There are a couple shelves of books behind her as well. I didn't even realize there was a reading nook in here.

"Mornin Mama Hazel." I greet. She looks up at me, and gushes on the spot. Putting a bookmark inside the page she was on, she stands up to walk over to me. I figured it was to greet me, and it was. I just didn't realize her way of greeting was hugging.

I hugged her back though, of course. It just caught me off guard. "I'm so glad you're here. You can finally lighten up someone's bad mood." She lifts up her hand, and points her finger at Milo discreetly. He rolls his eyes, and before I can even blink Mama Hazel grabs a towel and wack's his neck.

He groans, and rubs the sore red spot of tender skin. Go Mama Hazel. "Don't roll your eyes at me boy, it's the truth." Looks like Milo and Mama Hazel have been spending some 'quality' time together. I giggle softly into my hand causing Milo to send a glare towards me. For some reason his glare does nothing to me, and I keep laughing.

He turns away from me, but I swear I see him trying to hide a smile. Or maybe it's just the dark. Probably just the dark. I watch as Mama Hazel grabs her things, and starts walking towards the front door. "Wait, where are you going?" I ask. Milo turns towards her. "You guys got it. If you don't know how to do something, ask him." She points at Milo, and now I'm pretty confident she doesn't remember his name.

"No. I don't want to–" The door shuts behind Mama Hazel, and now we're both just standing here awkwardly, with one light that illuminates the whole place. I turn on my heels to face him, and give him a smile. One he does not return, in fact I'm pretty sure his face is turning red with anger.

I look at the tiny clock on the wall, and see that it's 6 on the dot. Meaning we have 30 minutes to now get the shop ready. "Ok...what do you want me to do?" He doesn't look at me while he starts heading behind the back door. "Go home." He mutters, then the door slams behind him.

Does he not remember he's my ride?

I huff in annoyance feeling my own anger rising, but instead of pursuing it I just shove it into the back of my head and put a smile on my face. It's 6 in the morning and I have a long day ahead of me. I need to make it a good day. Lord knows how my parents would act if I came home all grumpy ready for a barbecue.

I walk around the corner and follow through the back swinging door's that Milo just walked through.

I've got this.

The minute I see him my confidence falters. Oh no, I don't got this. He's kneading dough on a floured surface, causing the veins in his arms to pop out. I take a deep breath before circling around the table he's standing at, and stand across from him.

I place my hands on my hips, and try to scowl, but all I end up doing is ogling over his arms. Who knew I was an arms typa girl? "What?" He snaps, glaring up at me. I jump back at his harsh voice and watch his eyes turn from anger to confusion then back to annoyance within half a second. Ok, that was weird.

"I need something to do." I say in the nicest tone I can, but I'm not sure if it works. He rolls his eyes, and keeps kneading the dough. Before I even have time to think about the consequences that might follow, I dip my hands into a pile of flour, and flick it at his face. He stops, and looks up at me with a dead stare. His jaw is locked, and I think I might see steam floating out of his ears.

Oopsies.

I bite down on my bottom lip to stop myself from laughing, which doesn't help the situation. He picks up a handful of flour and chucks it at me, socking me in the face. I groan when my head flings back, and I cover my eyes with my hands. "That was," I pause and spit out flour. "Not nice." I finish, and wipe enough off to where I can squint my eyes.

Either there's flour in my eyes, or Milo is grinning. "You started it." I still see a small grin, but his voice is cold as ice. "I didn't throw that much at you." He shrugs, and goes back to what he's doing. I turn around, and start walking towards the door that says 'bathroom' and accidentally run into instead of opening it.

I don't have to look back to know that Milo would be teasing me if I did. Or laughing at me. He would probably call me a name, so instead I continue walking through the door this time and lock it behind me. I look like a ghost when I see my reflection.

This is going to be a long morning.

———

I've spent exactly 5 hours straight with Milo Wesley, and definitely dug myself a grave for him. After burning my hand with the hot water of the espresso machine, I gave up and walked back to try and bake something. That failed miserably when I forgot to set a timer for my cookies and burnt them all, nearly setting Mama Hazel's in flames. After that I gave up and worked at the cash register for the rest of the time, with the occasional waitressing for some people.

"Ow." I rub my forehead again, when I run into Milo for the 4th time in the last half hour. He's been dragging around a cart, switching his eyes from his phone to the aisle every 3 seconds. My dad sent us a list of food items to pick up from our local k-mark for the barbecue. He turns around sharply. "Would you stop that?" I smile tightly, and just nod my head.

It's not the best idea to try and pick a fight with a man that is definitely 6'0 if not more, and well over twice my weight. Also I'm trying to become his friend, but become his enemy. Although I think he already drew red horns and pointy teeth coming out of my face on a punching bag.

"Sorry." I mutter. He sighs deeply, and rubs his forehead as he walks over and over again through the same asiles. "Do you know what you're look-ing for?" I ask questionably. He looks lost. "Yes." He grits out, and stops abruptly again. I almost smack into him, but get a hold of myself before chaos is let free. He groans, and drags his hands through his hair twice each.

"What is it?" I yank the phone out of his hand making him growl in disapproval when I see one last item on the list. "You can't find the patties?" I look up at him to see his cheek's ting a small shade of pink. I walk over to the frozen meat area whether he's following me or not, and look directly at the empty spot that reads 'beef patties' "You can't find them because they're out."

I see a worker coming out of the back door, and stop her before she can go back in. "Hey, you guys are out of beef patties, do you mind checking the back to see if there's any in there?" I smile at her, asking politely. She smiles back at me before it drops, and she pops a piece of her gum. "Look lady, I have a job to do that I'm actually getting paid for. What I don't get paid for is to find you patties." She tries to walk back into the doors, but I grab her arm and pull up my big girl pants.

"Look here lady, I have an angry dad with a lot of other hangry people waiting at my home for food. On top of that I have an angry–" I look back at Milo, who has an amused look on his face, his arms crossed over his chest.

"--Him, and I just want to go home. I've been up since 5am. Have you? No, I doubt it. So I would really like for you to go check the back for at least 15 patties." I breathe deeply, while she opens her mouth to speak, but I beat her to it. "Or, I could find your manager. Do you think they would be very happy to know you are upsetting one of their customers."

She groans, and rolls her eyes. "I'll see what we have." She grumbles before stomping off. I shake off my sweat, and wipe my hair out of my face. "There, that wasn't so hard." I mutter, walking back to Milo. He still looks amused as he stares down at me, not saying anything.

"What? Is there something on my face?" I asked worriedly, touching around to make sure I'm in the clear. I would die if there was still flour on my face. It took at least an hour to get it all off. His grin drops, and his cool expressionless face floats back over. "No." Well ok then.

The lady walks back out with a full blown cardboard box full of beef patties. Score me I guess. She throws it into our cart, gives me a fake smile while smacking her gum, and then walks off grumbling something I could care less to hear. "Well damn." I do here Milo mutter though before he's pushing the cart off towards the self checkout line.

Chapter Five

—'In another lifetime we will be brave enough to love each other out loud.'~ J.B. ~ ——

Barbecue ~~Isabelle

We pulled into the driveway to Milo's house seeing no other cars in sight. I'm about to ask Milo where everyone is when he slams his car door shut and stomps over to the back. I sigh a long, breathy sigh, before swiping my face with my hand and stepping out of the car.

I walk to the back, and see Milo pick up the last grocery bag from the car before slamming the door shut. What the heck does this man bench? I follow behind him awkwardly, empty handed, over to my house where the front door is ajar. I can hear faint music coming from the back yard, and the minute we walk into the kitchen I see everyone through the window.

People on my deck, by the pool, and in the yard. A lot of people. "Did he invite the whole town?" I mutter under my breath, not hearable to anyone else but me. Although I wouldn't be surprised if Milo's super hearing heard it. If he did though, he doesn't show it.

I start unloading the bags, and putting them in their respective areas in the fridge, and pantry, then leaving some things out. Once all the bags are empty, Milo walks out back through the sliding doors without a goodbye, or even a glance back.

Seeing the items I have I began to make a salad, rolling my blue bell sleeves up to my elbows. Just before I began to add anything to the bowl, my mom came walking around the corner, gasping when she saw me. "Good lord Izzy, I love you, but please step away from the bowl." I look up at her confused until it hits me. "Mom, I can make a salad." She shakes her head and pushes me out of the way.

"You are not ruining my salad. People wait for your fathers barbecues for this." I roll my eyes, and grab a handful of grapes from the fridge before sitting at the island table we have. I look out the window and see Milo ruffling Luna's hair, and smiling. Ok, maybe it is just me. I sigh, and shove a grape—more aggressively then I attend to—into my mouth.

"How was work?" My mom asked, making me change my position so I'm looking at her now. She's looking at me with a knowing look. What she knows, I have no clue. "Uh, it was...good." I say slowly, remembering everything that went wrong, and the little that went right. "How's Milo?" She asks. I can feel my face flaming with color, as I try and chew my grape.

Instead of answering her question, I ask my own. "How long has he been like that?" My mom furrows her eyes brows, and begins adding the lettuce and vegetables into the bowl. "Been like what?" I shrug, trying to think of the right wording. "Distant? Quiet? Not happy?" She sighs, and gives me a sad expression. "I would be lying if I said he didn't change after you left, but there are also things that happened to him while you were gone. Things that aren't mine to tell." Good to know, now I have a mystery to solve.

"No I understand, I wouldn't want you telling him what happened to me." I mutter, laughing sarcastically. If I want to know why Milo is like this, I need him to tell me. If I want him to tell me, I need him to want to tell me. In order for that to happen, I need to make it up to him. I need him to somehow forgive me for leaving.

If you tell him what happened he will understand. I shove that thought into a grave 6ft under the minute it sprouts up in my brain. I am not going to trick him with pity. I don't want his sympathy, or pity. I just want him to forgive me on his own. Which means I need to show him what he's missing as my friend. Ok, that doesn't sound too hard.

I take it back, it sounds hard, but I love a challenge. I can do this. Operation get Milo back is a go.

——

"What are you doing?" I jump out of my skin when I hear Lotties voice whispering in my ear from behind. "Holy macaroni you scared me." I gasp, breathing in big gulps of air. "Sorry," she chuckles.

"So what are we looking at?" I move away from the big window in our kitchen and walk over to the counter. Jumping onto it swiftly, I begin kicking my legs back and forth. "I was admiring the nice sun beating down on the flowers." I say gracefully with a smile. She doesn't look convinced.

"Are you sure you weren't look at 'the sun beating down on your neighbo r.'" She mocks, giving me the same tone I gave her. "Nope." I say, popping the p.

She rolls her eyes and comes walking over to me. "Why don't you just talk to him?" Now I roll my eyes and cross my arms. "I have, he ignores me or silently flips off my back. I don't get what I did wrong?" I rant, throwing my hands in the air. Her expression softens, and she places her hands on my knees.

"Hun, you can't let him get to your head. He's like that with everyone." She whispers, holding the same expression my mom did when she was talking about Milo earlier. "He's not like that with Luna." I mutter, feeling jealousy coil in my stomach. "Him and Luna...after you left they got close. They were both sad you left, and Milo...well Milo was going through stuff and she just wouldn't leave him alone." Like me. I smile sadly, and softly.

"Anyway. Your mom told me to come in here and get you. Food is ready." I hop off the counter, and follow her out back where everyone is already seated and eating. "There she is." My dad smiles brightly and tugs me down next to him. I only realize after I'm seated that Milo's right across from me. Luna's next to him.

"Hey sweety you ok? You didn't really come out earlier." My dad whispers, rubbing my back while everyone else starts eating. I smile and nod my head. "Just tired." He gives me a stressed look, because the last time I said 'just tired' I was well over 'just tired.' "I'm ok dad. I had to wake up at 5 this morning." He smiles remembering my screech I presume.

"Cheers to Izzy being home!" Everyone clinks glasses, and then goes back to whatever they were doing. Talking, eating, messing around. I see lasagna on the table, and go for a big scoop of that when my hand knocks with someone else's.

I suck in a tight breath when I follow the veiny arm back to Milo's glaring face. You know, I used to think he was the sweetest, funniest, most innocent person ever. Even when people got scared when he walked in. Now I see it. I see why they were scared. He looks like an axe murderer. Oh my gosh, did I turn him into an axe murderer?

I give my farewells to my family, and friends. I will miss you all dearly.

"Go ahead." I mutter, letting him grab the lasagna first. I'm pretty sure that just makes him more mad by the way his slice slaps his plate. Luna is too busy on her phone to see what's going on. Not that she'd care, she'd probably laugh.

We eat in a comfortable silence for about 30 minutes before everyone is leaning back in their chairs, falling into a well needed food coma. I pick up my plate, as well as the people around me's plates and start walking towards the sliding door. My parents are protesting, but I ignore it and start washing all the dishes.

I plant all the dishes on the side of the sink, and one by one pick them up and start cleaning them. I throw soap, and hot water all over them while scrubbing like my life depends on it. How am I supposed to enjoy this last summer at my house, if my friend group is all messed up? Why can't things go back to the way they used to be?

I clear my head as best as I can so that none of this ruins the rest of my day, and take a deep breath. Once I'm finished with washing the dishes, I turn around to walk away but yelp when I run into a chest. Coconut hits me in the face, and when I crane my neck to look up I see Milo staring down at me. I smile, and grab the sink behind me. "What are you doing?" I ask, keeping eye contact.

More like staring at his eyes because they're so pretty. I ignore my thoughts by smiling wider. "Forgot a plate." He tosses the plastic in the sink, but it makes a loud noise causing me to flinch.

God I hate the new me.

His eyes furrow down at me, but somehow he's still glaring. "Ok, well, I gotta go." I point my thumb behind me, and slide out from in front of him.

I brush my hands off onto my dress, even though there's nothing on them except sweat and walk out of the sliding doors. Everyone's dispersed from the table now, and only lies the pan for all the food. I go to grab it, but my mom snatches it before I can get to it. "Go hang out with your friends and stop cleaning up." She scolds. I open my mouth to protest but she only slides the door behind her and disappears into the kitchen.

I follow her orders and walk down a step to the pool area. The wood deck changes into cement as I switch areas. With 5 o'clock rounding the corner, my feet begin to burn on the cement and I find myself running to a shade spot under an umbrella.

"Come on Izzy, the water feels nice."I hear Violet call, and look over to see Henry, Lottie, and Violet swimming around in the pool. Although I don't see Noah. "I'm not wearing a bathing suit." I call back, finally feeling my feet cool down. I yelp when I feel someone grabbing my waist, and then all of a sudden I'm flown in the air onto a shoulder.

I hear everyone laughing, and then finally realize who's shoulder I'm on. Noah has thrown me over his wet shoulder. "Noah! Everyone can see my spandex!" I scream, trying to cover my butt, but it doesn't seem to be working.

"Relax, the water will cover it up when you're in." I start thrashing in his hold, on the brink of tears. "Please Noah, I'm not wearing a bathing suit! This is a new dress!" I moan in anger when he picks up his speed. "Welcome home Isabelle." Then my body was off his shoulder, and I felt cold water hit my skin.

It travels all over my body, and soaks my hair as I fall under the surface. The world goes silent as I stay there appreciating it. Floating to the bottom before pushing off the ground and coming back up.The first thing I hear is laughter when I emerge from the water, and see Noah now in the water too. Even through my anger, I still feel a smile forming on my lips.

"That was very rude, and not funny." I say while laughing, and splashing them all with water. I burst out laughing for real, not being able to hold it in when they all attack me with water at once

"Ok, ok, guys relax." They do, and now we're all just messing around. I hop out of the pool and pad my wet feet towards the front door. "Where are you going!" Lottie cries out, throwing her arms up. "I'll be right back, I'm just changing into an actual bathing suit." She nods her head, and so I walk off into the freezing house.

My body automatically starts shaking from the AC, so I quicken my pace up to my room. "Izz, that you?" I stop, and hold back a groan as I call back a 'yes' to my dad. "Come here real quick." My teeth chatter, and I pull my arms up to hug my body for warmth.

I walk into the kitchen, and stand there awkwardly and cold. "Yeah dad?" He looks up at me, and catches in his words as his eyes travel my form from head to toe. "Don't ask." He laughs, and shakes his head. "You remember your birthdays next weekend?" My eyes widen as I do remember. My 18th birthday is next weekend.

"Holy sunflower seeds, that's coming fast." He furrowed his eyebrows at my choice of words, but didn't question it. When I was younger, I put myself on a cursing detox because of my mom always scolding me, and somehow I came up with random phrases to say now.

Then a thought pops into my head, and my smile drops a little. That also means its– "We were thinking of having a party for you and Milo? Since your birthdays are back to back." That's right. My birthdays June 1st and Milo's is June 2nd. I gulp, and shiver again. I blame the cold.

"Does Milo know about this?" I ask hesitantly. He nods his head smiling. "He seemed super excited about it." I snort, and hide my disbelief with a smile and a cough. "Really. Excited?" My dad nods, looking back at his phone. "Your mom and I are gonna leave for the night so you guys can have a party." My eyes widen as I choke on simple air.

I need to get this choking thing under control.

"Of course you don't have to if you're not comfortable with it. You know that right, sweety." His face changes real quick from happy to concerned and serious. I hate that I make them worry even 3 years after. "Of course it's fine. I would love that." I smile, and so does he, nodding his head.

I begin to walk away when I hear him whisper. "Don't tell your mom." I chuckle, and I know he hears it, but without looking back I dart up the stairs.

~~~~~~~~~~~~~~~~~~~~~~~~~~~~~~~~~

AN:I know it's a little repetitive, but I swear it'll start getting better.
~~~~~~~~~~~~~~~~~~~~~~~~~~~~~~~~~

Chapter Six

—'My head says, 'Who cares?'But then my heart whispers,'You do, stupid..."~ Unknown ~ ——

Squirt Guns ~~Isabelle

I kick my feet feeling too awake to fall asleep. It's the night before my birthday. Technically the day of my birthday. Specifically June 1st 4:45a.m It's not even the fact that it's my birthday tomorrow that I can't fall asleep. It's simply the fact that I'm having a party with actual people at my house tomorrow night.

I'm laying flat on my bed though listening to the quietness of the house. Nothings awake yet, not even the birds. I've been watching the repetitive flow of my ceiling fan turning and turning since Midnight. It's starting to make me sick.

I turn around, and get myself steady to my feet on the floor, stretching out my stiff limbs. I make my way downstairs slowly, tucking my messy bun flyaways behind my ear. It's humid, really humid in the house, but it somehow feels good to know what that feels like. It means I'm home.

I pour myself a glass of water, dropping a couple of ice cubes from the freezer as I do so. Then grabbing a straw because why freaking not–there really cute frogs ok–I slide the back door open and step outside. Surprisingly it actually feels better outside than inside. With a slight breeze I walk over to the pool that's lit up by underwater lights, and sit on the edge.

It's peaceful, I find, watching the water ripple from wind, or leaves occasionally falling. I feel so energized, I'm practically buzzing and I don't even know why. It could be because I'm nervous. I mean my parents are going to be gone all night, what if something happens? What if something happens and I can't get a hold of them? What if something happens to me? The thought sinks in like seeping blood, and I can't remove it.

It's like hot molten lava, making me shiver from its burn. My heart is beating about 100 times faster and I have to look up at the stars to calm myself. It's not as good as the view I had at my aunts, but it's still so pretty.

So many stars scattered in such a small portion of the sky. It's fascinating. I hear the sound of a sliding door moving, and look up to my house but see nothing there. I hear it close and realize it's not even coming from that direction. My gaze shifts to my right, where I see a figure in a hoodie and shorts, sit down on the cement.

I watch Milo, wondering what he might be doing when I see him holding something in his lap. My heart skips a beat when I see what he's holding. It's a sketchbook. It sends a rush of memories running into my brain that I had almost forgotten about. The times I would admire his face structure when he would be concentrating.

Or when it didn't even look like he realized he had paper beneath his fingers as he drew his quick increments with a small pencil. I try not to look at him, and look at any other possible thing out here but I can't tear my eyes from him. He pauses for a moment, like maybe he doesn't want to do whatever he's thinking about. But then he rips a page out, making a noise even I can hear.

He tosses it in his pool, but not harshly. Then he grabs the paper and quickly crumbles it up. Now all that it is, is a mushy piece of dead tree. I continue to stare at him, mesmerized by what he's doing. Was there something on that paper? Did he have a purpose for that? What is going on in his mind?

I lose all train of thought when he suddenly freezes, and turns his head towards me. He's not far. Across a flimsy fence that's nearby. I can see his face, make out his expression, and I don't know if it's the lighting, or maybe he's simply just as tired as I am but he doesn't look mad. He looks caught off guard, and maybe a little flustered.

Either way, I am very flustered, and embarrassed, so I pick myself up and walk quickly towards my house. I slide the door shut once I'm inside, and breathe a breath of relief. Then I sink to the floor against the glass and lean my head against the door. What am I doing?

———

I've cleaned everything. When I say everything, I mean this house does not have one scrap of dirt anywhere. It's polished, and waxed, and then cleaned again and again, and I dusted, and washed. Ugh, I've done too much.

My tie-dye sweater has been rolled up to my elbows for so long, I'm sure there's a mark. "Wow, this place looks. Clean?" I throw the rag I was holding into the sink, and smile up at Violet. "Hey. What are you doing here?" She shrugs, but I can tell it's definitely something. "Did you...clean?" She asks, almost looking worried for me. I nod my head, and walk closer to her.

"Couldn't sleep." I shrug. Her eyebrows rise in surprise. "You've been cleaning all night?" Now I shrug, feeling a little embarrassed. "Technically I didn't start till 5." She closes her eyes, and takes a needed deep breath.

When her eyes open she smiles widely, and jumps into my arms. "Oh my gosh, you're finally 18!! Do you feel older?" She squeezes my cheeks making me laugh. "Oh, is that a wrinkle?" She goes to touch my face again when I swat her hand away. "As much as I love seeing you, I would really like to know why you're here."

She rolls her eyes, and that's when I notice she has a bag on her shoulder. She re-adjust it, and looks around awkwardly. "Why didn't you sleep?" She avoids my curiosity with a question. "I was too energized for today." She doesn't believe me, I don't either. Partially because it's not the whole truth, and I'm a horrible liar.

"You know it's ok—" I shake my head, interrupting her. "Everything's fine. Today is going to be a great day. Now, stop avoiding my question and answer Violet Bailey, or I will call in reinforcements." She holds her hands up in surrender, and places her bag on the table between us. She pulls out a small notebook, not much bigger than my hand and hands it to me.

"We have officially planned the best 18th birthday of your life!" I'm about to ask who 'we' is, when Lottie comes running around the corner, looking like she just ran a marathon. "Ok, outfit secured." My brows furrow, as I crack the book open.

So much writing is the first thing I see before it's snatched away from me. "She can't know what we're doing." Lottie states in a duh tone. "Ok, now come on and get dressed. We need to get the stench of...is that toilet bowl cleaner?" I roll my eyes playfully, and make my way up the stairs to my bedroom.

Violet and Lottie flop onto my bed the minute my door closes, and I notice the outfit sitting on my chair. "What did you guys do?" I asked worriedly. "Well, we know that the party tonight might be a little overwhelming." Lottie starts. "So, we are going to have a fun day to try and ease your consciousness about tonight." Violet finishes. "Now go change. Lord only knows how long the others can wait." I'm about to question what that means, when Lottie forcefully shoves me into my bathroom with the outfit.

I look at it before changing. The more I look, the more I realize there aren't any undergarments. Only the blue bathing suit that I bought the other day. The actual clothes that they got for me though consist of a deep blue spaghetti strap dress with an open back that reaches my mid thighs. It's very comfy though so I don't object.

I change quickly, and look at myself in the mirror. My hair's a mess, and with the new found tiredness hitting me, I don't try to change it. My breath hitches when I find sight of a faint scar on my collarbone. You wouldn't notice it unless you were looking for it, or just that close in general, but it's almost as if I can feel the pain all over again.

I shiver, and walk out of the bathroom. "I told you it was perfect." Lottie growls at Violet. "Ok, ok, fine you were right." Lottie seems satisfied with that answer and looks up at me. "What do you think?" I smile, and nod my head, no words coming out.

"Good, it's good." I give her 2 thumbs up, and she does it back. "Ok, we got stuff to do." They both start dragging me down the stairs when I stick the heels of my feet into the ground and scream, "wait!" They groan, and laugh at the same time. "What is it now?" Lottie whines. "I need to tell my parents I'm leaving." I start walking towards their room downstairs when they pull me towards the front door instead.

"We already told them, they're ok with it." Wow, they've really planned this out. Once we were outside they shove me into the familiar blue Jeep, and take off down the road. "Where are we going first?" Violets driving, so Lottie looks back at me from the passenger seat and starts explaining. "Breakfast first, of course." We pull into the familiar parking lot of Mama Hazels, and make our way over to the front doors.

Throughout the last week, I've come here every morning and worked. Once Mama Hazel found out that Saturday was my birthday she forced me to take the day off, telling me that it was going to be slow anyway. I forgot how much I missed this place though. I've also found that windows in the back show off a great view of the sunrise over the water.

"We're just here to get coffee." I scrunch up my nose in distaste which catches the eyes of Violet because she rolls hers and huffs dramatically. "Or tea." I smile happily as the bell rings above our heads. I see Mama Hazel wiping down the counter looking peaceful, but when she glances up at the door she starts glaring at me.

Her stare is so intense that it almost scares me enough to walk out of the building and never return. "I told you not to come here." She says, rounding the corner and popping her knee out. Her hands on her hips in a disapproving stance. "I'm only here because—"

"It's Isabelle's birthday funday!" The girls yell from behind me. Mama Hazel smiles, going back behind the counter leaning her elbows on top of it. "Well then, what can I get you ladies?" I smile gratefully, and stare at the menu while Violet and Lottie blabble away.

Once it's my turn, I've decided on a drink already. My favorite drink on the planet. "Can I have a vanilla matcha with coconut milk?" Mama Hazel smiles like she might remember when I would order it 3 years ago. "Is that it?" We nod, and she turns around to start making everything.

I take this time to go and sit by the window that has a great view. The girls follow behind me. "So what else are we doing today?" Lottie opens her mouth, but Violet's hand quickly covers it. "It's a surprise." She looks worried for a second, but they both ease up when Mama Hazel lays our drinks down.

"It's on the house. Cheers to the birthday girl." She winks, and zooms away before anyone can protest. Violet glances down at her phone quickly, before standing up and beginning to drag Lottie and me out of Mama Hazels. "Come on, we gotta go." She whispers, as if someone's gonna be listening to us which obviously no one is.

"Time crunch?" I ask suspiciously. My two best friends only roll their eyes, and proceed to shove me into the backseat of the car like their kidnappers. Ya know, they are my kidnappers. I actually wanted to be able to hype myself up for tonight, maybe get some sleep in, but no. Here I am being kidnapped.

Before we start driving Lottie leans into the car, and wraps a bandana around my eyes. "Ok, is this really necessary?" I go to tug it off when they tie my hands together too. "Ok, this is very unnecessary." No one answers me, making me feel like I'm alone in this car but the feeling of the car taking off on the road tells me otherwise.

"It is necessary, with you and your nosey eyes, we can't have you seeing anything. It will ruin the surprise." Surprise of many to come, I believe is what she meant to say.

―――

The drive was very short, but that still gives me nothing because everywhere in Halings is a short drive, if not a fast walk away. They grab me out of the car, and the first thing that assaults my nose is the smell of the salty ocean. How could I forget that smell? Not only that, but Halings beach has a distinct smell to it. I don't know how, or if I've just really never been to any other beach, but there's something different about it.

I don't say anything though, worried that these sick physcos might tape my nose shut and continue walking as they guide me. My hands are undone now, so that it doesn't look like a total hostage situation, but my vision is still black.

What confuses me though is that they know that I can smell the beach, and hear the crashing sound of the waves getting closer, yet they still decided to blind fold me? That doesn't make any sense. "Can you guys just un-blindfold me already? I know where we are."

They both chant a 'no' in unison, electing a groan to rise from my throat. Little flipping gremlins. I even start to feel sand as we enter the beach area, and hear the seagulls getting louder. Ok, there's gotta be something more here than a beach.

Right as the thought hits me, I feel the tie on the back of my head being untied, and then the blindfold is being torn off my face. My eyes widen when I see the man standing in front of me. Strangely close. How did I not feel his presence? The same man that rid me of my sleep last night is staring at me with irritation. His angry face makes me want to do something to make him smile. I wanna turn his frown upside down. No one should have to feel this mad all the time.

Then my mind drifts back to what I saw last night, and my eyebrows furrow. As if he knows what I'm thinking he gives me a look that says 'you tell, I tell' as in we are both doomed if our friends find out something was wrong with both of us last night. "Why are you guys looking at eachother like you're going to die." Ok, I guess we're giving each other that face too. "I'm—we're not." I state, finally averting my eyes from his. He scoffs, and shakes his head.

"Is anyone going to tell us what's going on?" He speaks, his voice only slightly less aggravated than his expression. I watch the sun catch his green eyes, and suddenly wish he was smiling so I could see his dimples with his eyes. He's so handsome.

Ok, no, not a good thought Izzy.

I suck in a tight breath and recollect my thoughts. "Yeah, what is going on?" I ask, now noticing the 2 guys standing behind Milo. I get a sick feeling this was a set up. A birthday set up, because technically, his birthday is tomorrow. I get an itching feeling to rub it into his face that 'ha, I'm a day older' but I don't think that would fit the occasion.

I used to do it all the time when we were younger. Although we're not younger anymore. "Well," Violet gestured with her arms extended, stepping in between Milo and I. Lottie and Henry lock arms, surrounding us while Noah stood beside Violet.

"We have planned an amazing, extravagant birthday fun day before you have an even more fun party tonight!" I hope she wasn't expecting us to jump up and down in excitement, with tears of joy falling down our faces. Because that is not what happens. No, the complete opposite if not worse. Milo starts walking away. "You're not going anywhere buddy." I watch, almost as if in slow motion as Noah whips out a squirt gun—from freaking no where—loaded, and squirts Milo straight in the face.

I was expecting Milo to get angry, and maybe punch the sunshine off of Noah's face, but instead when I get a glimpse of his face, he looks like he's holding back a grin.

Then I feel water splatter on my face, and I'm stunned momentarily before a gun is placed into my hands. Now a smile is tugging at my face. "You will have fun!" Henry screams, squirting me while Noah does the same to Milo. It only takes a handful of seconds to realize Milo was handed a squirt gun and is beginning to shoot everyone as well.

So I do the only thing I can do. I lift the squirtgun in my hands, and spray Milo square in the face, because watching his face drop in mad amusement is worth anything the future holds.

~~~~~~~~~~~~~~~~~~~~~~~~~~~~~~~~

AN:Not sure why, but I really enjoyed writing this chapter lol.

This is the dress I imagine her wearing
~~~~~~~~~~~~~~~~~~~~~~~~~~~~~~~~

Chapter Seven

—'We were Just friends That spoke like lovers And that seemed to be enough for Two teenagers who were scared to love one another'~ k.a.t ~ ——

Birthday Party ~~Isabelle

"There was no humidity there?" Noah gawks, jaw dropped by my last statement. "Yeah, I'm not sure why but it was really nice. Never really got too hot either." Everyones staring at me while I bite down on my amazing cheese burger again.

I forgot how good they were down here. If there's one thing I've missed the most from Florida, it's this cheeseburger that has me drooling.

The sun is beginning to set, and the beach wind is hitting my face on the pier. We swam all day. I have the sunburn on my checks and back to prove it. Now we're all burned out, and relaxing, watching the waves hit the wood below us.

So burned out though, that I think Milo's given up on being mad at me today. I don't think he has the energy for it anymore and frankly, I'm really enjoying it. He's not looking at me, but he's not not looking at me if that makes any sense. He's simply just here, and so am I. Almost as if we were never friends to begin with.

Shaking off the sad feeling, I wipe all the ketchup and mustard off my face, and shove more fries into my mouth. Everyone else continues with their eating as well, and we fall into a comfortable silence. That is until Milo wrecks it. "Why did you leave anyway?" There's no anger in his voice, but there's no comfort in it either. Just pure curiosity.

I tense, and almost choke on a fry, but luckily waters on my side today, and washes it down before I can choke. I glance up at him, and see his arms folded and his structure leaning back in his chair. His black hair is still slightly wet, making it look somehow darker than it was before, and lays atop his head. His eyes are shimmering, and there's not even any sun on them.

How the heck does he just look like a god? A blush rises to my cheeks at my new thoughts about him, but luckily it doesn't show through my sunburn. I catch the slightest bit of tension from Lottie and Violet at the same time, and it's because we're all thinking the same thing.

Why did you leave Isabelle? Go on, tell them. My conscious urges on, but my voice never comes. This isn't the way I'm telling them, it's just not. Not on my birthday. I wanna have fun this summer, and wrecking it with my sad past is not going to help the future. "Uh, well–" I fish for words, but nothing comes to mind. Thankfully, someone comes to my rescue.

"It's getting late, we should get home and start setting all the drinks up." I sigh in relief, and shove the last of my cheeseburger into my mouth. Thinking about it after it's gone, really makes me think I should've appreciated it more. "Well then what are we waiting for!" Noah screams, and jumps out of his chair, momentarily spooking me.

It's astonishing how he just always has this much energy. The rest of us start following him back to the car slowly.

It doesn't take long to get back to the house, and when we do there's only a shred of light coming from the sky, the rest is pure blackness. My parents are already gone. My dad had texted me back while we were still at the beach saying that they were leaving, just as a heads up.

All 3 of the guys run into the house, leaving us girls out the follow suit. When I enter, the first thing I see is the door to my dad's office open, Henry and Noah searching through the open liquor cabinet. I'm too stunned to speak, that I don't even realize Milo isn't there. "What are you guys doing? My dad is going to kill me if he finds out we were going through his stuff." That's a half lie, I don't think my dad would honestly be that mad.

He doesn't want me to get stone faced drunk every night, but he does wants me to enjoy my summer here while I can. I'm pretty sure he would just plug his ears, and say something like 'I was never here' or, 'I didn't hear anything'. My mom on the other hand...

I hear a small crash from the kitchen, and instantly start remembering the fact that Milo isn't here, and is probably creating a mess somewhere else. I turn around, leaving Henry and Noah to whatever the heck they're doing and walking down the small hallways towards the kitchen.

I freeze when I see everything set up. Milo flashes me a Milo grin as I watch him pour alcohol–specifically tequila–into shot glasses, lined up on the edge of the counter. I completely ignore the flutter my stomach does at his small dimples poking out from his smirk, and avert eye contact.

Besides what he's doing, there's already bowls of chips everywhere, and almost a million solo cups stacked on the counter. "How many people are coming?" I stress anxiously. Milo only shrugs, not giving me a snarky remark or glare, confusing me

I try to break down his new found cheery mood, and figure out what could possibly be going on with him. Is there just a switch somewhere that he's flipped? Is it because this is technically for him birthday too? I mean he is turning 18 tomorrow.

I don't get much time to think about it, because I quickly hear pounding footsteps approaching the kitchen. Henry comes running around the corner, followed by Noah. Then Lottie and Violet come next. "Pre-game!" Someone shouts from the kitchen, and I can't even tell which one of the guys' voices it is. The girls push me into the kitchen, and over to where the shots are lined up. Violet shoves one into my hand, and whispers in my ear, "Only if you want." Which brings warmth to my heart, and pumps me up even more to take the shot.

I've only had alcohol one other time, and that was when my friends back in Oregon took me out for my sixteenth birthday. I took one beer, and puked it up the day after. My aunt then grounded me for the year following. I was peer pressured back then, and I think the fact that I don't feel like that right now makes me even more excited.

It's my 18th birthday. If I'm gonna get drunk, I miswell do it now. "Cheers to the newly adults!" Everyone laughs, clinks glasses, and then knocks the shots back. The minute the alcohol touches my mouth it burns, and the second it glides down my throat, it stings bringing tears to my eyes.

Even through my bleary eyes, I catch sight of Milo pouring more shots, but not taking any. He doesn't take one sip of the alcohol.

Once I've swallowed it, I start coughing ferociously, but don't have time to finish when something is shoved into my face, and I'm gulping it down trying to ride the flavor of whatever the heck that was. Once I pull away from my drink, Lottie is staring at me with half concerned and half amused eyes. "What was that?" I ask, referring to the shots we just took.

"Tequila babe, that would be tequila."

———

With my amazingly good aim, I throw another ping pong, and hit it into the rim of the cup. "God damn, you're really good at this game." The guy to whom I do not know the name of, laughs, and drinks the beer in his cup.

It's been about 3 hours, and I'm surprised that I don't feel too drunk. I can still walk, and talk with only a slight slur, but my mind is a bit hazy.

I was introduced to truly's about an hour into the party, and after about 2 hours I was introduced to beer pong. A game I am extremely good at. Although so is the other guy I'm going against, and with every drink I feel myself getting more and more hot.

My skin is buzzing, and I can feel the sweat causing my hair to stick to my forehead, and my dress that my brain has still somehow convinced me to keep on, is stuck to my body. It's hot, like really hot outside, and humid, and the alcohol is just making me warmer.

Although I have discovered that it's making me really happy, like I can't stop laughing, and smiling, and it's somehow making everyone else smile around me. "You are very good as well, mister." I point out, and drink from the cup he knocks his ping pong in.

I ditched my shoes before everything even started, and decided that my toes didn't need to be sweaty either. My freshly painted toenails are liking the attention though. The man across from me laughs, and looks over my shoulder. I follow his gaze and see Noah standing near me.

"Noah!" I scream, letting my arms flail into the air as I ditch my game, and rush over to him. His eyes don't look anywhere near as hazy as mine probably do, and only hold amusement from my state. I don't really care though.

"Hey Izzy, how you holding up?" He questions, placing a hand on my lower back to steady me. "So great. I just played beer pong." I shot my thumb in the direction behind me, and watched Noah's face lighten up when he saw something behind me.

I turned to see the man I was playing against smiling back. If I didn't know any better, I'd say– "Oh, I see you've met Xan." Noah explains, starting to walk back, pulling me along with him. "Xan! Great name." I nod, and Xan nod's, laughing. "I didn't know you knew Noah." He says, pointing behind me like I didn't know he was standing right there.

"Oh yeah. We're like. So close." I say, extending the word 'so' way past its limits, and grab my last solo cup, swigging it back. "Slow down there. You're gonna be passed out before midnight if you keep that up." Noah laughs, taking the cup from me and placing it back on the pong table.

Noah and Xan start talking about something, but I'm too focused on trying to tie my hair back into a ponytail that I don't hear anything there saying. I flip my head over, gather my hair, tie it in a high ponytail, and then flip my head back.

I ignore the still stuck to my forehead fly aways, and breath out a huff. A whine flys through my lips, as my dress becomes even more sweaty. "What is wrong with you?" Noah laughs at me again. "I'm so hot. It's too hot here." I grumble, but I'm not sure if my words make sense because he just gives me a confused look.

I laugh at it for some reason, and wave him off, walking towards the house. I pass the pool filled with people, and trip up the step to the house. Luckily, I catch myself in time, and walk through the already open sliding door.

Air conditioning hit's me like no other, and I find myself sighing out of relief, and whipping my hands down the length of the dress. Through dazed eyes, I take in the filled kitchen, and living room where music plays and people dance. More like grind. On one another.

I grimace, and turn towards the kitchen. Not as many people, so I walk over to the fridge and pull out a coca cola, then a solo cup. Thinking about what type of mixture I want to make, speaking from the fact that I've had no other liquor besides tequila, I think about it really hard.

"Rum's good with it." I jump at the voice close behind me, and turn around to see an unfamiliar face. The more I look though the more it looks like I should know him. Where have I seen him before? "Sorry, do I know you?" I ask, pointing my finger at him accusingly.

He laughs, and shakes his head. "Sorta, we meet briefly. Blake." He holds out his hand to shake, and I return it. "Isabelle." I try and think again, but his name still doesn't ring a bell. 'Huh, Isabelle. Pretty name." I get a weird, bad, gut feeling in my stomach.

He just gives off those vibes. Even through my drunkenness, I can tell something is wrong. I turn around, and pour rum with the Cola into a cup, and sip. It's not bad actually. So, I chug the whole thing off. I guess I didn't realize the effects rum would have on me because I instantly started getting dizzy.

That might've been my limit that I just passed there. Suddenly, I feel warm hands on my open back. "Wow, you ok?" Blake askes, holding me up. I must've started falling. "I'm good, thanks." I become aware of our proximity, and start walking away from him.

He tightens his hold on me, and I think that I might be falling again, but I'm not. "I'm ok, thank you." I say again, stronger this time, trying to walk away again. "Why don't we just go sit you down somewhere..." He starts pulling me off in a direction that I can't even decipher through my own vision.

I sober up quickly, not by much, but enough to rip myself out of his grip and know something is not right. "I'm just gonna go find my friends.." I trail off, walking away as quickly as I can, and out the back door.

Through my slight panic, I fail to remember the small step the door gives, and start tumbling down to the cement. Although, I didn't make it there.

I feel arms grabbing me, and pulling me upright. I want to get out of these arms. I don't wanna be touched right now, not after what just happened with barn...barry? What was his name again? Something about these arms though, make me feel safer than Mr.B's back there.

These are hot and cold at the same time, burning my arms. "Name yourself, unknown...man. Before I detain you!" I slur, rocking on my feet, and trying to stop my spinning head. Well now I know never to drink freaking Rum ever again.

I hear a laugh coming from the face high above mine, so to get a clear picture, I grab his cheeks and steady myself from moving.

Green...eyes. Black—no. I pull away, only enough to start falling in another direction, and then to be grabbed again.

Just let me fall in my embarrassment already.

It's like my brain knows what's going on, but my mouth just has a mind of its own. "Milo! Hey there buddy. How's it been?" I ask. At least, I think I ask, but the way he's looking at me makes me think that's not what came out of my mouth at all.

His hands are holding me by the waist now, sending a shocking feeling through my body. A feeling I haven't felt in years. "How much have you had to drink?" He asks, and I watch his eyes grow darker.

Good question Milo, good freaking question.

~~~~~~~~~~~~~~~~~~~~~~~~~~~~~~~~~

AN:Don't worry, next chapter will pick up with this night. It isn't over yet ;)
~~~~~~~~~~~~~~~~~~~~~~~~~~~~~~~~~

Chapter Eight

My Birthday ~~Milo

My body radiates heat as I throw the rest of my beer away, and make my way towards the house. I've shoved myself into the back corner of the yard where no one would bother me, because I can not handle more people today.

I wasn't too fond of this party idea from the very beginning, but how could I say no to the family that basically raised me? I love John like he's my own dad, so I can't exactly just say no when he seemed too excited by the idea of this.

Although the one thing I haven't been able to take my eyes off all night is Isabelle. Just thinking about her makes my jaw clench, and I don't even know why. I'm not mad at her, I'm more annoyed that I'm not. I should be right? I shouldn't want to do the things I want to do.

I sigh for the millionth time tonight, and shake my head, trying to release some tension in my body. Right before I can even walk into the house I feel my body colliding with somonelses. My hands fly out of instinct to catch the girl in front of me, but the moment my hands touch her skin, an electric wave shoots through me.

Ah shit. Blonde hair invades my face as her pony tail slaps my cheeks. A strong scent of roses and vanilla swipes across my nose, momentarily putting me under a happy spell. The moment I catch her face, I see her eyes phased over making me smile slightly.

This is gonna be just wonderful. Her bright blue eyes stare up at me, looking at me like I have two heads. "Name yourself, unknown...man. Before I detain you!" She spits out, slurring the whole sentence. I can't help the laugh that slips out of my lips.

I've never seen Isabelle drunk. I haven't seen Isabelle in general in so long, and it's nice. I'm still holding her up when she squints her eyes, and takes a hold of my cheeks. My eyes widen at the way her grip makes me feel. It's unnerving, like she's slowly tearing down every wall that I put up.

The moment her face holds recognition, she backs away and stumbles again, prompting me to catch her. "Milo! Hey there buddy. How's it been?" She says, to no surprise slurring her words, and patting my chest.

Oh god, I need to get away from her. I need her to get off of me before we both have a very awkward, not fun, problem down south. More like I'm going to have a problem while Isabelle continues to float around in neverland.

"How much have you drunk?" I question, detaching her from my side, but still making sure she's not gonna smack her head on the concrete. She shrugs, and doesn't answer, but instead starts walking towards the pool. I look around for someone I know, and trust, to watch after her but when I don't see anyone I sigh, and chase after her.

"What are you doing?" I question in panic, while she starts squirming out of her dress. "Swimming!" She yells, throwing her dress in the air, revealing the same blue bathing suit she was wearing earlier. I groan at the sight of her, and force my eyes away from body.

This is not helping me right now. She picks up a random can of someone's drink, and brings it to her lips but I grab it before she can drink it. "Isabelle. I think your night needs to come to an end now." She pouts, fucking pouts, doing something weird to my chest.

I go to reach for her, but she backs away from me. "Isabelle." I grumble, watching a cheeky grin fill her face. Oh my, her smile. Jesus help me. I glare at her while she shakes her head, and runs to the other side of the table we were standing at. Still very half naked. "Have fun Milo! It's our birthday!" She yells, drawing no one's attention because everyone here is drunk, and has no care in the world for me and her.

"I'm not doing this right now." She laughs, and wobbles on her feet. "Smile Milo. It's so pretty, and it's going to waist. Smile!" She smiles, and I ignore her statement, because I don't think that's something I'm supposed to be hearing right now. It's not something I want to be hearing.

She starts running and instantly trips over her feet, but luckily she's not far from me, and all I have to do is reach my arm out to catch her at the waist. She giggles, and attempts to pull herself up right. "Thanks for saving me, my knight in shining armor." She pats my chest again, her hands falling down my torso and dropping to her side, then her cheek falls onto my chest, because that's where it reaches.

I look up at the stars, holding her bare waist and swiftly grabbing her dress to throw back over her. She doesn't argue as I tie the straps around her neck and make sure she's fully covered.

Gosh she's so tiny. Why is she so tiny and fragile? It's awakening a protective part of me that needs to stay under wraps before I start killing anyone that looks at her. Her scent intoxicates me once again, and I almost stumble backwards at the power it has.

Shoving my feelings away, and grabbing her by the waist, I throw her onto my shoulder. The last thing I need right now is for her to go grind on some guy's dick, and have him take advantage of a drunk girl. My drunk girl. I groan out of frustration, and slight anger at the image my mind has conjured.

Walking to the side of her house, I swing the tiny gate open, and walk over to the one at my house, doing the same thing. It's instantly quieter as I walk through the sliding door, and into the kitchen. Our houses look more or less the same, and always have.

I would've thought that she would have passed out already, but her legs kicking my stomach lightly tell me otherwise. "Woah! Party is so fun!" She screams in the silent house, and thank god my parents aren't home. They never liked her family from the start, and let me tell you the start, was a long time ago.

I don't respond, and instead listen to her babbling as I make my way up the staircase. As much as it pains me to be hearing her voice, I can't just turn my ears off.

Once we get to the guest room, I set her down on the bed. Maybe a little harsher than I intended because she bounces, and falls onto her back. Her arms fly above her head and pull the ponytail she has in out, letting her blonde hair cascade all over the comforter.

God, she's so beautiful. I shake my head, and stumble into my room to grab her something to wear. I wish I could say it was for her, but if I have to stare at her in that dress for much longer, this party is gonna be taken somewhere else.

I grab the first t-shirt I find, and walk back into the guest room through the connected bathroom. When we were younger and we had sleep-overs–which for the record, nothing would have happened if we slept in the same bed–she would always sleep in the guest room, and we'd keep the bathroom doors open so we could still see each other.

I freeze when I don't find her on the bed. Scratch that, she's not even in the room. A groan that sounds more like a whine leaves my lips. Why, just why can't the lord be on my side? I just want to sleep, in peace, without her in my house.

Ever since she's come back I can't stand all the feelings it's given me, and it's making me mad. Which is then making me rude but I can't help it. I'm not particularly mad at Isabelle, at least not in that sense, but her being here still–if not more–just as gorgeous as when she left.

Why the hell did she have to fucking leave?

I come to my senses when I hear something down stairs, and instantly start following the sound.

When I get to the living room, because that's where it is, I see her sitting on the couch with a slice of pizza in her hand, and the TV playing Back To The Future.

Ok, how the hell did she do all of this drunk and half asleep? "Isabelle. What the hell are you doing?" I whisper, irritatingly. She looks over at me, when she hears her name and raises an eyebrow at me. "Eating pizza. It's cold though." She takes another bite of it, and chews slowly.

"You need to sleep." I walk over to her, and reach to take the remote from beside her, but she swipes it away and stuffs it under her butt. Oh hell, I'm not in the mood for this. "Give it." She shakes her head, eating more of her pizza.

"You're no fun, you need to lighten up..." She looks at the digital clock beside the TV and then mutters. "Birthday boy." Her words even more slurred and muffled as she stuffs the crust into her mouth.

I grow more frustrated, and swipe my hand up my face then through my sweaty hair. It really was so freaking humid outside tonight.

I glance back at the clock, and sure enough it reads 12:10a.m meaning it is in fact June 2nd. My birthday. I sigh, and look back at the drunken girl sitting on my couch. "I missed you." I tense at her words, another brick knocking down another wall.

"I wish I never left. Like golly guys it wasn't that big of a deal. I mean stuff happens and–oh my googly eyes what is that!" I'm so stunned at her words, trying to figure out what she means by that that I don't even turn to see what she's looking at.

It wasn't that big of a deal. Stuff happens. What happened that caused her to leave?

Her eyes are gushing down towards my feet, so I finally relent and look down. There stands Boeing, my cat, that I've only had for a year. He's mean, at least to me. Ok, not mean, just more like the devil reincarnated. He knocks shit over, pees everywhere, runs away–actually a lot–and never listens to me.

For some god unforsaken reason, I can't give him up. He rubs up against my legs, and I watch as the dark gray haired cat with black dots on his back jumps into Isabelle's lap. She gasps, and instantly starts petting him.

He purrs, the ass purrs like he doesn't have a single bad bone in his body, making me want to growl at him. Obviously, I don't. Isabelle looks up at me. "Name?" She questions. She looks like she's gonna pass out right here, but somehow she's still going strong.

"Boeing. He usually doesn't like people." I explain, but as I'm doing so, I glare at him and I swear–I swear–he smirks at me. Little devil. Isabelle's head starts to droop as her consistent pets start getting longer. "Come on." I reach out to pull Boeing off of her, and she doesn't resist this time.

Her eyes lazily run over me as I help her to her feet, and support her weight by wrapping my arm around her waist. She leans into me as we walk up the stairs slowly, and by the time we get to the guest room she's all dead weight. I place her into a sitting position and try to get her attention.

"Wanna change?" She nods, so I hand her the shirt and exit the room. Once I'm in my room, I change into pajama pants and a t-shirt, but before I can lay down in my bed, I hear her call out my name.

I walk over to the connected doors and open it, giving her a questioning look. I see her figure laying in the bed, her body curled under the blanket and her head towards me. She smiles when she sees me, and tugs her fingers out towards me.

I roll my eyes and walk over to her. "Yes?" Her eyes close briefly, but when she opens then she says, "I'm sorry." I tense at her sincerity, and wonder what she's apologizing for. Oh, wait. I don't respond, because frankly I'm not sure how I'm supposed to.

"Leave the door open?" I nod my head and get up from the bed that I had sat on. As I'm walking out the door I hear her call out, "night Milo." I look over my shoulder to see her fast asleep. "Good night Izz." I mutter before gently throwing myself into my bed.

Happy birthday to me.

———

"Come on Milo it's been over a year and I still haven't been able to go on the water." Luna whines, kicking sand up onto her board. "That's not true." She rolls her eyes, and props her arms up on her hips just like I've seen Isabelle do only about 100 times. It means she's definitely not putting this down.

"Ok, you let me on once." I nod my head, seating myself in the sand. "Yeah, and what happened?" Now she cowers back, probably remembering the way she ate about half the sea that day. "Mhm, that's what I thought." I reply smugly, a grin tugging at my lips.

"Now, show me the form again...and, maybe I'll let you try again at the end of this week." Her face lit up, even though 'the end of this week' was on Friday, and it was currently Sunday. She starts bouncing up and down, genuinely excited for an 'if' statement' just making me want to throw her out there even more.

About a year and a half ago Luna came barging into my house, no warning, demanding that I taught her how to surf. I was not appealed by the idea at first, speaking for the fact that I didn't want to see Isabelle let alone a spitting–slightly tinier–image of her.

Although over that time, I have now grown a real liking for Luna, also speaking for the fact that I spend almost all of my time hanging out with her, I really enjoy every second of it.

Have I ever gotten made fun of for hanging out with a 12 year old? Yes. Do I care? Fuck no. Luna's basically my little sister, and definitely family. No matter what anyone says.

"Why was Isabelle leaving your house this morning?" Luna asked casually, staring at her bent knees like it's the most fascinating thing in the world. I can see right past her exterior, and know exactly what she's really asking.

'Your really betraying me for her?' I sigh, and rub my hand across my forehead.

Isabelle was gone when I woke up this morning, the bed perfectly made, and absolutely no evidence she was ever there. Typical Isabelle thing to do though. I was actually surprised when I found the bed empty, and shocked that her body could wake up that early while being hungover.

I was up at 7, meaning she had to have left well before that without me noticing. Also makes me wonder why Luna was up that early.

I know Luna isn't too fond of her sister being here, or the fact that she left either. It kinda frustrates me listening to Luna talk about the same way I'm feeling when it sounds so stupid.

I mean, what are we even mad about anymore? It's just getting exhausting being mad all the time. It's not like it's all Isabelle though. Very, very true. I also have my parents to blame for my shitty 24/7 mood.

"She got drunk off her mind last night, so I let her sleep in the guest bedroom of my house." I answer honestly. There's no point in lying to Luna. I know her trust is a slim line that I am skating the ramps of currently, and I don't wanna break that.

"Seriously? She got drunk?" I see the smallest hint of a smile on her face before it's gone. Sometimes it seems like she's mad because I am. In other words, she's mad for me. The irritating thing is that I'm not even mad.

This is just bullshit, things need to go back to how they used to be.

Then I remember Isabelle's words from last night. The same words that unfortunately kept me from sleeping last night. I'm itching to know the meaning behind them.

'It wasn't that big of a deal' 'stuff happens' 'I'm sorry'.

Why can't I just let go of her drunken words, and let them be nothing more than nonsense she was spueing?Because drunken words are sober thoughts. Because there has to be a reason she left. There has to be. Or maybe I just need Mama Hazel to go tell me I'm a stupid boy again to drill that into my head.

I laugh, and nod my head at Luna. "Yes, she did indeed."

~~~~~~~~~~~~~~~~~~~~~~~~~~~~~~~~

AN:I enjoyed writing Milo's POV, he's kinda just a big softie under his hard exterior.
~~~~~~~~~~~~~~~~~~~~~~~~~~~~~~~~

Chapter Nine

Pink Journals ~~Isabelle

Yes, I did sneak out of my neighbors house half asleep this morning panicked beyond my limits. Not of Milo of course, but of the fact that I was laying in an oddly comfortable and all too familiar bed.

All it took was one look through the connected doors in the bathroom to see Milo's asleep, surprisingly not scowling face that had me make a run for it.

Obviously I made the bed first, because I'm not rude, but I didn't take off Milo's shirt. Franky, in my messed up hungover mind it didn't even register that I was wearing his shirt. It had only clicked after the fact that I was out of his house, not wearing my dress, that it must've been somewhere in his house.

Maybe if I wasn't so freaked out about the fact that I just woke up in Milo freaking Wesley's guest bedroom, I would've gone back in and gotten it.

Instead, I high tailed off his property way too quickly for my hazy mind to take me.

Once in the safety of my own quiet home–thank god my parents weren't back yet–did I not only realize the unearthly hour of the morning, but had I also, somehow, managed to make it to the bathroom before puking my intestines out.

And that's where I found myself for the next 3 hours. On the bathroom floor. At one point, I remember my dad walking in, no words said but a small chuckle leaving his mouth as he passed on some aspirin and water.

It's now noon, and I'm showered, and surprisingly feeling better. The hangover only lasted for the morning, and now I'm cleaning the kitchen...and the backyard...and literally everywhere else because this place is a mess.

A small part in the back of my brain has been nagging me all day about why I was at Milo's house, and what had caused me to end up there. I don't remember anything past the moment I started playing beer pong.

My mom yelled at me already, but once my dad explained to her that I had been awake since 6 in the freaking morning throwing up into the toilet–my new best friend–my mom just told me I had to clean up and I already got all the punishment I needed.

'I hope you've learned your lesson.' She had said, and indeed I had. So now, here I am picking something out of our beautiful garden, in a sweatshirt and shorts. My hair—I don't even want to talk about it. It's a big mop on top of my head, barely hanging onto the hair tie I put in.

I roll up my sleeves as I pull out–nope, nope! No! I shriek and drop everything I was just holding.

A shiver of disgust rolls through my body as I almost gag. I am never having a party again. I whine, yes I whine like a freaking child because this is not fair. If this party was half Milo's, why am I doing all the cleaning alone?

After regaining my composure—and my sanity—I tuck the loose strands of hair behind my ears and walk over to where I know there will be shade. Just out of view from the house, both houses actually. Milo and I's. I find the exact same trees creating the same exact shadows as I remember.

I sigh out in relief from the coolness, and slump onto the stump that again, has always been here.

Resting the palms of my hands onto my forehead, and staring at the green grass, I watch the light catch some sorta metal. Sucking in my breath, I squint my eyes thinking I might be imaging it but nope, I watch it reflect light again.

I lean my hand down, and grab a hold of the small object, and as I begin picking it up a slow string of metal follows after it. A necklace. How the heck did a necklace get lost here? This place isn't something you stumble upon at a drunken party, no this was my childhood spot.

Our spot.

Erasing my thoughts, I move so it's in the shade, and I can get a good look of it.

It's a metal, no color in it at all. It's so small, and fragile. It looks like it could break in one false swoop. The fact that it survived the impact of the ground is surprising. I lean back, and just stare at it.

It's beautiful. A flower, I realize. Instantly I notice it's a daisy, and the only reason I know that is because they've always been my favorite flowers. A small smile forms on my face as I run my fingers over all the small indents of the silver flower.

Upon flipping it over, my breath hitches when I see that there are words on the back. I suddenly feel my heart rate picking up, and guilt, like by reading this I'm invading someone's privacy.

Screw it, I'm curious.

I squint my eyes, and pull it close to my face to read the small handwriting. It actually looks....handwritten, if that's even possible with it being this small.

I finally get a clear shot of the words, and the minute I do my heart falls, as does the flower.

'Smile sunshine, it can't be night forever'

No...oh, oh god. I swipe up the necklace and race for my house. Quickly grabbing the trash bag as well, I stumbled around the pool, nearly falling in and racing inside.

I place the trash bag by the door, and run up the stairs on unsteady feet.

Smile sunshine, it can't be night forever

Smile sunshine,

It can't be night forever.

I lock my bedroom door the minute I'm inside, and sink to the floor against the wood. With shaky hands, I read it over, and over again. Thinking that I'm reading it wrong.

There's no way this is a coincidence. That's what he said to me. That's what he said to me. I suddenly feel queasy again, this time, not because of my intoxication last night.

I suddenly feel hot. Like I can imagine him staring at me, with those huge green eyes and adorable dimples. His black hair shaging, clearly in need of a trim.

There has to be an explanation to this.

He's the only other person that knows where that spot is.

I shuffle off the floor, and scrabble to my closet. I push through the door, and walk into the cramped space, desperate to find something else to wear.

I huff out a groan when I nearly miss eating the floor, and steady my feet in time to look down at the small cardboard box sitting on the ground.

My eyes furrow realizing I really haven't walked into my closet yet. I haven't seen his box in here. With the amount of dust on the top of it, it doesn't seem to have seen a person in a while either.

Looking around almost anxiously, I set the necklace on a shelf and crouched down towards the box. My hands open the top and dust fluters everywhere causing me to swipe my hand in the air, and cough into the dirty fumes.

The minute it's cleared, I set my eyes on the bright pink journal with the words, "DIARY" In big words, and bark out a laugh. No way these are still around.

Gosh I was obsessed with writing journals when I was younger. It was in my daily routine to write a diary entry everyday. My whole childhood is here.

I pick up the first one, and see so many more underneath it.

I fall onto my butt, sitting criss cross now, and get comfy.

The pink book pops from the spine as I open it, making it bluntly obvious that it hasn't been opened since I closed it 5 years ago if not longer. I look up again towards the door, afraid someone might walk in and steal them.

These were something personal to me. I mean I never showed anyone, not even Milo. Only two eyes have ever seen the words I've written, and they belong to me. The first diary entry surprises me with the sloppy handwriting, and when I see the date it all makes sense.

This was written nearly 10 years ago. Meaning it was 2nd grade me.

Monday, June 1stDear Diary,

Today's my birthday! I'm turning 8 years old! I know, it's so crazy. I'm still mad that I have to share my birthday with Milo though. I don't think it's very fair that everyone else gets their own personal birthday all to themselves when mine and Milo's are always shared. Although he is my best friend so I guess I'll let it slide. When I woke up this morning, I was greeted by a tray of fluffy pancakes with strawberries and blueberries everywhere. It was crazy. My mom bought me a new dress this morning to wear too! It's so beautiful. It's got these lovely daisies all over the dress that skims my knees, and even though she says I'm supposed to wear shoes, I don't.After I let my food settle, I of course went over to Milo's house. His parents didn't look so happy when they opened the door. I'm not sure why, but they never seem to be happy. At least not when I'm around. Milo came running out the door within minutes of my arrival and wrapped his big arms around my tiny body. Even though I'm older(Only by a day)he's still so much taller than me. Maybe I'm just short though. "You look pretty." He had said right when their front door shut. I giggled, obviously blushing like a total loser. I mean Milo called me Pretty! On my birthday! He never mentioned my blushing either."Wait right here, I gotta go get your present." He zoomed off then, on his two long legs up the stairs back into the house. I listened, and didn't move, only played with the hem of my dress. I was nervous, like so nervous you have no idea.Before I even knew it, Milo came running out the door again, this time with both his arms behind his back. I tried peeking around him, but one of his hands turned my face back to him. He looked nervous. He was chewing on his bottom lip, and staring at me with those big beautiful green eyes. His black hair was long, covering his forehead and nearly his eyes, but I could still see them."If you don't like it just tell me." He said, looking even more anxious. I only laughed and shook my head. "I'm gonna like it. Show me." A small smile covered his lips, bringing out his dimples. I looked down in his hand, to see a folded up piece of paper."What is it?" I whispered, taking it softly from his hands.He didn't look away from my face as I opened the folded paper, and gasped at the image. You guys don't understand how much my heart sped up at what I saw. It was a drawing. One Milo clearly drew himself. It was a flower though, a really, really gorgeous flower. It looked like I could touch it, and hold it in my hands. "Milo.." I gasped again, running my fingers over the paper. I couldn't stop looking at it. I still can't. Every small shadow caused by the flower was there.Every flaw the flower may have had was there. "Do you like it? If you don't–" I couldn't take it, I jumped into his arms, wrapping my hands around his neck. He had stumbled back a step, catching me by the waist. "I love it Milo, thank you so much." I couldn't stop the tear that fell from my cheek. I knew one thing for sure though. This was the best present I was ever going to get in my life.

I shrieked, dropping the book, and twirling around to see my dad standing at the door. I was breathing heavily from the fact that he had caught me by surprise.

I thought I was alone. I watched my dad lean against the door frame, and smile lightly. "Whatcha doin kiddo." He asked suspiciously, smiling wider when I stuttered and flushed ferociously.

"N-nothing." I kicked the box under a shelving unit where my shoes were supposed to go, and rocked on the heels of my feet. "Uh huh, sure." I nodded my head, subconsciously tucking hair behind my ear.

"Did you need anything?" I whispered, desperately trying to change the subject. "Yeah, how was the party last night?" No, not this type of subject change. "Oh, it was...fun." I started slowly, trying to remember anything that had happened last night.

He laughed at my face, I'm assuming the way I looked conflicted. "I hope you've learned your lesson, and are never going to drink again." This time, his voice held a hint of sturness in it, like this wasn't something he was messing around about. "Of course dad." He nodded, breaking into a small smile.

"Your friends are going to the beach, they want to know if you want to go." I feel bad for saying no, but a part of me doesn't really wanna go. I wanna stay here and freaking devour every grade school journal I ever made. The curious part of me though, the one that wants to read, doesn't beat the part of me that wants to go surfing again. The part of me that wants to see and hang out with my friends. "Yeah, let me just showerr first." With a nod of his head, he began walking away only to stop before he got out.

"Izzy?" He called back. I swallowed hard, fixing up the journals, and hiding them better. "Yeah dad?" I questioned still from the closet, not even being able to see him. "Don't think I didn't see whose shirt you were wearing this morning." Then I hear the door creak open, and close softly.

Blushing so hard I think I might sweat, I lean my forehead against the cool wall and groan. Loudly.

———

"Yes, I remember." I exaggerate, gripping the edge of my board as I try to walk past the barcade of people again. "Isabelle, it's really not safe to be going out on the water without practicing if you haven't gone surfing since you left." Lottie states, for the millionth time.

"I know, but I still remember everything and how it works." I smile, my eyes switching from Lottie, to Violet, to Henry, to Noah, to Milo. Who are all blocking me from the water. Milo hasn't said a word to me at all yet today.

It's giving me an itch or irritation because of the fact that I can't remember what freaking happened with us last night. I don't remember talking to him, or seeing him, or going into his house for that matter.

Every time he looks at me, my body gets all hot and tingly, making me feel like he knows something I don't. Or perhaps just something I don't remember.

"Izzy, it's not safe. You could get really hurt." I know how to surf, it's not like it's been a decade since I've been on the board. "You trust me right?" They nod–besides Milo, I notice–and finally move out of the way.

"Ok, now come on." I begin my march to the water, but as soon as my toes hit the nice, cool water, I'm being scooped up into strong arms, and my surfboard is being dropped. "What the heck! Put me down...Milo? Milo, what–ugh, let me go!" I'm over his shoulder, now, like a ragdoll he carries me.

"My board." I whine, and see Violet scoop it up. "Oh this is rich." I hear Noah snicker. "Seriously man, totally not caring." Henry mutters, and his words make me think I wasn't supposed to hear it. "Both of you shut up will ya." Milo grumbles, the sound vibrating his broad, hard shoulders, shaking me to the core.

He's like an ogre, or troll. Another fact that registers in my mind is that I'm not only over his shoulder, but we are deeply skin to skin at the moment. Like, my bikini has definitely ridden up, and I wouldn't be surprised if my poor bum was sticking out.

"Milo, everyone can see my butt." I hissed, trying–and failing–to reach behind me and cover my loose cheeks. "Let them." He hisses back, making me blush again.

He walks so far that I'm almost certain that we're out of the sand when he finally sets me back down. Harshly on unsteady feet, I wobble slightly regaining balance. "That was very inappropriate." I seeth, glowing crimson, and surprising both of us with my anger. Well, at least I'm surprised. Milo's as cool as a cucumber, standing way too close to me, with his arms folded over his bare chest.

He just stares at me, watching patiently as steam rolls out of my ears. "Why did you do that?" I ask, a bit calmer, but now standing with my hands on my hips. He shrugs, and looks away. "You should know better than anyone that it's a horrible idea to go out there with a board like that." I was shocked, for two reasons.

One: Those are the most words I've heard come out of Milo's mouth since I've been home. Two: He actually sounds...concerned? Worried? I don't know, but whatever it is, it isn't nothing.

"I would've been fine. If I recall, I was a better surfer than you." His eyes narrow, and I watch as his hands fist his forearms on each side. "Was; you used to be. So I suggest you get your pretty little ass on your board, on the sand, for us to judge before you get on the water." My anger dissipates quickly at his language.

Pretty little ass.

Goosebumps rise up on my arms as my brain tries to rack itself with ways to prevent myself from blushing like a flamingo. Too late, it's too late. I'm a goner.

My cheeks flush, and I'm starting to realize that I have blushed more times being just back here for 2 weeks then I have in my entire life.

Strangely, they all lead back to the man standing in front of me. Really close to me, actually. I duck my head, and change my position to cover my exposed skin, feeling way to naked in front of him right now.

Although I have a feeling that even if I was wearing the thickest coat along with the thickest pants I would still feel bare with his gaze on me.

"Ok, uh, yeah. Sure." I clear my throat, keeping my eyes trained on my bare pink toes. "Okay?" He sighs. Furrows his eyebrows.

"Okay."

Chapter Ten

—'They stood there pretendingto just be friends when all the while everyone in the room could plainly see that they were only existingfor each other'~ Unknown ~——

A Birthday Cake and Tears~~Milo

"No."

"No?"

"Yes, no." I emphasize again, for the millionth time tonight. "But there's so much sexually tension between you too. I can't even breathe when I'm near." Henry exaggerates, again. Noah nods his head along and flops down onto my bed.

"No, there isn't." I sigh again, rubbing my face up and down in annoyance. They won't let this go. They haven't let it go since the beach. "You're telling me you haven't gotten hard once since she's been back." Yes, I have. My eyes narrow at Henry's. "No, I haven't."

"I call bullshit." Henry states. "Your bullshit." I retorted. They both smirk, and I realize what I did. I fed into their claims. There fucking try to get a reaction out of me. "Don't even say it."

"You like her." I throw my hands into the air and shake my head at the ceiling. They're never gonna let this go. "I don't like her like that." I threw my clothes that were on the floor into the laundry bin. "Oh, yeah?" Noah asks, totally not convinced. "Yes." He jumps off the bed and runs off to the guest room.

Henry quirks an eyebrow smirking and folding his arms over his head. Noah comes back holding a blue piece of fabric in his hands. No, a dress. Isabelle's dress. "So what's this doing then." I go to grab it but he just moves his hand away. "If I remember correctly, wasn't Isabelle wearing this yesterday?" I actually blush. Jesus Christ

I feel the heat coming up my face and it only makes him smile more. God dammit. "Got something to explain Wesly?" Henry taunts. I groan into my hands and shake my head. "She was drunk out of her mind, I wasn't letting her stay there." I growl.

"Isabelle was drunk?" Henry asks, baffled. "Yeah, it was so funny." Noah laughs, shaking his head. "You saw her and then left her drunk and alone?" I growl at Noah. He holds up his hands up and backs away slowly. "Simmer down, you ogore." He laughs. I lunge onto him, knocking us both onto the ground.

He's laughing his ass off as I plan out his murder. His slow, painful death. "I hate you." I say with no violence in it. Actually a smirk rolling onto my lips. "I love you too buddy." He pats my shoulder and then pulls his hands away and makes a heart with them over his chest.

I roll my eyes and get off him. "Your such a weirdo."

"You know you love it." He winks, shuffling to his feet. "So, just cause you let Isabelle sleep here still doesn't explain why her dress is here." Henry states. Noah and I look back at him laying on his bed with his phone in his hands. "You know something." I narrow my eyes. "Of course I know something. You forget my girlfriend is her best friend."

"What is it?" He shakes his head and starts typing away at his phone. "Bros before—" Noah begins, but doesn't't get far.

"Finish that sentence and you won't have a tongue to speak with." Henry growls, his demeanor instantly changing. "You're so whipped." I state with a small laugh. "It's kinda disturbing."

Henry and Lottie have liked each other for as long as I can remember but only a couple months ago did he grow a pair to ask her out. "Not letting him call my girlfriend a hoe isn't being whipped. It's called human fucking decency." He grumbles.

"You can't even be talking Milo." Noah states with a snicker. Here we go again. I sigh, and start shoving t-shirts on hangers and into my closet. "Holding in all your feelings like this isn't going to get you anywhere." Henry states, with a hint of concern in his voice.

"I'm not holding anything in, ok, now seriously drop it guys." My eyes flicker between them both, and I'm guessing they get the memo because they stop after that. "Ok, well, I'm going to order Pizza then."

———

I pulled the cardboard box out of the fridge in the empty, quiet house, and set it onto the table.

At first the quietness bothered me. Always surrounded by noise, anytime my parent's would go away for a weekend trip I would lose my shit in the silence.

When I was 16 they took their first summer trip down to the Bahamas for 'work'. They weren't here for my birthday, and they weren't here for the fourth of July. Over the course of that summer, I grew quite fond of the silence.

I didn't like them arguing anymore, or their breaths breathing down my back every five seconds.

It's a tradition for them to leave over the summer now. Honestly, I really only see them for 2 months out of the year. And that's with days adding up; they're never here for more than 2 weeks at a time.

Usually I get a happy birthday text from them, but today I got nothing which bothered me. I was waiting for the text for the whole entire day. Even just a 'happy b-day Milo' would've suited. It's my 18th birthday and my parents didn't even remember? How fucked up is that?

Last year–the second year of being alone–the Everrest found out and forced me into their home every Friday to watch movies with them. They celebrated every single thing with me, and became my new family.

An old family that became a new family all over again. I honestly never talked to them after Isabelle left. The only contact I had with them was through Luna. Then Luna found out I was alone, and snitched on me. Which, for the record, I am really thankful for now.

I love Mr and Mrs E like my life depends on it. It really opens your eyes, and proves to you that blood isn't always family.

Sighing through my thoughts I open the cardboard box, and slide out the small, two layered cake that Mama Hazel made for me this morning.

I don't know how that woman found out when my birthday was, but ever since I remember, she's made me a cake. No one else has. No one else has really ever cared. She always acts like she doesn't like me, or doesn't know who I am, but I know deep down she has a soft spot for me. She watched me go through some bad shit a few years back, and actually had the balls to pull me out by the fucking ear.

The sun had set, and the guys left a little bit ago. I've been spending so much time with people, and now the silence doesn't feel right. It feels unsettling again.

I pulled out a candle from the drawer beneath me, and lit it with the lighter I had on hand. With the white of the cake, and the candle burning lightly over it, I closed my eyes and made a wish.

I know it's stupid, but sometimes wishing is the only thing I can do. Plus, I've been wishing for the same thing for 3 years. The minute I blow out the candle the doorbell rings. I stand up straighter, my heart beating quicker.

No body told me they were coming over. I didn't invite anyone over. After an aggressive knock is herd, I began walking towards the front door. Looking out the side window first I see a scowling Luna standing behind the door, her arms hooded across her chest and a glare set on her face.

I open the door, and the minute I do she swings it open and slams into me. Wrapping her arms around me in a hug. I stumble back a step, but nonetheless return her hug. I hear a small sniffle and pull away to see a tear falling down her face.

"Why are you crying?" My panic instantly rises, as does my concern. She sniffles again, and I realize that she's shaking—with anger—she looks really mad. "I hate her." She rasps out, walking past me and wiping her eyes. It doesn't take a genius to know who 'she' is.

I follow after her and sit beside her on the couch. "You don't hate her." Lunas glare slides to me with a look of disbelief. "Yes, I do. She didn't deserve to be welcomed home with open arms when she left us Milo." I sigh, and rub my forehead.

"Want some cake?" Her eyes furrow, but she nods nonetheless. I'm thinking that maybe the sugar will calm her down. I quickly cut us a slice and moved back to the couch to hand it to her. Boeing jumps up onto the couch after I've sat down and lies against my legs. "Can I stay here tonight?" She sniffles again.

"Of course." I reply instantly. "Only if your parents are ok with it though. They get so worried when you run away, you know." She rolls her eyes and stuffs cake into her face. "They know where I go every time." She mumbles with her mouth full of sweets.

"Why do you 'hate' Isabelle?" I finally ask, starting to eat my cake, and pet Boeing. "It's not fair." She finally says after swallowing, her voice tiny. "What's not fair?" I press on. She groans and sets her cake on her lap. "I don't wanna forgive her. I wanted a sister to help me grow up." She finally says, tears coming back to her eyes.

"But you know you don't hate her." She falls back against the seat, and sinks down low. "I want to." She whispers. "Me too." I sigh leaning back with her. It's silent as we finish our cake, and silent as I clean the plates. "Do your parents know you're over here?" She stays quiet, answering my question.

"Come on, I'll walk you back over." She doesn't move, only crosses her arms and shakes her head. "I can't stand being in the same house as her." I can practically feel her rage coming off of her, and for some reason a part of me feels bad for Isabelle.

"Your parents are great people though, and they don't deserve to be worried sick about you all night." She sighs, and looks over at me with pleading eyes. "Can we just watch a movie first? Let me cool down before having to go back over?" I nod my head and grab for the remote.

I hand it to her, and just for good measure I send a quick text to John telling him she's over at my house and I'll bring her back after. It's not the first time she's done this, so I'm sure they're not surprised. I don't want to give the poor people a heart attack though if they haven't caught on yet.

Boeing walks over my lap, purposely stepping on my dick with his back paw. I scowl at the cat as he lays in Luna's lap and starts purring. Do the Everest women have some secret cat power I don't know about?

———

"Don't act so sad. It's a good movie." Luna jokes, slapping my shoulder. "It's Tinkerbell and I'm a grown ass man." She giggles, and slips on her sandals. "That's why you were so engrossed in it." I roll my eyes. "That one just happens to be my favorite." She scoffs and leans back on the couch.

"Sure buddy." I'm totally getting talked on by a 12 year old right now, and I'm definitely taking it like a champ. It's now over 1am, and I'm still adamant about taking her home. "Come on, I'm walking you over." She groans, and grounds her feet when I try and tug her off the couch.

"She lives there, Luna, you can't run away everytime she makes you mad." Her arms cross over her chest, and she glares at me. Playful Luna instantly being swapped with angry Luna. "Oh, like you avoid her wherever she is? Hm? Don't think I didn't see that." I groan now, in frustration, because she's totally right and I am being a horrible role model.

I'm also being extremely selfish, and a hypocrite. "Ok, well, then, we'll both push aside our feelings and suck up being with Isabelle." Luna's eyebrow quirks up. "You're going to be nice to her?" I didn't say that. "I...well. I'll try?" She rolls her eyes and finally stands up.

"Ok, fine." I sigh in relief when she starts walking towards the front door. I never want kids. I can't even deal with Luna, how would I deal with a kid? I shudder, and walk with her out the house. "You don't have to walk with me, my house is right there." She points towards her house, which is completely pitch black inside.

"Yeah..I'll walk you." We made it to her front door quickly. She lifts her fist up to knock on the door, but stops and abruptly turns around. "What if we just watch one more—" I cut her off by reaching over her head and knocking on the door. She groans when I turn her back around.

It's quiet, for a hot second, before I hear footsteps and then see the lights turn on. The door opens slowly, and my eyes widen in surprise when I see a yawning Isabelle on the other side of the door. She's wearing a sweatshirt and sweatpants—which is making me hot just looking at—it's sweating balls outside.

Her blonde hair looks dark in the light, stuffed in a bun on top of her head. She looks like she just woke up. Shit. Her eyes widen when she finally sees me, and looks down to see Luna. "Oh my gosh." She's awake now, pulling Luna into a hug that Luna clearly doesn't recuperate.

Isabelle doesn't seem to notice this though. She just pulls her away and looks down at Luna in the eyes. "Please don't ever leave like that again. Someone could've kidnapped you, or worse, they could've—" Luna pulls out of her grasp and starts sidestepping her.

"Well I was just with him so you can calm your tits." I scowl at Luna as she looks back at me. She rolls her eyes and walks past Isabelle mumbling, "I won't do it again." Isabelle looks away from Luna, and back to me, her body sinking into the door. She rubs her eyes, and that's when I realize that they are red and bloodshot.

Double shit.

She was crying. A lot, by the look of her puffy eyes. A pang of guilt floats through me at the thought of her lying in bed, crying her eyes out, while I watched freaking Tinkerbell with her sister. She was worrying herself while I was eating birthday cake.

"Thank you for bringing her back. I understand why she's so mad at me. I really do. I'm mad at myself too and I just—she doesn't know..." She huffs out a long sigh and looks up to my eyes. "Just, thanks." I nod my head, not really sure what to say.

Her words—all of them—are just swimming around my head trying to connect somehow. Maybe they'll go together like a puzzle in the end. "Bye, MIlo." She whispers, her voice soft with sleep. Her black eye bags do nothing to hide her sleep deprivation. "Bye, Isabelle." The door closes softly in my face, and the light turns off.

I'm not sure how long I stand there just thinking until I finally force my body to move away. It's killing my mind with curiosity at what all of her words are meaning. I wanna know why she seems so different. I wanna know what happened when she left. I wanna know why she left.

Chapter Eleven

—'But what if he's waiting for you to start talking to him? And your waiting for him to start talking to you?~ Just do it, now

~——

A 20 and a 10 ~~Isabelle

"You're not doing it right!" Milo yells from across the table, and I can't really tell if he's more scared or mad at the moment. "Well I'm not having a very good teacher." I bit back, my anger just barely at bay.

Let's just say this has been a very long morning...and it's still only 8am. Although, I really–really–am trying to think on the bright side. "You broke the cash register Isabelle." He hisses, his breath hitting my check as he leans closer so that nearby customers won't hear.

"How was I supposed to know it was old?"

"It's not." He retorts. I gather all the money that is now all in one pile in the middle. "It's fine, I'll just...fix it?" Milo grunts, and stomps off past the back doors of Mama Hazels.

I ignore his man-child-like state, and start scanning my surroundings for anything that will work.

The cash register is one of those two layered ones, and one of the hinges just broke off, so the top half grew slanted prompting the money to practically slide out.

I guess 'just broke off' isn't very descriptive, but all I did was open it. Ok, maybe I tugged it a little harder because of how rude the customer was being. Stupid pricks need to be thankful for what I'm giving them.

The store has been pretty quiet this morning, so when I don't feel like anyones going to be coming, I walk towards the back of the store. There's a small storage closet, and when I open the door I realize it is indeed small.

This used to be my ultimate hiding spot when playing hide and seek with all my friends. Technically no one is allowed back here, but Mama Hazel always left it open, and nobody ever found me.

It was pretty funny, actually.

Only problem though, I don't remember it being this tiny, or cramped pack for that matter.

I flick on the light switch to my right, and a small bulb begins to buzz above my head. It doesn't do much for light, but it does give enough to where I see a small box of random materials.

When I was in Portland, one thing I took up doing in my spare time was creating things. I remember vividly raiding my aunt's attic and creating just worthless items to pass the time.

The older I got, the bigger my things got. I built a treehouse for my little cousins that were on the way, I built them a crib too actually. My aunt was having twins right before I left.

Besides the point, I shove a couple other things away until I get to the box I'm looking for. I need something that's going to be slidable, like a hinge that can move back and forth. Finding a broken piece of rubber band, and popsicle sticks, I walk back out to the front room–thankful no one came by–and get to work.

First, twisting one of the ends of the string to the stick, and then tieing the other end to the other one, I place one stick in the bottom shelf pocket, and the other in the top shelf pocket.

See, that wasn't so hard.

I finish up re organizing the spilled money, and shut the cash register at the same time someone clears their throat. I jumped, spooked, to look up and see a familiar brown eyed man. It startled me, his eyes. Momentarily stunned me.

"Isabelle? You alright?" I blink a couple of times, and laugh awkwardly. "Sorry, you just looked like someone else I knew. Wait, how do you know my name?" I know this man, that's for sure. I ran into him that day when Mama Hazel convinced me to work here.

"Oh, wait, Blake right?" He laughs softly, and nods his head. "You were ok the other night right? You were pretty hammered, and then just disappeared." Oh, that's right. It finally clicks that I saw him on my birthday.

It's a really faint memory that sweeps over my vision of us re introducing ourselves. "Right, sorry, I was out of it, but I–" My voice gets abruptly cut off as I feel another presence behind me. Warmth against my back. "She was perfectly fine." A voice grumbles from behind.

Milo's voice. I look back at him, giving him a quick 'what the freak?' look, before turning back around to Blake. The thing that confuses me even more is that he's semi glaring at the man behind me.

They seem to be having some silent conversation when I step forward, more or so that I wasn't feeling the warmth Milo was emitting onto me.

"Can I get you anything?" He looks back at me, smiles, and nods his head. "Yeah, I'll have–" I huff out a breath of air when my body is jolted quickly.

I don't even have time to process what's happening because I'm being shoved into the back room. I only see the smallest bit of Milo's face as he walks back out to Blake.

I stare, in both shock and confusion. How the heck did he just get me back here, and why did he put me back here? I groan out in annoyance and start stomping out the swinging doors when they swing open on their own.

I run straight into Milo's chest, but don't bounce off. I just stand there, breathing heavily as does he. His eyebrows are once again furrowed, and it looks as if he has an expression of pain on his face.

The doors are clearly open to the world to see us standing in between them, but I can't move. I can't physically get my feet to cooperate with my brain.

Either Milo get's this, or he just wants me to move but he starts moving forward, causing me to walk backwards so that I don't fall. He only stops when we hear the doors behind him swing shut.

The little noise that was being made out in the other room is now replaced with a deafening silence. It's silent, yet so many thoughts and words are being spoken through the air.

"What the heck was that for? You just push me away from my job and start talking for me to an actually nice guy who is possibly my friend? Are you trying to ruin my life?" My words hang in the air for seconds after with him just staring at me.

It takes me a minute for my words to catch up with my brain–and boy do they–which then has me clamping a hand around my mouth, eyes wide. "Oh gosh, I'm sorry. That was so mean–"

"Stop, talking." Milo sighs, no anger at all in his voice. "It's fine, you don't have to apologize, but that dude is a prick and whether you like it or not, I know him better than you; therefore, I get to say what type of person he is." I just blink at him, not believing one word coming out of his mouth.

"Milo, he's done nothing but be nice to me." Except for the weird, bad gut feelings I get when I'm only around him, and the sense of an eerie remembrance. I leave that part out though. "You're going to listen to me when I tell you to stay away from him." My eyebrows shoot up at his command, and then drop into a glare.

"Why am I listening to you? Give me one good reason why I should do what you're saying." I ask slowly. He grunts and looks up at the ceiling. When his face lowers, a look of pure worry is etched onto his face. "Because I'm asking you, Isabelle." His words are hard, but somehow soft at the same time.

I sigh and look down at my feet. "Ok." I finally whisper. He exhales loudly, and walks around me, towards the tables with pastries on them. "I'm being serious Isabelle." He tells me again when I walk over to him. "Yeah, so am I." He glances over at me, his eyebrows furrowed in a confused/glare kinda look. It's confusing me.

"Are you?" My eyes narrow in a confused look because what the heck else am I supposed to do? I am beyond the land of understanding what's going on. "You're really confusing me." I admit. "You're confusing me." He admits back, his voice going pitchy. I snort a giggle and look down at the tray of food he's got in his hands.

I then glance around the busy kitchen that holds 4 other people all doing different jobs. "Stay away from him." He whispers staring back at the pastries, scowling at them like he's ready to take them on. "Yeah, ok, but you're going to poison those poor treats if you keep looking at them like that." His eyes snap up to me set in a glare before he sees me sporting a smile on my lips. Then his eyes somehow soften.

I swipe the tray from around him, and push the swinging doors with my hips to walk out. I leave Milo behind when the doors shut, and I'm off delivering food to people. I do, fortunately, avoid seeing Blake. I'm not looking for him or anything, but I don't see him anywhere when my eyes sweep the café, making me slightly worried about what Milo could've said to him when they were alone.

Ignoring the past, I focus on the present and work the newly fixed cash register, watching the small breakfast rush hour run through, and then die down when noon circles around. People come in, buying books, and reading here. I watch people work, and drink coffee. Dates, phone calls. Basically intrude on everyone's personal lives and not feel a single bit of shame about it.

What surprises me is when Milo walks back out the doors, and leans against the counters next to me, just reaching my height with his hunch over the table. No one has come by the counter in a while, and everyone seems to be content so I lean next to him.

His eyes search the tables of people, until they lock on one particular table in the back and he finally speaks. "What date do you think there on?" I look at the boy and girl, probably around our age, give or take a few years. "What makes you think they're dating? They could be siblings." I glance over at him, but he's looking at them.

"No way, he's got his hand on top of hers, and he looks nervous." Milo points out. I stare at the two people more, and notice their faces looking very similar. "But look at their physical features. They are practically identical." We both stay silent for a few minutes, giving me time to absorb the fact that Milo is talking to me—willingly—and not fusing or glaring.

Change of heart?

"20 bucks there dating." He finally states. I stay silent, staring at them. "30 they're siblings." I challenge him. His eyes widen only slightly, for a second, then fall back into place. "Ok, you're on Everest."

I'm not sure how we are supposed to find out if they're dating or siblings in general, but being so friendly with Milo, and talking like it's normal is really doing something to me. Is this what we would be like if things had never changed between us? Would they be better than this?

My thoughts are interrupted by another set of elbows sitting themselves on the counter. I jerk backwards, clutching my chest at the surprise. "What are we staring at?" Violet questions, her big golden eyes blinking up innocently at me, then switching to Milo who has yet to acknowledge her presence.

He's so focused on the pair that I don't even think he realizes she's here. "Jesus cornflakes, you scared the nut sack off of me." I breathe, smoothing my hair back.

Two pairs of eyes slowly turn to look at me, giving me weird looks. Milo of disbelief, and amusement. Violet of..horror? "What?" I ask slowly, switching my eyes between them. "Scared the nut sack off of you? Isabelle, what the heck does that even mean." I feel my face glow red, but I don't get a chance to answer because Milo's head is snapping back to the two unknown people pair. "We need to work on your phrasing." I hear Violet murmuring while her eyes finally follow where mine and Milo's are attached.

"Why are you looking at the Montgomery twins?" She asks curiously. Although I barely hear her statement over the high squeal that leaves my lips. "Haha, I was right! Pay up mister." I beam with excitement, my face forming a huge smile as I hold my hand out extended for my money.

I've never seen a girl more confused in my life, but I don't even care anymore because all I can see is the pure look of shock on Milo's face. He watches them, slack jawed, walk up to the counter while the girl starts pulling her wallet out. "It's on the house." I tell her.

They both look at my ecstatic expression with a funny look, smiling slightly as if they can't help it. "Oh, are you sure?" The guy askes. I nod, giggling and looking back at Milo.

His expression hasn't changed one bit. "Of course. You two enjoy your day." I wave them off, and when I look back Violets sitting on the counter swinging her legs while Milo's standing crosses armed, leaning with his back against the counter.

I bit down on my lip to suppress another squeal in fear of scaring off any customers, and just held my hand out for him to put money in. I don't even want his money, I just want to gloat about the fact that I was right and he was wrong.

As petty and childish as that sounds, it's so freaking fun seeing his embarrassed and confused face as he fishes for a twenty and ten from his wallet. After slapping the money in my hand, I know I see him suppressing a smile as well. I laugh evilly, and stuff the money into my wallet as I take my apron off. "Will someone please explain what happened?" Violet askes, breaking the care free, light, silence. "He thought they were dating, and I said they were siblings." I reply slyly, snickering to myself. "Ya'll bet on it." She asked in disbelief. I shrug, glancing back at Milo with a smirk.

He's got a normal Milo glare set onto his face, and looks like it could also pass as a pout. "He started it." Violet takes a few cautious looks between us before bursting into a fit of giggles. "Oh man, you got your balls tied there didn't ya?" His glare shifts towards her slowly, his jaw ticking in annoyance. His ears ting a light shade of pink.

She slaps his back, rather harshly, and then jumps off the table. "Come on Izzy, we gotta get going. Our parents are getting a little hangry." He starts pulling me towards the door, but I stop her. "Wait, are you gonna be ok without me?" I ask Milo, right before exiting the door. He looks surprised by my question, but hides it with a cough.

"Yep." I take one extra long look at him before finally just exiting the doors.

~~~~~~~~~~~~~~~~~~~~~~~~~~~~~~~~~

AN:Truly love this chapter
~~~~~~~~~~~~~~~~~~~~~~~~~~~~~~~~~

Chapter Twelve

Lunch at Violets ~~Isabelle

"Ok, spill. What the hell is going on with you and Milo." Violet sputters as we pull out of the parking lot of Mama Hazels. My face turns hot red, and I know it. I feel it. "What?" I clear my throat. "What are you talking about?" She scoffs, glancing over at me.

"I thought you were all like 'me no like old friend' and he was like 'me hate old friend' but you guys seemed all buddy buddy in there." Her arm flays in the air, somewhat pointing in the direction of the store's parking lot were pulling out of. I sink into my seat, and cover my hot face with my cool hands.

I sigh, and attempt to sink back into the seat even more. "I don't know." I mutter. "That was the most I've talked to him since I got back. I don't even know why he suggested that stupid game in the first place." Violet senses my tension, and stays quiet, but her non subtle side glances tell me everything I need to know.

She pulls into her driveway, and the first thing I see are her parents standing at the end of the driveway waving so vigorously I'm afraid their hands might fly off.

Emily and Andrew–Mr and Mrs.Bailey–have always been like a second family to me. That and of course Lotties family, which I'm sure are somewhere inside.

My parents have been talking about having a 'get together' with everyone like we used to for a while, but only last night did my mom notify me that today was gonna be the day. She just said we were going to be having lunch with them, so nothing but a casual get together.

I hop out of the car as Violet takes the key out, and am immediately bombarded by two dark haired bodies. I laugh softly and hug them back tightly.

The minute they pull away from me, Emily takes my face into her hands and quite literally examines every part of me, and then runs her fingers down my hair. "Stop harassing her Ma." Violet scolds, murmuring something I can't catch as she walks back to the house. "Oh my gosh, you are just so gorgeous." Emily continues, ignoring Violet's command.

I don't mind though. I love Emily, and am just as happy to be back and seeing her. "I really missed you." I reply with. She pulls me back into her arms for another hug until Andrew has to drag us inside.

"It's good to have you back kiddo." He whispers, nuzzling me under his arm. "It's good to be back." I state, causing a chuckle to rumble his chest.

"Hey, that isn't fair!" I hear a faintly familiar voice filter through my ears. I think it's Jakes, and my suspicions turn out to be true when another voice chimes in. "Uh, yes, I'm older." Aiden says.

Andrew and I turn the corner, Emily leaving our sides when she sees help needed elsewhere. "Boys." Andrew draws, catching their attention. Jake, who I saw a couple weeks ago at the beach, still looks as handsome as ever, sitting in a t-shirt and shorts on the couch with a playstation controller in his hands. He's got black short hair, that flows well with his dark eyes and dark skin.

I do happen to see the same familiar red head tucked under his arms as well. Anna, I believe her name was? "Isabelle, it's good to see you again." Anna states, while Jake nods along with her, his eyes being pulled back to the screen.

I look over to the other side of him to see Aiden, Violet's older brother by 2 years sitting on the couch. She had told me previously on the phone that he goes to college out of state, but is back for the summer.

He has blonde dusty hair that's cut sharp on top of his head. Leaving the sides shaved, and a lump of blonde curls on top. His eyes, I can't see from here, but I'm pretty sure he used to have green eyes. Of course different from Milo's.

"Holy shit! Your back!" Faster than I can breathe, I'm being scooped up into two strong arms and being twirled around in the air. I squeal, and laugh as he sets me down lightly. My dress swaying at my knees. "You look so pretty." He coos.

Although I blush—because I can't freaking help it—there's nothing romantic about his words. From the minute I laid eyes on Aiden Bailey, he took me under his wing, protecting me from literally anyone or anything that tried to hurt me. He's as much of a bigger brother to Violet as he is to Lottie and I.

"You don't look too bad yourself either. Have you got anyone hooked yet at college?" I question playfully. He leans back, and that's when I realize he's wearing a muscle shirt. Not only that, but he also decides to lift up his arms, flexing them outward to show said muscle. "Only every girl that lays eyes on me."

I scrunch my nose up in distaste, and shake my head. "Don't ever do that again." I laugh. "Don't worry, I'm flattered, but you're definitely more of a sister to—ow! What the heck!" He whines like a little girl when his dad smacks him upside the head.

"Don't be a douchebag." He grumbles, walking back to the kitchen where his wife is setting the nice, big, table. "Come on, sit down." Aiden wraps an arm around my shoulder, and drags me to the couch where I prop myself up on the edge.

"Where's Lottie?" I don't question where Violet is, because odds are neither of them have seen her. "She had a lady incident and Violet took her upstairs." I snicker, and start to get off the couch and Aiden tugs on my arm. "No, don't leave yet." He whines, and you'd think he was younger than us.

"I should go check on her." He reluctantly lets me go to trudge up the stairs alone.

I get a little queasy at the feeling of walking up these stairs again. From the last time I was here...

A hand starts tugging on mine causing me to jump. I stop staring at the door I didn't even realize I was staring at, and look over to see Violet holding my hand. "Hey, you ok?" She asks softly.

I nod my head, and follow her when she pulls me to the other side of the stairs where her bedroom is. The door opens, before we get to it, and Lotties standing here looking a little frazzled. "Oh, hi Izzy." She smiles, twisting a braid in her hand.

"Your brother said you had a ladies incident. Are you ok?" She rolls her eyes at her brother's words, and nods her head. "Yeah, but bleed through a little, no worries. All fixed up." I nod, and start following Violet back down the stairs as we all make our way to the living room. "I think your brother has a slight obsession with me, Violet." She snickers to herself, looking over at me as we start walking towards the living room.

"He's obsessed with everyone that's smaller than him. He has a problem." I agree, just not out loud. "And they return!" Jake throws up his arms, the controller now at his side as he dramatically announces our entrance. This time though, there is another person in the room.

It takes me a hot second to recognize that person as Leo, Violet's younger brother. Who is currently sitting way too close for comfort to Luna. He's got the same dark hair as Violet, practically looking like a spitting image of his older sister.

They're both staring at a phone, but I can't tell what they're watching. "Leo, you remember Isabelle right?" His eyes snap up to me, and it takes him a minute but soon recognition fills his eyes. "Oh yeah! We went to—ow! Hey." He rubs his ribs where Luna shoved her elbow in.

She whispers something to him that I can't hear, but it seems to change his whole mood, because with one more look back towards me, he shifts closer to Luna, and they resume whatever it was they were watching on the phone.

"Come on." Violet urges softly, pushing me by the small of my back to continue towards the kitchen.

My sad mood instantly rises when I see Lotties parents standing in the kitchen, bickering like an old married couple, which for the record they are getting dangerously close to. I laugh quietly at their playful scowling faces towards each other.

"Mom, dad." Lottie calls out, causing both their heads to snap towards me. Lotties dad–Ben–is white, with brown hair on top of his head, while her mom–Row–is African American, with the same braids that Lottie has. "Oh, my baby!" Row yells, launching herself onto me into a hug. "Don't kill the girl." Ben mutters, taking me into his arms once Row is done.

"You're all grown up now. All of you are. You've all just grown up to be such beautiful young women." Row coo's running her hands over my face.

I let her do as she pleases, because what the heck else am I supposed to do? Not let them miss me, and see what I look like?

By the time everyone is finally done with saying their greetings, I'm ready to find my dad and huddle close to him for the rest of the afternoon. "I'm gonna go find my parents." I tell Violet and Lottie shortly from where they are sitting on the couch.

Both their gazes snap to me with concern. "Why?" Violet askes. "Is something wrong?" Lottie askes. I shake my head, and start backing up a little. "No, I'm just gonna make sure they know I got here alright." They both nod their heads, still looking unconvinced.

Once I know they won't pounce on me, I walk quickly out of the room, past all the warm bodies and make my way outside. I already knew I'd find my dad at the grill, and wherever my dad is my mom isn't far.

It really should be harder than this to find them in a crowd.

I walk swiftly towards them, barley missing the corner of a table on my way. My mom spots me first, smiling with a wine glass in her hand.

I don't know what I look like, but whatever expression I seem to have, wipes her smile right off. "Honey, are you ok?" She asks softly. This gets my dad's attention, and soon after, he's turning around towards me.

I give them both a soft smile, but that doesn't stop my dad from wrapping his arms around me, and pulling me into a hug. "What's up? Did something happen?" He asks softly, no rush in his voice at all.

I give myself a minute to breathe, before I pull away and run my fingers through my hair. "Yeah, I'm ok. Just everyone is kinda making me anxious, and, ya know...being back here..." I laugh lightly, trying to diminish the bad mood, but neither of their expressions change. "Do you want to go home? I can drive you." My mom chimes in, already grabbing her purse and keys.

"No, no! I don't need to go home. I mean, we're going to be having a lot of these right? I need to get used to everyone around. I was just so isolated in Portland, it will just take a little bit for me to warm up to everyone." I explained quickly.

My dad's eyes narrow before he shrugs, and turns back to the grill. "If you say so..." My mother says skeptically, but nonetheless sits back down. I breath out the breath I was holding in, while I just sit next to my mom on the patio chairs.

Don't get me wrong, I love all my friends and their families to death. I really do, but sometimes everyone needs a break. "I know we talked all the time on the phone, but you never really mentioned how things were going when you lived in Portland." My mom, not so subtly, asks me. Well, I know what she's implying.

"Um, everything was good I guess. I missed you all like crazy, but I made some pretty cool friends at school. Oh I also got into crafty things like making Aunt Sarah's new crib for the twins." I point out.

"Really? You'll have to start making stuff for me soon then." She laughs, but I hear all the seriousness in her voice, making me smile.

My mom still doesn't look satisfied, so I finally answer the question she's been nagging at. "I also had a really good support system." I whisper softly. She turns towards me, with a sad but happy look on her face.

"Oh, honey." She whispers back, laying her head onto my shoulder. "I love you." She states, almost breaking my heart in two. I know my parents love me, and it was proven when they went to hell in back for me 3 years ago.

It also pains me though to see them hurt so much for me. "I love you too, mom."

"Are you two done being sappy over there? We got some Chicken to eat!" My dad yells, sticking his tong's up in the air—clutching chicken might I add. "Dad, don't ruin the chicken before we can eat it." I laugh, standing up slowly so I don't give my mom whiplash.

"Go tell everyone that the food is ready, Izzy." My dad waves towards the door without even glancing over at me, as he fights with the grill. I'm laughing as I walk back inside the house, and I'm laughing as I sit at the picnic table eating chicken at noon.

Because sitting here with everyone, watching Aiden and Jake bicker;Leo and Luna play around in the pool. Having my friends at my side? How could this get any better?

I know! An internal voice chants over and over again. If Milo was sitting beside you! It calls again. Which makes me realize something. Having him here would be better. As greedy as that sounds, I'm not giving up on him just yet.

~~~~~~~~~~~~~~~~~~~~~~~~~~~~~~~~~

AN: Just a short fun chapter:)
~~~~~~~~~~~~~~~~~~~~~~~~~~~~~~~~~

Chapter Thirteen

—'Making someone laugh after they've just finished crying, is one of the most painfully beautiful thing to ever exist.'~ (via lovelysadness) ~ ——

Pink Fluffy Clouds and a Stale Cupcake ~~Isabelle

Wednesday December 20th Dear Diary

Today was the last day of school before Christmas break. It was only a half day, but I was still dreading it. My dad had basically dragged me out of bed, and forced me to change into my clothes. I was mad at him for a little bit, but after he got Milo and I mcdonalds for breakfast, I forgave him.Milo had a sleepover at my house last night. His parents had an unexpected work thing or something, and so my dad glady said he could stay with us. Since my twin bed wasn't big enough for both of us, we threw every duvet and blanket we owned on the floor, with pillows and had a butt load of popcorn while watching Tinkerbell. I've practically forced Milo to watch every Disney movie ever, but I think he's finally starting to like them.Milo and I have had plenty of sleepovers before, but this one just felt different. It wasn't planned, and everything was last minute. We got to school around 7, when our class started at 7:30. All of the 2nd grade teachers brought their classes into the library to have a christmas party so we all got to be together. Milo, Henry, Noah, Lottie, Violet and I claimed the table in the back as ours and ate all the treats the teachers would allow to our hearts content. I couldn't help but giggle every time Henry said something towards Lottie because she would blush every time! She definitely has a crush on him. Though I think he has one on her too. Honestly, I totally ship. I was talking about it to Milo on the drive home today, and he said he agreed with me. My dad then scolded us for talking about our friends behind their backs, but I bet he secretly knew it too. Oh my gosh, I almost forgot to tell you, today when we all went outside for recess, I was so cold that my teeth were chattering and you know what Milo did? He hugged me until I got warm again!This might sound a little weird, but he smelt so good. It was like a combination of mint and coconut. I was basically smelling him the whole time we hugged. He only stopped when I stopped shivering.Lottie and Violet wouldn't let it down when we got back inside, and I assumed that Henry and Noah were doing the same to him. We played games and split into groups of boys and girls. Overall, it was honestly the best day ever. I can't wait for Christmas though! I already got Milo his present, and I just know he's going to love it. Well, I hope at least.

I close the very first journal that I ever finished writing, and set it next to the box in my closet. It was early. I'm not sure the exact time because I haven't even opened my phone yet today, but the sun has only just risen.

I just knew that as soon as I was awake, I had to continue reading. I barely remember any of this stuff, and reading it is like opening the floodgates to my childhood.

Apparently it's a thing that if you go through something traumatic, your brain can kinda shut down, and close out memories. It's just crazy to be reading all this stuff again.

It's honestly very therapeutic.

It's been a slow week of working at Mama Hazels, but with it finally Friday–my day off–I intend to go to the beach. I've been aching to go surfing again. Like it's right there and I can't do it.

Lottie and Violet said everyones going down to the beach today anyway, and it's going to be a perfect day to go surfing anyways.

I'm not sure why I woke up so early, maybe anticipation? But whatever it was had me clambering out of bed, and flicking on the closet light switch just to sit inside of it and pull out my journals.

There's countless more. I mean, I had to have written at least 2 a year. It's fascinating to see what my 2nd grade brain thought about my best friends. Reading about all the good times we had? It's funny too, because as I read I could replay the memories in my brain so it was like I was living it all over again.

I don't let my brain get ahead of itself thinking about the last things I wrote in the year I left. I'm not there yet, just slowly reading my way through time. Reading through my childhood.

I think all I can take today was the rest of that journal, so I close the box, flick off the light, and start making my way downstairs.

The sun shines brightly through the big window in the kitchen, exposing our beautiful green backyard. The sun is just barely touching the trees, I admire it for as long as I can. I missed this view. After the sun is completely over the horizon and shining way too brightly for....7am, I read on the clock.

I debate about making anything other than a bowl of cereal, and quickly decide against it, speaking for the fact that I do not want to be cleaning up this house again.

I mean, I just got the stench of alcohol out, I do not need burnt pancakes to add to that.

I take in the silence, and realize that I haven't actually been alone with my thoughts since being home, because of everyone I have been surrounded by.

Don't get me wrong, I love it, but now that I'm actually feeling healthy, and happy, the silence is comforting. I'm not afraid anymore, ya know? Well, at least not constantly. Not everyone is completely perfect, but I'd say I'm completely average now.

With a smile on my face, I eat my cheerios against the window, curling my tiny legs up to my chest. I can't help but feel excited for the day to come.

Yes, I have to put up with Milo, but it's not so bad anymore. It's kind of...dare I say amusing? I giggle to myself at what Milo would say if I told him that. "What are you laughing at?" I jump so far out of my skin, I'm afraid I might've lost a few bones when I hear the familiar voice ask.

More specifically, mom's voice. I'm breathing heavily, resting my hand on my chest as I stare at her wide eyed. Her eyebrow quirked in a questioning, but suspicious way at the same time. "Geez, you scared me mom." I laugh nervously, running my fingers through my tired hair.

Ugh, I need a shower.

"So?" She questions further. I groan, thinking about drawing myself in my cereal bowl, then quickly realizing that's not going to be possible, and stick with a half truth of sorts I can tell her. "I, well, am happy to be back." I blurt. She snorts, and starts brewing herself coffee. "Isabelle." Her stern voice has me gulping for that peaceful morning air I had earlier.

"I'm happy to get back out on the water today?" I try again, rising my voice in a question like tone. Gosh darnit. My cover is blown. "Isabelle Mona."

Uh-oh, she used the middle name. "I'm happy to see...Milo?" I whisper, again questioning but not because it's a lie. Because I'm afraid of how she's going to react.

Laughing was not what I expected.

"It's not funny." I mumble, staring at the few remaining cheerios in my bowl. "Sorry, excuse me, but isn't that obvious? I know you miss him, he misses you too honey." My ears perk, but my head stays down. "No he doesn't. He's always arguing with me." Except for earlier this week, but I don't spill that small, vile piece of information.

"That's because he doesn't know how to talk to you anymore. You think he's changed? Look at you Isabelle." I don't move my head, but glance up at her with my eyes to see her leaning against the counter with a mug in hand. "Do tell." She sighs, taking a long sip of her hazelnut roast.

"You've both grown up. He's scared. He's scared to let you in again." I don't blame him. I'm scared too. "Oh." Is all I say though. No confessing today. "You all were planning on going out early today right?" She asks, thankfully changing the subject.

I carry my empty bowl towards the sink, rinse it out, and quickly load it into the empty dishwasher. "Yeah," I sigh. "I should probably start to get ready." Violet and Lottie are picking me up at 8 to get the good morning waves in before all the kids start coming out. Which gives me an hour to get ready.

I head upstairs quickly, hopping into the shower just to wash my body, throwing my hair into a claw clip quickly.

After washing myself, and getting out I change into my baby pink bathing suit Violet got me for my birthday, and throw a strapless dress on over it.

The doorbell rings as soon as I finish sliding on my sandals, and turn the light to my room off. "Bye mom," I called over my shoulder, waiting for her response before walking out the door. "Bye honey." With a small nod to myself, I exit the door quietly and instantly float into an aroma of crazy smells fallowing Violet.

My nose scrunches up in distast as I stop in my tracks to sniff the scent. "What is—" I get cut off by Violets groan and Lotties, 'aha'. "I told you, you smelt weird!" Lottie wags her finger in Violet's face as a way of saying gross. "I know." Violet whines back.

I snort out a laugh, and walk off the small porch as they start walking to the car. "So, you've gotta tell me what happened now." I explain, jumping into the jeep after them.

Violet stays quiet, but luckily Lottie speaks up. "You know how Luna slept over at their house last night?" I nod my head slowly, wondering why that has anything to do with Violet smelling like pink fluffy clouds and a stale cupcake. "Well, she brought over a bunch of her old perfumes; Leo and her sprayed Violet in her sleep." She snickers as I hold back a giggle.

"Why would they even do that?" I ask, chuckling softly to myself. "I don't know!" Violet yells, hitting the steering wheel, and accidently honking the horn. After giving an apologetic wave towards our neighbors she continues talking.

"Ok, well, I do know." This earns another laugh from Lottie. "What did you do?" I ask cautiously. "I accidentally turned all of Leo's white clothes pink in the wash. Including his favorite shorts. And all his underwear." I can't hold it in. I burst out laughing, falling sideways in the back row of seats, slapping my leg as I giggle my butt off.

"Oh my gosh Violet." She groans an "I know," as Lottie joins in on my laughter. "Ok, ok, we're here. You guys can stop laughing now." As soon as

the car turns off, Violet jumps out and pulls the boards she had in the back
of the car out.

Lottie and I follow behind her, all of us carrying at least one surfboard in
our arms. I forgot the way the boards feel in my arms. I missed carrying
these heavy bastards.

Not many people are on the beach, so it doesn't take long for me to spot
the small group of all our friends. Well, all our friends and more. A twang
of something goes off in my stomach, maybe alarm bells, but whatever it
is off putting.

There sitting on a beach towel is someone I frankly completely forgot
about in the last couple weeks. Ava, basking in the sun, her tan smooth skin
way prettier than mine could ever be. I suddenly feel super self conscious
and just want to go home. Or preferably, to the other side of the beach.

"Why is she here again?" Lottie whispers between us. This makes me confused. "Ugh, I don't know." Violet grumbles. "Wait, do you guys not like
her?" I ask, confused. I thought everyone would've liked her. "No, she's got
Milo wrapped around her finger, but we all see through her facade."

I'm still beyond confused, but I don't get to ask anything else because the
guys are soon running up to us and taking our boards. I try, really, really
hard not to stray my vision from anything lower than Milo's face, and I do
succeed...for a little while.

The minute he turns around, I see a perfect line of vision of his toned
back, and perfectly plump butt in his bathing suit bottoms. Oh lord have
mercy. He has tattoos. I gulp for air through my dry throat, and almost
start coughing from my lack of air.

I really need to get this under control.

"You got a little drool there." Noah whispers in my ear, startling me, and a cough finally arises. I sputter, looking over at him with widened eyes.

It's just us now, everyone else has walked back over to our spot. Noah's hand finds my back, patting slowly as he sets the board long ways in the sand, still holding onto the front of it in his hands. "I mean, it is a fine ass, but jesus Isabelle." He laughs, earning an elbow to the ribs.

"What, I was agreeing with you." He exaggerates, but the smirk he has drawn on his face gives it all away. "Don't worry, I stare at it a lot too." He sighs sarcastically, and when I look over at him he's literally staring at Milos butt in the distance.

I slap him upside the head right before he grabs the board and darts off ahead of me. I chase after him, laughing because I can't help it. This is so fun.

He drops the board, and darts for the sea, to which I rip off my dress, kick off my shoes and follow suit. We're only deep enough to where the eaves crash into our knees, but that doesn't stop me from scooping up a load of water and flinging it at him.

He stands there, hands on his hip, water dripping down his chest as he shakes his head. "Now, that wasn't very nice, was it? My sunscreen was definitely not done soaking in yet." I giggle, and then try to run when I realize he's walking towards me.

He reaches me, of course, and bends down to pick me up by the knees. I'm flung over a wet shoulder, a huff leaving my mouth as I start fighting against him. "Noah! Put me down." He pats my calf, but doesn't say anything. I lean up on his back by my hands and see our friends staring at us with anticipation.

Then I realized we were going deeper.

"Noah...I'll buy you ice cream!" I blurt out. To my despair, he does stop, but only to resume a second later with a chuckle. "As tempting as that is, Violets already got dibs for food tonight. Hold your breath." I don't have time to react before I'm being thrown.

I do as told, and hold my breath, my eyes squeezing shut as my body penetrates the water, and my ears are filled with silence. We must not be deep though, because I feel the sand immediately and push off the ground to resurface.

The sun shines brightly in my eyes, as I have to shield it away with my hands when I open my eyes again. Noah is grinning from ear to ear, standing triumph in the water.

I try not to grin, holding my arms over my chest and popping my knee out. The waters up to the top of my torso now, right below my breast, but the waves are softer now, forming more when they get past us.

"I will get you back." He nods his head with a laugh. "Sure ya will." Then his name is being called, and when we look behind him, our friends are walking out to the water.

I take this as my opportunity to body slam him from behind and push him under water. He goes down easily, and I'm not sure if that's because he's being nice or he knew it was me, but either way it makes me smile even bigger.

I stare at our friends for a split second, and wave to them as I sit over a drowning Noah. Well, he's not drowning, I wouldn't let him drown. He wouldn't apparently either, because I'm soon again being flung off his back and into the water again.

~~~~~~~~~~~~~~~~~~~~~~~~~~~~~~~
~~~~~~~~~~~~~~~~~~~~~~~~~~~~~~~

AN: I love Noah and Isabelle's relationship. :))Literally platonic soul-mates.

Chapter Fourteen

—'I'm worried that nothing else will ever feel like love again after you.'~ Unknown ~ ——

Beach Day~~Milo

This is bad, like 'internal panic, external chill' type of bad. My head falls under the water again, and I just wish that my body wouldn't come back up. Maybe I can just stay down here forever.

Sadly, the need to breathe wins, and reaches for air above the water.

My eyes, also sadly, land on her again. She's laying on a towel, sipping god knows what out of a cup while smiling so wide my chest hurts.

She's laying face down, but her head is propped up on her elbows so she can stare at whatever Lottie's rambling about at the moment. Her legs kicked up in the air, covering the perfect view I had of her ass again. Yes again.

Her silky smooth golden hair is tied up in a low bun at the nape of her neck while baby hairs stray out to frame her face.

I can't get my eyes off her.

She's so damn beautiful.

"What are you doing silly?" My eyes draw away from Isabelle with much needed force to look at the girl I've been preoccupied with for the afternoon.

I'm not mad about it. I met Ava at the beginning of the year, and we've been friends since. Well, I know she likes me, and I wish I could recuperate those feelings, but she just doesn't give me the same feelings as...

Her laughter flows through the ocean air, hitting my ear drums, causing my heart to speed up rapidly. I can't think, my throat has gone dry.

Why the hell can I even hear her out here?

"...Milo? Are you listening to me?" Shit. I shake my head. "I'm sorry, I zoned out. What were you saying?" She frowns, and I instantly feel guilty for not listening to her.

"Do you know what you're doing for Fourth of July yet?" Now I frown. "Yeah, my neighbors throw a party every year. I always go to that." She knows this. I told her. Which means she either wasn't paying attention, or wants something else.

She moves in closer, her hand trailing down my chest, and disappearing past the water, nearing the danger zone. I tense, and I'm instantly cursing myself, because she definitely takes it the wrong way.

My hand grips her's under the water, and I slowly move them back to her side. "Oh," Yeah, oh. "I'm sure you're more than welcome to join if you'd like." I offer, knowing it's what she wants. Her face lighten's before it diminishes and her gaze moves to look over towards the beach.

"Yeah, but it's with her. Wouldn't you rather spend it with me?" She asked innocently, her voice holding no anger. Maybe jealousy? Or I'm just hear-

ing things. "I don't go because of her. You know this. They are my family."
I answer proudly. John and Lea are equally if not more like parents to me
then my own. She opens her mouth to speak but doesn't get the chance
to because another voice is interrupting us.

"Hey love birds! Pack it in, kids are here!" Violet, I realize, is screaming for
us. My gaze shifts behind her and I see Luna, and Leo walking onto the
beach, laughing together at something one of them must have said.

Everytime I question her about it, she blushes and starts mumbling and
stuttering like crazy. I personally think it's cute. Nothing better than young
love.

Although I do not recommend it.

"We better get going." I started walking closer to shore when I feel Ava grip
my wrist. I glance back at her questioningly, waiting for her to state her
reason as to why she suddenly doesn't wanna leave.

"None of them like me." She whispers. "That's not true." She looks down
at the water, and nods her head. "Yeah it is. Why don't we leave and go
do something together." She looks up at me hopefully, spasming another
guilty pang to my chest.

"I promised Luna I'd help her surf." Her gaze instantly changes to one of
hope to one of annoyance. "You never want to hang out." Then she pushes
past me, and stomps back to shore.

I sigh, and follow after her, although make no attempt to catch up.

Girls are so exhausting.

Except for Isabelle.

I hold back a groan because for the love of god, how did my mind just
drift like that? I just upset a friend of mine, who is for the record making

it sound like we're a couple–where we are most definitely not–and I'm thinking about her again?

"Ooo, pissed off the bee didn't ya there buddy? Better be careful before she comes back and stings you in the ass." Noah laughs, slapping said ass.

"Touch my cheeks again, and I will personally see to your inability to ever sit down again." He doesn't react to this. In fact, he keeps a straight face, and continues with my strides.

"Ya know, some people find that rather kinky;I'd be careful who you say that too–" His words soon turn to whines as I tug him by the ear, and quicken my speed so I'm dragging him forcefully behind me.

"Care to repeat?" He laughs, and opens his mouth, but another hand is quickly being slapped into the side of his head softly, and I let go. "Noah, save it for your dreams." Violet whispers tugging him by the arm down onto a picnic blanket that rests on the hot sand.

He laughs, and reaches for a bag of goldfish.

What a child.

Grinning, I snort, and lay myself down onto the blanket. A water bottle is soon being thrown at me that I catch quickly, and chug in one go.

It's nearly 10 in the morning, yet I find myself hungry again even though I ate breakfast this morning. Two bodies crowd around me, sitting flush against my side and shoving food into their mouths like barbarians. Or maybe chipmunks because I don't think they swallow any of it.

"When do I get to go surfing?" Luna pries, bouncing way too eagerly for a pre-teen this early. "Yeah, this is a really exciting day dude." Leo comments, causing me to look over to the other un-matured-pre-teen sitting to my left. "You two should be investigators or something. You're freaking me out right now." My comment causes them to just laugh and huddle closer to me.

What am I? Mama bear?

"Answer the question." Luna chants, over and over again. "Well you gotta eat, then wait 30 minutes for that to settle then practice–"

"Don't feed me that 'wait for 30 minutes' bullshit." Luna retorts. "Hey, language." Isabelle–who came out of nowhere, and might actually kill me if she doesn't get out of here–scolds, reaching into the cooler beside us.

"Mhm, yeah. Ok." Luna grumbles. I glare at her when Isabelle visibly de-shines. Is that even a thing? A word? I don't know but Isabelle definitely just lost some happy glow she's been carrying around all morning.

"Sorry." Luna fixes, her tone not changing, but it still lifts Isabelle's smile before she glances over at me. I watch as if in slow motion, and it's like we become the only people here, she slowly trails her eyes down my body and checks me out.

Once she realizes what she's doing, her eyes snap back up to me, and a quick red filters her face. Then she scurries away back to her towel merely 10 feet away from me. My heart beat is still freaking crazy as I fear I may be having a heart attack.

Is this what it feels like? Chest constricting, heart pounding, hands sweating, heart attack. Oh god, I'm dying.

"Why don't we like her again?" Leo questions, leaning forward to get a view of Luna from the other side of me. "Because we don't. You're my best friend. You shouldn't question me."

"Don't manipulate him." I scold. "You don't have to be mad at her Leo." His eyes brighten as he glances back over at her. "Yes he does." I glare at Luna.

Poor Leo probably already got threatened with something involving his balls being detached. God save us all will ya?

"You can surf when I say. I promise I'll get you out there by today." She punches a fist into the air before hip-hip hooray-ing, and attacks me with a hug. "Thank you, thank you thank you..." Her praises get drowned out by a sad looking Isabelle staring at our interaction.

Shit, I didn't even think about that. She's here trying to build a relationship with her sister while I'm practically stealing her. "You need to behave though. Especially towards Isabelle." Luna pulls away, looking no less happy. "Ok!" She cheerfully agrees, and I get a feeling she didn't hear anything that came from my mouth.

———

"Your knees are bent right?"

"Yes they're bent, look at them." Luna grumbles. I know I'm stalling, but after all this time I can't help but be...scared? Luna is my little sister as much as she is Isabelle's. I don't want her to get injured.

What if she gets seriously hurt in the water? What if she drowns? What if she breaks a bone? What if she falls off and gives up?

No, the Everest girls never give up. That thought draws a smirk out onto my face. "Ok, grab your board. Let's get you in the water. I'll be standing on shore watching you and–" She squeals, and jumps off her surfboard so fast I'm surprised she didn't get hurt.

"I swear Luna, if you don't be careful–" She's running off, away from me so fast I don't even get to finish my sentence. "That girl is going to kill me one day." I mutter, like a broken record mother who is watching their kid grow up.

If this is what motherhood feels like, I don't want it.

"You'll be ok, ya big hunk of meat." I don't even have the energy to scowl at Noah's stupid funny comments anymore, so instead I just snicker and shake my head as he passes by.

It's nearing 1 p.m now, and I am rapidly beginning to feel my lunch hunger set in. I love days on the beach more than anything, but they leave me exhausted.

I'm drawn out of my thoughts when I hear a small whimper coming from somewhere behind me. I whip around quickly, trying to find the source of the noise. I'm starting to believe I was hearing things when I hear it again. Although this time it seems to be out of pain, morphing into a groan.

I walk towards the cars, because that's where it's coming from, and when I reach it, I finally spot the source.

Blonde hair, tied up still as Isabelle leans her forehead against the side of the car. "What are you doing?" I ask, concern seeping through my voice. She startles backwards, clutching her chest and staring at me wide eyed.

When she moves forward, I can't help but catch the wince her face makes. "I, uh, forgot to put on sunscreen, and, um, I think it's too late but I was trying to get some onto my back..." She trails off grabbing her shoulders with her hands.

I walk around her, to get a gaze of her back, and wince at the sight of it. "Jesus christ." I mutter, taking a better look at the bright red skin that's almost blistering. "Oh gosh, is it that bad." She whimpers, sagging her head again.

It really is that bad.

But I don't wanna freak her out.

"No," I cleared my throat. "Let me grab some coco butter." I dash off to my car that isn't far at all, and throw my body into the scorching front seat to fish for my small container of coco butter lotion, and get out just as fast.

She's still standing in the same position, not one muscle moved. She must really be in pain.

I hand it to her, but her brows only furrow. "Milo..I can't reach my back." My eyes widened for a split second, imagining my hands running down her smooth back with lotion.

Sweet baby jesus. I clear my throat, and stare at the ground with my jaw set. "I guess...I'll do it." I take the bottle from her hands, and walk behind her again. She takes a deep breath, putting her hands on the top of the car and leaning into it just so that her forehead can rest again.

I do not like the way this is making me feel. How intimate this is. How wrong this feels. God, how right this feels. Against my better judgment, I pour some of the lotion into my hand, and slowly begin rubbing it into her skin. She tenses, and groans at the contact.

The coco butter has some SPF in it as well, so it should act as sunscreen until the burn goes away. I make sure to only get the spot needed, but I can't help but shiver at the nosies she's making.

Her skin is so smooth.

I know all of the noises she's making are ones out of pain, but the big man down stairs doesn't seem to register that one bit. It's more like, 'women make good sounds' and bam. I have no control anymore.

Just think of dear old granny Milo.

"Is that ok?" I strain to say, finally taking my hands off her. She turns around slowly, and wipes the sweaty baby hairs out of her face. "Yes," She breathes out. "It was great, thanks." Her voice whispers, which surprises me because she was never a quiet talker when we were younger. "Yeah...of course." I whisper back, because at the moment it feels illegal to speak any louder.

I know I'm half caging her in right now, but I can't move. I'm just staring at her, taking in her new features for the first time. Her blue eyes, and her freckled face. Her button nose that's pressed lightly against her skin.

My gaze drops slightly to her collar bone when a white line catches my attention. Actually, 2 white lines. Scars. They're almost making the shape of a circle, but they cut off in the middle. The only thing swimming through my mind though is that they weren't there before.

They're new.

They're so faint, it's hard to see them, but the light is doing a pretty damn good job at showing it off. I open my mouth, to say anything. Just something to break the tension but a different voice beat's me to it.

"Milo! There you are! I was looking for you..." Ava's voice fades slowly as does her pace when she rounds around the car.

I jump away from Isabelle so fast, it causes her to jump as well. Ava stares at us, looking shocked and angry at the same time. "Hey, what's up?" I ask. Not knowing what to do with my hands, I place them behind my back and clasp them together.

"I was looking for you. Why are you guys together?" She asks through a smile. A genuine smile. Well, it looks genuine, but you never know what's going through her head. "She burnt her back, so she was helping her put coco butter on." Ava's smile doesn't falter as she moves in on Isabelle.

Although, I've known her long enough to know she doesn't have the best intentions. Sometimes when we're alone, Ava tells me how she doesn't ever mean to be mean to people, it just happens and she always feels bad.

I believed her because she's never given me a reason not to. She's nice, and she's my friend, but I can't help but feel protective over Isabelle.

Either she's blind or she doesn't notice the look Ava's giving her, but she smiles brightly and waves at her. "Hi. You're Ava right?" Ava nods, smiling back at her.

"Yeah, it's nice to see you again Isabelle." Her voice is off. It doesn't sound nice, and it's a little scary that her face still holds pure kindness.

They stare at each other, and then I watch Isabelle's smile diminish and she starts walking backwards. "I should get back to Violet and Lottie." She laughs awkwardly, and then scurry's away.

Ava turns around, looking content and sly. Apparently too much so that she doesn't even see my confused face. "What was that?" I finally questioned when she reached me and intertwined our fingers.

Ok, this is getting a little out of hand.

She starts dragging me back towards the beach when I abruptly stop and tug on her arm gently. She turns, and gives me a puppy dog eyed stare. "What the heck just happened?" I ask again.

"Nothing happened. Let's go." I tug on her arm again. This time, when she turns around she looks aggravated. "You know, I don't...like you like that."

She laughs, and continues to tug on my arm. "I know silly. You're like my best friend." Oh, ok. That makes me feel better. I sigh in relief and finally follow after her.

~~~~~~~~~~~~~~~~~~~~~~~~~~~~~~~~

AN: Guys, I literally love Noah so much. I can't even— although I also wanna try and do something later on with Henry more. Give him a one on one with Izz or Milo.

Let's just not talk about Ava right now lol.
~~~~~~~~~~~~~~~~~~~~~~~~~~~~~~~~

Chapter Fifteen

—'You and I, always almost. Again and again. We were always on the verge of almost. Never nothing. Never something.'~ Unknown ~——

Sleepover~~Isabelle

"Why are you acting so weird?" Lottie pokes me in the stomach again with her freakishly sharp nails. "Ow Lottie! Stop poking me." I groan, rubbing the sore spot on my stomach.

She smiles sheepishly, and mutters a quiet apology. A couple more seconds of silence before she scoots closer and whispers, "Did something happen with Milo?" I hold back another groan and drop my head into my hands.

Of course something happened with Milo. Something is always happening with Milo and I. I hate to admit that I maybe, kind of, possibly liked his touch on me. I haven't been able to stop thinking about it for 3 freaking hours.

So, I have come to the conclusion that I have a problem, and I have a feeling Milo is stuck somewhere in the middle of it.

"Where's your boyfriend, shouldn't you guys be like...I don't know...cu ddling?" She laughs at this and tugs at the ends of my hair lightly. "Stop avoiding the question." I sigh, knowing I'm not going to get out of this.

"Milo helped me put cocoa butter on my back." She stays silent, looking at the ocean in thought. There's still a decent amount of daylight left in the day, but the color of the sky is starting to change a bit orange.

Lottie begins to nod slowly, and then looks at me with confusion. "What's wrong with that?" She questions. Before I scream at the top of my lungs in frustration, I take a deep breath and try to keep my voice low.

"He had his hands on my back." I whisper, trying to get her to understand what I'm saying without having to actually say it. "You've lost me." She states. This time, I do groan, along with the blush that rises on my face. This is ridiculous.

"I can't stop thinking about it. I, um, liked it?" Lotties face breaks out into a wide grin that spreads across her face like jelly on bread, and I understand what she was doing. She was messing with me. She just wanted me to say it.

"Aww, I'm so happy for you." She tugs on me, wrapping her arms around my neck causing me to fall into her side. She squeezes what's left of my breath out of my lungs in a hug.

"It gets worse." I stress, pushing off her to get her reaction. "Ava showed up, and I feel bad because she already told me she likes him, and wants to make sure nothings going on with us–"

"Whoa wait, she's talked to you about this?" Lottie questions, irritation taking over her features. "Yeah," I nod. "I kinda caught them doing it in Violet's car the first night I was here." Lotties eyes bulged out of her head at my statement. "Why didn't you tell us that! Oh my gosh, I need to clean her car with bleach." She shudders.

"Um, sorry? Anyways, she approached me the day I got the job at Mama Hazel's, and told me the stuff about her liking him. I don't think she likes me very much now." Lottie just stares at me in astonishment as I wrap up my story. "I am going to kill her." Lottie starts standing upward, causing my eyes to widen, and my hands to tug her back down.

"What are you doing?" I whisper-yell. "Going to beat a bitch." I shake my head rapidly. "No, what, why?" She sighs and rubs her temples. "I know you weren't here to see any of it, but Ava's been obsessed with Milo for nearly a year, and he's made it very clear that he doesn't like her. Every time he confesses that though, she always reassures them that they're 'just friends' even though that's not what she really thinks."

"Oh." I whisper, lifting my eyes to stare at them talking. "Well then why have they had sex?" Lottie rubs her eyes slowly, looking about one second away from losing it. "I don't know. It happens when he gets drunk. Of course it's just another thing that Ava has told him is just platonic though."

At her words, I start to feel anger rising in me. No one deserves to be manipulated like this. No one deserves to get played, especially Milo. "You get it now?" Lottie stresses. I nod my head slowly, narrowing my eyes at Ava's hand that runs down his arm.

They're laying on a towel together, and Milo doesn't seem to be comfortable with her touch. "I wish I still knew him like I used to, so he could at least talk to me." I confess. Lottie visibly softens as I lay my head on her shoulder.

"Maybe you should tell him." I tense, pulling back suddenly. "No, he hates me. He would blame me–" Lottie cuts me off. "Whoa, hey, I know he may be mad at you, but he's not going to blame you for being–"

"Lottie." I hissed. She shuts her mouth instantly. "I'm sorry, it's not my place." She sighs. "It's ok. I know you only mean well." We both fall into a comfortable silence of just watching Noah be a weirdo with Violet, and Henry work with Luna on surfing. She's been doing a really good job.

"I'm starving. Can we go get something at Mama Hazels now." Noah whines, running up to us. Violets not far behind. "Yeah, me too." They're heaving dramatically in front of us, causing both Lottie and I to start laughing.

"Yeah, I'm cool with that." I say, smiling back at them. "Go get the others, me and Lottie will go get the car started." They both nod and dart off to our friends.

Lottie and I start walking back to the car, but as hard as I try, I can't help but look back at Milo.

He's looking straight back at me.

———

I'm really really trying to give Ava the benefit of the doubt, but the more my mind races the more I just come up with reasons to not like her.

I don't like not liking people. I truly believe everyone deserves to be loved, and cared for, because you never know what someone could be going through.

She never came out to eat with us after the beach. Milo may have taken her home, but I'm still not that sure. Here we are though, sat in Mama Hazels, and I can't stop thinking about Ava.

"Isabelle?"

I mean seriously, why is this girl trying to force herself onto Milo? She's practically sexually assaulting him by putting her hands where he doesn't want them.

"Isabelle."

And the fact that even when he speaks up about it, she just manipulates him into thinking she 'just wants to be friends.' She told me to my face she likes him.

I was trying to actually let her get her shot, but now–

"Isabelle!" I jump when I hear my name being screamed in my ear. Violet places an arm on my shoulder, but I just shrug her off, still feeling mad. I don't like being mad in general. Even more so at people.

"Are you ok?" My face heats as all of our friends stare at me with a mix of concern and confusion. I clear my throat, and let out a small, nervous laugh. "Yeah, sorry. Just got lost in thought."

Nobody believes me, but no one mentions anything either. "Anyway, we were thinking of having a little movie night. Your house has always been the one we used to go to...so, we were wondering if you were cool with that?" Noah askes, sipping on his Dr.Pepper.

"Oh, yeah. Why not?" Everyone else smiles at my response, even though I'm still a little flustered from a few seconds ago.

Noah is right though. We used to have weekly sleepovers where we would make forts on the ground in front of my Tv, and watch Disney movies all night long.

It was indeed always at my house. That was only because my mom made us the best snacks, and my dad always let us stay up for however long we wanted.

It's dark outside now, but still very humid. It's always humid here though.

Once everyone is done with their drinks, we paid, and began driving home. We had dropped Luna and Leo at my house before coming here, because I believe they are also having a sleepover together. I doubt my parents will let them in a room alone together. Although they did let me and Milo alone together.

So with that, the guys drive their car, and us girls drive in Violet's car.

We get home quickly, and the guys are already racing into the house before we can even step foot outside of the car. They all seem more relaxed than normal. Ok, Milo seems more relaxed than normal, especially since Ava's gone. Is that mean to say? That's definitely mean to say.

I really need to drop this problem I have with her. It is getting ridiculous.

It's not just today though either. Milo has been a lot more relaxed with me since his birthday, and I'm not really sure why. Maybe he's finally warming up to the fact that I'm home.

The three of us walk inside to find Henry scrolling through the Tv, Noah carrying so many blankets you can't even see his face, and Milo in the kitchen searching for food.

"Mom? Dad?" I peek my head out the back door, and see them both silently chatting on the deck. "Hey guys." They both smile over to me. "Hi honey, how was the beach?" My mom askes. "It was," I think it over for a second. "Good, actually. I'm really glad I went." I just don't mention the part where Luna ignored me, and Ava...became a problem.

"I'm happy for you Izzy." My dad praises. "Yeah, me too, dad. oh also, everyone came over. Well, just the usual, but we were going to have a movie night in the living room if that's alright. I promise I'll clean it all up in the–"

"It's ok Izz, go have fun with your friends." Dad chuckles, and when I look over at mom, she's smiling and biting her lip. "Go on." She urges. I thank them quickly, and duck back into the nice air conditioned house.

"They're cool with it right?" Lottie askes, and I notice she's now huddled up to Henry's body. "Of course." I answer, walking over to the kitchen.

I regret it immediately when I see the catastrophic mess Milo's making. "Oh my gosh, what the heck are you doing?" I gasp, then giggle into my hand.

Milo looks up at me panicked, but the minute he sees me laughing at him his face softens. Oh gosh, his facial features aren't all hard and tense anymore. He has such a baby-man face. Does that make sense?

Of course it doesn't Isabelle. Right, right whatever. "Here, let me help." I grab a bigger bowl from the dishwasher, and pour the overflowed bowl of chips into the bigger one. "Want me to make popcorn?" He questions?

I nod my head, only glancing up at him slightly to make sure he sees my head gesture.

After I see that he has, we fall into a silent routine of getting all the food together, and it feels right. It feels a little too comfortable for the way things have been.

It almost makes me feel like we really did just go back to being friends, and that Milo isn't really mad at me for leaving. Then I look up at him, and he has a hard and stoney look on his face again, and I know that's not that case.

"Aren't you tired of fighting, and being mad all the time? I whisper, turning my head to the side trying to analyze him. His face contorts into one of pain, and I know it's hurting him.

"You don't get it, Isabelle." He answers gruffly. "I have to, you don't understand what you did when you left." You don't know why I left! I want to scream, but it wouldn't change anything. His voice is edged, and sharp, and painful. He's in pain because of me.

Even if I wanted to explain, he won't hear me if he doesn't want to.

"I know but–" I get cut off by the voice of someone else.

"Guys, hurry up. Henry is starting Tangled, and I am not rewinding because you guys missed it." Noah exaggerates, throwing his hands in front of him to show that we need to come.

I grab a couple bags of chocolates and sweets before we walk into the living room. I stop short when I see everything. It's so beautiful. I forgot how much fun this used to be.

They have pillows propped up against the couch, and so many fluffy blankets and bedspreads that there's no way you can feel the ground beneath it.

Lottie and Henry are in even more of a cuddly position, watching the beginning of the movie start to play. Violet steals the popcorn from Milo and starts chowing down on it.

Noah sits beside her and takes handfuls of popcorn as well. God, they're such hethens.

I lay myself against the pillows, and snuggle under the blankets. I'm so exhausted from the long day in the sun and swimming that it doesn't even register in my brain how close Milo is sitting next to me.

I eat a little bit of chips, and then a handful of skittles before I find my eyes starting to shut.

I try to keep them open, as we're no more than 30 minutes into the movie yet, and I really do love this movie, but my sleepiness is winning right now.

My body starts to shut down as I feel my head falling to the side. It lands on something hard, and I instantly tense. I pull my head up just enough to see Milo staring at me.

I rub my eyes and yawn before saying, "I'm sorry, I didn't mean too..." My eyes start drooping again. A soft hand presses on the side of my head, guiding it to his shoulder once again. Oh my gosh is this Milo's hand? What the heck is he doing?

"It's ok, go to sleep sunshine." He whispers softly, and I don't even fight it. I'm out like a light within seconds.

~~~~~~~~~~~~~~~~~~~~~~~~~~~~~~~~~

AN:Just a short fun chapter:) don't worry, they'll start getting closer soon.
~~~~~~~~~~~~~~~~~~~~~~~~~~~~~~~~~

Chapter Sixteen

—'If two people can't seem to stay away from each other maybe they aren't supposed to.'~ Unknown ~——

SPIDERS~~Isabelle

I love having a plan for each day. I like waking up early so that I can process what I will be doing that day. I'm never late to parties, or when meeting up with someone. If anything, I'm early. I need to be productive during the day because if I'm not, my brain swallows me whole.

Which all leads back to why I don't like rainy weather. You can't plan, or predict when the rain will stop and start so you can't plan around it.

It sucks.

So the first thing I wake up to on Saturday morning is a headache, because it's already raining, and my head is already in a swirl.

I was instantly awake before everyone else–totally not anywhere near Milo Wesley, because that would be crazy–and sulking because I knew, I knew exactly what those dark clouds were going to bring.

I was eating an apple, slouched on the seat in the kitchen, drinking a glass of water when I heard the first sound of thunder.

I've always tried to stay in a good mode, and not only for myself but for others. I don't like being sad, or grumpy, and I most definitely try to find the best in every situation.

Although I don't think there is a 'best' scenario when it's raining.

My spine straightens when I hear footsteps coming from the stairs. My friends are all still asleep in the living room, and my parents bedroom is behind the stairs.

That means it could only be one other person.

A tired, half awake looking Luna comes waltzing into the kitchen, barely standing on her feet. She doesn't seem to notice my presence as she grabs a glass of water and starts filling it up at the fridge.

"Good morning." I exclaim cheerfully, smiling at her when she looks over to me. She looks startled, wide eyed like a racoon caught in your trash can.

Then her eyes narrow, and turn back to her water. "Morning." She grumbles with a croaky voice, and stumbles out of the kitchen.

Progress.

I nod my head to myself with a smile, thinking maybe this day won't be too bad. Although my happiness is short-lived.

I suppress a 'jaw drop' moment, when Milo now walks up the small step into the kitchen from the opposite side as Luna. The side that also leads to the living room to the right of me.

His hair is a mess sticking every which way, and he's freaking shirtless. He's shirtless. That's all my brain can think of. That's all my brain can comprehend.

I think I may be drooling, which I hope I'm not because that would be embarrassing, but I can't stop looking. Not just at him. I mean don't get me wrong, he's got abs, and sweet sweet muscles—no, ok, no.

I'm mostly looking at the tattoos though. I've seen them before. Obviously I saw small glances from afar at the beach, but here, now, I can see them a lot more clearly.

The biggest one is on his shoulder, which flows down half of his right arm to the elbow. I think it may be a person, but it's hard to see from here. The rest are scattered on his chest. I can only make out a couple hearts, and maybe a snake but everything is in such precise detail its astonishing.

Whoever did those are flipping amazing at tattoos. There is something tiny—one thing—on his left arm that's too out of sight to even make out the shape of.

The real question that I have though is how he even got those. He just turned 18 a week ago. Those are definitely from more than a week ago.

A throat clears, and it's not mine, which causes me to jump and finally stops staring at him. Oh god. I was just staring at him.

We lock eyes, and I see that he's smirking, and leaning against the counter that's across from me. He's got a cup of water in his hands. When did he even get water?

I blush so hard it dips into my stomach and makes me queasy. A good queasy that's given me a big rush of adrenaline.

My eyes finally darted down to my water, and it is very interesting now that I think about– "Just ask what you wanna ask Isabelle." My eyes move back to his freaking emerald glowing ones, while my mind stays one step behind on his voice.

I take deep breaths, to clear my head of...well, just Milo in general before attempting to speak. Milo has literally infested my mind, and is killing me.

"Oh, uh. How did you get all those tattoos?" I stutter, and then clear my throat when it suddenly goes dry. "I did them myself." It takes a second for his words to register in my brain, because I'm still a step behind, but once they do all I can do is gape at him.

"You did all of those by yourself?" I squeak, completely flustered and confused. He shrugs like it's nothing. "A couple I couldn't, and those I got done by one of my friends that's practicing tattooing." He explains with ease, as if it's the most normal thing in the world.

"Your parents don't mind?" It still feels weird to be having a normal conversation with him where he's not getting mad, which causes me to inevitably get mad. I can tell by the way his body is tense that he doesn't exactly feel comfortable with this topic of discussion.

"They don't care to know." He answers more coldly this time. I drop the subject from there. "So, is that what you're doing then?" I whisper softly, taking a big gulp of water to cool my heated face. "Doing what?"

"Tattooing. Are you going into tattooing?" He doesn't answer right away, and looks to be thinking hard about my question. "I don't know." He whispers, looking off to the side in deep thought. It seems to be something he's been thinking about a lot lately.

Although, I do know that he loves drawing, and is in fact a really good drawer so maybe that has something to do with it. "Well, they are really pretty." I mutter while swirling the glass of water in my hands.

When he doesn't say anything else, I take a quick glance up at him only to see that he is staring at me. His face looks constricted, and concentrated and as his eyes run over my face I realize he's trying to read me.

Diverting my eyes once again, it gets really quiet, and uncomfortable in the room. We never used to be like this. We always knew what to say to each other, and even when we didn't, the silence wasn't bad.

We both jump when a grumble is heard coming from the doorway of the kitchen. Henry walks in, with Lottie following after him. They're both dragging their feet, but Henry stops half way through, causing Lottie to run right into him.

He looks between us, and then groans again. "I feel like I just walked into a cloud of tension." He mutters through a yawn. I ignore his comment and ask, "Are Violet and Noah still asleep?" As if on cue I hear a load of muttered cruses coming from the living room.

Then a second later there's a scream, and Violet comes running full speed into the kitchen. Everyone is on high alert now, trying to figure out what just happened. "Are you ok?" I ask, standing up and rounding the table.

She shakes her head, breathing hard and holding her hands on her hips. "No, there was a–"

"SPIDER! GET IT OFF ME!" We all jump, and run back into the living room where Noah screamed bloody murder from. Thank god my parents are already gone.

Noahs sitting with his back against the couch, holding his arm out and flailing it all over the place. "Noah, stop, don't move!" Violet yell's over his wailing. He stops instantly, and shields his eyes with his other hand.

"Get it off! Get it off! Is it off yet!?!" He yells, and I think he may be crying now. I snicker, not feeling bad at all for laughing at him, because the way that Violet has her arms extended out in front of her, like it might protect her as she approaches Noah is killing me.

"Oh god it's still there! It's crawling up your arm!" She squeals and runs away behind Milo, using him as a human shield. He's laughing too, I realize.

Noah stands up instantly, and starts running, but I quickly grab a hold of him and examine his arm trying to find it. "Please get it off Izzy! I think I may faint, and die. Oh god, what if it kills me." I giggle when I spot the tiny creature who looks just as freaked out.

"It won't kill you." I laugh, and then scoop the little thing off his arm. He slumps once it's gone, and wiggles out his body. "Get it away from me." He steps back, making sure his arm is out in front of him to protect himself.

"Relax, I think you gave the thing a heart attack." I whisper, walking towards the back door and sliding it open. It's drizzling now, but I don't have any other choice but to let the spider crawl off of my hand into the grass past the deck.

Once it's off, I speed walk back to the house and slide the door shut after I get inside. The minute it's locked, the clouds finally release their water and it starts pouring down rain. I sigh, and rub my forehead to try and get rid of this stupid headache.

"Is it gone?" Violet whispers, causing me to turn around to see everyone staring at me with anticipation. I put my headache to the side, and smiled, wipping my hands on my legs.

"Yep, now he can live out the rest of his happy little life in peace." I walk back to the kitchen where everyone is seated at the counter, and hop up the small step before I trip.

"That little crawling bug doesn't deserve peace." Noah shakes his head in disgust, sipping on a glass of water. I roll my eyes, and throw the rest of my apple away. "Don't be so dramatic. It wasn't gonna hurt you."

"You're just saying that because you love bugs." Henry chimes in, and Lottie nods with him. "I don't love bugs. I just treat animals the same as I'd treat a human." I shrug, and shudder when it thunders again.

"That's not normal." Milo adds while the rest of them nod along, but I can hear the playfulness in their voices, and see them all smiling at me. I've always liked animals, and they've always attacked me for it.

"Oh shush, it's who I am and you can all deal with it or else you'll start finding bugs in your house." I wouldn't do that, but it's fun to taunt them. "You wouldn't." Noah gasped, looking at me wide eyed.

I laugh, and shake my head. "No, I wouldn't, but it was worth threatening to get that reaction out of you." He narrows his eyes, but breaks out into a smile anyway.

"I hate to admit it, but I definitely missed your 'save the plants and animals' talk." Noah exclaims, smiling brightly at me. "Ok, it wasn't exactly–"

"Me too." Milo whispers. Everyone's head turned towards him, but he doesn't give any type of emotion off. He simply leans back in his chair and crosses his arms over his chest. His–thankfully– clothed chest.

He shrugs his shoulders, and drains the rest of his water.

I suddenly feel hot, and itchy, and maybe....like I wanna cry? Henry clears his throat and nods, smiling towards me. "I agree." Lottie and Violet both nod their heads while scarfing down lucky charms from a cereal bowl.

They already gave me their 'we missed everything about you' spiel, so I just find it amusing.

A loud crackle of thunder fills the room, and lightening brightens the room before all the lights suddenly flicker. Violet laughs nervously, shaking her head while she drains the milk from her bowl.

"Let's pray that we only get a flicker. Ya know it would really suck if—" Violet stops talking as the lights flicker for the second time, and then go out. "Violet." Noah groans, dragging out her name along with everyone else's collective moans and groans.

"Well this shall be fun." I mutter, feeling my headache grow worse.

——

I've always had a mutual feeling about the dark. It never particularly scared me, but I wasn't exactly best friends with it either.

I slept with my room pitch black, but every door needed to be closed before I could fall asleep. It never scared me because I never had a reason to be scared.

When I was younger it was always the monster under my bed, or the scary creature lurking in the corners was going to get me. As I got older though, those fears started to wear off.

I didn't need a night light, I would walk outside in the dark between the houses, play until my parents forcefully dragged me inside.

It wasn't until the end of Freshman year, during Violet's beginning of summer party did I begin to fear it again. It wasn't a slow burn back into it.

I didn't gradually grow afraid of it, or watch a horror film that brought it back for a weekend. That night, in that bedroom...everything changed.

After 'it', I physically didn't sleep, I couldn't. I needed sleeping pills, and even then I was always tired after waking up. I didn't leave the house ever.

I needed every single light on in the house, I needed to be able to see every possible corner that could go dark.

It was scary honestly. It became a phobia of mine, that gradually with therapy I began to overcome. I was ok to sleep in the dark again, but I needed the hallway light to glow up my room.

I could go outside, but with the exception that I wouldn't be alone. When I came home, I finally felt normal again. Like just maybe everything would be ok, and I could forget anything that ever happened.

But right now? At this moment? I can't see anything, and all I can hear is the storm becoming louder and louder and louder and–

"Hey Izzy babe, you ok?" Lottie askes warily, and I notice my hands are starting to shake. I snap out of my thoughts instantly, and try to blink away the darkness.

Didn't work then, isn't working now.

I take a deep breath in, and wipe my sweaty hands on my shirt. "Why don't we go sit down." I realize I hadn't answered her yet, which is probably freaking her out a little bit.

"Oh, I'm uh, ok Lottie." I smile at her and laugh softly. She still directs me towards a stool, and sits me down. That's when I notice everyone else staring at me with concern.

My eyes jump to Milos, and his eyes are furrowed, racing across my face for more info. "Seriously, I'm good." I laugh again, swallowing the lump in my throat.

The rooms tense again while everyone just has silent conversations with each other. No one speaks, but so many words are being said. "Why don't we bake something? You have a gas stove right? Fudgy-no-bakes?"

I'm a little shocked at Milo's suggestion, but at the same time I feel that weird thing happen in my stomach again. God is Milo Wesley giving me butterflies?

No, of course not. I smile, and slap my hands on the counter. "That's a great idea." From there, the girls and I get started on what needs to be melted while the guys get all the dry ingredients together.

We struggle, and laugh, and make the most fun out of this situation. Any chance of a panic attack, or PTSD episode is vanished as we are all screaming at one another to get all the ingredients in at the right time.

By the time it's finished, we are worn out, and all just a big mess. I'm picking up the first goody that's dry to test taste when the lights suddenly turn back on.

"Oh my gosh, I'm putting on Beauty and the Beast!" Noah screams, flinging his body into the living room. "No! We are going to watch Cinderella!" Violet yells following them.

Henry takes handfuls of our chocolaty treats as he trots off into the living room, oblivious to anything else around him. "Are you ok, for reals?" Lottie whispers, stuffing the treats into a napkin.

"I'm ok, for reals." She smiles and walks away.

Well would you look at that, it's just Milo and I. Again. Although this time, I find myself smiling up at him as I eat my fudgy heaven.

"Admit it. You had fun." He snatches one of the treats off the parchment paper and rolls his gorgeous green eyes. "Sure, whatever." He mutters. I laugh, and start to walk away from the kitchen as well.

"Ok, fine, you win. I had fun. Thank you Izzy." Izzy. He called me Izzy. Maybe we are making progress.

Chapter Seventeen

Finally Surfing~~Isabelle

I'm laying flat on my back, in a starfish position on my bed staring at the ceiling. My bedroom is a decent size, it gives me space on both sides of my bed, and a good amount of room between my desk and my bed.

I've always loved my room, because it's always been me ya know?

I sigh, lost in thought, and turn my head to the side to see the curtains open on my window. It gives a straight view to Milo's window.

I remember when I became obsessed with the song You Belong With Me by Taylor Swift, and forced him to re-enact the video of it with me.

We had Violet and Noah film it for us. It was awesome.

I frown, thinking about all the fun memories we had, and find myself sitting up and walking over to the window. I wince at the blaring sun, and have to blink a few times before I can see outside properly.

His curtains are closed, which makes sense speaking for the fact that it's only 7:30 in the morning. It's also a Sunday, which happens to be one of the few days Milo and I have off together.

I tap my finger against the railing, squinting my eyes at his window like maybe I'll be able to see through it. If he opens his curtains right now, I think I'd cry, and then probably throw myself out of this window.

I look like a creep.

Before I can get caught, I turn around sharply, and walk over to my closet, already knowing what I'm going to change into.

After pulling a soft thin dress over my bathing suit, I tie my hair back into a low bun and trudge down the stairs. It's quiet in my house, and I don't think my parents are awake yet.

This is too, a day they both have off. I surprisingly walk out the front door with ease, and make a sharp left turn towards my neighbors house. AKA Milo's house of course

Without a second thought, I take in a deep breath and give his front door 4 loud knocks. Once I'm done, I nod to myself, smiling already at the day to come.

I almost think he may have not heard me, and then start to feel bad for possibly waking him up when the door flies open. I startle for a moment, before composing myself, and watching a half awake Milo stare at me with confusion.

"Isabelle? What the hell are you doing here?" Oopsies. Turns out I did wake him up. He's also shirtless. Ugh, why is he always shirtless?

It's making my voice very hard to create words here. I clear my throat, and laugh nervously. "We're going to the beach." I speak confidently. His eyes narrow, and then a sarcastic laugh escapes his throat.

" 'We', are not doing anything." The door starts to close when I wail out a pathetic "Wait!" And slam my hand in the middle of the door. It stops, and opens slowly with a very upset tired man-child looking thing, standing in the doorway.

"Listen, you told me I couldn't surf because I haven't in a while, so I won't, ok? It's not fair though that you guys keep telling me no when no one will help 'show me' how to again ya know? So, come on, you're teaching me." I state, breathing in loads of air when my speech is over.

He stares at me blankly before groaning and looking up at the ceiling. "Fine, whatever. Just let me get ready first." I squeal as he walks away–leaving the door wide open–and fist pump the air above me.

He stops, and turns to look at me with a questioning brow. I clear my throat, feeling myself harshly blush. "I mean, uh, thanks." He laughs softly and runs up the stairs.

Oh my gosh. I just got Milo to laugh. Did anyone else see that? Crap, why didn't I video that? Ok, now I'm just being mean.

I suppress another fist pump to the air, and instead, walk inside his dimly lit house. Well this doesn't look fun. Before doing anything, I open all the blinds to let in the sunlight so that his house looks a little less scary.

I sigh, hearing the water running upstairs and decide to make myself comfy. I remember bits and pieces of the night of my birthday, some being in his house, but most of it's just a blur.

With that in mind, it's a little strange to be in his house again, fully sober, and seeing everything for the half-first time again.

It's a pretty house, surprisingly clean, making me wonder where his parents are. Now thinking about it, I haven't seen them at all since I've been back.

Has Milo been alone all this time?

I'm distracted from my thoughts the minute I hear a small 'meow' coming from below me. I gasp and look down at the little cat that rubs up against my leg.

"Oh well look at you. Aren't you a cutie?" I gush, and pick up this unknown cat's name into my arms. I hazeley remember seeing him before, but I just can't for the life of me remember his name.

He's cute, with a dark shade of gray fur all over his body, but then also these cute tiny black spots all over his back. He looks kind of old too, but I could be totally wrong.

He starts purring as I pet the top of his head, and run my fingers through his back. "Aww, you are just the cutest freaking cat in the world. I could just squish you." I giggle, and place myself in a criss-cross position in the middle of his living room.

I pull at the cat's collar, examining the name tag until I come across the name Boeing in a very pretty cursive font. Boeing, well that suits him. I don't know why, it just does.

I place Boeing on the carpet, and watch him roll onto his back, then proceed to let out a loud meow. I laugh again and rub his belly. His purring picks up once again.

I search the living room until I come across a small stick with a string and feather attached to it. I grab it, and dangle it over Boeing. His eyes shoot open and he instantly tries to claw at it.

I giggle again, and continue to stare at him with love while he entertains me.

"Ok, you ready?" I turn slightly to my right to see Milo coming down the stairs in a black t-shirt with black swimming trunks. Well that definitely goes with his 24/7 mood.

His eyes follow the play toy in my hands, and then his eyes widen and I feel a sudden sting coming from my finger. I wince, and turn down to see Boeing's claw in my finger.

"Ow." I whine quietly, pulling my finger free and dropping the small toy on top of him. He takes no mind of me while I watch blood start running down my finger.

I jump when I feel a hand covering my wrist and lifting my arm up vertically. "I don't want blood on the carpet." Milo grumbles, and pulls me softly to my feet.

"Oh, sorry." I mumble, ignoring the slight sting in my finger. There's quite a lot of blood, and it's starting to trail down my finger.

Suddenly, we are in the kitchen, and my finger is being placed under the water. All the blood washes away, but I can't even feel it over the soft fabric of a shirt against my back, and Milo's breathing over my shoulder.

He is extremely close, and I am way more ok with it than I should be. He stays focused, as he grabs a paper towel off the counter, and wraps it around my finger. "Hold this, I'm going to go find a bandaid."

I feel intoxicated by his coconut scent as he walks away from me, leaving me a little dizzy. I try to stop the swirl in my stomach, and the race of my heart but it doesn't work.

Milo is helping me, and my heart is melting away from me. I feel like my insides could just explode right now.

Milo comes back into the kitchen quickly, with a box of bandaids that have a picture of superheroes on them. "Uh, I don't use bandaids often, so this is all I got." I laugh softly, and shrug my shoulders.

His expression changes to one I can't really analyze when I laugh. He stares at me for a second as he's pulling the paper off the bandaid before he diverts his eyes and shakes his head.

He walks back over to me, as I'm leaning against the sink still. I stare into his eyes, and try to at least come off as if I might not quite literally pass out from lack of oxygen right now.

He doesn't break eye contact until I feel his big hand cover my wrist and pull it in between our bodies. He pulls the paper towel away, and inspects the small cut that's starting to slowly bleed again.

Quickly, he rubs some neosporin on it, and then grabs a hulk bandaid and wraps it around my finger. "Hulk?" I question, trying to ease my chest pains, but only succeed in getting my voice to go croaky and high.

He shrugs, finishing sticking the bandaid on lightly. "It was the first one I grabbed." He doesn't let go after he's done, just holds my hand gently, and looks back up to my face.

I feel the air sift between us, from one of tension to one of comfortable silence. He searches my face, before his eyes drop down to my neck.

"Where did you get this scar?" He whispers, trailing his fingers lightly over the mark on my collarbone.

All of a sudden, it feels like we are best friends again. It feels like he's never hated me, and nothing ever changed. It feels like I could laugh, and joke, and like we just went for a night walk around the block 5 minutes ago. It feels like I could tell him where my scar came from.

But I can't, and reality comes crashing down on me again. His question brings me back down, showing me that things have changed, and that things aren't normal because what 15 year old goes through something like that?

I take in a shaky breath, and look to the side so that I'm not as consumed by him. His hand leaves my body, and falls to the side as he stares at me, waiting for an answer.

"I'll tell you," I whisper. "But not today." He sees my sudden sad expression, and nods his head sharply, stepping away from me.

I feel as if I can breathe again, and gather simple thoughts as he walks past me towards the front door. "I have an extra board in the back of my car that you can use." He calls out to me as he leaves the house.

I stand there, stock still, just replaying the strange moment we just had. The way his eyes held concern, and a little bit of fear as he asked about my scar.

I used to try and cover it up, because it made me feel disgusted anytime I caught sight of it. After a year of hard core therapy though, I've learned to love it about me.

It shows a part of my past that I've been through, and made it out alive. At least that's what my therapist said. Maybe it's just all a load of crap that I'm happily believing.

I sigh loudly, and finally walk myself outside of his house. The cement is still partly wet from the storm yesterday that also lasted through the night, and the air is more humid than normal.

I climb into the SUV quickly, already feeling sweat from under the bun my hair is in. "I still don't understand why I have to 're-learn', it's not like I just forgot how to surf."

Milo begins backing out of the driveway quietly, then turns the nod for the volume up just enough to give the car a slight hum of music.

"It's just for safety. You could literally drown if you don't know what you're doing." He states in an obvious tone, like I should already know that.

I stare down at my hands with a frown. "But I do know what I'm doing." I state, getting a little more agitated. Leave it to Milo to bring the anger out of me.

"Again, it's just to be safe." He mumbles, with an annoyed tone clipping his voice. We pull up to the beach quickly, and he's soon unbuckling, trying to get out of the car as soon as possible.

This was a bad idea. I should've just stayed home with my little over dramatic brain running a million miles a minute. But no, I had to come and be the problem fixer and try to solve Milo.

I'm so frustrated I can't think properly, and I barely have the coordination to walk out of the car without staggering, or letting hot molten lava pour out of my ears.

No, I will not let Milo have this effect on me. I'm bigger than this. I take a couple deep breaths, before smiling, and rounding the trunk to help drag out a surfboard.

He gives me a strange look, one I've never seen before, but it's gone before I can even begin to process what it could mean, and he's rolling his eyes and walking away. With both the surf boards might I add.

"Hey! I was going to help, dingus." His head slightly cocks to the side at my statement. "Wow, did you just insult me? Thought I'd never see the day." I laugh lowly, shaking my head and poking the inside of my cheek to hide my annoyance.

Calm Isabelle. Calm Isabelle. Deep breaths. He's trying to agitate you.

"For you? Glady." I murmur, speed walking too catch up with him. I didn't bother with socks this morning, so the sand burns the soles of my feet right off.

I'm used to it, and I think that most of the skin cells on the bottom of my feet are dead, so it doesn't hurt too bad. "Ok buddy, let's get started," I smile, and snatch one of the surf boards out of his hands.

Throwing it onto the sand, I hop onto it and bend my knees with the placement I know I'm supposed to have. "See, I got it." He shakes his head, and groans, while getting on top of his surfboard.

"Don't watch your feet, make sure you're aware of your surroundings. Keep your arms out, but bent at the elbow." I follow his movements that I obviously already know.

Ok, I'm definitely not taking this seriously, but it is sort of ridiculous. It's bluntly obvious that I know what I'm doing here. He sees this, because why wouldn't he, which causes him to jump off his surfboard that's mere feet away from me and stomp over.

My body goes rigid as he comes behind me, and gently places his hands on my hips. Even through the material of the dress, my skin burns under his finger tips.

"Relax." He whispers quietly, then pushes my feet outward with his own, to show the right placement. My body seers with heat, and I am so glad he can't see my face because if he could, he would know just the effect he has on me. "See, then you extend your arms hafeway..." He mumbles, while his hands glide towards my arms and then lifting them to the appropriate position.

"Got it?" He asks softly. I don't trust my voice, so all I do is nod my head yes. I've been touched by Milo more times since I've been home than I had been with my time away in Portland.

It's getting only slightly concerning. I am now realizing why Luna likes him as a teacher so much. He's doing a great job. At showing me how to surf. Just surf, that's it.

"Ok, let's try in the water now." He comes back around me, but before I catch his eyeline, I flip the dress off of me and lay it down in the sand. When I'm done, I'm hoping that my face has cooled down slightly, and now it just looks red from the sun.

I'm wearing a light pink bikini, that's not too showy. I like it. It's also one of those types that I know will be secure enough to surf in. Some bathing suits would slide right off my body the minute a wave pushes me over.

Trust me, I know from experience.

Milo takes a quick glance down at my feet, probably examining the nicely done hot pink that I painted onto them last night, and laughs to himself.

I frown, trying to see why he's laughing at my feet. I don't get the chance to ask though, because he's soon grabbing his board and walking over to the water.

The water is surprisingly calm today, but also with big waves. The waves are normally ruff, but they don't look that bad today. If you want good surfing waves, like me for example, it's better to do it during high tide.

Which it is right now.

There aren't too many people here either. Only a couple adults, which is better than kids. Kids get in the way, and could possibly get very injured. Then their parents get mad, and try to sue, and it just gets very messy.

The minute my feet touch the shallow water, my heart starts beating harshly against my rib cage. I find myself nervous as we hit knee deep, and the waves start to crash into my upper body.

Milo glances back at me, I assume to make sure I know what I'm do-ing—which, all of a sudden, I don't think I do. My hands are sweating, and my breathing is getting heavier.

It's just surfing. You used to do this to calm yourself. Remember? Right, right. Yeah. I get my breathing under control, and begin paddling with my hands, laying flat down on the board, belly down.

"This is a good one!" Milo yells over the sound of the crashing water behind us, and instantly my fear is gone. My brain takes over, and I don't even think while I push up on the board, catching the wave perfectly.

I smile enormously, as I ride it out, and only feel complete ecstasy. God, I forgot how good this feels. A laugh gurgles its way through my lips as I come down from the wave, slightly closer to shore.

My head whips towards Milos who's now standing beside his surfboard, with wet hair.

I don't think, I just do.

The next thing I know, I'm jumping onto Milo and latching onto him like a sloth. His arms go around my back, and I squeal– probably a little to loudly–in his ear

I pull back and stare into his eyes. "Oh my gosh. That was so fun! I forgot how the wind feels when you're riding out the wave. Or nervous when you're catching it! Oh my gosh Milo, did you see me?? Was it good?! I told you–"

"It was great, Isabelle." He smiles.

He. Freaking. Smiles. His dimples give way, and his green eyes shimmer with the water against the sun. My chest heaves as I take in his beautiful features.

Then, as my breathing slows down, and the waves grow quiet, my actions catch up with me. I suddenly feel my bare legs that are around his bare waist, and my arms that are around his neck.

My checks flush, and I instantly pull away from him, throwing myself back into the water.

"Oh gosh, I'm sorry." I laugh, pulling my hands up to my checks and squishing my checks, hoping that I'll pop like confetti. His eyes widen and then his cheeks flush, the tips of his ears going red.

He clears his throat, and looks off into the distance of the ocean.

"Why don't we get a couple more waves, to let you get the feel of it again?" I nod graciously letting him direct us back out into the noisy water.

I fear that without the noise, my thoughts may become too loud for me to handle.

~~~~~~~~~~~~~~~~~~~~~~~~~~~~~~~~~

AN: Guys, I know nothing about surfing so please bare with me lol.
~~~~~~~~~~~~~~~~~~~~~~~~~~~~~~~~~

Chapter Eighteen

Sickening Sweet Cheeks~~Isabelle

I'm in love.Ok, so I'm only 9, and in 4th grade, but I am definitely in love. The moment my eyes locked onto his, it was love at first sight. Milo says I'm not in love, but every time I lay eyes on Harry Styles, a piece of me melts. Milo said I can't be in love with a man I've never met. I just think Milo's jealous that he can't have Harry. I told him so this morning. We had a sleepover last night because his parents had to run out for some big law related thing. I had said, "Milo, I am in love with Harry Styles." Milo looked at me with those big green eyes, and laughed.He smiled, showing me his cute dimples and shook his head. He said, "Have you not seen the movie Frozen?" I had in fact. We went and saw it in theaters together last weekend. I memorized all the songs, and forced Milo to re-enact all the scenes with me. Obviously he was Olaf, and I was Anna. That's not the point though. I laughed at Milo's dumb question and shook my head yes. "We watched it together." He rolls his eyes, and places both his hands on my shoulder."Remember Kristof's famous words. You can't marry someone you just met? It works the same for you." He shrugged. "You can't fall in love with someone at first sight." I giggled again."You're wrong.""No I'm not." Then we proceeded to argue back and forth for at least 20 minutes. My dad had to break us up and suggest milkshakes at Mama Hazels. At least that was something we could agree on—

"What are you reading?" A distrangled, slightly horrific scream flies past my lips as I snap the book shut, and shove it under my butt.

Not my most favored action ever, but it got the trick done. Milo stares at me with a half curious half amused look on his face. Then a knowing smirk forms on his lips.

"Was that one of your diaries?" I grow red—because that seems to be my new look—and clear my throat, sitting up straighter. "Nope, don't know what you're talking about." I shrug, and look away from him so he can't see my face.

"Mhm, sure." He drags out the word sure silently, and walks through the swinging doors of Mama Hazels. It's Thursday evening, with the sun setting outside and the place getting quieter.

Rush hour ended about half an hour ago, so now we're just dealing with late night couples, or families looking for a small snack.

Neither of us normally close, or do night shifts, but Mama Hazel said she didn't have anyone else to close up, and she was going to see her new granddaughter, so she couldn't be here like normal.

I'm not sure what she had to threaten Milo with to get him here, but I gladly said yes. I was also in the middle of reading one of my books, so I decided to take it along.

Apparently that was a bad idea.

I haven't been feeling particularly the best today, and I'm not sure why. I'm hot, my throat hurts, and my head hurts. I was in bed when Mama Hazel had called.

How could I say no to that poor old woman? She can barely stand on her feet anymore. Plus she was going to go meet her newly born grandbaby.

Although, the more my eyes droop, the more I realize maybe I should've just left this up to Milo. He's a big boy, he can take care of this shop by himself.

All of a sudden, I get an insanely rude itch in my nose, and find myself releasing a sneeze. Darn, this may be bad. I shake my head, clearing the slight fuzziness, and stand up slowly.

My body thrums softly, feeling stiff. I sigh, twisting my neck around, and then walking out the swinging doors. I grab one of the tubs we use for dirty dishes, and make my way to all the empty tables.

I stop slowly at each one, placing all the plates and cups into my tub until it's full, and making my way back to the kitchen. I walk into the doors going backwards to push it open with my butt, and twirl around to walk through once it's open.

I spot Milo immediately, seeming as we are the only ones left here, and see him placing pans into the freezer.

He doesn't seem to notice me, which is great, because I don't think I could deal with his nonsense talking right now. Ok, I'm being a little mean now, but my head is throbbing, and my nose is running.

I sniff away the snot, and begin washing all of the dishes. I place them one by one on the drying rack, my movements getting slower, and slower, and my body getting heavier by the minute.

I ignore my mind's wishes to sleep, and lean down to open the dishwasher to begin emptying it. Unfortunately for me, I stand up a little too quickly, and my body starts falling backwards. I grip the edge of the sink, and squeeze my eyes shut, willing the dizziness to go away.

This is really just a horrible day for me isn't it.

Suddenly I feel a hand gently press to the small of my back causing my eyes to spring open, and spin around. "Wow, are you ok?" I nod my head, swallowing and then wincing at my dry throat.

Milo frowns, examining my face before reaching up and placing his hand on my forehead. I instinctively close my eyes and lean into his cold hand. I hadn't realized how hot I was until I felt his coolness radiating off him.

My eyes burn slightly when I open them again. Milo's still standing in front of me, and watching me like a hawk. Frown still present upon his face. Although it looks to have deepened, and now he's got creasing marks on the sides of his mouth.

"Are you feeling sick? You're burning up, and your checks are all red." He states matter-of-factly. "No." I murmur, feeling my mood plummet further. I try to smile, and turn around to walk away but he catches me by the waist and keeps me from moving.

"Well, it doesn't matter if you don't feel sick. You definitely are. Here, sit down, I'll get you some water." His tone sounds light, and exhausted, but not angry or irritated.

I would try to figure it out, but my clogged up brain won't allow it. So I comply, letting him lead me to a chair for me to slump into.

"Just give me like, 20 minutes to close up, and I'll drive you home." I frown, trying to stand up, but instantly sit down when I grow dizzy again. My body feels weak, and my hands are shaking.

"Drink the water." He mumbled before darting out of the room. I would argue, but my throat feels like the sahara desert on a very hot day, so I listen to him once again, and chug my water.

Not even thinking about it, I lean my head against the cool, metal, counter, and close my eyes. I'm not sure how fast time is passing right now, but my brain begins to wander over to what I'm doing this weekend.

Violets having her annual summer party that she throws every year. Well, apparently she hasn't actually had it since I left–makes sense–but she wanted to continue the tradition since I'm back.

Although, it may end up with me having a full blown panic attack. Or getting drunk, but I don't think I wanna drink again. Like ever. That was a horrible experience.

I mean it was fun being drunk, but the not remembering part, and the sick part in the morning was not. I'm not sure how I feel about this party anymore actually.

I wouldn't tell her that though. She's been chatting my ear off about it for the last week. Then cuts in to say, 'we don't have to have it if you don't want though' after telling me how excited she is again.

Yeah, I'd rather not dim her happy spirit.

"Hey, wake up. I am way too tired to carry you." I groan, not wanting to lift my head up from the table that I've now warmed with my heated body.

I feel my body being shifted into a sitting position, causing me to groan from the light. "Wake up." Milo shakes me softly, making me feel nauseous, so I open my eyes and stop him.

"I will throw up if you keep doing that." He stops immediately, but doesn't move away. "Come on, time to go." I scrunch my forehead up in confusion. "It's been 20 minutes already?"

I swear I just put my head down. "30, actually." He groans and looks around tiredly. I stand up slowly, and feel my knee caps shrivel from under my weight. "I'm sorry, I couldn't help you." I mumble, walking slowly with Milo's hand on my back to support most of me.

"I wouldn't want your slimy sick hands on anything anyways. Trust me, you did Mama Hazel a favor." I smile at that. At least I could do something right. We walk outside of the building, and I feel Milo let go of me to lock up the shop, but my body still sways from the loss of support.

"Don't short circuit now, we're almost there sweet cheeks." Ah, there's the Milo I know and have come to deal with for the past month. "Your just so nice." I mumble sarcastically. I hear his laugh, and try to open my eyes to see the dimples but it's gone by the time I see him.

"What?" He asks when he sees me looking at him. I frown. "I missed the dimples." This draws another laugh out of him, just showing one small indent on the right side of his face.

He places me in the passenger seat of his car, and rounds the front to get into the driver's seat. "Hey, what about my car?" I ask, looking around, trying to see through the darkness.

Gosh when did the sun go down? I really am out of it.

"You can get it tomorrow." He sighs, and then looks both ways before backing out and driving down the short road to our houses.

The car is quiet, but everything still hurts, and I feel like I might puke. "Milo?" I whisper. "Yes?" He whispers back, but I'm not sure why. He seems to follow along with my vocal levels when I change to whispering.

He's strange like that. He pretends not to care, but then does small things, like keeping me sane. Ok, that's not so small, but you get what I mean right? "Isabelle?"

"Hm?" I mumble back. I see him looking over at me with a confused face. "Why did you say my name?" Oh right, I forgot about that. My brain isn't working properly. "My head hurts."

He sighs, fisting the steering wheel. "Have you been feeling like shit all day?" I silently nod, and lean the other direction so my face is laying on the glass window.

"Why did you come into work then? You know you get sick days right?" It takes me extra long to answer his question, because even though I know the answer, my mouth won't move the way I want it to anymore.

"Mama Hazel called. Said she needed me so I was here." I hear another obnoxiously loud sigh. Such a drama queen. "I would've been able to do it myself." He grumbled.

"Nu-uh, you would've burnt the place down and then probably blamed it on that poor cash register." I open my eyes, and stare at the night sky in confusion. Why did I just say that? That made no sense.

"Sorry, I don't know what I'm saying anymore." I mumble, and then groan as he jerks the car into park. I stay rooted in my seat, not moving at all as he rounds the car and opens my door.

I start falling forward without the window to help keep me up, but of course Milo catches me. What a sweetheart. I could totally see him being the reason someone falls and then has to catch them though, so maybe not.

He helps me walk towards the front door of my house, but as he opens the door, my knees buckle, and I groan out in pain. "Jesus Christ." I hear his mutter along with a couple other explicit words I'd rather not say.

"Ahh, fuck it–" I feel my body being lifted into the air, causing my eyes to widen. "Oh god, I'm gonna be sick." I mutter, squeezing my eyes shut, and stuffing my face into Milo's neck. His scent is intoxicating, and only helps my nauseousness slightly.

"If you throw up on me, I will drop you." He grumbles, carrying me slowly into the house. I don't know exactly where he's taking me, because if I open my eyes there will be no stopping the bile from rising further into my mouth.

"Milo." I whine, feeling everything that was once aching, quickly intensify. "Hold it." He grits out as if that's even a thing. Can people actually stop throwing up from coming out of them? I doubt it.

"Oh my gosh, Izzy. Is she ok." I hear a faint gasp, and I think it's coming from my dad. I relax further into Milo, shivering from the hot and cold. Everything feels wrong, but I just blame it on my body malfunctioning.

"She's fine, just decided to come into work sick. She definitely has a fever though." Milo's chest rumbles against me with every word he speaks, and for some reason I find comfort in it.

"Take her to her room. I'll get some medicine." I can tell we're walking up stairs, as all the sounds fade out, and then I'm being placed on my bed. I open my eyes to see a bleary Milo staring at me with a frown on my face.

"I'll take your shift tomorrow." I whisper, hoping maybe that will cheer him up. It only seems to make him frown deeper. "Why would you do that? You shouldn't even come into work tomorrow." I shake my head, and curl into a ball, sinking into the mattress further.

"Yeah, but, you had to do–"

"Isabelle, if you say it's because I closed up today I will fucking lose my shit." My eyes widen at his words. "But–"

"No buts. You need to stop pleasing other people for them, and start doing what's right for you. I'm sick and tired of you walking around with a smile on your face, and doing whatever anyone asks of you even if it doesn't make you happy. It's killing me."

I stare into his eyes, trying to figure out why he's telling me all of this, but come up with nothing. Before I can ask, he stands up and leaves the room.

I suddenly feel like crying. I didn't want him to leave. I sigh, and pull the comforter up over my head, and try to get some sleep.

It's short lasted though, because quickly after my eyes shut, I felt someone lifting the blanket off my head. I groan, and squint at the light.

"Thought you could get rid of me that easily?" Milo, is back. He's smirking, and holding a glass of water with some pills now too. I sit up on the bed, and watch through hazy eyes as he plants both in my hands.

"Drink." He commands, and I have no other choice but to listen. Once it's done he pulls out a thermometer and commands–again–for me to open my mouth. He places the cold object below my tongue, and then we wait.

In the meantime, I start taking in his features again. He's really tan, and his curly hair on top of his head looks darker than black. He's got a sharp jawline, and a little stubble on his chin.

"Why are you taking care of me?" I whisper once the beeper goes off. He examines it for a second before sighing and taking a seat on the edge of the bed.

"Because as much as it pains me to say it, I care about you." My eyes widen for a fraction of a second before dimming again. I don't know what to say, so I just stare at him blankly.

"Get some rest." He sighs, and begins to stand up, but my hand shoots out and clamps around his wrist. I don't know what I'm doing, but I'm in pain, and I want comfort.

"Stay?" He looks conflicted, and stands stock still for several seconds. My eyes are starting to droop, the medicine is starting to kick in, and I really just want him to sit down so I can relax.

"Please?" He gives in, sitting down beside me, over the blanket instead of under. I scoot over more, giving him room, and finally relaxing back into the bed. He lays beside me, not moving at all until I feel his hand encase mine.

"Milo?"

"Hm?"

"You're the best, ya know that?" He doesn't answer, and it doesn't bother me one bit, because even though I know I'm going to wake up alone, I fall into the most peaceful sleep I've had in years.

~~~~~~~~~~~~~~~~~~~~~~~~~~~~~~~~~~

AN: I swear this is like a turning point for them. There gonna get closer soon I promise :)
~~~~~~~~~~~~~~~~~~~~~~~~~~~~~~~~~~

Chapter Nineteen

—'You'll know..not just in the way they look at you, but in how they're not looking anywhere else.' ~ Butterflies Rising ~——

Violets House~~Isabelle

I did indeed wake up alone yesterday morning. My eyelids were heavy, and I just knew, I knew that my bed was empty. Of course I was in it, but it just felt...cold.

I still had a slight fever when I woke up, and honestly I hadn't really remembered anything from the night before. Thursday became a blur after we left Mama Hazels.

I felt absolutely horrible for having to call in sick, but apparently, when I had called Mama Hazel, she already knew. Milo ratted me out because he probably thought I was going to come into work anyways.

I haven't seen or spoken to Milo since Thursday night, and that's saying a lot because we're neighbors, but today is Violet's summer party and it's slowly starting to freak me out.

Even if I was still sick–which I'm not–I would feel horrible for canceling on Violet, so past my better belief, I'm still going over there.

Violet is supposedly out shopping with Aiden to get things for the party. I am at least happy to see him again. I know he'd protect me if anything went wrong.

Plus Jake and Anna will be there. Thinking of all the people that will be there, instead of who, or what could possibly happen, is already making me feel better.

See, being positive is always the answer. There's no reason to be negative when you can be positive. There's always a positive.

Since Violet's shopping, and Lottie doesn't have a car, Henry's picking me up. He's also picking up Milo.

My stomach goes into a knot thinking about seeing him again. No matter how sick I was two nights ago, I will never forget what he said. I care about you. If he still cares about me, then there's a way for me to get on his good side.

Whatever that good side may look like, it's gotta be better than this...different person that I don't even recognize.

Today is probably the hottest day it's been since I've been back, so I quickly find a white simple tank top and pull it over me, then slide some comfortable jean shorts on. They have cute flowers on the back pockets.

I do two quick small braids on the sides of my head to keep some of my hair out of my face, but also keeping my long hair down. It's too much work to deal with all of it.

I slip on my Birkenstocks, knowing they'll probably be off my feet by the time I get to Violet's house. I hate shoes. I don't think there's a point in wearing them, especially in the summertime.

"Izz, your friends are here!" I hear my dad call from the bottom of the stairs. I didn't respond, just skipped down the stairs instead, and met my dad at the bottom.

He looks more nervous than me. "Are you sure you'll be ok? Don't take drinks from strangers, don't walk off with anyone you don't know. Stay with at least one of your friends the whole–"

"Dad," I cut him off, placing my hands on his shoulder. "Breathe, it'll be ok." He does as I say, and lets out a raggedy laugh. "Yeah, ok. Just please be safe." I give him a tight hug, knowing he needs it more than me, then make sure I have my phone and walk outside.

"Call me if you need anything." I look back from the door and nod my head. "Wouldn't dream of calling anyone else." He smiles, this time for real, making me feel ok to leave him inside.

I see Henry whispering something to Lottie, and her saying something before looking around and spotting me. Her eyes widen, and then she sits stiff in the seat, not looking at me or moving an inch.

I slowly get into the car on the right side, and give them both odd looks. "Why do you both look so suspicious?" I ask slowly.

"We're not." They answer at the same time, then take a quick glance at one another. "Lottie Maddison..." She looks back at me slowly, giving me a nervous smile. I can practically see sweat beads rolling down her forehead.

"Yeah?" She answers weakly. "Tell me." She sighs, then opens her mouth, but doesn't get one word out before Henry slaps his hand over her mouth to muffle all her speaking.

"You suck at this babe." He whispers. I tense when I hear the car door opening, and then closing. Milo has now entered, and he's sitting really freaking close to me.

Well, only as far as the car will let him go, but his long legs are bumping into mine. He's a big man, and I'm a small woman, but this car still isn't fitting both of us comfortably.

"What is going on?" Milo askes, a little hint of concern in his voice. "Lottie and Henry are hiding something." Lottie nods her head anxiously, and Henry's hand stays over her mouth.

"If I let go, are you going to tell them?" Lottie shakes her head no, but the minute his hands are gone she starts talking all over again.

"Henrytoldme–" The rest gets muffled by Henry's hand again. He sighs, and shakes his head downwards. I slap a hand over my mouth to hide my giggles.

Henry waits a few more seconds, letting Lottie calm down before finally removing his hand. This time, she doesn't say anything, but she does stay unbelievably tense in her seat.

Henry starts backing out of my driveway, and down the street when I see a hand coming into vision. I startle backwards, and whip my head to the side to see Milo looking at me in a strange way.

"What are you doing?" I ask, worried. He grabs the seatbelt from the other side of me, and slides it over my front before clicking it in place. "You weren't buckled." I wasn't, and it hadn't even crossed my mind at the moment.

"Oh...thank you." I whisper meekly, and then mentally kick myself in the face for my small voice. If you want something, you've gotta be confident about it. That's what my mom always says.

Or used to say at least.

It's not very hard to see that I wasn't exactly the most confident person when it came to things like this. I've never had a boyfriend because of it, or my first kiss for that matter.

I gotta up my game if I wanna succeed in life.

Although that is a lot easier said than done.

"Where is Noah?" Milo asks, breaking the horrifyingly gross tension. The tension back here is so different then the tension in the front seat, but nonetheless it's here, and it ain't leaving.

"He's riding with one of his friends. I think his name was Xander." A memory clicks in my brain from the night of my birthday. "Oh, I met him, he was really nice. Also really good at beer pong."

Milo turns to look at me slowly. "When did you meet him?" He asks, sounding something I've never heard before. I can't put my finger on it, but it sounds a little bit like unease, and...jealousy?

"Uh, at our birthday party thing." I reply shyly, squirming under his gaze. Is it hot in here? uh, it's really hot in here. I start twirling the ends of my hair around my finger, almost cutting off circulation before unwinding it, and restarting again.

I kick off my shoes, and pull my legs up into a criss-cross position. All still under the knowledge that he's still looking at me. I glance over at him, and mouth 'what?' he shrugs, and looks forward again.

"Oh, also, I told Mama Hazel that I'd work next weekend because of how much I missed." I explain quickly to Milo. He doesn't even look at me when he says, "No." I hear Henry let out a loud laugh, and glance back at us in the rear-view-mirror.

"What do you mean no? I already told her–"

"I mean no, I already told you, we are given sick days for a reason, you used one Isabelle. One." He holds up one finger to physically show me. I shiver at the way he says my name, but don't let it shake me. "I already told her that I'm doing it Milo. No taking it back. I wanna do this."

This time he looks over at me and narrows his eyes. "You don't wanna do it, you just feel bad that you were sick yesterday, which, by the way, there were plenty of people working and it wasn't even packed."

"So? She's still paying me for the work I barely did on Thursday, so I'm making up the hours next weekend." I shrug, feeling my jaw tick without my control. "You're working for free?" His jaw tightens, and I watch the muscles move up and down on his cheek bone.

"Why are you getting so worked up about this?" I ask, confused. "Do you not remember any of the conversation we had two nights ago." No, I only remember the part where you said you care about me. I don't tell him that though.

Our argument gets cut off when the car stops, and I realize we're already at Violets. By the looks of it, her and her brother just got back too.

We all get out of the car, and I wish we could leave that conversation back in the car, but it follows us around like a dark cloud of rain on a bad day.

It's not gone completely, but I'm still able to shove it into the back of my head where I can forget about it until tomorrow. Or hopefully never again.

We all walk into the house at the same time, and hear Violet and Aiden in the kitchen. Their arguing, of course. "Why would we put out stuff now? People aren't coming until later." I hear Violet say.

"Because your friends are here now. Are you trying to starve them?" I snicker softly as we enter the kitchen to see them both gripping opposite ends of a lays chip bag.

It's not us that stops the arguing, but rather what Milo says. "Ava is coming over in 30 minutes, just so you know." Did I say stop? I meant redirect. Violet drops the bag, causing an oblivious Aiden to snatch it and start pouring it into a bowl.

I think he just wanted it for himself, and was using us as an excuse.

Instead of being in the middle of the fire that's about to erupt, I slide past them, and walk over to where Aiden is munching on handfuls of chips.

"Hey kid, how's life been?" I furrow my eyes up at him. "I'm not a kid, I turned 18 like, two weeks ago, and I just saw you not even two weeks ago." Aiden looks down at me because of his freakish height and laughs.

"You are so tiny, and most definitely a kid," He bumps my shoulder. "And when I say life, I mean you and Milo." He whispers. I immediately go up in flames, and shove chips into my mouth to stop myself from spewing all my life problems.

"What?" I mumble through the chips. "Don't know what you're talking about." He stares at me before sighing and slinging his arm over my shoulder. "Ya know I see the way he looks at you." My eyes darted to Milo, who is at the moment arguing with stubborn Violet.

"He's not looking at me." I whisper back, trying to breathe through my tomato face. "I mean before you left, when you guys were kids." I dare to say he just called me a kid twice for two different points of my life, but then think better of it. Definitely not the time.

"Oh, don't you have glasses? You were probably seeing something wrong." I laugh nervously and pat his hand that's over my shoulder. "I see the way you look at him now."

"Are you some love expert like the ones from Frozen, or are you just being a dimbo." He laughs at me again, and tugs on the ends of one of my small braids.

"Stop thinking in your head so much, and live like it's your last day. I know it sounds dumb, but what is something you'd regret not doing if you were to die tomorrow?" He makes a valid point, because there are lots of things that I'd wanna do today.

"Where is all this wisdom coming from? I've never heard you ever give advice like this." He pats my head, and unwraps his arm from around me, then eats more chips.

"I don't know, that took a lot of energy out of me, I think I'm gonna go take a nap now." I laugh loudly at his statement, and shake my head to myself as he walks away rubbing his temples.

The minute he's gone, Milo and Violets arguing starts flowing through my ears. "She's my friend Violet, and frankly, very upset that you guys always treat her like shit." Violet rubs an aggressive hand down her face and groans. "She's fucking manipulating the shit out of you! Don't you see that?" Violet yells back, practically turning red from anger.

I hear the front door open, and see Noah and Xander walk in, whispering to each other. Violet and Milo are both blind to the newcomers, and continue arguing.

I look out for Lottie and Henry, only to see them on the couch, flicking through the TV channels. I guess this isn't new. "Violet, you're just being petty, there's no reason for her to lie." Milo's comeback is strong...if you were seeing things from his side.

Knowing everything I do, not so much. I keep quiet though, not wanting to intervene between Mrs and Mr Godzilla. Noah and Xander are stopped, watching the fight now with concern.

Violet lunges for Milo with an inhumane growl leaving her lips, but before she can attack, Noah grabs her around the waist and catches her mid air, swinging her over his shoulder.

Xander seems amused by the whole thing, watching Noah carry Violet out of the room. Once they're gone, and Milo has walked off somewhere else, Xander looks around until he sees me and starts walking over.

"For the record," He pauses when he gets to me. "I totally thought you two were a thing." I scrunch up my nose in confusion. "Violet and I are both straight, and–" Xander burst out laughing, clutching his side for support.

"No, I was talking about you and Milo, I see I was very mistaken." My face burns hot as I frown. Geez give the poor girl a break. The poor girl being me.

"Sorry, I didn't mean to upset you or anything." Xander apologizes, no amusement left in his voice. "Oh, no, you didn't. It's just that a lot of people keep saying the same thing, about Milo and I."

His eyebrows raise, before falling and a smirk lays on his cheeks. He's got dimples on his round chin, and now that I think about it, he's got a baby face going for him. "Ah, I see."

"See? See what?"

"Well after your birthday, and I saw him carrying you over to his house I had assumed you were a couple, but now I see it's more of a 'not relationship, but obvious feelings.'" I sigh in defeat.

"I don't have feelings for Milo." He raised an eyebrow at me, throwing a chip in his mouth. "I don't think I do? Ugh, this is hurting my brain." I groan, massaging my temples.

Maybe I should go take a nap with Aiden. "It's ok, don't hurt yourself." He laughs, inching closer to the chip bowl, and eating some more.

"It is nice to see you sober though." I lean against the counter, and lay my elbows down on the table placing my chin in my hands. "Yeah, you too."

~~~~~~~~~~~~~~~~~~~~~~~~~~~~~~~~~

AN: Don't worry, this isn't the last of this night ;)
~~~~~~~~~~~~~~~~~~~~~~~~~~~~~~~~~

Chapter Twenty

—'Sometimes fear does not subside and you must do it afraid.' ~ Elisabeth Elliot ~ ——

Summertime Party ~~Milo

I am so tired. I don't wanna be at this damn party, but I know being at my house is only going to lower my mood. Violet's words won't leave my mind, and it's giving me a headache.

Ava isn't manipulating me. I'm better than that. I mean, what would be the point in lying to me? If she liked me, then she would tell me, and I would reject her. Easy peasy, it would be done like that.

We could still be friends. I'm not as cruel as I look. I wouldn't just drop her because she had a small crush on me.

The thought of drinking sends a spike of pain through my stomach, which just makes this even more depressing. I'm sober as can be, at a party I don't have any business being at.

Ava came, stuck to my side like a leach, and then started dancing with some other dude. It doesn't bother me, but the way she keeps glancing over at me makes me think she wants it to.

My eyes search the room, until they come upon the blonde headed girl that I wish was sitting beside me, tucked into my side, where I could keep her safe. I don't know why I want to keep her safe, but I'm starting to see a pattern with my behavior at parties.

I don't want her hands on other guys, and I don't want other guys hands on her. I don't want guys simply looking at her. So many fucking emotions that I can't even cling onto one, just making me look down right mad.

I am mad, but I'm also jealous. Jealous that all our other friends get to have her back while I don't. Which is again, my fault. So, I'm also sad because I can't have the one girl I actually want.

She's standing ridiculously close to another guy, and she's laughing at something he said. Her smile is so beautiful, and her laugh is so pretty that it makes me want to be the one to put it there.

It's fucking contagious, and I have to fight my face from smiling because of it. I feel my jaw tick, and I shift in irritation. She's not even trying to get under my skin, yet she's somehow burrowed and implanted herself there.

I study the guy's movements more, and it's obvious he's not trying to get anything with her. He's simply just talking to her like a friend. Now that I think about it, he looks like the guy Noah walked in with.

What was his name again? Xavier or Xander? I don't remember, and I don't really care enough to think about it any harder. I'm at risk of a migraine at the moment.

"Can I join your pity party? Or is it strictly prohibited to dumb fucks who are in love with someone they are so prone to pushing away." My scowl turns slowly to my left as Noah slings his arm over my shoulder and sits down on the couch.

"Shut up, I'm not fucking in love." I growl, siping the bottle of water I have. Noah does the same, but with a beer bottle instead. "Ok buddy. You keep telling yourself that."

"What do you want, Noah?"

"Why? So you can go back to wallowing in self pity?" I roll my eyes and down some more water. "I'm not wallowing in shit." I give him a forced, sarcastic laugh and then go back to staring at Isabelle.

This is just pathetic. "Maybe you should start by apologizing for being such a dick. You know she'd forgive you." I do know that, and it's scary as fuck.

She forgives me, then what? We go back to being best friends and ignoring the way we find each other insanely attractive. Well, I can at least speak for one of us.

Everything has changed. I changed, and went through some hard shit. It's obvious she's changed, and gone through stuff. I open my mouth to tell him just that when he cuts me off. "I know you both are two different people now, but that is no excuse to not be at least on good terms with her."

I feel like a broken record here, going in circles and circles that are endless. My jaw clenches looking at her. "Who's that?" I question, pointed at the guy she's talking too. "Xander." He sighs wistfully, making me look over at him with an assumed smirk on my face.

Looks like someone is denying their own feelings to themselves. He stiffens when he sees the way I'm looking at him. "Friend to friend, you should probably work out your own love life before trying to fix mine."

He opens his mouth several times, looking like a fish out of water as he searches for words. "I don't–that's not." I laugh, and shake my head.

"Don't worry, you've got this." I nod my head at him, standing to my feet. "You suck at giving advice." I shrug, straightening out my shirt. "Yeah... good luck in your...what did you call it? Pity party." I smile down at him while he bluntly lifts his hand and flips me off.

The minute I finish my water, and throw it away I realize I have to pee, and start heading to the upstairs bathroom. The whole town is practically here, and I can already see the line for the one downstairs skimming around the corner.

Violet says since were her friends we get to use her personal bathroom, but only for actually using the bathroom. She told me, straight up, no fucking in her room or bathroom.

She told me she can't control what happens outside of those rooms, but if she found any trace of sperm in her room, she was going to skin me alive.

That woman scares me, and most people don't. Besides Mama Hazel. I think it's the fact that they don't bluff. it isn't in there nature. It's obvious in their tone that they will threaten, and follow through with it.

Unbenounced to a lot of people, I don't sleep around as much as I make it seem. I've only ever slept with 2 people. Once sophomore year when I lost my virginity. I never saw her again after that, and it didn't seem like she cared at all.

Then second being Ava, and the only reason I've slept with her more than once is because—well, I'm a man and I need release, and she doesn't ever seem to care. She knows I'm using her, because she's using me too.

Although now I'm starting to doubt myself. Maybe she's been using me more than I thought.

I do my business quickly, and then get on with it and begin leaving Violet's room. For her personality, it's strangely clean. I shake my head, and open her door to leave her room when I ram into someone.

More like someone rams into me.

I get deja vu instantly from the party on our birthday when I look down and see Isabelle, shaking her head as If I just winded her. I wouldn't be surprised if I did.

Not to be egotistical, but I do have a hard chest, and she's a tiny person. When she looks up and meets my eyes, she takes a large step backwards, and her face flushes with color. Her blue eyes are so beautiful I would get lost in them.

Jesus, and who knew vanilla could smell so damn good?

"Oh, sorry." She mutters, and that's when I realize she looks angry. Her face is flushed, but her hands are also clenched into fist. It's dark, but it's not dark enough for me to see that the once white shirt she was wearing is now see through.

My eyes snap to hers and see her look down slowly until she realizes. "Oh my gosh! I'm so sorry. She freaking spilt her drink on me and it didn't even register that I–" She cuts herself off, looking up at me wide eyed.

Her rosy cheeks deepen. Hell, she's so pretty. She smiles sheepishly, and crosses her arms over her chest slowly. "Who spilled their drink on you?" Suddenly, the smell of alcohol wafts through the air. Coming off of her. She doesn't look like she wants to answer me either.

My anger spikes only for a minute before I look down at her again, and she calms me instantly. I realize we're still standing in the hallway, for other people to potentially see her.

Yeah, no.

I grip her shoulder softly, and guide her back into Violet's room. I flick the light on, and the room finally glows to life with light. "Oh, this looks different." I hear her murmur softly to herself, as she walks towards her closet.

I don't know why I'm still here, but I feel like I have her in my grasp, and I don't want her to leave yet. I can't stand losing her again.

I examine the pictures Violet has of all of us when we were really little. Ranging from birthday parties, to school field trips, and not one of them is missing any of us.

Violet may be a pain in my ass for 95% of the times we are around each other. But that 5% shows itself a lot in the way she loves. She's got a big heart, and she isn't afraid to show it.

"Oh, you're still here." I turn around to see a flushed Isabelle staring at me, with a hand over her chest like I scared her. She's now, instead of her soaked shirt, wearing a large graphic t-shirt of Violets that has spongebob plastered across it.

That is totally something she'd wear. We stand in silence, but for once it's sort of relaxing. She blows out a long breath of air, and glances at Violet's bedroom door. "We don't have to go back out." Her gaze snaps to mine, and then she smiles softly.

"Really? Thought you were a partier." I shrug, taking a seat on her bed. "Looks can be very deceiving. You'd know that better than most." Her smile falters, and I mentally punch myself in the face.

That came out harsher than I meant it to. "I didn't mean it like that. It wasn't–"

"It's ok, you're right." She gives me a sad smile this time before padding over, and taking a seat next to me. I realize she's not wearing shoes and smirk. She's never been a shoe typa gal.

I also notice her toes are painted hot pink as she kicks them against the bed. She was never much of a fidgeter when we were kids.

I sigh, feeling another wave of emotion hit me. A collection of them actually. "Do you not like parties?" I ask her. She looks over at me, and then pops her legs up into her lap and crosses them.

She shrugs, down casting her gaze, and fiddling with her fingers. They're also pink, except lighter.

Cute.

"I guess not." She whispers, but it seems to hold so much more unspoken words. "Thank you, by the way." She says quickly, blushing again, but not as much this time.

"For what?" I ask, staring at her, trying to figure her out. She's an open book with so many words it hurts to read. "Helping me, when I was sick." I laugh, causing her to look over at me and bite down on her lower lip.

"Don't be so hard on yourself. You practically worked yourself to exhaustion." She flames red again, and diverts her eyes. "You do too, ya know." She speaks quietly. Not soft enough to be considered a whisper, but if I wasn't sitting right next to her I wouldn't have heard her.

"Who poured the drink on you, Isabelle?" I ask, needing this answer. People don't just do that for no reason. She doesn't meet my gaze when she answers, more like stares at the wall behind me. "Nobody."

It's an obvious lie, and she doesn't even try to hide it. Before I even know what I'm doing, I reach out and grip her chin softly to direct her eyes to mine. "You can tell me." I whisper, feeling myself soften for her.

I don't know how she brings this part of me out, but she does it pretty damn well. She visibly gulps, and then her eyes run over my face before settling at my lips. She snaps her eyes to mine and blushes softly.

"Uh, just someone I upset. It's ok." I frown at her words. She doesn't even seem confident in her answer. "Then why can't you tell me." It flashes in her eyes before she can stop it. She doesn't wanna upset me.

"Izz." I whisper. Tears look like they want to topple over, and cover her checks completely. "I'm not gonna be mad." She shivers from the contact and I realize my hands now on her cheek.

I retract it immediately, and almost blush myself. "You promise?" The vulnerability in her voice has me breaking open wide for her. "Of course I promise, I won't be mad." She sighs, and looks down in her lap.

"Ava poured her drink on me." I have to look away, and then breath through my nose to calm myself. "You said you wouldn't be mad." I look over at her, to see her staring at me. "I'm not mad at you sunshine, I'm mad at Ava for doing that." I pause. "Why did she do it?"

This time she completely blocks me out and shakes her head. I know I'm not going to get an answer here. Her sad mood makes me want to cheer her up.

"Do you remember when you thought you could fly, so you jumped out of Violet's window and landed on me, and we both broke our wrist." She snorts, and looks behind her at the window.

"We had just watched Peter Pan for the first time. How was I supposed to know it wasn't gonna be like the movie?" She looks over at me, and flashes me her smile that makes me melt, and wanna jump around her until she doesn't stop smiling again.

I can't even stop myself from smiling. Her eyes slowly, so slowly, trail down my face until they land on my lips. Again. She doesn't look away this time though.

Her smile falls, and her lips part before she bites down on her bottom one again. "Don't look at me like that Isabelle." My voice causes her to shiver, and look up at me. Her eyes are darker, barely any blue left in sight.

"Like what?" She whispers, while her eyes fall, and fall. "Like you want me to kiss you." She blushes, and looks me straight in the eyes. "Maybe...I want you too." She seems hesitant, like I might run, or scream at her.

"You want me to kiss you?" I ask, my body somehow moving closer to hers. She stares at my lips, and nods her head sharply. "Izz." I grumble, lifting my hand and cupping her cheek.

"Say it." I whisper. She gulps, and blushes. "Kiss me, Milo." I pause. "Please." And so I do. Leaning down, and lifting her chin to capture her lips with mine.

I don't know what happened when she was gone, or if she ever kissed anyone else, but shes fucking good at it. My hand moves up, and around her head to the nap of her neck, and then I'm pulling her closer to me deepening the kiss.

Her lips are soft, so fucking soft and she kisses me carefully like I'm a feather she doesn't want to break. It takes me a moment to realize her hands have fisted my shirt, and pulled me closer.

She makes a noise in the back of her throat, and then all of a sudden her lips are gone. I open my eyes in time to see her gasp, and cover her hand over the lower half of her face.

"Oh my god," She mutters, standing quickly and darting for the door. "Wait, no. Isabelle–" It's too late, she's gone.

~~~~~~~~~~~~~~~~~~~~~~~~~~~~~~~~~~

AN: So...yeah that happened.
~~~~~~~~~~~~~~~~~~~~~~~~~~~~~~~~~~

Chapter Twenty One

Mistakes~~Isabelle

It has been just over 9 hours since the 'incident that will not be named' happened. My hands haven't stopped trembling, and my mind won't shut off. I didn't stay any longer at Violets, and had Aiden drive me home like a wimp.

If I had told Violet I wanted to go home, she would've known. I know it.

Aiden knew. I know he knew, and he knew I knew he knew. Does that make sense? My face was flushed, I guarantee my hair was a little messy, and I was shaking.

Plus, he has literally been the one that had said to 'live in the moment', if I remember correctly. I blush, again, frantically speed walking around my room and pulling on random articles of clothing.

When I got home last night the first thing I did was jump into the shower and wash off all the sticky alcohol. I reeked, and it was not nice. Whatever she was drinking definitely had a faint hint of peach, but the vodka sadly overpowered it.

I was simply talking to Xander, when he walked away for one second. One, he was literally going to get us another soda when Ava came stomping over to me. Well, maybe she wasn't stomping, it could've just been the heels, but the way she looked at me was as if she was satin, and I was a freaking pawn in her game.

It scared me enough to cower away. That wasn't enough though. She smirked when she got to me, a smirk that could easily be bypassed as a smile, but I knew. I knew what it really was.

"Oh my gosh Izzy! Hi!" She had squealed, and somehow over the music I'm pretty sure my ear drums shattered just a little bit. Nonetheless, I pulled up my big girl panties and said, "Hi Ava, it's good to see you." I wasn't going to be rude.

The merciful glare she gave me was one to kill. "There's nothing going on with you and Milo right? He was staring at you, and I was just making sure since ya know..." I nodded my head.

"Nothing." An apparent lie. If only I knew the events that were going to follow. "Oh goodie! Well I'll get out of your hair now." She had leaned down, maybe to hug me.

I wouldn't be surprised if she air kissed both sides of my cheeks with a small 'salut' and waltzed away like a hot french supermodel. Although she never got that far.

She tripped on what I could only assume was air, and her drink toppled over me. She really could have pulled it off as tripping over her heels if the smirk she gave me didn't already give me my answer.

She is such a nice girl, with such a cold heart.

I would love to say that seeing Milo walking out of Violet's room off set my mood more, but it only made my day. It may have not been normal, but it was obvious he was trying to cheer me up, and that alone made me happy.

Then I kissed him. Milo freaking Wesley kissed me. My childhood best friend kissed me at a party that I didn't want to be at due to some intense traumatic memories after commanding me to tell him.

It was so hot.

Oh god no. My flushed face rises as I trip over my feet and land with a huff on the ground. "Are you alright?" My dad peeks his head around the stair landing and raises a question brow at my half inside half outside body to my room.

"Great. So, great." I mutter, scrambling to my feet and slipping on my slippers. My hair is in a lazy bun on top of my head, and I'm wearing an oversized t-shirt with alvin and the chipmunks on, and athletic shorts.

I slip on my car-sunglasses and back out of the driveway, feeling more riled up than anything. The thing that really gets me though is that I feel good. Like I could go do 20 backflips and then give Milo another kiss at the end.

God, I am never going to forget how his lips felt, and how freaking soft them were. How he took control and played with my hair.

Does this change things? Are we going to go back to what we used to be, or is it going to be different now? Good different, or bad different?

Barely 5 minutes later, I find myself walking into Mama Hazels, and thanking the lords that she's chatting with another customer right now. She isn't always at the store, and I really need her right now.

I wanted to first tell my dad, but then I realized that would've spread quickly, and if my mom found out she might quite literally kill Milo with her own bare hands. Then again, they do both love him.

I think it's a given why I can't tell Violet or Lottie. Yeah...that was a no. Then it just circled back around to the man himself, and I obviously can't talk to Milo about the kiss we shared together.

Actually, that would probably be the most logical thing to do, but I need time to digest this, and get my thoughts together. I don't lift my sunglasses from my face in fear that my eye bags might give someone a heart attack and stride over to the woman herself.

The customer she's talking with walks away, and when she turns to me, no words are exchanged. She simply looks me up and down, sighs, and then calls through the doors. "Hazel, get the register for me please." She turns back to me and gives me another once over.

I probably look like a pile of hot dog diarrhea. I feel like a pile of hot dog diarrhea. "I'm going to get you some tea, and then we are going to have a talk."

———

It takes all but 10 minutes for me and Mama Hazel to be seated outside on the pier, with my green tea for me to spill everything. Starting with Ava, and ending with my miserable, embarrassing ride home with Aiden.

I swear he's a worse version of Violet.

You see what I mean now?

Mama Hazel is silent, and after speaking everything out I feel good, re-lieved. The waves crashing against the wood, and the nice, small breeze feels good.

We're in a more secluded area, behind her cafe but still with plenty of eye sight of the water. Thank god, because I was truly getting worried for other people's well beings.

People who actually looked at me, gave me wide eyes, and then pity stares. Yeah, I wasn't ready for that yet.

"You told him to kiss you honey." I groan, and sink into my chair further like a child. "I know." I mutter hopelessly. "Did you want him too?"

I don't have to think twice about my answer. "Yes." I'm doomed.

"Do you still like him?" I gap at her. Still? "I didn't–"

"You two used to walk into my shop at least once a week with dirt covering yourselves, and ordering milkshakes. I may be old but I'm not blind." I sheepishly cower away again.

This lady is scary.

I swallow another gulp of my drink, and push my sunglasses up from the nose. "So what do I do?" She looks over at me, then back to the water and sips her drink thoughtfully.

"The fact that you're asking that means you already know. Do what you think is right Isabelle." She sips again, and starts to stand up from her chair.

"Wow, wait, where are you going?" I start to panic, because there has to be more than that. Why does she have to say everything in a wistful way that makes it seem so right. Yet so confusing.

"You really think Hazel can run that register for long? I put her in the back for a reason." Mama Hazel shakes her head, but stops for a moment before walking away.

"Izzy? Make sure you go home and get yourself looking...decent before speaking to him." Then she walks away and throws her empty cup into the trash before re-entering her store.

I blow out a huff of air, and look around awkwardly, before picking myself up and walking back to my car. I only get about halfway there before a high pitched voice comes into focus.

"Oh god yes, he was all over me." My steps halt, and my ears perk against my will. I don't like eavesdropping on people, but the fact that it's Ava's voice I'm hearing has me a little bit intrigued.

"He's so fucking naive, I can't believe he thinks I'm his actual friend." My heart hammers faster against my chest, and I finally will my body to move and peek around the building's corner.

I see Ava, obviously, and what I assume to be her posse. I also realize that there's no other way but to pass them then to walk by them.

"I know," One of the girls laughs. "I thought he was an f boy, but I think he's just stupid now." The other one laughs. I get an invision of a highschool movie scene–me having to walk by the 3 scary mean girls as they talk trash about people.

I suck in a deep breath, and walk as close to Mama Hazel's as I can; wishing I had just walked through the actual store. I do get to my car, and the door opens, but a voice stops me from getting into my car.

"Isabelle? That's your car right?" Ava asks, her voice softer, and more nice now. I spin on my heels and give her a bright smile. "No, my dad, but he lets me drive it. No point in getting a car if I'm not staying here." I laugh nervously, and force my mouth closed.

Ava gives me a once over, but doesn't show what she thinks of it and then continues to talk. "You're not staying?" Darn it. I said too much. "Only for the summer." I shrug, and inch closer to my car, trying to slither my body into the driver's seat.

Ava steps forward, and laughs but I swear it's evil. "Well that's good, don't need to worry about getting attached to anyone." My smile twitches, but stays in place. I'm glad that at least my eyes are blocked, because if looks could kill, I think Ava would be dead.

"Guess your right. I gotta get going, but it was nice talking to you." She nods her head, and gives me a weird hand finger twinkle thing like she's some princess from the BC's or whatever the heck it is.

I wave her off, and then pull out of the parking lot faster than Violet chases us when she's mad, and trust me, it's fast. I finally breath once I'm out of sight from her and began driving around aimlessly, not wanting to go home.

A nagging feeling pulls at my chest, and tells me I know who those girls were talking about, and then again when I was talking to Ava.

Her voice sounded like it was truly curious, and interested in what I had to say, but the voice I heard talking to her friends was so completely different.

Talk about two faced.

———

The gas is on the empty tank when I finally pull into my parents driveway, making me almost feel bad for not filling it up.

Almost.

I get out of the car, shutting the door and then leaning against the side of it. I've got Milo's house in my periphery, giving me the view to spy a little.

His house seems dead, no cars in the driveway, but his garage is closed so it could be in there. No lights on, no curtains open–then again, I do remember how dark it was in his house when I went in a couple days ago.

I come back to thinking about where his parents could be. Could he really be living alone? If that is the case, where the heck are they? Did they just ditch him? Did they die?

I start sweating under the sun, and finally walk into the nice ACed house. I walk straight to the kitchen to see my dad sitting at the counter with a cup of coffee. His night glasses are still on.

"Hey dad?" He looks up at me and then winces. "Hon, why did you go out like that?" I look down at my sad excuse of an outfit, and rip my sunglasses off my face. "It was an emergency, but that's besides the point." I wave my hand in front of my face, and collect my thoughts.

"Ok, what is it then?" He asks softly, giving me the loving dad tone that warms me up inside. "Where are Milo's parents? I haven't seen them since I've been here, and that's almost a month." My dad sighs, and shakes his head.

"You should really ask him that." The kiss comes back into my brain full force making me a little shaky. How do I ever even talk to him again?

I thought we were finally getting somewhere, and now it's all ruined. One stupid kiss. That's all it was. Nodding my head slowly, I begin walking up the stairs and heading for a shower.

Stripping out of my dirty clothes and then hopping into the shower quickly. The water soaks through my hair fast, and soon my body.

I'll just walk over to his house like a civilized human, and we will talk like normal people. I'll explain to him how it had been a long day, and it didn't mean anything.

Except it meant everything.

Ok, well, then, I'll ask him his thoughts first. I'll just see if he felt the same way I did about it, and then go from there.

I walk into my new clothes-filled closet and pull on a short sundress. My hair is still damp, and tangly so I grab my brush and start softening my hair. I smile, and sway my hips while I stand in my room. My eyes draw to my window, and widen when I see that Milo's is open.

I try not to look, but I'm now interested, and can't stop myself. Setting my brush down on my nightstand, I walk over to the window and peer into his like a stalker. A tiny voice in my head is telling me this isn't good, but I can't stop myself.

Then all of a sudden two frames come into the view. Milo. And Ava. Kissing. My eyes widen, and a hand shapes over my mouth. Before I can look away, Milo looks up and sees me. I gasp and drop dead on the floor. Cowering away so that he can't see me.

I tug on my curtains from both sides until they're finally covering the window whole, and I'm laying there with my face shoved into them.

I think I know how Milo felt about our kiss now. Obviously he was drunk or something—There was no alcohol smell—and he probably doesn't even remember it.

I don't even realize I'm crying until I feel the wetness drip down my neck and coat the opening of my chest. I keep my hand over my mouth, and cry silently to myself. Alone, again. Like always.

Chapter Twenty Two

—'We both drowned under the waves of words we weren't saying.' ~ Ben Maxfield ~——

The Start of a Friendship~~Milo

Pulling up my slacks, I run my hand through my hair and stare at a sleeping Ava. I stare and stare and stare trying to feel anything for her but I just don't. I walk over to the bathroom, and open the last drawer, pulling my sketch book out.

I haven't drawn in a while, and I've been itching for a new one. Maybe I can make it into a new tattoo. Get one that's actually legal this time. As I stand up, I take in my messed up appearance. Eye bags, hair sticking every which way. I didn't bother with my shirt so all my tattoos are on full display.

I don't have that much, just a couple small doodles and one large one. It's a joker on my right shoulder, and the only one that has full color. I sigh, and walk out of my bathroom, then walk downstairs.

I don't even know what I'm doing anymore. My whole life has just been falling apart, and I can't pick all the pieces up.

I pick up the pencil, and start drawing. Letting my hand decide what to focus on.

Two years ago, was when it was really bad. I was lashing out because of how fucking sad I was. I didn't know how to cope with being alone, and being in the quietness all the time.

It was screwing with my head. I started doing drugs, and it became my only escape. It made me forget, and pass out for long periods of time. I would wake up passed out in random houses, or on the streets.

I was hanging out at the Everest at the time, but they weren't really there for me yet. I was still pissed at Isabelle for leaving. I was pissed at my parents for leaving.

Everyone was just leaving me all of a sudden. A 16 year old kid. The drugs soon grew to a need, and not a want anymore. I had to have a joint, or snort something just to get through a single day.

I felt so depressed, no, I was depressed, and all I could do was get high and drunk to numb the pain.

I went too far at a Fourth of July party. I went into the down stairs bathroom at the Everest party and stuck a fucking needle in my arm.

I was already drunk, and practically passed out instantly. The only thing I remember, which is still hazy, is John's fingers down my throat forcing me to throw up everything I had taken.

He took me to the hospital that night, and they still had to pump my stomach. Apparently I hadn't been eating properly, and when all you have in your bloodstream is alcohol and drugs, it can get you killed.

I could've died. Or had a seizer and been even more fucked up then I am now. I remember when I got out of the hospital, John made me pack a bag and shoved me into the first rehab center he could find.

I hated him so much, but I knew he was just worried. No one ever yelled at me, and told me I was a druggie, but instead tried helping.

The only people that visited me were John, and Mama Hazel. I don't know how she figured out what had happened, but she did, and she didn't let me go.

A year later, I relapsed at her store, and she held me while I cried. She told me it was ok to have a down, but it was important to stand right back up and beat the shit out of this. Her words, not mine.

Even though she acts like she doesn't like me, I know she loves me. She acts like that because it's what I want. She knows I don't want her to look at me like a lost puppy, so instead she looks at me like a vicious wolf.

I love her though. I love all of them. Especially John and Lea. They have been my biggest supporters, and practically only ones.

Noah and Henry don't even know. No one besides the adults do. I distanced myself from everyone, and as far as they know, I was staying with my grandparents the month before school started.

People think I always get drunk off my ass, but in reality, I haven't had more than a bottle of beer in two years.When I'm drunk, I could trigger myself and it could spiral badly. Plus, now that I'm not high, the taste of alcohol is pretty disgusting.

I don't know what's going on with me anymore. I was treated for depression, and I remember what that felt like, which isn't this. I just feel kind of lost. Like I was thrown off my path and I don't know what to do. I don't know how to find it again.

For example, why am I still sleeping with Ava? She's my friend, and she probably thinks I have feelings for her. Then again, we started out as friends with benefits, so I don't understand why it's getting out of hand.

I glance down at my drawing, and realize I've finally finished. My hands caked with lead from smearing my palm over the paper, and my pencil is down to its last life.

My breath hitches when I see what I actually drew.

Isabelles sitting on the edge of the peer, her arms leaning back and glancing off at the sky. Her hairs blowing in the wind harshly, but you can still see her pained expression.

She always looks sad. Someone took her spark away, and I fear I might be the only one that can see it. She smiles all the time, and tries to appear fine, but her smile isn't bright like it used to be.

So that's what I drew, and you can see it in my picture. I flip my sketch book shut, and rub my eyes with my thumb and pointer finger. Then lean my head against the couch and let out a deep, long, breath.

I sit up straighter when I hear soft footsteps coming from the stairs. Ava comes around the corner slowly, dressed in her clothes from yesterday but her hairs combed, so she's probably ready to leave.

At least I think that's what she's doing until she turns towards the living room, and drops down on the couch next to me. It's quiet, and we both know why. We both know what's coming.

"Ava.." I turn to look at her, and all she does is give me a small smile. "I think...I think this needs to stop." She nods her head along with me.

"I've kind of been a bitch to you." She whispers. "I've been a bitch to Isabelle too." I know Ava comes off mean, and cold, but she's just like me. I think that's part of the reason why we get along so well.

She's gone through a bunch of shit with her parents, and I guess we just bonded over that. "I guess I just thought that if we kept doing this, you would eventually get feelings for me. I sound so pathetic." She wipes her eyes quickly and looks the other way.

"I see the way you look at her." She breathes out, meeting my eyes again. "Yeah, I know." Silence, again. "Ava, I'm really sorry I couldn't give you what you wanted." She shrugs, giving me another lazy smile. "I think I knew, from the start. Just the way you'd talk about her. I knew you were in love with her." I don't deny it.

"I really think you're going to find someone. Someone that will love you the way I couldn't." We both stand up, and I walk her to the door. Right before she leaves though, I engulf her into a hug.

"Don't be too mean. It's not you. Let someone break that hard shell of yours." She laughs softly and pulls away. "Yeah, you too Milo. Seriously, I'm rooting for you two."

I give her a soft kiss on the cheek, a friendly type, and then watch her climb into her car and drive away. As soon as she's out of sight, I close my front door and run upstairs.

First of all, I need a shirt, so I pull one over my head and then walk to the bathroom. My shoulder tattoo peaks out from the bottom, but it always has. My hair still looks a little crazy, but I need to do this now.

I walk down the stairs, and slide on my berks before walking across the little grass patch between our two houses.

I shudder when I remember the way she looked when she saw me and Ava last night. I just need to talk to her about it. I'm done with not communicating. I want my friend back.

I open the door, because John has insisted, no, commanded that I don't knock when I want to come over. The house is quiet, and strangely dark.

I walk down the short hallway until I come to the kitchen on my right, and glance around. No one is here. Although it is a Monday morning so I'm not surprised. I'd still be asleep, if I was sleeping at all.

Isabelle and I have to work later too. We get the afternoon shifts the first half of the week, and then the morning for the other half. With the expectation of one day where we close.

I run up the stairs quickly, and stare at Isabelle's bedroom door. It's slightly ajar, and dark inside. I walk slower this time, opening the door slowly.

I began to say, ' Hello, ' but only get half way through before I feel a hard impact coming to my head. "Ow." I whine, falling backwards onto my ass. The light switches on and I hear a gasp.

"Oh my gosh, I thought you were a murderer. I am so sorry." I feel slight dizziness as Isabelle comes full force into my vision. She's looking at my forehead with a pained expression on her face.

"Yeah, that was my fault." I realize now, that she is a teenager that's home alone. I'd probably hit whoever it was too. I'm assuming the object of choice was a hairbrush, because it's sitting on the floor next to my foot.

"No, no. I'm so sorry." She keeps muttering over and over as she pressed down on the spot that took the impact and I wince. "I'm so so so sorry." Then I see something fall down her cheek.

"Hey, no. Don't cry. It isn't your fault. You were just trying to protect yourself." I brush the hair away from her face, and stare at her blue eyes, which are staring at my forehead.

"Oh god, it's bleeding. Hold on." She runs into her bathroom, and comes back in surprising time, peeling a bandaid as she speed walks back over.

She places it so gently on my forehead before smoothing it over, and I can't help but realize how soft her hands are. "Ok, uh. Do you want any ice? Or to rest, sit down. Wait, what if you have a concussion. Should we go to the doctor? Or the ER? Yeah, no, don't sleep yet–"

The rest of her words get muffled by my hand. "I'm ok Izz." I whisper, making sure she's looking at me. She's kneeling down in between my legs, really close to me right now. When I remove my hand slowly, she sighs and hangs her head low.

In the silence with no movement, I finally get a chance to take in her appearance and she looks exhausted. "Ok, yeah." She looks at me with a smile, and tries to stand up but I hold her down with me.

Her eyes are red and puffy like she might've been crying, and there are bags under them, indicating that she hasn't slept either. Somehow she's still smiling as she stares at me. "Yeah?" She whispers.

I furrow my eyebrows. She's got a messy ponytail on top of her head, but so many pieces out in the front, like she can't stop playing with them. She's wearing a t-shirt, and shorts.

My t-shirt, I realize. The one I gave her on her birthday. I don't make any comments though, in fear of scaring her away. "Milo?" She whispers again, grabbing my attention.

"Don't hide it. I see the way you fake it with everyone else. Not me. Please don't fake it with me." Her head tilts to the side in confusion. "Hide what?"

"When was the last time you slept?" I changed the subject, feeling this may be more crucial. Her smile falters a little, and I get a glimpse of how she's really feeling before her walls go straight back up.

She stands, ignoring my protest and walks over to her bed. "You were with Ava last night. What happened to her?" She asks, and my heart breaks because she doesn't even sound mad. She sounds thoroughly sad with curiosity.

"I was with Ava last night, but this morning we talked it over and thought it would be better if we stayed away from each other. We're kind of toxic for each other, and she deserves someone who will treat her right." Isabelle nods her head slowly.

"You don't like her?" Again, with the sad tones. "No. Not the way I should." I reply, sitting down next to her. Not the way I feel with you. I want to say. "Now, when was the last time you slept?" Her eyes widen for a second, before she clears her throat, and smiles. Again.

I realized that she thought I was going to forget about the sleeping question with Ava. "I...don't know? Before the party?" She whispers. "Why not?" She stares at me, internally debating weather she should tell me or not.

"I had insomnia for a while after I left, and I had sleeping pills for it, but about a year ago It kind of went away and so I didn't need them anymore." My first thought is why she had insomnia in the first place, but I'll save that for later.

"And you're having it again?" She shrugs her shoulders, slouched and scrubbing her eyes. "Well that just won't do." I sit up straighter, getting a weird look from her. I stand up, pulling her with me. "Milo...what are you doing?"

I start dragging her down stairs and into the living room. I make sure she's seated on the couch before walking over to the blinds on the window, and pull them open. "That's better." I mutter, and wonder if that was what my house always looked like.

I walk over to their junk drawer, and find a sharpie, then grab a bag of chips and walk back to the living room. I place the chips down, and place the sharpie in my pocket. Then I run back to the kitchen and grab us some water bottles.

Once I'm back on the couch, with Isabelle on my right, I grab the remote and scroll to disney +. "Are you going to tell me what we're doing yet?" Isabelle askes, a tiny bit annoyed. "We're gonna watch Tangled, and eat chips." And she's going to sleep, but I don't tell her that part.

I click on the movie and it starts playing with Flynn's voice in the background. "Really?" She whispers. I glance over at her to see her sitting there with a cheeky grin plastered on her face.

"Can I draw on your arm? Only if you want." I pull the sharpie out and wag it in the air. Her smile gets bigger. "Yeah, I'd like that." I smile, and inch closer to her.

I grab her left arm, and start at the wrist. Drawing a flower with fine detail, and working my way to her elbow. We only get half way through the movie before her head sags onto my shoulder, but I don't stop drawing.

I think it might actually be helping her fall asleep. "Thanks Milo..." She murmurs, pulling her feet up under her butt, so she's more of a ball attached to my side than a human.

"Of course, anything for you." I whisper back, knowing one thing for sure. I like this, and I don't want it to change.

~~~~~~~~~~~~~~~~~~~~~~~~~~~~~~~~~

AN: Finally learned a little entail about Milo's past. ;)
~~~~~~~~~~~~~~~~~~~~~~~~~~~~~~~~~

Chapter Twenty Three

—'You will never be able to escape from your heart. So it is better to listen to what it has to say.' ~ Paulo Coehlo ~——

Tattoo~~Isabelle

"Shut the fuck up." Someone whispers harshly from behind me. "But aren't they so cute? This is so cute." Another voice says. "You're going to wake her up." The first voice hisses.

I wiggle a little, feeling comfort on the couch. Suddenly light hits my face, and I wince, opening my eyes. "Great job Noah." I look up to see Milo staring daggers at Noah. I follow his gaze and see Noah standing with Henry, and they're both holding cameras.

"What's going on?" I murmur, turning my head away from the sun, and burrowing into Milo. I'm laying on his lap, with a pillow below my head, but I'm so tired that I can't decide if it's good or bad.

"Nothing, just go back to sleep sunshine." Milo whispers. This feels very intimate, but I am also very tired. "Oh my gosh Henry, did you hear that?" Noah gasps loudly, making me jump slightly.

"Fuck yeah I did." Henry says, but whispers instead of yells. "This is earth shattering, this is amazing!" Noah yells again, making me jump again. "Would you stop doing that?" Milo grumbles, covering my ears with his hands to muffle their voices.

I sigh in content, and begin relaxing again. Still listening in on their conversation though. "You do realize it's 4 in the afternoon right now, right?" Someone askes, but the voices are too muffled for me to tell who it is.

Geez, I've been asleep all day. I guess that's what you get for not sleeping for over 24 hours. "I'm aware. Izz has been having sleeping issues, and she hasn't slept in two days." I can tell that Milo says that one.

"Shit." The other two boys mutter. "What happened to your forehead?" I grow flustered, and twist my head so it's hidden against Milo's stomach even more.

He knows I'm awake now, and that I'm probably not going back to sleep, so his hands slowly move from my ears. "Don't you dare." I mutter, inhaling his scent.

Milo laughs. "Isabelle thought I was a murderer and hit me with a brush." He explains. I sit up, and move away from Milo on the couch, rubbing my face slowly. I already know my hair is a freaking mop.

"Damn, girls got strength." Noah whispers, plopping himself beside me, while Henry does the same next to him. I yawn, and lean my head back against the couch.

A small headache erupts behind my eyes, but it could also be from the fact that I haven't been drinking or eating properly lately. I should probably tell someone, because it's not good to keep things locked up like this, but I think it's just stress.

My mind is running on overdrive right now. I think it just needs some rest. "Earth to Isabelle." I open my eyes and look over at Noah, who is staring at me. "What?" I ask, my voice cracking.

"What do you want to eat? We're gonna order food." I ponder on this question, thinking of all the food places we have around here.

"McDonalds?" He smirks, and then ruffles my hair. "That, my friend, is a great answer." I laugh, and let myself steal a glance over to Milo. He looks down for a split second, and then back up.

Confused, I look down, and realize I'm wearing his shirt. I haven't done my laundry in so long, and it was the only clean thing I had left.

I blush, and push myself off the couch, walking into the kitchen. His shirt falls down to mid thigh, looking like a dress on me. I could probably get away without wearing shorts underneath it.

I reach for a glass to get water with, but stop short when I see my arm. My mouth hands open from surprise, seeing the beautiful drawing on my arm. "Wow..." I whisper, examining the fine detail of the flowers and vines.

"You like it?" I turn around on my heels to see Milo standing across from me, leaning against the kitchen island. I look back at it, an idea popping into my head. "Can you tattoo it?" I look up at him hopeful, seeing his eyes widen. If I'm not mistaken, I think he is...blushing?

"You–what? I'm not an actual tattooist or anything." I step closer to him, making sure he's looking at me when I speak. "I've seen the work you've done. Plus, I'm 18. So technically it is legal." He stares at me for a split second, before rubbing his jaw nervously.

"You know it's permanent right? You really want that on you forever?" I nod my head. "Why else would I ask." A small smile grows on his face. "So can you?" His eyes widened slightly. "Now?" I shrug, rolling my eyes and smiling.

"When else?" He nods his head, moving away from the island. "Yeah, sure. Let me go get my stuff from my house." He starts moving towards the door while I move to the stairs. "Ok, I'm gonna go take a quick shower." He nods, leaving the house.

I smile, biting my lip from how much I wanna laugh. I'm gonna have a tattoo. This is literally the best day ever.

——

"You've got to tell me if it hurts ok?" I nod, and giggle at his nervousness. He has the machine thing set up, gloves on, and ink sitting on the table.

Our food got here a little bit ago, so I'm chewing on fries while Noah and Henry stare intently at my hand. I had asked them where Lottie and Violet were, but apparently they both got grounded for getting caught sneaking drinks around their house.

"It's gonna be fine Milo. I'm excited." and I really am. He nodded his head, extending my arm closer to him, and held it down.

He turns on the machine, and brings it down, testing out a spot and then looking back up at me. "Good?" I nod my head, not even feeling what he did. He gives me a small smile, and moves it back on. I feel a slight sting the longer it goes, but most of the time, it feels like a small tickle.

"You've got some real balls." Noah exclaims, and Henry nods along with him. "I can barely even feel it." I tell them. My gaze moves back to Milo, who is so concentrated that I see his arm muscles flexing and his brows knitting in focus.

My face heats up, and I have to look away from embarrassment. Milo pulls the machine away and turns it off. "All done?" I ask, breathing in heavily. He nods, and grabs a disinfectant wipe. "You'll have to keep the plastic on it for the rest of the day, and try not to get it too wet for the next week. I'll check back, and if the scab is gone by then, you can go back to normal."

I don't look at Milo's face as I stare at the flower on my arm. The skin around it is becoming a little red from irritation, but it doesn't stop it from looking so beautiful. "The shading is so good." I whisper.

When I look up, I see that Noah, and Henry are both gone. Milo finishes wrapping my arm after cleaning it, and glancing down at it. "I practice a lot." He shrugs like it's no big deal. Little does he know he just did the best thing anyone has ever done for me.

"Oh my gosh." I gasp, covering my mouth. Milo looks up at me confused. "My parents." His small smirk drops and he covers his mouth. "They're going to kill me." He mutters. "I mean, I am old enough." What if they think I'm acting out?

Right as the thought hits me, the front door opens. "Oh no." I whisper. "Shit." Milo whispers at the same time. I pull my arm back behind me right as my dad walks into the kitchen.

He stops when he sees Milo and I sitting here, probably looking as suspicious as mother Gothel from Tangled. "Hello..." He says, walking slower, and giving us both a look. I gulp, and I think I see a little sweat on Milo's forehead. His whole body is covering all his equipment right now.

My dad walks and gets a glass to grab water, and I actually think we're in the clear. I breathe a sigh of relief until I hear footsteps entering the room. "Is it done, can we see it now?" Noah askes all jittery.

My dad turns around quickly, ears perking. "See what?" Noah looks confused, pointing at me. "Isabelle's tatt—" Henry's hand comes out of nowhere, covering over Noah's mouth while he continues to talk.

My dad turns to look at me with a questioning, almost sinister look. He glances at my noticeable hidden arm. "What's on your arm Izzy?" I shrug, wigging my tingling fingers. "Um, skin?" I try, but my lying skills are the worst, and everyone here knows. My dad walks over and pulls my shoulder so that I can't hide anymore.

He gasps, and yanks it closer. Not in a way that would hurt though. "Oh my god Isabelle Mona." My face flushes, and I cower away. I look over at Milo, but he's staring daggers at Noah. "I mean it's beautiful, but why wouldn't you tell us? Your mom is going to kill you." He mutters, twisting my wrist to see it better.

"Uh, well. Milo drew it on my arm earlier, and then just tattooed it. It was kind of a last minute—" My dads gaze snaps to Milo. "You did it?" There's no anger in his voice, but Milo still hits my other shoulder. "You just ratted me out." I bite my lip and look over at him.

"But you did do it. What was I supposed to say, some random person—" Milo groans, and rolls further into his scat. "I can't believe I did this." He groans again. I look over at my dad, but he's just smiling. "What? Are you going to kill him? Because I promise I told him to do it and he's done a bunch on him before." My dad stays silent.

"You are 18, and you did a good job..." Milo looks up at my dad hopefully. "As long as you tell me before something like this happens again. I'm ok with it." I hug him, and lift my arm so it doesn't touch him.

"Although, I can't speak on your mother's behalf. You know how she gets about this stuff." He rubs his forehead, almost stressfully, before standing up and going back to his drink. "Just because I'm ok with it this time, doesn't mean you can just do it again though." My dad looks towards me, and then at Milo. Giving both of us a pointed look. "Yes sir." We both speak at the same time.

He gives me a funny look, and I'm about to ask what it is when he starts walking out of the room. "I wish my dad was like that." I hear Milo mutter, but a part of me thinks I wasn't supposed to.

"Speaking of your parents. Where have they been? I haven't seen them since I've been back." I ask, looking at my tattoo. He doesn't answer, so I lift my gaze to see him glaring at the table. I instantly feel regret. That's his personal life. I shouldn't have asked.

"That's none of your business." He hisses out quietly, but there's a hint of something else there. Maybe sadness? "I'm sorry. I didn't mean to upset—"

"It's fine. Whatever. They're just working." My eyebrows scrunch up together. "Have they been home at all?" I whisper slowly, trying not to anger him. He sighs, and rubs his face thoughtfully.

He shifts uncomfortably, and looks up for what I assume to be an escape. "Not really." He mutters quietly, as if he doesn't even want me to hear, but I do. "Not really, or no?"

"Look, it's really not important right now ok." He snaps, and I flinch. His eyes soften immediately, but I don't let him get anything out. "Yeah, yeah of course." I smile, getting to my feet.

"Wait, Isabelle, I didn't mean—" I waved him off. "It's personal, I get it. Seriously." I turn around to walk away, but his voice stops me. "No, they have not. I haven't spoken or seen them since May." I stop, and turn around slowly.

"They didn't call on your birthday?" He looks down, and blinks rapidly. My heart shatters into pieces on the spot. "Milo..." He stands up, and tries to walk away.

Maybe it's sadness, or fear, but I grip onto his forearm and keep him in place. He looks down at me and askes, "yeah?" I just shake my head

Before I know it, I'm rising onto my tiptoes and wrapping my arms around his neck. He tenses for a second, and I think I've just screwed everything up, but then in the next second he's slowly wrapping his arms around my waist.

His head leans down, further, and then further, until it's stuffed into the side of my neck. His stubble that's none-visible from a far, tickles my neck and I shiver. It's slight, and most likely not noticeable.

My hair is only slightly damp, but he doesn't seem to mind. The only thing I can focus on is how warm he is, and how much I've missed hugging my best friend.

"I'm so sorry." He whispers. I gulp, and close my eyes. "Yeah. Me too."

~~~~~~~~~~~~~~~~~~~~~~~~~~~~~~~~~

AN: Not that long of a chapter, but I enjoyed writing this one.

Get ready for a few more filler chapters like this one.
~~~~~~~~~~~~~~~~~~~~~~~~~~~~~~~~~

Chapter Twenty-Four

—'Can you remember who you were, before the world told you who you should be?' ~ Charles Bukowski ~ ——

Separately, Literally, Dying~~Isabelle

You know that feeling you get in your stomach when you're on a roller coaster. The tightening, almost sickening feeling that forms right before the drop?

Milo's that feeling for me.

Anytime I see him, or any time I'm near him. I mean, just thinking of him sends my stomach into a frenzy. I would've thought that after I got home, and actually interacted with him that those feelings would disappear.

It did everything but disappear. It freaking evolved. They grew, and now I don't even think I can contain it anymore.

Maybe this is a disease, and I'm actually dying.

"Izz!" I turn around quickly, and rush past people walking around, trying not to bump into anyone. It would be tragic to see all these glasses and plates break.

"Isabelle!" I push through the back doors with my hip, and rush over to the sink where I discard the dirty dishes I was carrying. "I'm coming!" I scream back, knowing Mama Hazel is about to scream my name again.

I rush out of the kitchen, tripping over my feet only slightly, until I take a sharp turn and make my way towards the back room. "Yes?" I question through a loud huff of air, and lean my body against the door.

Mama Hazel stares at me with her hands on her hips, and her grandma glasses low on her nose. "I've been calling for 10 minutes." I sigh with a small smile on my face.

"There's like three people working right now, and I was trying to clear the tables so there was room for more people." She sighs dramatically and shakes her head.

"What am I ever going to do with you?"

"Let me work so that you don't get swamped?" I question, and she finally cracks into a smile. "Come here, I've got some stuff for you." She waves her hand over into the small room that I didn't even know could fit more than one person at a time.

Nonetheless, I shimmy my way into the dim closet, and heave when she suddenly places a box into my hands. "What...is all this?" I question through deep, heavy breaths.

Backing out of the closet and spinning on my heels to head to the front, I glance back and see Mama Hazel following close behind. "Just old junk I thought you'd like." She shrugs.

I set the box down gently, behind the counter and mentally set a reminder to not forget it later on. Straightening back up, I get bombarded by two faces.

"Excuse-mio?" Violet questions in a terrible French accent, while rubbing her fake mustache. "Hm, lets ah see. What shall wi-wi have?" Lottie askes–also in a horrible accent–looking over at Violet with a deadpan face.

I suppress my giggle, leaning over the ledge and giving them both a straight faced look. "I would suggest two hugs, and apologies for being grounded?"

They finally break character, and shuffle around the small curve of the corner and hamer into me. "It was totally Violet's fault." Lottie mutters into my left ear while Violet mutters, "It was all Lotties idea." Into my right.

"Don't worry, look what I did." They both pull away, and I extend my new tattooed arm. Milo told me that it's ok to get it wet now, and all the swelling is gone, so it looks way better than before.

"Holy shit." Violet curses, and pulls my arm close for her to see. "We leave you alone for two seconds." Lottie mutters, stealing my arm from Violet.

"Technically, I wasn't alone. Henry and Noah were there, and Milo's the one who actually did it." They both look up at me awestruck, mouth agape like I might be freaking Jesus.

"We are sitting down right now, and you are going to tell us everything." I smile nervously as Violet and Lottie pull me over to an open table in the back next to a window.

I still haven't told them about the kiss. I mean, I haven't seen them since Violet's party. As if it could get worse, I haven't even talked to Milo about it either. It's been killing me.

Everything was perfect on Monday. Milo and I had a real life person conversation, but as the week went on it just got awkward again. It was very obvious that we were both thinking about the kiss, and that neither of us wanted to talk about it.

It might be crucial if we don't though, for this new found friendship that's beginning.

"So, what are we missing? What happened to you?" Lottie askes, while they both stare at me intently. I can't lie, and they will know if I do.

"Yeah, why don't we start with when you left my party early." Violet accuses and my eyes widen. My face flushes remembering Milo's hand on my neck, or his soft lips against mine...

"Oh shit." They both mutter. I clear my throat, and rub my neck nervously. "What?" I croak out. When did my throat get so dry? Nerves tickles the bottom of my spine, beginning to shrivel up and grow.

"I kissed Milo, alright." I blurt, then flush again. "Well, I mean. He kissed me, but I told him to kiss me? Technically he told me to tell him to kiss–"

"What!?" I jump at their sudden loud voice, and force my mouth to stay shut. This is not how I planned my nice Saturday to go.

"Um." I laugh, clear my throat. "Milo and I...kissed?" I whisper softly, my voice coming out as a question even though it is most definitely a statement. A very real fact.

"When, where?" Violet askes, both of them smiling widely.

"At the party Saturday." Then, everything comes out.

"I didn't really wanna be there because...ya know, and then Ava spilt her drink on me, and I went to borrow one of your shirts, and Milo was in your room, so then we both stayed there and talked a little because neither of us wanted to go back down stairs. Then, we uh, kissed, and yeah. I got Aiden to drive me home because it was my first kiss since everything happened, and I was embarrassed."

I took a couple deep breaths, realizing that I hadn't inhaled at all during my speech. Neither Violet nor Lottie say anything. They just stare at me with blank expressions.

"Continue?" Lottie gestures with her hand. I sink into my chair until my backs slumped, and my butts no longer on the seat. I moan like a child, and cover my face with my hands.

"There's more?" Violet questions, no anger in her voice, but something. Something that sounds a lot like pain. "Well she still didn't get to the part where she got the tattoo." Violet nods agreeingly, and then looks back over to me and nods her head as a sign to continue.

"Milo came over on Monday, we watched Tangled, and then I fell asleep for like, the whole day, and then Noah and Henry showed up and got us food. Milo drew this on my arm," I wave my tattoo to show them.

"And I asked him to tattoo it since he's done his own, and he did it. There, all caught up now." I finish with a smile of relief, deliberately skipping over the part where I didn't sleep for two days, and that I saw Ava and Milo...well.

They both nod, not asking for anything more. It's silent for a while, letting me breath for a few seconds, feeling like a weight is lifted off my chest from finally saying all that. See, this is why it's good to talk about your feelings.

That is until Violet decides to speak. "Why didn't you say anything about not wanting to go to the party?" She whispers sadly. Guilt crawls slowly under my skin, making me swallow hard, and rub my hand over my arm.

"You were so excited to be throwing it again, I didn't want to ruin that." Her eyebrows knit in pain, and I realize I've messed up even more. "No one would've been mad. We would've just had a small party, with the six of us, and probably Aiden." This time, Lottie says.

"We promised we wouldn't keep secrets anymore Isabelle." Violet says.

"I'm sorry." I whisper, looking down at the pretty daisy that's etched onto my skin. No words, yet it says so much. "Don't be sorry, seriously though. We've gotta work on this communicating feelings thing." Violet says, with a playful hint to her voice.

Then I feel a hand enclose mine, and look up to see Violets hand over mine on the table. She gives it a small squeeze and smiles lightly at me.

Violet has never been good with talking about emotions, but she shows the way she cares through actions, and I admire that about her.

"If we're sharing things that happened this past week, I've got some real good stuff." She says, a long, sly smirk growing on her face. Lottie looks between us with concern.

"You were grounded." I told her. She nods, and bites her bottom lip. "I met someone." Lottie and I both scoot our seats closer to the table. "Well go on then." Lottie urges, causing me to giggle.

Violet starts turning red, and smiling even wider. "Oh my god, Violet." I laugh, and she blushes harder. "I was out walking, after I snuck out because I was already grounded, so what the heck right?" Lottie rolls her eyes.

"Anyways, I was walking at around Midnight, near the beach, and then there was this man." I quirk an eyebrow at her, confused on where she's going with this. "Are you sure he wasn't stalking you?" Violet growls at Lottie. Literally growls.

"Let me speak, women." Lottie backs off with a small laugh, while Violet composes herself. "I think he's new here, because he seemed lost, mind you, it was like, 1am, but we just walked on the beach." She pauses.

"Anything else?" I ask. "Oh yeah, so we talked for like an hour. Then we kind of broke into Mama Hazels and made milkshakes." My mouth drops. "You broke in here?" After I had closed?

"How?" Lottie askes. Violet shrugs. "There's no alarms, and one of the windows was open." I cover my hand over my mouth, and then feel the urge to laugh. So I do. "Oh my gosh. That is so bad V." She shrugs again, looking around the place, probably making sure no one heard her illegal confession.

"What was this mystery guy's name?" I ask, and Lottie nods her head with me. "That's the thing. We didn't exchange anything. He was all like 'if we see eachother again, then that's that', and I was kinda diggin it." She giggles, and covers her mouth.

"Oh my gosh. Guys." She clutches her chest, and starts sinking into her chair. "What?" Lottie, and I question at the same time. She starts giggling, and clutching her chest harder. "I think I'm dying. My heart is beating, like, really fast."

That gets a laugh out of me. "Welcome to the club honey." Lottie shakes her head. "I felt the same way when I first started liking Henry. Remember?"

"You mean when you would spy on him from behind the slides in 3rd grade?" I ask. Lottie scowls, and shakes her head. "Ok, so, I will admit. I've liked him for a while, but I mean when we were like 16."

Violet, still rubbing her chest, laughs a little and nods her head. "You mean when you had a meltdown because he took his shirt off. You passed out, and he ended up carrying you back to the car." She starts laughing harder while my eyes bulge out.

"Lottie!" She shrugs, her face now red with embarrassment. "He was sweating, and really tan ok." She mutters, causing me to burst out laughing.

Violet rubbing her chest, Lotties face burning, and me laughing so hard I'm crying, we probably look a little crazy.

"Why do you guys look like you're dying? Separately, literally, dying." I jump, still laughing at the voice of a man coming from next to us.

I cover my mouth to stop the laughs, and look over to see Noah leaning against the table, his hands on the edge gripping for support. Violet giggles again, and rubs her chest harder. Then she moans. "Izz, I can't breathe."

"She's having boy fever." I squeeze out through deep breaths, tears still running happily down my face. Noah's eyes jump to Violet. "Is she broken?" This comment helps snap her out of her weird meltdown.

Then Noah's eyes move towards Lottie. She's got her hands covering her burning face, while making very distorted noises. "What's up with you?" Lottie shakes her head, and slams it against the table. "She's remembering when she would pass out from the mention of Henry." This draws a smirk from Noah. He opens his mouth, probably to say something that would make everything worse, but someone else stops him.

"What did you do to my girlfriend?" Henry, now at Lottie's side, askes. I start laughing again. Rich, horrifyingly loud laughs and I can't stop. Noah even starts snickering.

"Why are you crying?" I look up to see Milo standing besides Henry with his hands on his hips, staring at me with concern. I lean into Noah, to my right, and continue to quite literally die of laughter.

"Can't stop...laughing." I stutter, squeezing my fingers to my eyes while I get the last of my giggles out. "Is this really what it looks like when they get separated for just a week?" Milo askes, full concern etching his voice.

"It's a little scary." Henry mutters while Noah just lifts me up so I'm standing. He stares into my eyes, and then hugs me. I don't know what's going on, so I just hug him back.

~~~~~~~~~~~~~~~~~~~~~~~~~~~~~~~~

AN: things will make a little more sense in the next chapter for Noah.

Guys i swear, i love this friend group so fucking much. There my babiesss
~~~~~~~~~~~~~~~~~~~~~~~~~~~~~~~~

Chapter Twenty Five

—'Maybe I can't stop the downpour but I will always join you for a walk in the rain.'~ Word porn ~——

Secrets~~Isabelle

Today was a little strange. It was our last day of 5th grade, and saying goodbye to all our teachers. We had a big party out at the playground with all of our classes. Luna was having her last day of pre-k at the same time, and she was also super bummed about missing all her friends.There were multiple times that I had to get her to stop crying, and explain how she was going to be with the same people next year.Violet was sick with the flu, so it was only Lottie and I with the guys. Lottie finally confessed today about her crush on Henry. She was blushing so hard. It's so obvious that he likes her back though, I don't know why she's so scared.While we were playing outside, I had decided to go and pick some flowers for everyone as a going away present, because I hadn't gotten anyone anything.I was wearing the new sundress my mom bought me. It's got ruffled short sleeves and reaches to my knees. She also put a couple cute clips in my hair for me.I would be eleven already like the other kids if I didn't have such a late birthday.Milo did make me feel better about that though, because of how close our birthdays are. We are both still ten. Only one more week and we will finally be with the other kids.While I was picking daisies, because they are my favorite, another boy came up to me. He had dark hair, but not as dark as Milo, and his eyes were brown like puppy dogs. "Hi, do you want a flower?" I extended my hand out to him, and he smiled big. That's when I noticed his puffy eyes. He sat in the small field, just out of view from the teachers with the flowers.I sat next to him."Are you ok?" I asked. He sniffled, and looked away. "You don't gotta be embarrassed to cry. My dad said that crying shows your strength." I told him, just like my dad told me when I skinned my knees on the cement.I had been playing tag with my friends when I tripped over the creases in the ground, and fell face first into our patio. "My parents are getting a divorce." He said quietly. "They were fighting about who had to pick me up." He finally looked over at me, teary eyed, while his lips formed downwards.So I did the best thing I could, and wrapped my arms around him. It was a little awkward of a position, but he accepted my hug, and recoperated it.When we pulled away, he quickly wiped at his eyes and looked down again. "You can come home with me. We could have a sleepover with the rest of my friends. They're always fun. We watch a bunch of Disney movies and eat a ton of popcorn." This brought a smile to the boy's face. "What's your name?" He asked. I smiled, and extended my hand. "Isabelle. My friends call me Izzy or Izz though. We're friends now. What's your name?"He shook my hand, and smiled widely. He had a really pretty smile. "My name's Blake." I had never–

I shut my journal quickly, but softly and shoved a hand over my mouth. My brain searched for the memory of ever meeting Blake when we were kids, but I can't think of it.

Was this the same Blake that I've seen since I came back? It couldn't be right? He would've told me if he remembered me. It is a small town though. What if he just forgot too?

I was too distracted by my own thoughts to even move to open the journal again, when I heard a light tap on my window. I jumped so fast, I was surprised my bones had time to follow, and ran towards the window. I flinched when the sound was heard again.

I opened the window, and poked my head outside to see the view of the ground. Before I could see anything, I felt something hit my check. "Ow." I whisper.

"Izz? Are you there?" My eyes scrunch, and I move to see someone standing on the ground, no shoes, a ragged shirt, and plaid pajama pants. "Noah?"

"Sorry, did I hit you? I didn't wanna wake your parents up with the door." I blink down at him, and then hold up my hand. "One sec." He nods, and I go back into my room.

I look at the time on my phone quickly, and see that it's 2am. Why the heck is Noah over at my house at two in the morning? I run downstairs quietly, and creak open the door to an inch.

"Noah?" I whisper, and open the door wider. "Yeah?" I jump at his loud voice, that's closer than I thought it would be. "Be quiet, and get in here." He lowers his head like a child in trouble, and walks into the house.

He walks to the kitchen, so I follow, turning on the lights as I walk. Once I see his features completely, I notice how exhausted he looks. He takes a seat at the table, and starts to shake his leg up and down.

His fingers tap against the table in a fast paced rhythm. "Hey, Noah. Are you ok?" I ask softly. He looks up at me with large eyes, weaning his round glasses, and shakes his head no. "Ok...do you want some tea." He nods his head yes this time, so I set the tea pot.

My parents got me this old fashioned tea making kit for my birthday, and it's so cute.

While the water starts to heat up, I walk over, and take a seat beside him. "What's going on?" He looks over at me, and bites his lip.

"I have a secret." He finally whispers. I nod my head in encouragement. "Ok, what's the secret?" He stays quiet for a long time, and I start to get worried that he might not answer.

"I...I don't know." He finally says. I don't push him on the matter, and instead stay quiet. "Just know that I'm here for you when you want to talk." He nods his head slowly, so I stand back up and walk over to the pot.

The house is quiet, so I try to be quiet along with it, not wanting to wake anyone up. I turn around and glance at Noah. He looks nervous, and a little scared. Then an idea pops into my head. "I have a secret too." I whisper, glancing down in sadness.

His head shoots up, widened eyes. "Really?" He asks, his voice cracking only slightly. "Yeah," I swallow the lump in my throat. "A really bad thing happened to me." I take another breath, then laugh at myself. "It was the reason I left in the first place." I look back at him, and he's staring at me with interest.

The room is quiet again. "I know I'm more of the 'friend who makes jokes' all the time, but I'm a really good listener, if you ever want to talk. Seriously." I smile at him, and nod my head. I hear a light hum from behind me, and turn around to see steam come out of the kettle.

I take it off, and pour the hot liquid into two mugs, then plop the tea bags in them. I hand him his, and sit beside him again. He takes a long sip of what must burn his tongue, but he doesn't say anything. When he finally sets the cup down, he looks over at me and takes a deep breath.

"Ok, so. You remember Xander?" I nod my head, smiling at the memory of that nice guy last weekend. "Yeah, ok. So, he's my...boyfriend." He pauses, probably trying to gauge my reaction. "Like..." I let him finish the question, just to be sure of what he's saying. "Gay, I'm gay." He breathes a sigh of relief, and laughs to himself.

"That feels good to say." He mutters. I smile, tears glistening in my eyes and engulf him in a hug. He startles, but excepts my gesture. "Oh my gosh Noah, I love you. Thank you for telling me." He laughs, and hugs me back. "Thank you for accepting me." He whispers, almost like he's embarrassed.

I pull away, and glare at him. "If that's the reason you haven't told anyone, I want to tell you that you are far off. Everyone here loves you, and they will accept you for who you are Noah," I pause. "And if they don't, well then fuck them." He gasps, smiling widely.

"Did you just say fuck."

"It was definitely the right time. Don't expect it ever again."

———

My brain feels broken. I can't stop thinking about what I read about Blake. The description I gave sounded like him, but there had to have been at least one more Blake at the school I went to. Then again, this is a small town, and we were a small class.

It's Sunday, and early, and all I want to do is go back home, and open another journal, but instead I'm working at Mama Hazel's with Milo. We get off at 11, in an hour, and I've just been watching the clock tick forward.

It's been slow, probably because most of her customers go to church in the morning. "What's wrong with you?" I flinch backwards when my vision un-blurs and I see Milo leaning on the table, head to head with me. He doesn't sound angry or mad, just curious.

"Hm?" His eyebrows clench together meeting at the bridge of his nose. "What?" I ask again, searching his eyes. His green, emerald eyes. His black hair has gotten fluffier since I've been home, so it's a huge fluff ball on top of his head now.

"You've been blanking out the whole time we've been working here." I smile, and shrug. My face begins to heat up under his gaze. I'm not used to his attention, and it's making me nervous. "Just tired, I guess."

He moves around the counter, and takes a seat next to me. He lifts my arm—making me shiver from his chilled hands—and examines my tattoo. "How has it been?" I shrug, and rub my eyes with my other fist. He looks up at me, expecting an answer he's not going to get.

"You slept last night right?" No. "Yes." He doesn't look convinced, but he also doesn't press on the matter. "You should come to the beach after we're done working. I'm taking Luna to surf again." My eyes widened. "Uh, she wouldn't like that. I think it's best if I just give her some space." I say quickly, and quietly.

He sighs, and looks down. "We need to talk about it." I blurt out, my face flushing, and my heart rate rising. He looks over at me again with confusion on his face. "Talk about what?" It's only been a week, why is he making me say this? My face grows hotter. "Uh, the thing. At Violet's party.." I leave my statement open ended, and watch as his eyes show recognition.

"You mean the kiss?" My face turns red from the casualty of this tone. I nod my head sharply, and go to stand up, but his hand comes down on my shoulder. "What about it?" He asks again. I clear my throat, and look at him. "Well...what does it mean?"

It obviously wasn't his first kiss, but it was mine, and it meant something to me. He gave me control, and I didn't have that before. I'd never had that before.

"I mean, it was late, I don't know about you, but I was really tired." I nod along with him slowly. "I barely remember it." He laughs softly, and stands up. Tears brim my eyes, but I push them down. "No, yeah. Same." I laugh, but it sounds pitiful. He turns around, pauses, and opens his mouth to speak. He stays like this for a minute, and then shakes his head, and turns around.

I sit fully into the seat again, and internally scold myself. How could I be so stupid? Of course he doesn't remember it. It was a simple fluke, a mistake. It wasn't real. It felt real. No, no it did not.

~~~~~~~~~~~~~~~~~~~~~~~~~~~~~~~~

AN: sorry, again, for the short chapter, but I'm going to try and make the next few longer. :)

Im sooo sorry that Milo keeps being the bad guy but y'all gotta remember he's going through his own stuff still and doesn't really understand his feelings either.

Please go easy on him.
~~~~~~~~~~~~~~~~~~~~~~~~~~~~~~~~

Chapter Twenty Six

—'I am still learning how to go back and reread my own chapters without feeling like I want to set all of my pages on fire.' ~ E.V. Rogina ~ ——

Journals Truth~~Isabelle

I pull my feet up under my butt, and crack open a new journal. This one's from when I was in 6th grade. I didn't write much about this year because I thought it was stupid to be journaling. Then 7th grade, 8th grade, and lastly 9th grade. My last year of writing before I left.

I shiver thinking about the things I wrote during my last couple weeks here. It was dark, and I'm scared to read it again. I also think it will help though. It will help me realize that I've overcome what happened to me so much since then.

The first written entry from 6th grade was during Halloween.

October 30thI'm a chipmunk. Ok well, technically I'm Britney from Alvin and the chipmunks. Violet and Noah are Simon and Janette, Henry and Lottie are Theodore and Elenore. Last but not least, Milo is Alvin. Violet was freaking out over how cute we all looked. Of course, Noah is Simon because of his glasses, but Violet had to go out and buy fake ones. Lottie and Henry are practically in love, which I think is hilarious. Milo really pulls off Alvin though. I don't know why, he just gives me Alvin the chipmunk vibes.We're all having a sleepover tonight, and then hanging out tomorrow and going trick or treating.This is the first year that our parents are actually letting us go all by ourselves. We usually venture off by ourselves anyways, because this is a very small town, and everyone knows everyone.We do have a curfew to be back by 10:30 though, which isn't too bad.We obviously still need time to sort through our candy, and swap whatever we don't like. Luna's going trick or treating with Violet's little brother Leo. They're literally best friends, and Leo is such a sweetheart. Aiden's going to some party with older kids though, so I probably won't see him. He's like an older sibling I've never had, and has helped me in lots of situations. Oh also, Blake is staying the night, because his parents are fighting again. After they got a divorce a year ago, they kept being an on and off thing for a while. When they separate though, no one ever wants to take Blake.He has an older brother, but his older brother isn't around much. He's only around Aidens age, a couple years older so maybe they're friends.

My mouth drops open, but I urge myself to keep reading. What the heck am I missing here?

I have to stop writing soon, because they're going to be here in a couple minutes. Actually, I don't really know when I'm going to be writing again. Some girls at my school found my journal and stomped all over the page s.They said I was too old to be writing 'diaries', which I don't really think of them like that. I haven't told anyone what happened yet, because they'll probably just say the same thing again.

I forgot about that. Why can't I remember any of this? My therapist said that sometimes after traumatic events, my brain can shut out some of the memories that had happened prior. But all of them?

April 24thOh my gosh, I haven't written in so long. The last time was during Halloween. Today was the last day before spring break, and I know I shouldn't be writing because it's kind of stupid, but what happened today was crazy, I just had to write it down.Milo and I were in a slight disagreement this morning. There was this guy at my school, who hadn't been leaving me alone and he keeps asking me out.Every time I would tell him I wasn't interested, and didn't want to get into anything.I mean, after all, we're only in 6th grade.Anyways, I was telling Milo it was fine, and that I could deal with it, but he was getting frustrated. He had said, "You're too nice for him. He needs to leave you alone." I started getting a little frustrated as well, but I kept my cool, and walked away from him.During Lunch Ben (the guy's name) came over to the table that my friends and I were all sitting at. He squeezed himself between Lottie and I, and placed an arm over my shoulder. "Can you please go away?" I had asked. He scooted closer. It was making me very uncomfortable.I looked over at the guys, who were all glaring at Ben."I saw you, thought I'd come say hi." He looked over at me, and smiled, but I didn't like it. I tried moving over, and Violet—who was on the other side of me—gladly gave me room. "Move along buddy." Noah said, squaring him up.Ben moved closer, and his hand moved to my waist. My eyes had widened. I don't know if that's what did it, or maybe he was just that mad, but Milo stood up. Actually they all stood up. Lottie had yanked his arm off of me while Violet helped me stand up and back away. The guys stayed still, as if daring him to try something else. He didn't, but that didn't stop Milo from actually walking over to us. He pulled Ben out of the seat, and held him by the collar. Milo was taller, and I could see the fear on Ben's face.I had looked around nervously, trying to spot a teacher, but I didn't see any.The next thing though, was absolutely crazy.Milo reached behind him, onto my food tray, grabbed my chocolate milk that I hadn't touched. (I don't like the schools drinks, and he knew that) He poured the drink over Ben's head!! Of course that was when the teacher actually came in, and grabbed both of them, dragging them to the office. I just stood there, stunned by the whole thing.Milo and I weren't in an argument after that.

June 2ndMilo's sitting right next to me right now. He found one of my journals, and asked why I stopped writing them. I broke, and told him about the girls. He told me that I shouldn't listen to them, and do what I want to do because I want to do it.Now he's forcing me to write. Although, I actually have something to talk about.It's 3 in the afternoon, and it's Milo's birthday. Mine was yesterday, so we had a sleepover last night at his house.Milo's been staring at a sketchbook page, dragging some sort of led or graphite(he calls it that, but I say that words a little extreme) across it for about an hour now. His whole hand is dark now from rubbing on the paper back and forth.I'm actually glad he's not watching me write though. It makes me uncomfortable when people stare at me.On another note, Milo and I are finally twelve. One more year and we will be teenagers. That's such a weird thought to think about. We won't just be kids anymore. I can't wait to get older. I can't wait till we can drive—even though we can walk everywhere—or when we can buy our own things.I can't wait till we can go to parties, and live the perfect teenage life.Milo says he agrees. Anyways, this was a shorter journal than normal. Hopefully I'll be writing again soon. I forgot how much I missed this.

I close another journal, and move on to my seventh grade one. I start reading the first one, but don't get far, and end up just skipping around through the book. Most of them are very repetitive, saying how my day was, or what happened.

Nothing that new for any of them.

Then I see the name 'Blake' and stop my flipping. I turn back slowly until I see what page it's on, and realize that it's the start of my 8th grade year. I guess I didn't write as much as I thought about seventh grade either.

September 8thI didn't have my algebra class with anyone that I knew. I'm ahead, in a highschool class, but I'm with other smart people. I was getting more nervous, until the teacher called the attendance and said Blakes name.I searched the room, and there he was in the back corner. He looked different. His hair was cut sharp, but not low, and he had glasses, which he didn't last time I saw him. Now that I think about it, I hadn't seen him in a while. I picked up my things, and moved over to him. No one seemed to care, or pay any mind to my sudden movement."Hey," I'd said. He startled, and looked up at me. Then he smiled, but my smile dropped. There was a bruise on his cheek, that swam up like a sea of dirty water to his eye. I sat down in the seat next to him, and whispered quietly, "What happened to your face?" His expression fell, and then his face began to change color. "Nothing." He whispered back. I smiled softly at him, and nudged his shoulder. "You know you can always talk to me." He smiled, and nodded his head. I knew he wasn't lying either. He had talked to me that first time in the field in 5th grade. The time that we became friends. We didn't talk for the rest of class because the teacher was talking about himself for the whole class.A part of me felt weird though, like something wasn't right. How could he have gotten a bruise on his face?Did someone hurt him?

I skip the next few diaries until I find one that says Blakes name again.

October 1stIt was Blake's birthday today. It's Friday, and I know he said not to get him anything, but I made him a small cake. I walked into school smiling, with the box in my hand and then frowned when I hadn't seen him in first block.I sat the cake on his table, but he never showed up. It was slightly weird, but it was his birthday so maybe he was doing something with his mom or dad.Lunch came quickly, and I was still holding the box when I finally spotted him sitting a few tables down. We were outside today, enjoying the nice weather, but he was sitting alone, with a hood over his head.I excused myself from my friends, and started smiling as I walked over to him again. "Hey!" I said, plopping down beside him. He jumped, and flinched backwards. I didn't understand why though. "Happy birthday. I got you something." He didn't speak, or look up at me. I smiled, and tapped his shoulder. "Blake?" He slowly, so so slowly looked over at me. I slapped a hand over my face. "Blake..." I had said. I remember so clearly trying not to cry. He had a busted lip, and his eye was swollen. Really swollen. "You can't tell anyone Izzy." He whispered. His voice was raspy, and thick with puberty. But also with pain. "What happened?" I asked softly. He shrugged, and cleared his throat. Then repositioned himself. "My brother...he just gets a little mad sometimes." It had–still does–makes me sick thinking about it. "Your brother hurt you? The older one! Blake, we gotta tell someone. You–" He had cut me off, and I almost didn't notice because of my thoughts racing faster than my mouth."No. You can't tell anyone." He had said. A small tear rolled down my face without my consent. I'm tearing up just reciting this.His hand came down softly on mine. "Don't worry. I've got thicker skin than you think." In that moment, when he smiled through his pain, all I wanted to do was hug him. So I did."No one deserves this. I'm going to help you. I promise.""Don't make promises you can't keep." He whispered, and hugged me back.When we pulled apart, he shoved his hood off, and opened the box of cake. "You made this?" I nodded, and handed him a fork. "All for you man, and me of course." He chuckled softly, and so did I, as if what we had just talked about never happened. But it did, and I didn't forget it. I don't think I could ever forget it. I won't forget about you Blake.I promise.

I couldn't read anymore. That was the year before I left. If I opened the next book, and read what I went through I might just puke.

I think I'm going to be sick actually. Blake was abused by his older brother. His older brother that's Aidens age. Did he ever know Aiden?

Where's his older brother now? Is he still hurting him. No, Blake could protect himself now. Right?

I hold a hand to my stomach, and stare at my wall blankly. Why would Blake have given me such a bad feeling if I knew him? He was my friend. How could I forget all these moments I had with him?

I had classes with him.

A tear rolls down my face. Then another, and another. It's dark outside, something I hadn't even seen happen. I didn't know what to do. I couldn't move. I couldn't process what I had just read.

I've gotta find Blake. How do I find Blake?

~~~~~~~~~~~~~~~~~~~~~~~~~~~~~~~~~

AN: ok, so this one's still a little short lol but now we know more about Blake, I can't wait for ya'll to finally figure out everything. :)
~~~~~~~~~~~~~~~~~~~~~~~~~~~~~~~~~

Chapter Twenty Seven

—'Maybe it's not about happy endings. Maybe it's about the story.' ~ Albert Camus ~ ——

Drugs~~Milo

My body is betraying me. My chest is tight, and no matter how many times I rubbed my hand across it, the pain never went away.

I slammed my head against the steering wheel, gracefully missing the horn, and groaning out loud. It's 5 in the afternoon, and I still have to go meet Luna at the beach for more surfing lessons. She's getting really good out in the water really quickly, but she still needs more practice before going to the big waves.

In some way, I feel like a proud mother watching their kid grow up and achieve their goals. One thing I'm sure of though is that I will be talking about Isabelle with her. I need Luna to try and somewhat forgive her sister.

It's not so bad once you've crossed the bridge. I like having her back, even if it's not fully yet, it is definitely better than before. Luna needs to see that. I'll give her a little bump in the right direction. Across the bridge.

I pull up to the beach quickly, and spot Luna sitting in the sand on her surfboard, eating a banana. She smiles when she sees me, and waves me over. I smile back, and lock my car before heading over to her. She stands up, and starts bouncing on her feet.

"Come on. Come on. Come on!" A small laugh leaves my mouth at her excitement, so I jog the rest of the short way to her.

Once I reach her, I open my mouth to speak, but she beats me to it. "I've been practicing for 10 minutes, and I'm ready to go back into the water again. Pretty please can I go back in now?" I laughed at her frantic tone, and get the first part of my head nodded before I remembered what I was going to say.

"Wait, no. Not yet. I need to talk to you about something. Non-surfing related." Her eyebrows pinch together while she takes a deep breath and nods her head slowly.

"Ok, what is it?"

I don't know how to approach this. She doesn't know how close Isabelle and I have gotten since she's been back, and I don't want her to hate me for this. But I also can't keep lying to her.

"It's about Isabelle." She rolls her eyes, and starts to smirk. "Ooo, what'd she do this time? Are you finally going to call it quits on this 'being nice to her' thing?" She snorts, and starts grabbing her surfboard from under her.

"What—no." She freezes, and glances up at me. "Uh...ok. What then?" I clear my throat, and rub my hands together. All of a sudden, they're sweaty, and I have a feeling it's not from the heat of the weather.

"She's been home for a month," I start. Luna nods her head, no expression on her face. "And?" She urges, with a now annoyed tone lacing her voice. Uh oh. This is already south and I haven't even gotten to the best part.

I internally groan, and feel my heart tightening again. I hate this stupid day.

"She's been here for a month, and I think it's finally time you...hear her out. Try to talk to her. I mean, maybe she left for a good reason. I just think that it's not fair to her–"

"Not fair to her?" She snarls, interrupting my soon to be ramble. Maybe it was good she stopped me before I ended up saying something worse, like the kiss I had with Isabelle. I shiver at the thought of Luna knowing that. Then my jaw clenches at how I handled that situation earlier.

"Luna...She's different. Somethings wrong with her. Something happened to her, and I think it might be why she–"

"What?" I freeze, confused, momentarily stunned to silence. "Why she abandoned me, Milo? Why she left you? Or anyone else that cares for her? What could possibly be worth that. She was selfish." She spits out, and her hands ball tightly at her side.

I breathe quickly, and rub my chest harder, wincing at the pain. What the hell is going on with me today? I push it down, and shake my head.

I need to stay focused. "Please Luna. We don't know any of that because we've never asked. Just listen to me." She turns around, her hair wiping around her back, while she stomps over to me.

Even though she's practically half my size, her anger is way higher than mine at the moment. "I don't owe her anything Milo, ok?" She takes a deep breath, and I can't tell if it even helps. "What did she do to you? You weren't like this before she got back. Did she seduce you? Manipulate you into thinking she was the victim." I clench my jaw, and suppress the urge to grab my chest, and rip the skin off.

"Shit," She whispers with hurt evident in her voice. "Milo. What did she do?" Her voice rises again. "She didn't do anything–" She pounds one fist on my chest. God. Jesus, thankyou. I stumble back a step, regaining myself quickly.

"Luna—" She cuts me off with another hit. "What did she do!" She yells. "What does she have that I don't!" My eyebrows furrow at her next question. She keeps hitting me, and eventually, I have to forcefully grip her wrist to stop her.

Then it hits me. The realization slaps me across the face like a deer in headlights. "Luna," She's breathing heavily when I whisper her name. "Forgiving Isabelle doesn't make you weak." Her bottom lip wobbles, so she sucks it into her mouth behind her teeth, keeping it captive from her emotions.

"I've been waiting...for her to come home." She says so softly, I almost miss it. "And now she's back, and all I want to do is hug her. Why can't I hate her?" Her voice, now, no anger left in it, only pure sadness.

"If I let her in. How will I know she won't break my heart again?" My voice gets caught in my throat, so instead of words, I pull her slowly to my chest, and wrap my arms around her. "I understand what you're feeling, but I've seen the way Isabelle looks at you. She's trying so hard Luna. Please just try too." She pulls away, and rubs her nose quickly.

"Hey," I nudged her arm. "It's a lot better from this side of the line. Seriously. Just talk to her." She rolls her eyes, but I can tell it's not out of anger, but playfulness.

After a few beats her shoulders sag downwards. "I can't Milo." I sigh, and wrap my arm around her shoulders. "No surfing today. Let's just go home for the night. Yeah?" She nods, and lets me drag her to the car, her surfboard being dragged behind me.

It's a quiet drive back to our houses. A quick one, but quiet, and my chest pains resurface like a brick falling from the sky. I rub my hand over my heart, feeling it pulse faster in my body.

Luna looks out the window the whole drive, and jumps out the minute I turn my car off in my driveway. I watch her retreating form run off to her house in more silence.

God, what is with this silence all of the sudden?

I stumble into my house, and shut the front door behind me. Tears start pricking my eyes at the pain. It's crawling up my chest like a spider, and entering my throat. Why can't I breathe?

What is going on? My vision blurs, and I drop to the floor. My back pressed against the kitchen table. I'm sweating, so I grip the ends of my shirt, and lift it over my head. My bare chest rises at a speed I know is abnormal, and the only thought that comes to my head is, I know what would help.

I shake my head, and pull my knees up to rest my elbows on and lower my head between them. One line, and the pain will go away. The voice is small, but so damn powerful.

I don't even think as I pull my body to its feet, and clumsily walk over to the pantry. It's a walk in closet, so I flip the light on, and make my way towards the very back.

In an old fruit snacks box, I reach my hand in and feel around until I feel the plastic. Pulling it out, I see the white powder sitting peacefully at the bottom of the tiny button sized baggy.

My hands tremble as I open it. Don't do it. Don't do it. Don't do it. A different voice chants. My voice. It's growing hard to breathe again, and the urge is just becoming stronger.

My body jolts backwards when I hear the doorbell ring. I suck in a tight breath, and try to breathe but it doesn't work. I stumble back out of the closet, and grip the edge of the kitchen island, throwing the small packet across it. I slide to the floor so that it's not in my vision anymore.

I can't do it. I've worked so hard to not do it.

"What the fuck." My eyes dark up to see Henry standing in front of me. How did he get here? When did he get here? I didn't even hear him walk inside. Now that I think about it, everything is ringing.

My head flinches backwards when I see Henry knelt down in front of me. He grabs my face, and forces me to look at him. "What's wrong? What's going on Milo?" I shake my head, and fling my hand to my chest.

"Can't–breath." His expression changes, and in two seconds, he's sitting down next to me. His hand grabs mine, and places it on his wrist where I feel his heart beating.

It's a strange feeling, how slow his heart rate is going when mine is going so fast. "What?" I pant. He shakes his head. "Don't talk." He says. "Follow my breathing." I try but it's not working, and my vision is beginning to black again.

"Hey? No. Milo, come on. Breath it out with me. Trust me. Let it go." I try taking in longer breaths, and letting out even longer ones. Soon enough, it starts to work, and I feel my body becoming my own again. He lets go of me, and scoots away a couple of feet.

"Now," I look over at him. "You're going to tell me what the hell just happened."

——

Starting from the moment I got into drugs, to this very second, I tell Henry everything. He stays quiet, and surprisingly doesn't ask any questions the whole time. My voice breaks once, when I mention what had happened on Fourth of July.

I've never told anyone willingly about it, and it feels really good. He doesn't judge, and once I'm done, it feels like a weight has been lifted off my shoulders. Henry walks over to the counter where the pack of drugs sits, soft white bits splayed across the table.

My face burns hot from embarrassment. I almost relapsed. I almost relapsed. He grabs the trash can, and drags it to the end of the counter, then proceeds to clean the table. "You don't have to do that, man." He shakes his head, and sticks up his hand to silence me.

"You think I'm about to let you relapse in front of me?" I sit quietly, and watch as one of my best friends cleans up my addiction. A small, such a small part of me wants to scream and take it all. A better, smarter part though, knows that it won't stop with this one, and it will take over again.

He turns around, heaving a loud breath of air, and giving me a stern stare. "There more?" I look down guiltily, and nod my head slowly. I stand up without his command, and walk back into my pantry, where I just hand him the fruit snack box.

He looks at me, with no pity or disappointment. Instead, "I'm proud of you, dude. Seriously." I look at him surprised. Only one other person has said that to me, and it was John. I nod at a loss for words, and follow him back to the kitchen.

"So, what do you wanna do with it?" Surprisingly my first thought to that question isn't snorting it. "Let's flush it." He smiles, and then turns around and starts walking to our downstairs bathroom. "What do your parents say about this?" He pours the powder into the toilet, and hits the flush immediately.

I scratch the back of my head, and lightly bounce on the heels of my feet. "Uh, I guess they don't really know?" He looked over at me with a confused expression on his face. "What do you mean, they don't know?" I shrug my shoulders, and rub my hands over my hair.

"They know about my drug addiction, but John was the one who put me in rehab. He visited me, and then watched me for the first couple months after I got out. My parents didn't know about my stash though, no one did." I pause. "They weren't really home when I got back." I shrug, and turn around to leave the bathroom.

It's dark outside as I climb up the stairs towards my room. I don't have to look backwards to know that Henry is following me up the stairs. "I guess that makes sense then. Why you're so close to the Everest now." I nod my head, and enter my room, only taking a slight glance at my window.

Isabelle's curtains are closed, but I'm not surprised. Instantly I'm wondering if she's sleeping. I sigh, and throw myself onto my bed, stuffing my face into my pillow. I turn my head to see Henry sitting in my spinny chair and twisting around in it. "Wait, why did you come here in the first place?" He stops spinning, and that's when I notice Boeing is on his lap.

He shrugs his shoulders. "Noah and Violet suggested that we all go to the carnival on Fourth of July, before going over to Izzy's house." I nod my head slowly. "Yeah, sure." I stuff my face back into my bed, feeling sleep begin to take over.

Henry intruded on my soon to be peaceful sleep with a question. "What's going on with you and Isabelle?" I look over at him again, with foggy eyes. I shrug my shoulders. "Something happened to her." His eye brows furrow. "What?" I shake my head and turn away from him.

"I'm going to sleep." I don't hear him reply, nor do I wait for one.

~~~~~~~~~~~~~~~~~~~~~~~~~~~~~~~~

AN: If anyone was confused, this was basically taking place at the same time as the last chapter.
~~~~~~~~~~~~~~~~~~~~~~~~~~~~~~~~

Chapter Twenty Eight

—'We're all just a bunch of addicts, struggling with our drug of choice.' ~ JmStorm ~ ——

Avoidance ~~Isabelle

I rub ice cubes under my eyes to try and reduce the bagginess of them. I didn't sleep a wink last night, and everything's getting a bit foggy. I searched up how to get rid of the under eye but I think I may just be too far gone.

It's currently 7 in the morning, and I'm already ready to go to the carnival. Violet and Lottie came over last week and told me about the plan. Obviously I was on board.

Since I read those journals about Blake, I've been so busy with work that I haven't even had time to find him, let alone talk to him. Which leads back to why I didn't sleep last night. I may or may not have been searching him up, and trying to find his address.

Ok, that just sounds really bad now that I think about it.

Above that, I've also been secretly avoiding Milo. I took all the shifts I knew he wouldn't be on, and made sure to keep my blinds closed. I'm still slightly embarrassed about the kiss we had, and the fact that it even meant something to me.

I know he doesn't know that, but I do, and I know it wasn't anything special to him. I shake my head, and cover the ice over my eyes long enough for it to go numb.

"You up Izz?" I jump off the ground at my dads voice coming from my bedroom door. I drop the ice into the sink, and dry my face with a towel.

Peeking my head out of the bathroom, I see my dad standing—well, leaning against my door frame. "Yeah," I smile at him, and walk over to my closet.

"I'm going to the carnival with everyone in a little bit." I hear his feet patting the floor, telling me that he's walking over to my closet.

When he doesn't speak, I turn around and raise an eyebrow at him. "Is everything ok?" I ask. He looks at me questionably. "Are you ok?" He finally asks.

His question surprises me off guard, and it takes me a minute to recover. "Uh, yeah. Why?" I ask back. His head turns sideways ever so slightly, looking somewhat like a dog.

He shrugs. "You haven't really told us how you've been since being back. You told your mom and I all about being in Oregon, but not once have you said anything about being back home." I frown, realizing he's right.

Then I smile, and turn around towards my clothes again. "Yeah, I'm good. It's just been busy being back. Having all the company now." I let out a small—very fake—laugh, and grabbed some dark denim overalls from the shelves while also swiping a green bathing suit for under.

I haven't worn the overalls yet, and they've got cute flowers on the ends of the shorts. I choose a sage green cropped t-shirt to wear underneath, matching my bathing suit. When I turn around my dads still standing there.

"Come on. Talk to me Izz." His pleading voice sends a wave of guilt over me. My dad has always been my number one best friend. So why is it so hard to tell him what's going on?

A part of me wants to tell him about what happened with Milo. The kiss, I mean, but Milo said it didn't mean anything. There's no point in getting his hopes up when I know there's never gonna be anything of it.

"I'm very excited for your barbeque tonight, and I'm very excited to go to the carnival, and to see the fireworks tonight." My dad frowns at this. "Izzy..." I shake my head, and walk into the bathroom to change. "I'm ok dad. Seriously." I hear him sigh behind the door, and finish quickly.

As I'm walking out, I begin parting my hair, and dutch braiding the left side first. "You promise that you will tell me or your mother if anything's wrong?" I nod my head, and walk closer to him. Finishing my braid, I wrap my arms around him, giving him the hug I know he needs.

"Of course, I promise." He breathes out a huff of relief, and hugs me back strongly. Once he pulls back, I start grabbing the other side of my hair to braid it. He shakes his head with a grimace. "How do you even do that? Don't your arms hurt." I laugh, and shake my head.

"I've grown used to the pain." He gives me a pained laugh, and then leaves my room. Once I'm done with my hair, I grab my phone and see text messages from the group.

The Dream TeamViolet - Who's ready for some PART-A!Noah - Me!Henry - Whose driving?Milo - You Lottie - YouMe - YouViolet - Girls with me? Guys with Henry?Henry - Why am I always the driver?Me - Because you can driveHenry - Milo can driveMilo - NoNoah - Are we all spending the night at your house Izz?Me - Sure, if you guys want. My parents don't care.Violet - Good, because I don't want to drive home late at night.Henry - I second thatLottie - What time are you picking us up Violet?Violet - Park opened up early this morning, so I can come over now.Me - Sounds goodLottie - YupHenry - I'm heading over to Noah's then Milos.Noah - I'm still showeringMilo - Why are you on your phone in the shower?Noah - Don't worry about it.Me- EwLottie - Gross NoahViolet - LMAO

I shut off my phone with a laugh, and tie my high top pink converse on. Walking downstairs, I see my mom sitting with Luna in the kitchen.

"Morning sweetie." Luna doesn't greet me. "Good morning, mom." There's a quick pause, "Good morning, Luna." She looks up ever so slightly, and then looks down again. "You're going to the amusement park. Isn't it right by the beach?"

I nod my head. "Yeah, some of the shops are on the pier." She nods her head, and then brings her cup of coffee to her lips. Her head turns towards Luna, while she softly nudges her shoulder. "Are you gonna go with Leo?" Her head perks up at his name, and then her face flushes with color.

I smile slightly as she looks up at me, and then scowls. "Uh, yeah." She clears her throat, and stands up from the table. The doorbell rings, causing me to say my goodbyes, and walk towards it. What surprises me though is Milo, standing behind it.

My eyes widen, and I quickly go to shut the door, but he stops me. I reopen it slowly, and laugh nervously. "You've been avoiding me." I give him a pathetic laugh, and scratch the back of my neck. "What? No." I shake my head vigorously until I start to feel dizzy, and then lean against the door for support.

"Yes you have. Mama Hazel told me you specifically asked for different shifts."

"Maybe I like working at night better."

"You don't." He answers instantly, not even giving me time to object before pushing the door open wider and walking in. I hear footsteps coming from the kitchen, and look over to see my mom walking out of it. "Oh, hey Milo. I haven't seen you in a while. How have you been?" She smiles warmly at him, but he only stares blankly at her.

"Actually, really bad." My eyes widen as he crosses his arms over his chest, and pouts like a little kid. "Your daughter has been avoiding me." My moms eyes turn from concern to annoyance as she looks over at me. "Have you been avoiding Milo?" I can feel my face burning red, but I still try to play it off.

I got this.

"No." Her eyebrows rise in a motherly way of 'try that again'. I look over to Milo, who is now smirking, and popping his hands on his hips. He pokes his tongue out at me from where my mom can't see.

I gasp, and look back at her. "He just stuck his tongue at me!" She doesn't look away. "Isabelle Mona." I scoff again, and groan. "Fine, whatever. I was just taking different shifts then him at Mama Hazels." I admit.

"On purpose to avoid me." I narrow my eyes at Milo. "What are you trying to get out of this, why—" I get cut off by the front door opening—no knock—with Violet and Lottie bursting in. Violet stops when she sees us. "I told you he would be here!" She yells back at the empty doorway.

Then not even a second later, Henry comes through the door, and stops right after walking inside. It's quiet, and Henry opens his mouth to speak, but gets cut off by a force running into him. He makes a pained noise, and stumbles forward.

"Henry! Why would you stop right in the doorway!" Noah yells, and finally comes walking around Henry, rubbing his forehead in pain. "Why would you run into a house?" Henry growls. After taking a moment to regain his thoughts he begins to speak again. "As I was going to say, before I was rudely interrupted," He glares at Noah, then shakes his head.

"Milo. I was looking for you."

"I thought you got kidnapped." Noah shrugs, and walks further into the room. "Mama E!! I missed you." Noah engulfs my mom in a hug, that she laughs at and recuperates. "Hi Noah. I missed you too." Her voice holds slight sarcasm, but also love and adoration.

"Come on, I wanna go. This is taking too long." Violet whines, and stomps her feet. I snorted at her child-like state, and started walking towards the door. "No! I am not done." Everyone stops, and glances back at Milo, who's staring straight at me.

With everyone's attention on him, I begin slowly inching towards the door, trying to get to the safety of Violet's car. Milo's not driving with us, so maybe that will give me some more time to think of a better answer then right now.

Right now, I have no answer.

"Don't you move Isabelle." I pause, and everyone looks at me. "Milo, for the last time I didn't—"

"Lea!" He screams for my mom, but she only pokes her head out of the kitchen slowly. When did she even leave? "Milo and Isabelle, you both need to work out whatever's going on, but I am not going to be in the middle of it." Milo scowls, and narrows his eyes at me.

"I didn't do anything!" I scream, throwing my arms up over my head. "Yes you did—"

"What the heck is going on?" Noah askes, and when I look over at him, he's smiling at us. "I don't know, I don't care. I want to ride the Ferris Wheel, and get ice cream." Violet grabs Lotties arm, and walks towards the door, then grabs mine on the way out.

I smile at the un-noticed save she just gave me, and happily walk back to the car with her. We all get into our respective seats—me in the back, Lottie in the passenger seat, and Violet in the driver's seat—and Violet begins backing out of the driveway.

Although we don't get far before she's pulling over on the side of the road and turning around to look at me. "Now, tell us what the hell was going on, because I am deeply interested." I sigh, and lower my head in defeat.

—-

We pulled into the parking lot of Mama Hazel's almost 30 minutes after leaving my house. I had to tell Lottie and Violet about me somewhat, only barely, avoiding Milo. Since I had to tell them that, I also had to explain why I was doing that.

It shouldn't have taken as long as it did, but I was very resistant. I walk behind my two best friends into the small cafe, with my head down looking at the marbled floor. Violet had said that we can walk to the rest of the fair from here, and Mama Hazel's has good parking, so we are just getting some drinks and then heading out.

I finally look upwards when I see Henry and Noah waving us over to a circular booth in the corner. By the looks of Milo slumped into the side of the table, I think Noah and Henry did the same thing to him. It only eases my embarrassment slightly.

We walk over to the table, and sit down beside the guys who instantly start talking. "We ordered you guys your drinks and foods that you always order." I smile at the fact that they just know what the orders are.

"Thanks." I say at the same time Violet and Lottie say it as well. "So, here's what I'm thinking," Noah starts. "We play some games, go swimming for a little bit, and then end the night with the Ferris wheel." I take a quick glance at Milo, and he's already looking at me, causing me to blush and look away.

Milo and I used to ride the Ferris wheel together on the Fourth of July every year during sunset. It has the best, and prettiest view over the water.

A waiter brings over our food quickly, and soon enough we are all eating away quickly. In a comfortable silence, we eat and drink, with the occasional speaking from Noah whose mouth is full of food each time, telling us about what he wants to do.

A part of me feels bad about blocking his voice out, but all my brain can think about it Milo. The sad thing is, I don't even mind it.

~~~~~~~~~~~~~~~~~~~~~~~~~~~~~~~~~

AN: ok, ok, LAST short one lmao

Also.....i am sooo sorry but its very unlikely that i will be posting this weekend, because i need time to write a little more and i have to help set up for a party.

Hope you all have a great day!
~~~~~~~~~~~~~~~~~~~~~~~~~~~~~~~~~

Chapter Twenty Nine

—'I want a second chance at falling in love with you for the first time.' ~ highpoetssociety ~——

Fourth of July ~~Isabelle

"My dad said he wanted us back by 5 so we can still eat before the fireworks." I state as we make our way towards the arcade. "But then we won't get to see the sunset." Noah pouts. I shrug. "The view will still be pretty though." The girls nod along next to me.

We all just got ice cream cones, and it really is helping with the hot weather. Although, it kind of sucks that they're melting so freaking fast. I finished mine a minute ago, and now I'm just holding my hands out, not moving them because of the stickiness.

"I gotta go wash my hands." I mutter, and dart for the bathroom door. I walk to the sink, and quickly turn it on with my elbow. I breathe out a sigh of relief as I feel my hands growing cleaner. I'm getting ready to leave the silent bathroom when I hear a sniffle.

I freeze, then when nothing happens I continue out the door. As I'm opening the door I hear it again, and a quiet sob. I close the door slowly and look back at the stalls. Only one is closed. I knock on it, and a small gasp echo's through the tiny stall, then shuffling around. "Are you ok in there?" I ask quietly.

"Yeah, I'm fine." The door opens, and out walks the last person I would have ever thought I'd see again. Sadly, this is a small town, and I can't really stop it. "Ava?"

"Isabelle?" She sniffles again, and wipes her eyes. "Oh god. This is embarrassing." She laughs quietly, and walks over to the mirror. "Are you sure your ok? I'm a good listener." She turns to look at me with surprise.

"You want to listen to my problems even after I was rude to you?" I shrug, and smile softly at her. "I don't like thinking about the past. It's just better to focus on the present time. If you let yourself stay in the past with grudges, you're never gonna grow." She smiles at me.

"He deserves you." She whispers. I don't have to ask to know who he is. "You deserve someone too." She grips onto the edge of the sink and shakes her head. "My step brother is being a dick." She mutters. "It's not just me either. He's always mean to Blake as well—" My eyebrows furrow. "Is Blake your brother?" I ask.

Is this the Blake I've been looking for? Is this the older brother that Blake said was hitting him? "Step-brother. My mom just married his dad." I know this town is small, but dang. I never knew it could be useful. Is Blake even an uncommon name though? There could be at least three Blakes in this town.

My hope dims ever so slightly. "My older step brother is Blakes biological brother." She explains, probably thinking I'm confused. Everytime she speaks, it just makes this sound like the same Blake from my journals more and more.

"Oh...have they lived here their whole lives?" Her eyebrows scrunch up in confusion. "I'm not sure. I think so." She whispers. Her eyes glance down to her hands, and then I see it. There's a bruise around her wrist. "Ava?" She looks up at me with saddened eyes. "Yes?"

"Does your step-brother hurt you?" I whisper, scared I might send her into a panic. Her eyes widen and I immediately get my answer. I think she realizes this, because she doesn't try to convince me I'm wrong. "It's not Blake." She says quickly.

"I'm so sorry." I whisper, and take a step closer to her, trying to see if it'd be ok to give her a hug. When she doesn't protest, I wrap my arms around her neck and pull her into a hug. She cries quietly on my shoulder. "I'm so so sorry I was mean. I was mad—" She stops as her voice cracks.

"It's fine. I forgive you." We pull away after a few seconds, only when she's ready and I watch as she cleans herself up. You know we can get you help." She shakes her head. "It will only make it worse." She replied sadly.

I'm getting deja vu from what I read in my journal, expect I don't even remember it happening. "Do you want to hang out with us? I know that you haven't really been—" Her head shakes vigorously. "No, no. You guys have fun. I don't wanna upset Milo, or Violet. Or really just any of them." She huffs out a laugh, and then wipes her hands down her face.

"I'll be ok. Blakes picking me up, and we were hanging out at his mom's house today." I think for a moment before asking for her phone. "Let me put my number in just in case ok?" She nods hesitantly and lets me put it in.

I smile softly at her, and we walk out of the bathroom together. It opens up to the outside of the arcade where you walk into the front door to get there.

I pause when I see Blake. Blake is standing, leaning on the doorway. My eyes widened. Seeing him is completely different when I know everything now. It's like cleaning a pair of dirty glasses, and being able to see for the first time. Jesus it is Blake. My Blake. My journals Blake.

Everything finally falls into place, and it makes me a little woozy.

He glances up at his step sister, and smiles softly at her, then looks over at me with a confused face. "Isabelle? What are you doing?" I clear my throat, and try to avoid eye contact. "I was just in the bathroom at the same time?" I laugh nervously, and scratch my head.

He looks at me intently, and for a second I think he knows, but then he sighs and turns his attention back to Ava. "You ready?" She nods her head, and begins walking closer to him. He takes another glance at me, this one holding a small smile.

He gives me a small wave, and I recuperate his actions, adding a smile to go along with it. The moment him and his sister are out of view, I blow out a breath of relief, not even knowing what I should be relieved for.

I'm going to need to find him again, and actually talk to him. I cover my face with my hands, and groan.

I jump when a hand comes down on my shoulder. "What are you doing? Everyone's inside?" Milo, askes slowly. "Gosh, you scared me." I mutter. He doesn't respond to my statement instead, askes his question again. "I was using the bathroom." I finally answered.

He nods, and turns towards the arcade. He opens the door, and holds it open for me, but instead of walking I stay rooted in my spot. I turn to look behind me to see people walking around. Moms with their kids. Brothers, sisters. Friends, toddlers. No Blake or Ava anymore.

There both getting hurt right now and I know about it. If it's Blake's brother, and it's been going on since my journal, that means that he's been abused his whole life. I can't just stand by and watch. I need to tell someone. How do I even tell someone about this?

My heart speeds up at the thought. Who is Blake's brother anyway? Why do I feel like all the answers are right in the front of my brain and I just can't remember. "Isabelle." I turn my head back to Milo, who's got an eyebrow raised. "You comin? We don't have all day." I nod with a smile, and follow him inside.

The smell of popcorn, and hotdogs hits my nose as does the cool air from being inside as the doors shut. I don't start moving until I feel Milo's hand on the small of my back, urging me forward. "Are you ok?" He whispers, and I shiver at his hot breath against my neck.

"Yeah, why wouldn't I be?" I clear my throat, and fidget with my fingers. His hand reaches out gently, and pries my hands apart. "Stop lying to yourself. You don't have to be ok all the time." There's slight frustration in his voice, but also disappointment.

"I don't know what you're talking about Milo." I pull away from him, putting space between us. He frowns. "Why can't you just—" I cut him off. "Will you just stop? Please?" I whisper. He doesn't answer, and I can feel the tension as we walk towards our friends.

We find them next to a clown throwing game while Lottie and Violet were violently throwing the red balls at the clown's faces. Not gonna lie, they are pretty good at it. I smile as the guys throw basketballs at the game besides them.

Once both of their games are done, they turn around, smiling at us. "Oh, hey guys." Lottie says. Violet opens her mouth to say something when

Noah walks right in front of her, facing me. "I won. Say I won." He demands. I laugh and shake my head.

"Won what?"

"I just won, Isabelle. Say it." Henry walks in front of him and looks at me. "I won. That dumbo is lying because he sucks at basketball." He points his thumb behind his head at the same time Noah slaps his head.

"Don't listen to him Izzy." I look between them, and then back at the game. "I'm sorry Noah." Henry smirks and crosses his arms. "Yeah, you did great, babe." Lottie nods, walking up and attaching herself to Henry's side.

"Milo. They are ganging up on me." Milo laughs and shakes his head. "I'm not getting into this." I gasp, ignoring their argument when I see my favorite claw machine across the arcade. I can't believe it is still here.

Milo and I would always compete, trying to get a prize, but neither of us ever got anything. I start walking towards it and pull out my money. It's only a dollar so I grabbed two ones, and stuck one in. I feel more bodies behind me, telling me that my friends are standing there.

I look through the prizes, and see that most of them are still the same as when I used to come here. I see a cute tiny pink bear. Just about the six of a milk jug. I locate the claw over it, and finally press the button. It falls, and lands over the bear, then it rises with the bear in it's grasp, but before it can drop it in the slot it falls out and lands back with the rest.

I sigh, and put my other dollar in. The same process repeats, and I don't get the bear. I turn around to my friends and give them a smile. "Didn't get it." I shrug, and they all turn around to look for another game.

Milo stares at the claw machine, before shaking his head and following us all.

———

It's late, almost 6 o'clock. My dad texted me an hour ago, saying we could stay till 6:30 instead of 5. We're all tired, and worn out, ready to leave.

We are making our way towards our car when Violet and Noah stop us. The rest of us just stare at them confused and exhausted. "Wait, we need to ride the Ferris wheel." Noah demands. "I won't leave till we do." Violet agrees, nodding her head.

Everyone's quiet for a second, before I speak up. "Ok, well let's get going." We walk back towards the peer, where the Ferris wheel sits, right near the water. The line is short, and we make it to the front quickly. Violet and Noah jump into the first one. Henry and Lottie jump into the next one, and then there's one left open. "I'll just wait for the next one." I say, moving over so Milo can take it.

"Sorry, it's two to a seat." The operator says. Milo gets in first, and then I stare at the open door. I can do this, I got this. I breathe a shaky laugh, and hop into the ride. It begins moving up slowly, stopping with every cart at the top, giving them time with the view.

It's quiet, and awkward, and no matter how far I scooted to the side our knees were still grazing one another's. It's making me antsy, and I need to speak, but for some reason my throat gets caught.

It gets to us, and stops at the top. I turn, looking over Milo's side at the water. The sun is still fully in the sky, just barley dancing against the ocean. "Wow." I whisper. My eyes glance over to Milo, who is also looking at the view.

I turn my head back, and look at my lap. "It's beautiful." I whisper. "Yeah, it is." I look up, back towards the sky, but see Milo looking at me. Was he just... "Milo."

"Isabelle." My eyes skip over his face, taking in his features, and his eyes. His eyes are everything. "What—" The ride starts moving again. I shut my mouth, and turn stock still, facing forwards, and staring at nothingness.

———

We pull up to my house that's buzzing with life. There's soft chatter echoing through the backyard, telling me that most of my dads friends are already here. Meaning Lottie, Violet and probably Henry or Noahs parents are here.

It was a quieter ride back from the pier, because everyone was tired, and nobody felt like talking. I was sunburnt. I am sunburnt. I never remember to put sunscreen on when we go swimming, and then the sun beats on me, literally.

We walk through the front door, that's instantly quieter than outside. A few people are standing around, including Lotties parents. Her mom is also wearing a pretty purple sundress. "Hey darling." She smiles down at Lottie, and kisses her forehead, then does the same to Violet and I.

She pulls Henry into a small hug as well, and mutters something into his ear that I don't catch. I find my own mom in the kitchen cooking on the stove. "Hey mom, whatcha making?" She turns around towards me with a big smile.

"Hon! How was the fair?" I look at the table, and grab a handful of chips to start eating. "Really good. I had a lot of fun." I peer over her shoulder, and see her stirring chili in a pot. "I love chili." I mutter.

She laughs and nods her head. "I know, that's why I made it." I smile at her, and walk back over to the chip bowl. The kitchen doesn't stay silent, because soon enough the others are walking in.

"Dinner will be ready soon, you all are still hungry right?" My mom asks hopefully, turning around to glance at all my friends. "I could be about ready to explode, and I'd still eat your food Mrs.E." Noah exclaims, rubbing his stomach with a smirk on his face.

"Oh my gosh, I am sweating." Henry groans, and wipes his face with the front of his shirt. "We could go swimming. If we have time?" I look at my mom, and she nods her head. "I'd say you have about 30 minutes." She smiles.

"That is exactly what I need right now." Lottie sighs. "Onward!" Noah points like a pirate towards the sliding doors, and we all follow after him.

We walk around the swarm of adults, until we reach the empty pool where we all start stripping. My bathing suit is still a bit sandy from the beach, so feeling the nice clean water as I get it, feels extremely good.

Everyone else soon gets in, and we're all relaxing, talking about nonsense. "Wait." Noah gasps. "We should have a chicken fight." Violet laughs loudly, and climbs onto Noah's shoulders, forcefully grabbing the front of his face as she gets on. Lottie starts swimming towards Henry, and then I realize that Milo is the only one left.

Not this again. Why is this happening again? First the ferris wheel, now this? "You comin?" He quirks a brow, and I instinctively blush.

I swim slowly, blaming it on the water, and stand behind Milo. He lowers himself enough for me to float my legs overtop of his shoulders, before he rises back to his full height.

We're all in a strange looking triangle, while the guys make sure they have a good grip on all of us. I lay my hands on top of Milo's wet hair, and feel his hands hold my calves in place.

My cooled skin is getting heated by the warmth from his hands, making goosebumps arise on my skin. "Ready?" Lottie askes? I nod, and Violet smirks deviously.

The guys soon walk closer to each other, and as soon as Violet is close enough she tickles Lottie in the ribs. She starts laughing, and losing her grip while Milo wrestles with Noah below. I wait until I see Lottie finally topple over, laughing and falling into the water before I start attacking Violet.

She wasn't exactly ready, and loses her balance, but only for a second before she regains herself and fights back. Milo is slowly shoving Noah under the water against his will, causing Violet to shrink.

I laugh, and lean my head back smiling. They go down, and I don't even have to do anything more than fist pump the air. "Milo, we won!" I exclaim, shaking his head vigorously.

"Damn straight." He mutters. He starts lowering himself to what I assume is him letting me down, but then all of a sudden he jolts back up, and throws me off his shoulders.

~~~~~~~~~~~~~~~~~~~~~~~~~~~~~~~~

AN: Yay! A longer chapter lol.

I still have more planned for this night so get ready... it was getting too long so I just decided to split it into two ;)

Also, sidenote, ya'll i literally wrote NOTHING over the weekend. Dont worry tho, i still have this chapter and another one before i need to write more lol
~~~~~~~~~~~~~~~~~~~~~~~~~~~~~~~~

Chapter Thirty

—'Words do not express thoughts very well. They always become a little different immediately after they are expressed, a little distorted, a little foolish.' ~ Hermann Hesse ~ ——

Broken Pantry~~Isabelle

Our 30 minutes went by quickly, and we were soon being called by my mom to come get our food. We were all now seated around a small table in the backyard, away from all the adults, and eating by ourselves.

I was peacefully enjoying my chili when Noah spoke up. "Do you guys remember that one time we stole a golf cart, and then crashed it." He smirks.

"Technically, it was only Lotties, and she was there. So was it really stealing?" Violet questions, shoving another spoon full of beans into her mouth, and twisting her drying hair around her finger.

"Yes, Violet. That is still stealing." Henry sighs. "My parents were forgiving." Lottie shrugs.

"Mine weren't, I spent the whole summer paying that damage off." Noah says, a little frustrated. "We all did, Noah." I remind him. I still remember having to go over to the Maddisons every afternoon, and help clean their house.

It wasn't hard though, because we all ended up making the best of it. Plus it just gave the 6 of us more reason to hang out.

It goes quiet again, and my mind starts to wonder back to Ava and Blake. She had told me this morning that she and Blake were going over to his dads house for Fourth of July.

Had they really left though? Did they go back home to grab something, and never make it out? Could Blakes older brother really have that much power over them? How do their parents not know? Do their parents know? Are their parents also abusive?

I bite my bottom lip hard. So many questions that can't be answered. I mean, in my diary, it said that Blake's parents fought over not wanting him a lot, so maybe they didn't even notice.

"Do you guys remember Blake? He hung out a couple times you guys were over. Went trick or treating with us once." Milo's jaw clenches unknowingly. On the other hand, the rest of them stare off, thinking thoroughly.

"The kid with the glasses that always sat alone?" Henry askes, but his voice doesn't hold any anger. I nod my head. "Yeah." I whisper. The rest finally nod along. "He was always so quiet." Lottie states, probably remembering how he sat alone with a hood over his head everyday.

Little did they know what was under those hoods. "Does he still live here?" I glance over at Milo, who's being suspiciously quiet, and strangely still. I nod my head. "I've seen him a few times since being back. I didn't even remember that I knew him."

It's silent, before I choose my next words carefully. "Did you guys know that Blake and Ava are siblings? Well, step-siblings." This time, Milo does move, but it's only his brows scrunching up.

"Really?" Violet askes, surprised. I nod my head. I want to say more, there's so much more I want to say, and yet I don't even know how to say any of it, so instead, I don't say anything at all.

———

"We're going to watch the fireworks that they set off at the beach. We'll be able to get a clear view from here." Just like when we were kids, he gives us the rundown of what we are doing, even though I haven't forgotten any of it.

I stop walking when I see my mom coming towards me. "Hey hun, could you go get some candy for the little kids from the pantry? Be careful though, the door broke a couple days ago, and locks from the outside. Make sure you leave it open." I nod my head, and smile.

Walking over to the kitchen, I run my fingers through my hair that's dried, and clip one side of my overall top over my shoulder, then leave the other one undone. I leave the door open like she had said, and walk towards the back of it, rummaging through all the foods until I find the candy.

I grab the bag, and stop short when I notice I'm not the only one in here.

"Milo? What are you doing?" His hands on the door, holding it open, and then all of a sudden he lets go of the door. "I wanted to talk, and you've been avoiding me all night again." The door starts shutting, quicker then it should, and I try to rush to stop it, but it doesn't work.

"No, no, wait—" I hear the hinges click, and immediately try to open it, as if maybe it will work for me now. It doesn't. "Milo." I groan, and yank on the door again, before finally giving up and setting my head down on the door.

It's almost pitch black, and the light switch for the pantry is on the outside wall right beside the door. "What? Why isn't it opening?" He sounds panicked. Good, he should be, he just locked us in here. "It broke and now only opens from the outside."

I sigh in defeat, and turn around to lean against the door with my back. "I didn't know that." A wave of anger hits me out of nowhere, and I feel my face getting hotter. "Why are you even here?" I can barely see his facial features, but I know he's standing in front of me.

I wonder if he can see me.

"How do you know the thing about Ava and Blake?" Of course this is what he wanted to know. A sarcastic laugh bubbles in my throat, and I don't fight it. "I saw her at the fair, she told me." He nods his head, and I can feel him back away from me.

My eyes have adjusted to the lighting, and now I can see him better. Just his eyes, his face, and his figure. "That was it? You got us locked in here, so I can't see the fireworks, and it is because you wanted to know something about Ava?" He stares at me, at least that's what it looks like.

"How was I supposed to know it was going to lock?" I groan, and slide to the floor against the door. "You shouldn't have even come in here." He sighs. "Why are you so mad at me?" He finally asks. I look up at him, and see that he's also on the floor, but on the far wall opposite of me.

"Why don't you like Blake? He has done nothing to you. You don't even know him." I bite out, not even feeling bad about it. "You weren't here. If you were, maybe you'd know but you don't." I flinch at his words.

"I'm sorry, that was mean." He whispers right after. I take a deep breath, and rub my hand over my face. "I'm sorry too, that's not what I'm upset about." I sigh, and lean my head on my knees.

It's quiet, and I don't hear anything behind the door, so I assume that everyone is already outside watching the fireworks. All I can hear are my deep breaths, that I'm trying to use to calm myself.

It's not Milo's fault that Ava and Blake are being hurt, and it's not his fault that he didn't care about the kiss. I can't blame him for any of this.

"I have a problem." I look up, and squint my eyes at him to see him better. "What?" I ask, confused. What problem? Is he in trouble, does he need help? "A couple years ago, I got into drugs. I don't really want to get into it, but it became a need over a want." My eyes widened as I realized what he's saying.

"Oh." I whisper. "Yeah, oh." He repeats, no sarcasm, or rudeness in his voice. He takes a deep breath before speaking again. "Blake was the one that gave me the first line." My eyes widened even more. "He didn't know I was addicted, and I didn't tell him," He pauses, and shakes his head downwards.

"I'm sorry. I'm being stubborn, and that's not an excuse—" He stops himself and doesn't continue. "You can't just be mean to him, when he doesn't even know why. You don't know him or what he's been through." I don't either, I only know him through my younger selves perspective.

"I didn't realize you knew him when we were younger." He states calmly. There's no more anger in the room, just sadness. "Me either. I was reading my journals and saw things that I wrote about him. Like how he—" I stopped myself before I told him something I promised I wouldn't tell anyone.

I sigh loudly and stare at his dark face, finally being able to make out his facial features clearly. "Is that what's been bothering you?" He finally asks, probably putting it all together. I nod, not even sure if he can see me through the dark.

I assume he can when he doesn't ask again. "I'm sorry I locked us in here. I know how badly you wanted to see those fireworks." He whispers. I shrug, and look down at my fingers. "It won't be the last time I see fireworks." I try to joke, but it comes out sadder than it should.

It's quiet again, only our breaths being heard, but strangely, no tension like the other times we've been left alone together. I lean my head back against the door, and tap my knee lightly with my finger. "Isabelle?" I open my eyes, and glance at Milo who is already looking at me.

"Yes, Milo?" I whisper back. He doesn't respond immediately, as if he's choosing his words really carefully in his head. "I'm sorry for how I've acted towards you. There's no excuse for me being mean, but I want to change that. I really want to change that. Will you let me?" My mouth hangs agape for a moment, unsure of how I should answer.

He doesn't give me time to answer though before he starts talking again. "I just wanted to be mad at you for leaving, ya know? I wanted to hate you, and never see you again, but I didn't. All I could think about was you, all I can think about is you." He stops, and shakes his head then groans. A pang of guilt hits me again. I shouldn't have left.

"It's ok, I forgive—"

"No, don't do that. I don't deserve it. Not yet. Let me earn your forgiveness." I stay silent, processing his words over and over again in my head. "Ok, yeah. I'd like that." I smile, even though I'm sure he can't see it.

He stands up and walks over to the door. I stand up, and move over to the side. "Surely there has to be a way to get this open." He mutters, and jiggles the nob again. It moves back and forth, but the door stays stuck. "Milo, seriously, it's fine. We'll just wait it out until someone notices or just opens the door."

He doesn't listen, and shakes the door harder. "Milo—" I place my hand on his shoulder to stop him, and he finally slows his aggression. He backs away with a huff, and crosses his arms. "This is stupid." He grumbles.

I ignore his grumbles and mumbles, and walk around the pantry. Then I grab the candy that was supposed to be for the kids, and seat myself towards the middle of the pantry. "What are you doing?" Milo asked curiously. I shrug. "If we're gonna be stuck in here, might as well have some candy." He laughs softly, and sits down in front of me.

I pour it out, and squint at the candy to try and read what kind it is. Milo goes to grab one, but I stop him. "Wait, we should eat some of the candy, and guess what it is." I tear open a small rectangle and bite a piece off. "Oh, that's definitely a KitKat." Milo snatches the rest of it out of my hand and pops it into his mouth. "Mmm, yeah I agree."

He grabs a small plastic bag, and opens it, grabs whatever is inside, and pops it into his mouth. His face scrunches up in distaste as he swallows the candy down. I laugh softly. "What was it?" I ask, once I know he's in the clear.

"Whopper, here have the rest." I take them cheerfully and eat the rest. It doesn't take long for us to finish the candy, and now we're just sitting in pure silence.

I'm not sure how I feel about it. "Hey Isabelle, can I ask you a question?" I nod my head slowly, and wait for what he has to say. He takes a deep breath, and looks around a little nervously. His nervousness is making me nervous.

"Did you want to leave?" He finally whispers after seconds of silence. I wasn't expecting that to be his question, but for some reason it doesn't make me tense up like it normally does. I feel a wave of confidence wash over me, one like I've never felt before.

I open my mouth, and no sound comes out. I don't know what to say. I mean, I know the answer, but I don't think now is the time. I'm not ready for him to know yet. "You have your secrets Milo," I start slowly. "And I have mine." I finished. He nods his head, and doesn't ask again.

A simple answer would have just been plain and simple. No, I didn't want to leave, but that answer would have been more complicated than just a simple yes or no, and I think we both know that. I hear a quiet hum coming from outside of the room, and smile to myself.

"I can hear the fireworks." I tell him. Another small blow is heard, and I smile wider. "Yeah, me too." I close my eyes, and imagine like I can see them when I hear it again. A small laugh falls from my lips at this.

I open my eyes, and see Milo looking at me like a lost puppy. His head is turned to the right slightly, and he's staring at me. I smile at him and laugh again. "Maybe it's not so bad being stuck in here with you." He smiles softly, and I see the shadow of his dimples.

"I'll make it up to you, I promise." He says confidently. "I'll hold you up to that Wesley." His smirk grows. "Oh, are we going by last names now, Everest?" A weird feeling rolls over me, making me feeling jittery. Like I wanna giggle, and fall onto my back like a little girl.

Like I could go run a marathon with a smile on my face. Like when Milo had his lips on me. My smile falls slightly. Remember, it didn't mean anything to him, and it didn't mean anything to me. "What?" He questions. I blink rapidly and fix my posture.

"Huh?" I mumble, confused. His eyes furrow. "You just look like you got lost in thought, and it made you sad." I smile, and shake my head. I can't think of the past. If I think of the past I'll get stuck in it, and I can't do that again.

"No, just thinking." I shrug. He opens his mouth to say something, but gets cut off by the door opening. I squint, and blink at the suddenly bright light. I watch Milo do the same, and turn around the look at the door since his back was facing it.

"Oh my gosh, there you guys are. You just disappeared." Lottie exaggerates, with Henry standing next to her. "We got locked in." I state, blankly. Then my dad appears behind them. "What are you two doing?" He asks, suspiciousness lacing his tone.

"The door is broken, so it locks from the outside." I tell him, even though I think he already knows. "Yes, Isabelle, I'm aware. I'm asking what you two are doing." My eyes widen when I realize what he's implying. Milo groans, and looks down. "Dad." I groan, and move my soon to be flustered face.

"What?" I look up and he's grinning. So are Lottie and Henry. "I believe they need a cleansing Mr.E." Henry shakes his head. "Henry." Milo growls, and glares at him. "Dad, we weren't doing anything." I tell him, and he laughs. "I had to ask, ok? you both are growing teenagers who—"

"Dad!" He stops, and laughs, turning around to walk away. "You're dead." Milo exclaims, pointing towards Lottie and Henry. Henry laughs. "That was worth it." He snickers, and finally turns to leave. Lottie gives us both one more glance before leaving.

Milo stands up, and starts walking towards the open door. "Milo," He stops, and turns around. "Yeah?" I stand up, and glance around the room. "Thank you, for telling me about what you went through." He smiles softly.

"Yeah, I trust you." He turns around and walks out the door, back to god knows where.

~~~~~~~~~~~~~~~~~~~~~~~~~~~~~~~~~~~~

AN: we LOVE the new found communication lol

Also, I'm going to be changing the posting schedule, I'm thinking one or two chapters a week so I have more time writing.

I hope you all have a great day!
~~~~~~~~~~~~~~~~~~~~~~~~~~~~~~~~~~~~

Chapter Thirty One

—'My past is an armor I cannot take off, no matter how many times you tell me the war is over.' ~ Jessica Katoff ~

Tree House ~~Isabelle

The AC in the Lowe's I'm in right now is getting dangerously close to the temperature outside. I don't know if it's the windows, or maybe they really don't have any air conditioning, but I am sweating.

It's not helping either that my hair is down, which is causing the back of my neck to drip with sweat. I sigh, and grab another six by ten slowly to lay it on my cart. As soon as it's down, I see a guy walking towards me.

He smiles sweetly, and stops a couple feet away from me. "Hey there, do you need help with anything?" He's wearing a Lowe's shirt with a name tag, so I assume he's an employee here. "No, thank you though." I turn back around to grab another piece of wood, but he comes beside me and tries to grab it.

"Why don't I help you with this?" He takes it, and lays it on my cart. "No, I'm really ok." I smile at him, and wait for him to walk away, but he doesn't move. "Do you...need something?" He shakes his head and laughs softly.

"I can't help but notice your...size, so I just wanted to offer my help." My smile becomes strained. "Excuse me?" Is all I can think of saying. He laughs, like what I just said was funny, and goes to grab another plank. "How many do you need?" I finally frown, and cross my arms.

"I don't need your help. I would like it if you could leave me alone, please." I asked politely. Again, he laughs. "You really think you can lift these?" I grab it from his hands, and place it on my cart. Then two more, and start pushing my cart away.

Then, before I completely leave, I turn around and stare him down. "You shouldn't say stuff like that. It's very disrespectful. How would your boss feel about you disrespecting their customers?" His face pales slightly, and he soon scurry's away.

I smile to myself, proud, as I walk around the rest of the store and get everything I need.

Yesterday, I was outside when I noticed the old tree house a little further in the woods that my dad built for me and my friends when I was younger. It looked beat down, and the wood had turned rotten, which gave me the idea to start rebuilding it.

It's more or so for Luna and Leo, then whoever else they want, but I also want to see it again. It was the place where we conspired all our plans, and even had a few sleepovers. It brought me joy, so maybe it will do the same to her.

I pay for my things quickly, and walk back towards my dads truck where I load everything into the back. My mom insisted I took her buggy, to which I had to explain that the wood I was getting was not going to fit into her car.

Lottie and Violet are coming over as well to help. Actually, they're probably already at my house, waiting for me. I think Lottie said something about

Henry coming over, which means Noah's coming over, which then also means that Milo will most likely be there.

I saw him yesterday at work, and it was surprisingly not so bad. It wasn't awkward, but we also didn't get to talk that much because we worked during the rush hour. He did give me a ride home though. I still don't know how to feel around him. It feels weird for me.

Maybe I just need to tell him how I feel, just to get it out of the way. Just to get the air cleared up. That doesn't sound so bad, right?

No, it sounds horrible.

I pull into our short driveway, and shut off the car, then see Violet's car just as I suspected. I shut my dads truck off, and make my way into the house before getting any of my things out. Violet and Lottie are sitting at the table with Luna and my parents, eating sandwiches.

"Hey." I give them all a small wave, and then see a plate with an untouched sandwich on it. "That's for you, Izz." My dad exclaims. I thank him quietly, and take my plate to the table they're all sitting at.

It doesn't take much for me to tell that I'm eating a peanut butter and jelly sandwich right now. Although, I'm not opposed to it. I love PB&J's. As I'm eating it, my mom starts asking questions. "What do you have planned for today?" She asks, taking a sip of her water.

I glance up at Luna quickly, before shifting my gaze onto my mom. "I was going to rebuild the tree house we used to play in all the time. Maybe Luna and Leo can get use out of it like I did as a kid." I can practically see Luna's ears perk up at this. Her eyebrows raise slightly, but she doesn't look up at me.

"Oh, well that's sweet of you." I shrug, and take another big bite of my sandwich. "The guys are coming over to help with the heavy lifting." Violet adds. Then she smiles, and looks over at Lottie. "Hopefully, we won't have a problem with Lottie passing out over Henry's bare chest again." My mother shakes her head downward like she saw this coming.

Luna snickers from her seat.

"It was only two times!" Lottie growls, turning a light shade of pink. I laughed. "The fact that it even happened once is crazy." I state, causing her glare to roll over to me. "You're no better, maybe you haven't passed out, but I saw you gawking at Milo at the beach."

Luna, and my mom's eyes move over to me. I cower away, and pray to god that my sunburned cheeks hide my blushing. "I—" I cleared my throat. "I don't know what you're talking about." Violet laughs, and shakes her head.

"You both are so love struck." There's no way my tomato face is hidden anymore. Love. I don't love Milo. I'm not love struck. "What about you and your—" Her hand covers my mouth so fast that My words become muffled behind her hand before I just stop talking all together.

Lottie smirks, and finishes her sandwich. "Yeah, your night—" Violet's other hand slaps over Lotties mouth. "Don't listen to them, Mama E, they're both delusional." She rolls her eyes, but it would take a blind man to miss her rosy cheeks right now.

Maybe we're all doomed.

———

This may be a little exaggerated, but I may pass out, and it's not from the heat. My eyes are wandering against my will. How is it fair to us girls that all these men get to take their shirts off when it gets hot, and not only do we have to keep our clothes on, but we have to watch them glisten with sweat.

Ok, I'm only watching one out of three of these men. I think Lottie agrees heavily with me right now, except for her, it's ok to stare at Henry. In fact, he's been encouraging her to 'take it all in,' as he says.

Although, I am wearing a bathing suit top with jean shorts as are Violet and Lottie, which is helping with the sun. "Wait, wait, wait. I'm about to drop it." I look back at Violet who is at the other end of the board we're carrying from the truck to the backyard.

"Violet." I groan quietly again. This would be the second time we've had to stop so she could change her gripping on the wood. Henry and Noah pass us, walking by with multiple planks over their shoulders. We're all sweating the same, and dying for a drink of water.

"Hey, at least I'm not Lottie." I smile, and nod my head. "True." Lottie actually dropped the board because of Henry passing us. Her excuse was that his muscles were flexing. Violet quickly fixes her hold, and we start moving again.

Once we reach the back yard, we both set the wood down and quietly heave. "Why couldn't we do this in the winter." Violet groans, and re-ties her ponytail in her hair. I just rolled my hair on top of my head, leaving a slightly messy bun that's now slopped down to the back of my head.

Why can't we do this in the winter Isabelle? Because I won't be here. I sigh at the devastating thought. I still don't know where I'm going, or what I will be doing after Summer ends. I applied to a couple colleges before moving down here, but I haven't gotten any responses yet.

Maybe I won't leave. Maybe I will just stay in the small town of Halings Florida for the rest of my life and die old, and alone. Ok, no. Another part of me tells me that maybe I shouldn't even go to school. What if I just left, and traveled the world? Although, I don't have any money, so I think that's out of the picture.

I sigh, and start walking back towards the car. I'm not sure if all the wood is out yet, but I'm going back just to make sure. I glance at the back of the truck bed, and see it empty, so I just flip up the back and lock the car shut.

On my way back, I spot a shirtless Milo leaning against the side of the house, lightly banging his head back and forth. I look down, and see his hands slightly shaking. "Milo?" His head jerks off the house, and over to me. "Isabelle?" He questions back.

"Whatcha doing?" I lean against the wall beside him, making myself even smaller, my head now reaching his shoulder. I hate being short. "Just thinking." He responds shortly, and when I look down, his hands are fisted against his side.

"Are you ok?" I ask softly. He looks down at me with a raised brow. "Yeah. Why wouldn't I be?" He asked calmly, and I'm happy to hear no anger in his voice. At least he's not mad at something. Or someone. I shrug, and look off at a bush that's in front of us.

"You seem stressed." Is my answer. He sighs, and looks off in the other direction so that his face is facing away from me. "Just...hard day, I guess." I take that answer, not pushing him further. If you would've told me a month ago that I would even be having a conversation with Milo, I would have laughed and told you that was ridiculous.

The thought of how far we've come, brings a smile to my face. "Hey," He turns back to me. "Wanna go to the beach tonight?" I don't answer right away, trying to figure out why he would want to go to the beach late at night. "It's not the smartest idea to go surfing at—"

"No, no. Not to surf." I hold my breath, and stare into his eyes. "What for, then?" This question brings a slight smile out on his face. Oh god. A shirtless smiling man, with dimples. I might have a stroke. I clear my throat, and look away, more flustered.

"It's a surprise." I bite my bottom lip, and grin downwards. Once I'm sure the blush is gone, and I know the only red on my face will be from the sun, I look up at him. "Sure. Why not." Now he smiles wider and nods his head.

We're just staring at each other, smiling like idiots. We probably look a little creepy right now. He clears his throat. "We should get back to them." I nod along with him. "We should." I say back, yet neither of us make a move to leave.

This is your chance. This is the moment where you tell him how the kiss made you feel. This is the moment where he says he lied, and it meant something to him as well. I get grounded back to earth when two more pairs of feet come walking around the corner. I turn, step away from Milo, and look behind me to see my younger sister and her best friend.

She stops, and looks at me, then Milo. Slowly examining each of us. "Hey, what are you doing?" I ask them. "Leo wanted to see how the tree house was coming. He's really excited for it." Luna deadpans.

I look over at Leo, and his face flushes with color. "Uh—yeah. Luna said you were building it, and—um. Yeah." He nods his head and bounces on the heels of his feet. I smile down at him. "Yeah, we're starting to put the wood on now." I explained.

Luna grabs Leo's arm, and drags him off towards the backyard. I watch them enter the small, back gated fence, and disappear behind the house. "Looks like someones got a crush on you." Milo mutters, with a small laugh that follows.

I look over at him confused. "What? Who?" He looks at me in disbelief for a second before pointing at where the two pre-teens just walked away too. "Leo. He was stumbling over everything he said." I think back to our conversation that happened seconds ago.

Huh, I guess he did seem a little flustered. I shrug. "He'll get over it." Milo shakes his head downwards. "That's what they all say." I hear him mutter quietly. "Hm?" I hum back. He shakes his head, and turns around towards the backyard.

That's what they all say? What does that even mean? Milo gets to the latch in the fence, opens it, and then turns to look at me. Quirking an eyebrow, with his lip raised into a smirk he nods his head backwards in a small come-on action.

When I don't move, he turns to look at me fully. "You comin? This tree house isn't going to build itself." I nod my head, finally, and will my feet to move. Still thinking about his statement.

~~~~~~~~~~~~~~~~~~~~~~~~~~~~~~~~

AN: In honor of my birthday I give this treat to you guys because i love all your comments and opinions on the characters!!
~~~~~~~~~~~~~~~~~~~~~~~~~~~~~~~~

Chapter Thirty Two

Fireworks~~Isabelle

My mom made us tacos for dinner. Let's just say they were exactly what I needed to end a day of building in a tree. Of course I wasn't alone, but that only meant we all suffered together.

Everyone had left afterwards, which wasn't a surprise because we all looked like walking zombies with blistered fingers and ankles.

I had completely forgotten about going to the beach with Milo until he came knocking on my door 30 minutes later, only slightly after the sun had set.

I'm now seated in his car, the windows down, and waiting patiently as he drives us to the beach. My tiredness that was dragging me on my feet, now completely gone, replaced with adrenaline.

What could Milo have wanted to show me at the beach after the sun was down. We aren't going in the water. At least, I don't think we are. What else could it be?

Milo on the other hand, was looking antsy, like he was scared. Sort of like he did when he wanted me to like something he made for me. "Are you going to tell me what we're doing again?" I ask as he parks the car.

I squint into the darkness, and only see faint shadows of the water crashing against the sand. "Nope." He sighs, popping the 'p', and hoping out of the car. I follow suit, opening the door slowly and jumping out.

I round the car, just catching a glimpse of him shutting the back of the car, and walking off with a bag. His muscles are constricting as he carries the bag over to the beach, which makes me wonder what could be inside.

I jog lightly to catch up with him, and by the time I do, he's setting the bag down, and beginning to take out boxes. It's too dark for me to get a clear view of what it is, but it almost looks like...fireworks?

"What is that?" I whisper. He takes out about 3 boxes, and sets them in the sand. When he turns to me, he's fiddling with his hands, and looking everywhere but at me. Even through the dark I can see his ears ting pink.

"I told you I would make it up to you, so I bought fireworks, and instead of from your house, you can watch them from up close." He explains quickly, and a little quieter than normal. "Milo," I start.

Fireworks. That sounds like such a stupid thing to get emotional over, but he's doing this for me. Milo went out of his way to do this for me, because he felt bad. "This is," I pause again. I have so many feelings, and things I want to say with no time to say any of it.

"Thank you." I finish, and leave it at that. I assume that he can hear the emotion in his voice because he smiles slightly and nods his head. "It's the least I can do." Then he turns around and places the boxes a few feet away from us. I back up more, giving him room to light the firework.

He pulls out a lighter, and does so quickly, jogging back to where I am. I watch the quiet, soft yellow light dim and fall into the box. Then within seconds, light shoots out of the small space.

My eyes brighten when I finally hear the sound that it makes in the sky. I smile, and stare as more flow into the starry sky one after another. Green, Red, Pink light up, filling my heart with warmth.

"Wow. I missed this." I mutter. It finishes up, and Milo goes back to start another one.

While the second one is going, I glance over at him, and he's just staring at me. It startles me for a second, until his gaze softens and a small smile rises on his face. "What?" I ask, confused. He shakes his head, and looks down. I hadn't realized how close we were until he crossed his arms, and his elbow bumped me.

"Your face does this thing when you see something you like. It's like your whole face brightens, and your eyes deepen, and you just become so entranced with it." He states. My face flushes, and I look down quickly to avoid more embarrassment.

My whole face brightens? Whole face. I feel his hand lightly lift my chin back up to see him. I bite my bottom lip between my teeth to try and hold back the shiver he gave me. I just stare at him, and watch as another firework lights the side of his face up.

He leans down, so that our noses are almost touching. Our lips, our lips almost touching. I suck in a deep breath, and hold it. "Milo?" I whisper. "Isabelle?" He whispers back. "What are you doing?" I ask, slight panic entering my voice.

"I don't know." I let myself take a moment to soak in his warmth. The way his body makes me feel light, like I'm flying. The way I can smell coconut coming from him. Then, with all the strength I can muster up, I push him lightly backwards, and take a step back myself

"I can't—not, no. You—you said it didn't mean anything to you. You said the kiss didn't mean anything. I can't do that again. It—it meant something to me Milo. You don't understand." I take in another deep breath, and will my body to let it go.

I shake my head, and turn myself around. I don't hear Milo call after me, and I don't listen to hear if he does.

I open his car door, and get into the passenger seat silently. Five minutes go by, and the back door opens. I assume he puts his bag into the car, because seconds later he's shutting the door and getting into the driver's seat.

The whole drive home goes by painfully slow, where neither of us mutter a word. Our breaths are quiet, and our hearts silent. The only thing keeping me from losing my mind is the soft hum of music made by the radio.

He pulls into his driveway, and I fly out of the car as quickly as possible. "Wait, Izzy." I pause, and turn around. "Yeah, Milo?" I question softly. He sighs, and lays a hand on top of his car. "I'm sorry." He says.

"You keep saying that, Milo. Do you even know what you're sorry for?" He opens his mouth, and then shuts in quickly. I turn around and begin walking away again. I hop the step up to the door, and crack it open when it gets shut by a force behind me.

"Please, Izzy." Milo whispers. I look upwards at the closed door and see his hand extended from behind my shoulder. "Just. Let me explain." I turn around quickly and push on his chest.

"Explain what?" I try to express anger. I try to show my frustration through my voice, but all that comes out is desperation. "You don't understand. It's hard for me—"

"Hard for you?" I interrupt. I push on his chest again, and he finally backs up a step. "You're doing this to me! Your hurting me Milo!" My voice rises as I point a finger at myself.

"You hurt me! You already did. You broke me when you left without telling anyone. What scared you off? What made you so scared you had to leave? I see it on your face every damn day! What were you so scared of." He heaves and runs a hand through his deep, dark, black hair.

My eyes furrow in pain while I look away. "It's none of your business." I bite out. "Then let me in," he takes a step forward. "Tell me what's happened to you." He's asking me so much more than he thinks. He doesn't get it. He couldn't get it.

I shake my head and open my mouth to say something when the door opens. "Oh, Izz. Your back early." I glance at my dad quickly and then look back at Milo. He's begging me with his eyes to stay. I can see him silently asking to not walk away.

"Yeah. It didn't take as long as we thought." I answer him, still staring straight into Milo's vibrant eyes. "Hey, Milo." My dad greets. "Hey." Milo responds just as I did. "Ok, well. Do you wanna come in for some tea, or coffee?" Milo opens his mouth, but I beat him to it.

"Milo was just leaving." I don't have to see my dad's expression to know that he's confused. Probably wondering what would make me stubborn like this. Why I'm acting distant.

"Goodbye, Milo." With that, I turn around and walk past my dad into my house. He stays at the door, so I assume he's talking to Milo, but I don't linger down stairs long enough to find out. I beeline for my bedroom, and the minute I get inside, I shut my door and lock it.

I'm breathing heavily, and I can't tell if it's because of the stairs I just climbed or everything that happened prior. Leaning my head against the back of the door for support, I lift my hands and squeeze them to my eyes.

When I open my eyes, I catch the sight of a small flower on my shelf in my closet. I walk towards it and pick up the necklace. It feels like it's been years since my birthday. Since I found this charm in the dirt. Did Milo have it? Did Milo plan on giving it to me? Or did I just find a random trinket in the dirt after a night of partying?

I walk over to my bathroom, necklace in hand, and unclasp the backing. I slowly wrap it around my neck, watching it carefully in the mirror. I hold it together in the back and twist and turn like it might give me a better answer. A better understanding of the flower.

When no special sparks glow, I let go of one side in the back and let it fall into my right hand. Shutting off my bathroom light, I walk and do the same to my bedroom one.

Laying on my back in my bed, I stare at the old stains on my ceiling from the glowing stars I used to have.

As much as I tell myself to move on, my mind still stays behind. I don't want to linger on the past, yet it's still here. Hovering over me like a ghost, taunting and pulling.

Maybe I'll never get out of this nightmare.

———

I drag another plank of wood over to the saw to cut into smaller pieces. We got the main walls up, and now I'm going in with the smaller ones as reinforcement along with more nails and bolts. It's been cloudy today, the sun staying hidden away behind the clouds.

I'm wearing a light zip up jacket over a sports bra, the sleeves rolled up to my elbows. I underestimated the suns power to keep the air hot even when it's gone. I drop the wood, and wipe the back of my hand over my forehead to draw the sweat away before it has the chance to drip into my eyes.

Yesterday, I enjoyed working with all my friends, talking and laughing. Today, though, I just feel like doing it alone. At least getting the structure complete before I paint it. I've actually been prolonging this process all morning.

I finally figured out where Blake lives. It took some deep searching though. It turns out Blakes has been to Juvy before for drug dealing, which makes sense due to what Milo had told me. I don't think Blake's to blame though. Who knows why he needed the money. Maybe drugs were what he needed to make it through a beating with his brother.

Is that why Milo needed it? I shake my head, set the rest of the cut wood into a pile, and finally make my way into the house. After all this time, trying to figure this all out, now I have my answer and all I want to do is walk away. I want to forget all of this, but I know it's not that easy.

I need this. I need these answers. There has to be a reason that Blake was blocked out of my memory. Blake has to correlate with him somehow. My shower goes by quicker then I would have liked, and I'm soon getting changed into a white tank top with a mesh oversized cover up over it.

I lazily braid my wet hair straight now my back, which just falls over my shoulder as I bend down to pull my jean shorts on. I grab a ball cap style hat—one I may or may not have stolen from my dad—and slip it snug on my head.

My parents are at work, and Luna's at the beach so I slip out of the house silently, locking the door behind me. I don't have a car, and It just so happens that Blake actually doesn't live that far from me. Closer to Mama Hazels, but the walk will only take 5 minutes at most.

The sweat has already begun to stick my hair to my forehead, even from under the hat. I walk confidently, and quickly down the sidewalk, only seeing a few cars pass by me. They wave politely, and I wave back.

I see his house coming into view, and a new thought enters my mind. What if Blake doesn't come? What if his brother answers the door? It's ok, I could just say I'm an old friend wanting to catch up. I mean, I'm not lying. Technically, I do want to catch up with him.

There's one beat down Honda in the driveway, that creates tension between the house and its dirtiness. Their house is big, just like all the other houses in the town, and it looks well kept. They have a small path created with stones that lead toward the door.

I notice the pretty tulips and roses in front of the window that are barely even reaching the bottom of the frame. Their curtains are drawn, leaving anyone outside wondering what could be going on inside. I walk slowly now, feeling nervousness drag my feet backwards, wanting me to turn back.

It's as if my body knows this is bad. My brain knows that something doesn't sit well here, and yet I push through. I get to the door, and realize up close that it's rusting, and peeling at the corners. I raise my fist to the door, noting that they don't have a doorbell, and knock three times.

It takes a hot second, then a minute, and my nerves bring more sweat to my arms and legs. The sun is still beating down on my back, yet the heat is nothing compared to my shakiness as fear strikes me deep in the gut.

I hear rustling, and suck in a sharp breath against my will. I hear a lock turn, and it jolts the whole door making small flakes of paint fall off. Then, the door finally cracks backwards, looking as if it's falling back into the house. It probably would if someone wasn't supporting the door.

It isn't Blake that answers the door, but my brain instantly relaxes when I see Ava on the other end. "Isabelle?" She whispers. "What are you doing here?" She steps out of the door, and it would take an idiot to miss her obvious limp. She shuts the door quietly, and folds her arms over her chest.

My brain stutters, and my mouth moves like a fish out of water. Why am I here? What am I doing? Oh right— "I need to talk to Blake. If that's alright." She stares at me for a hot second, her eyebrows furrowed in confusion. "Uh, yeah. Ok. He's in his room. I would invite you in..." She shakes her head. "Let me go get him."

I nod at her leaving form, and wait all but two minutes before the door is opened again, and it's not Ava this time. Blake gives me a strange expression. Like he did when he saw me at the carnival. I smile at him, and wait for him to recuperate, but he doesn't.

"I was wondering if we could talk? I found some old journals of mine and—" I stop, and see realization finally take over his features. He flushes, like younger me described younger him doing countless times. "Mama Hazels is only a two minute walk? Do you want to talk there?" I nod, and finally see him smile softly at me.

~~~~~~~~~~~~~~~~~~~~~~~~~~~~~~~~~~

AN: School has been kicking my butt guys. Lol. Hope you enjoy this.
~~~~~~~~~~~~~~~~~~~~~~~~~~~~~~~~~~

Chapter Thirty Three

—'The finest souls are those who gulped pain and avoided making others taste it.' ~ word porn ~——

Hospital ~~Isabelle

Our two minute walk, just like everything else today, felt so much longer than it actually was. We were quiet, but I didn't expect either of us to talk. It was sort of like an unspoken rule that we shouldn't talk. That it would be too complicated until we get seated in a cooler area with water.

Or maybe the heat is just finally getting to me. The bell above Mama Hazel's rings as we step inside, and I instantly feel like I can breathe properly with the air circulation.

Blake walks ahead to a small, more secluded area with two chairs facing opposite over a small round table. A waitress comes by, one I recognize as Kelly–who I've never spoken to–and asked us what we wanted. Both of us say water, and that that will be all.

Kelly walks away, leaving a strange silence between us. How do I even start this? I clear my throat. "I found the diaries, like I said." He nods. "I–I wrote about you in them, but it was weird because I couldn't remember knowing you–I can't remember ever knowing you." His eyebrows raise silently before they fall back to normal, and a paleish color runs over his face.

"I know," I breathe in a deep breath. "I wrote about your brother as well. Your older one." His eyes furrow. "Both?" Now I'm the one confused. "Both what?" I ask slowly.

"Did you write about both of my brothers?" Two. He has two? What? I blink several times, and try to remember if I had ever mentioned two different' older brothers, but I can't.

"No. I–you have two older brothers?" He nods, and looks down, as if he has realized he said something I shouldn't have known. Like he crossed a line.

"Yeah. They're twins." He whispers, while his face gets even paler. "Oh ok. Wait. Can you explain this? Do you know what's going on? We were friends. You were my best friend and I can't even remember–" I blow out a huff of air in annoyance, and look at anything but his face.

A saddened look takes over his features. "We were friends." Is all he says, looking down as if he's remembering something from the past. "Why didn't you tell me? Why did you act like you didn't know me?" He shrugs his shoulders, and rubs his arm anxiously.

"Once I realize you didn't remember me, I just assumed it would be better if I didn't bring it up." He's still giving me vague answers. Circling around the prize with a fishing line, just missing every time. But he wants to miss it.

There is something he doesn't want me to know that apparently my mind didn't want me to know either. I opened my mouth to say just that. To demand an answer. Maybe stomp a foot. Whatever I was going to say gets cut off by his phone buzzing.

He doesn't answer, but he does stare at the caller id for a long moment, before sighing and stuffing the phone back into his pocket. "Listen. I need to get going." I hear the regret in his voice. The sadness. I want to know why. What is he hiding from me?

"Ok. I hope we can talk again, soon." I say quietly. He gets up, lays a 5 dollar bill on the table and leaves all whilst I stay seated in my chair. Kelly freezes when she lays the waters on the table, and stares a Blakes seat in confusion. "He had to go." I explain, and she finally nods, walking away. After a couple more minutes of getting nowhere and nothing done, I sigh and stand up to leave.

As I'm walking out to leave, the door rushes open, and in walks Milo, looking hectic and a little scared. He searches the shop very slowly until his eyes land on me, and I finally see how pale his face is.

Suddenly, all the anger I have had for him in the past few days vanishes and is replaced with instant fear. He speed walks over to me, getting a few questionable looks from other pedestrians, but he doesn't pay any mind to them. "Milo?" I whisper, suspense and fear striking my own voice.

"Isabelle," He sighs, and runs his hands stressfully through his black hair. "We need to go. We need to go now." He stops, and clenches his eyes shut. Then they open, and I can tell he's been crying. "What is going on?"

"It's Luna. We were at the beach, and she got—she was stung. It—It didn't look that bad but she started shaking, I thought she was having a seizure. It was something poisonous." His voice cracks, weavers on the line from ok to completely broken down.

Something lodges itself inside of my throat, something that feels a lot like bile, but I push it down and nod my head. If Luna needs us, we can't fall apart on her. "Ok. Ok, let's go." He nods, and turns around sharply with me following close behind.

———

I've only ever been to the real deal hospital once. I've only been a concern to the doctors once. I can still remember the fresh minty, almost stale air. The bright lights.

The alcohol stench. The white. God, why are hospitals filled with white?

The only difference this time is that I'm not the patient. I know what it feels like to be in a waiting room with other sad, miserable people, waiting to know what's going to happen next.

I don't think I actually realized how difficult it is being the loved one of the person that's hurt.

My parents are back with Luna, or talking to a doctor. All I know is that they are beyond the doors that these ladies in blue are so persistent on keeping us out of.

It's just Milo and I, sitting–waiting. Well, technically Milo did just go off to find some sort of decent edible thing that they may have, which leaves me temporarily alone.

Who knew hospitals could be so sad? Yes, people die here, but countless more get helped. Children are brought into the world here. Maybe if they made the walls pink, or yellow. Or even blue. Blue is supposed to be a calming color.

I have to physically close my eyes to attempt to block out the headache white that's surrounding me. Suffocating me. "Hey. Don't go dozing off on me now." Milo's voice is the only reason I open my eyes again.

It's not even night. It's probably only been an hour, maybe two since we've been here. It's only the afternoon. Milo's smirking softly, as if he's trying to make me feel better, so the only thing I can do is muster up a smile back.

He takes his seat beside me, and that's when I finally notice the two bags he's holding. He extends one of them over to me, that I can now see has doritos in it. "They only had cool ranch." He shrugs, and drops it in my lap.

"Thank you." I mutter, and tear open the top. When I look over, he's sporting the same snack size bag in his hands. "Their vending machine options were shit." He mumbles, but I have a feeling he would have said that regardless of what food he brought back.

We haven't talked, not really anyway, since we got here. Just sitting, and staring, or texting because our friends are going a little crazy. They know what's going on, we just insisted that they don't come and crowd the hospital.

I stop eating, and look over at him again. "Do you think she'll be ok?" He freezes, tenses, but doesn't look over at me. "Yes," but he's staring downwards when he answers it. "I don't know what type of animal it was. A Jellyfish, maybe? I don't know how bad it was, but I worked fast, and she was still talking–" He stops his ramble, and sighs.

Without thinking too much into it, I reach out and take his hand in mine, squeezing it. Words won't do anything at this moment, so I'm hoping my gesture can show him how much it means to me. You did the right thing. You saved her. He looks over at me, and then flips his hand over and squeezes mine back.

The silence becomes deafening again, and I can hear everyone else's cries, or whispers of excitement. "Do you remember when Luna was born, and your mom was in labor for hours?" I shake my head slowly. "No, I don't think so." He laughs softly and shakes his head. "It was just us kids in the waiting room with Mama Hazel. It was the middle of the night, and all our friends had fallen asleep." He pauses, and looks over at me.

"You started bawling because you didn't want to have a little sister any-more." He laughs again. "I had to calm you down so we wouldn't wake anyone up." I smile faintly, his words jogging my memory.

"You got the nurse to give us sympathy ice cream." I look over at him, smiling softly at the memory. "She was so reluctant because it was the middle of the night, but when she saw you crying she finally gave in." I do remember that. Luna wasn't born until somewhere about six in the morning the next day.

I wasn't even awake when it actually happened. I don't think Milo was either. "We got to skip school for that." I remind him. "Greatest excuse ever." He whispers, and leans his head backwards, so that he's staring at the ceiling.

The big swinging doors that we weren't allowed to go behind, swing open slowly. Milo and I both jerk, and glance over to see my mom and dad walking out. My mom has puffy and red eyes while my dad looks on the brink of a breakdown. I shoot out of my seat, and rush over to them. "Is she—where." My dad places a hand on my shoulder to stop me.

I take a deep breath, shaking with nervousness and look between them quickly. "She's ok. She wants to talk to you." I freeze, and tense. "Me?" My voice only a whisper when I speak, pointing my index finger at my chest. They both give me one firm nod, and walk past me.

A nurse that I hadn't noticed was there before, walks up to me holding a clipboard. She smiles, a little too widely for the circumstances. "Isabelle Everest?" I nod and she jerks her head backwards to indicate where we will be going.

I follow her closely while we walk past the swinging doors. A hallway is in front of us stretching out narrowly. We walk down the hallway and then take a right where she stops outside of a door. She smiles and turns to look at me. "We've got her kicked up on some painkillers, so I will warn you, she isn't exactly herself." I nod wordlessly, and try to muster up the best smile I've got.

She opens the door and ushers me in where she follows behind and shuts the door afterwards. I instantly suck in a sharp breath when I see her. She has wires attached to her arms, and something under her nose that I assume helps her breath.

"Izzy." She mutters quietly but her voice somehow holds excitement. The nurse walks around me and does something to the machine beside my sister. "Hey Sal." She looks at the doctor—Sal—as she speaks. "Hey Luna. How are you feeling?" Luna shrugs and rubs her nose.

"Hi Luna." Her eyes zone in on me again, and another huge smile covers her face. "When did you get here?" She giggles, and waves me over. I inch closer and clear my throat. "I missed you so much." She slurs, dragging the word 'so' out for an extended amount of time.

"I missed you too." I whisper, then search the room quickly for a chair. Once I find one, I pull it up beside her bed and take a seat. "They said you wanted to speak to me?" She nods, and tilts her head to the side. "Why did you leave?" I tense, and dart my eyes up to the nurse, who is on her way out of the room.

"I'll be back in a little bit." She says briefly, before leaving. Luna's eyes don't leave mine. I open my mouth to try, to try and give her the answer, but I can't. For some reason if I say what happened, it will become real again, it reveals a part of my past that I've secretly locked away.

Luna speaks again. "I didn't want you to leave. You weren't here for the things I needed you for. You missed everything. Why wasn't I good enough for you to stay?" Her voice holds so much sadness, and not a hint of anger.

As if she's just been putting on an act, pretending to hate me this whole time, when she was really just sad.

A tear slips from my eye, and I look down, ashamed. "You're crying." She states. I look up at her, and notice how she doesn't look as tired as she did when I walked in. She doesn't look loopy, or high. She looks confused.

"I'm so sorry." A sob racks my body, and I cover my face with both my hands. "It wasn't your fault. You were more than enough for me, Luna. I needed to leave for myself, not for anyone else. I didn't want to. I swear I didn't want to."

I wipe my eyes, and look back up at her. She has a tear stained face, now matching my own. "Will you tell me why, then?" I nod my head, and take a long shaky inhale. Be brave for Luna. Be brave for yourself.

My eye lock with her pale, blue eye, identical to mine. I don't know what's going to happen after this. Maybe she'll hate me more, maybe she'll understand, but I'm down with the 'maybes'. Not only am I revealing a part of myself to her, but it's almost as if I'm reassuring myself that I'm ok. I made it through this.

Finally building up the courage to say the words, I open my mouth. "When I was fifteen years old, I was raped."

~~~~~~~~~~~~~~~~~~~~~~~~~~~~~~~~~

AN: This isn't the end of the scene, just wanted to get out a chapter for ya'll. :)
~~~~~~~~~~~~~~~~~~~~~~~~~~~~~~~~~

Chapter Thirty Four

— 'We'll never be those kids again.' ~ Frank Ocean ~——

Welcome Home~~Isabelle

The room shifts almost immediately. Tension seeped through the bottom of the door, through the cracks of the window. As if it's being sucked in by my words. Yet, through the tension, somehow I feel lighter. My body feels more open to sharing everything that I've been through.

My spine straightens almost immediately, feeling confidence flutter throughout my arms and legs, leaving a tingling sensation where it came from.

Luna, though, looks absolutely and utterly destroyed. Her body deflates, and tears glisten against her face. "What?" She whispers, yet her voice is still higher pitch than normal. A tear slips.

She clears her throat, and pays no mind to the tears rolling down her cheeks. As if she doesn't even feel them. "Luna–"

"You were...raped?" She interrupts, and I can hear the hesitation in her voice at the word rape. Yeah, that took me a long time to say too.

I feel my hands shake slightly. It's one thing to regain, and contain your own emotions, it's another thing to ignore someone else's.

"Yes, I was," I pause. "It was too hard to be here. This town was suffocating me, making everything ten times worse. Was I going to see him at the store? Was I going to see his..." My voice trails off, but not because of what I was going to say.

A strange assortment of memories flood my mind, smacking my face, and knocking me backwards. A sharp pain flows throughout my head, and then the memories are gone, like they were never there.

"His what?" Luna askes, her voice weak. I blink rapidly, twice, and glance over at her. What the hell just happened? I shake my head, and open my mouth to finish what I was going to say, only, I can't remember.

"Um, his–him, see him." I finished slowly, knowing that wasn't what I was going to say. What was I going to say? I shake my head softly again, and regain myself.

My body sags further into the chair, and I blow out a long sigh of relief. Although my relief is short lived, because a loud, quick beep fills my ears. I look over, and see Luna's heart monitor rising rapidly.

My eyes scrunch up, and dart towards my sister. She's covering her mouth with her hand, and breathing heavily. "Luna, hey–Luna." I stand up, and sit on the edge of her bed.

My hand lightly rubs up her back, and I slowly remove her iron grip from her face. "Hey, I'm ok." I whisper. She falls against me, her breaths coming in short pants. "I–no. I was so mean." Her voice cracks, and a sob fills the room. Her sob

My eyes cloud over, fog taking over my vision, and it occurs to me that I'm tearing up. No, hold it together. I clear my throat, and pull her into my side. Lying myself further into the bed.

She quickly hugs me back, and cries, hysterically, into my shirt.

"It's ok. It was three years ago. I'm ok now." I whisper, trying to soothe the ache that I feel vibrating off of her. "No, no, no. It's not ok! I was awful to you, and you were–" Another sob. "I should've listened–" Her voice cracks. "I'm so sorry. Please forgive me." A tear falls silently down my face, and I don't have the hands to swipe it away.

It tickles my chin, and runs down my neck, stopping once it meets the neckline of my t-shirt. "I forgive you. It's ok. You did nothing wrong Luna. I love you so much. None of this has ever and will never be your fault." Her heart rate slowly decreases.

I sigh in relief, when it evens out, and I feel her slump against me, half on the bed, half on top of me. Knowing she's asleep, lets me finally relax. Resting my head against the pillow, I finally let the tears out.

The door cracks open after a quiet knock, making me jerk–which thankfully doesn't walk up my sleeping sister. My mom's eyes soften when she sees us, and then widen in alarm when she sees me, crying.

"Honey, what–" I shake my head, and swallow the lump in my throat. "I told her." I close my eyes, and breath out the air I was unconsciously holding in. "I told Luna." I say again, and open my eyes when my mom doesn't respond.

She's just staring at me with pure sympathy. Then the next thing I know she's at my side, and gripping my arm. "I'm so proud of you." She whispers, and I can't tell if it's for Luna's sake, or mine. Probably both.

"I'm proud of myself too, mom." She smiles at me, and I find myself smiling back. Really, smiling.

———

"What did you do!" This time, it's not me who's getting yelled at, but me who is the one yelling. "No, no no no." I grip the middle of Milo's t-shirt from the back and yank him away from the baking bowl.

He spins around quickly, looking at me with confusion and aggravation. His left hand holding a measuring cup filled with what he thinks is sugar. In his right hand he's holding the jug that we hold our salt in.

"That's salt." His eyebrows lift, and he swiftly looks down at the bottle he's holding that reads the word, salt, on the front. "Oh.." I nod, a stressful laugh flowing out of my mouth.

He clears his throat at the same time a light glow of pink fills his cheeks and the tips of his ears. "Oh my gosh, are you blushing?" His eyes narrow at me slightly, and his face gets redder.

He must feel it, because he turns back away quickly, and switches the salt out for the actual sugar. "Shut up." He mutters under his breath, and continues adding the ingredients to the cake recipe.

I adjust the strapping of my bikini top, and get back to adding all the wet ingredients together. Once we're both done, we have to add them together and bake it. I'm praying that it will turn out decent, because this isn't for us.

Luna is coming home today, after only being in the hospital for an additional day, and Milo and I wanted to make her a cake. Ya know, throw a little welcome back party. Obviously Milo and I are already in our bathing suits. As is everyone else who is already in the backyard.

There is a speaker that we have set up, playing music for us as we bake. I know I suck at it, Milo's...ok at it, but together maybe we can make each other slightly better at baking. I mean, we do work in a place that makes food like this.

"And they say I'm bad at this." I mutter, but keep it loud enough for Milo to hear. I glance over my shoulder, smirking, and watch as he turns sharply, ready to rebuttal until he sees my smiling face.

He falters, and a smile slowly pulls his lips upward. He shakes his head, and leans against the table, crossing his arms over his bare chest. "You do suck at it." I turn fully, and match his pose against the opposite counter.

"Say's the one who just got salt and sugar mixed up, when they're labeled." I make the mistake of grabbing the carton of eggs I have, and swinging it over to the front of me, because the whole dozen go flying out of my hands and crashing to the floor.

It makes a loud, painful sound as it hits the floor, letting us know that they are all clearly broken. Egg gew splattered everywhere, along with shells. A worried giggle slips out of my mouth, and I'm quickly scurrying to pick it up.

Another bad idea on my part, because seconds later, I'm slipping on the yolk and slipping right onto my butt. My back followed soon after. I let out and groan, and lay my hands on my stomach.

"Oh shit," I hear Milo whisper. "Are you ok?" I blink, confused when I see his head upside down, leaning over me. "I would help, but I don't want to slip." He shrugs, like it's no big deal and keeps staring at me.

I groan louder than necessary again, and squeeze my eyes shut. "I think my butt is broken." I whine, and turn to my side like I might die. I pay attention to Milo though, who is slowly inching closer to me.

"Hold on. I got this." He mutters, and takes careful steps. I reach my hand outward, hoping he'll take it to help me up. He does, but instead of pulling me up, I wrench backwards and watch as he stumbles forward right into the eggy mess.

Out of panic, I watch him reach for the counter to grab onto for support. Fortunately, he misses and continues towards the ground. Unfortunately, his hand swipes the bag of flour that was on the counter, which is now following him as he falls.

Milo lands on his stomach, groaning into the ground while the flower bag lands right onto the middle of his back. A soft, small amount of flower coats his side, sadly the rest of his sputters outward into my face and neck.

The impact made me gasp, and fall back onto the floor. My eyes shut tight. I hear the sliding door opening, and then another gasp. "Holy hell." My dad, I believe, mutters while I just listen to his feet getting closer.

Then louder, and more footsteps follow. Curiosity getting the better of me, I wiped the flour out of my eyes, and opened them slowly. Both my parents are staring down at us. I see that Milo has also turned over so he's sitting up now.

I sit up slowly, and brush as best I can at my face. "Shit! This is rich!" I glance over and see Noah giggling like an idiot with his phone out, taking freaking pictures.

Of course he's taking pictures.

I look over at my mom, who looks beyond furious, and then to my dad who looks thoroughly amused. "You are both grounded." She growls like a rampant animal. "Oh go easy on them Lea. They obviously didn't do this on...purpose." My dad answered with a laugh.

My mom shakes her head, but I see the smile that she's trying to suppress as she walks away. Lottie and Henry walk in, oblivious to the situation until they come up behind Noah, and actually look at us. "What the..." Henry mumbles, shaking his head, and letting out a low chuckle.

"You better be planning on cleaning this mess up." My dad gives us each a pointed look, and then walks off back to the yard.

I drop my head into my hands, and just start laughing. I laugh so hard my body starts shaking. Then, out of nowhere, I feel a hand land on my back and rub. "It's not that big of a deal." I hear Milo say warily.

I look up at him, confused, still laughing. His eyes widened. "Geez, I thought you were crying." I snort another laugh, and then slap a hand over my mouth. "Did you just snort?" He chuckles, and then when I don't stop laughing, his smile grows and grows wider.

It's like the whole world lights up when he smiles. When the indents on his cheeks pop out, and his eyes glow. How are they even glowing? It's contagious. His smiling face, his laugh, is just making me laugh harder.

I don't know what this means, or if it even has to mean anything, but all I know is I don't want it to stop. I don't want this to ever stop. God, please don't ever ruin this.

———

"She's here!" My dad whisper-yells at all of us, telling us that my mom has finally arrived back home with Luna. I shove a strawberry into my mouth, and then dart behind the couch.

A strange, 'oof' noise comes out of me, when the rest of my friends cram into the small, very tight space. Violet lays long ways while Noah and Henry sit on either side of me, Lottie sitting on top of Henry's lap, and looking highly uncomfortable.

I'm freaking uncomfortable. "Milo hurry!" Noah whispers out quickly, waving his hand over to us. "No way am I going to fit in there." He whispers back, and looks around worriedly for a spot to hide.

I hear the door start to open, and quickly reach up–without thinking–and pulling on his forearm. He comes slamming down on all of us, like a domino set we got down.

Violet cackles softly from behind me, and Noah quickly shoves him off as he jumps up to say 'surprise.' Henry follows soon after, with Violet and Lottie, and then it's just Milo and I, in a very compromising, awkward position.

I shift to try and stand up, hearing everyone screaming around us. Milo groans, and stops my movement with his hands. "Don't do that. Let me get off." My face flushes when I feel what he's talking about. "Right, uh ..sorry?" He groans again, and grips onto my legs for support in standing up.

I gasp at the contact, not feeling repulsed by the feeling of a man's touch like I have been for three years. No, Milo's hands make me feel hot, and antsy. I want him to touch me.

Not in a weird way.

His hands are gone too soon, and he pops up, smiling at whoever is on the other side of the couch. Then he looks back at me, and reaches out with his hand to help me up.

I take it quickly, adjusting my shorts and bathing suit top while everyone that's in the room comes into vision. Luna's smiling, bubbling around the room to see everyone that's here.

She's got a slight limp from where the jellyfish had stung her on her upper thigh, but if it's in any way hurting her she doesn't show it.

Her eyes scan the room again, and she's soon seeing Milo and I standing beside each other. I smile, still a little nervous from the very serious, very open talk we had merely two nights ago.

Luna surprises me by taking off in a sprint that I wasn't sure she could do, and plowing into me. I hear my mom faintly telling her to be careful, but her voice gets drowned out by the warmth of my little sister hugging me.

"I missed you." She whispers. "I saw you this morning." I laugh, and hug her back tighter, not ever wanting to let go. "Still." She shrugs. I smile widely, closing my eyes while we stay put.

When I finally open them, I look over at Milo who is staring at us both with affection. Our eyes lock, and a million different things to say go through my head. So many things that I could tell him, or thank him for. None of them seem right though. "Hey, where's my hug, kid?" Luna turns around, laughing, and rams herself into Milo just as she had with me, and I finally see it.

I see how Luna confided in Milo when I was gone. I see how Milo found comfort in having a little sister around, and I don't feel that small spike of jealousy that I normally feel when I see them together.

I just feel love. For all of them. For my mom, my dad, the girls, Noah, Henry, Milo. And for the first time I'm not mad that I left, because if I had stayed, I wouldn't have healed the way that I did. I would have still been the same scared girl I used to be.

Chapter Thirty Five

—'And if love be madness, may I never find sanity again.' ~ John Mark Green ~ ——

The Sun and the Moon~~Isabelle

My happiness from yesterday was short-lived. After eating an impressively made cake, and swimming in the backyard all day, I welcomed my bed with open arms. Only, my bed didn't keep me safe.

The last time I had a vivid nightmare about what happened was a year ago. I had to accept the fact that I can't control my dreams, and sometimes they don't even need to be triggered to happen.

Although I have a sneaking suspicion that this one was caused by the conversation I had with Luna when she was still in the hospital. It was bound to catch up with me eventually.

This one just happened to be a very bad one. I woke up in a panic-like state, thinking he was in my room. It took about an hour for my body to finally give up and realize that it wasn't something real that happened. Just a bad dream.

Though, even after I had calmed down, my mind was still a little messed up, leaving me an overall mess. I took a long shower around 5 a.m, and now it's 6:30, the sun slowly starting to rise.

I dressed myself into a hoodie, and sweatpants, despite the heat that I was feeling. I didn't want my body to be exposed. I need to chill out, just for a second and I'll be good.

I was going to have everyone come over to work on the tree house again, but that idea flew out the window, so I just texted the group chat that I was sick, and they shouldn't come over.

To be honest, I feel sick.

I've pulled the curtains in front of the window, hiding the light that's trying to peek through, and leaving my room in complete darkness. I'm laid in my bed, bundled under all the blankets as if they might protect me.

I haven't closed my eyes though. At least it doesn't feel like I've closed my eyes, not since I woke up. There's a light knock on my door, and then a pause and I know it's my dad. He always waits until I tell him to come in.

"Yeah," My voice is croaky from being used for the first time today, and soft. My voice is so soft. "Can I come in?" My dad askes, and I feel bad to wreck his good mood, knowing he's going to start worrying the minute he walks in. "Yes." I say, even though I just want to say no.

He opens my door slowly, letting bright light flow in, causing me to squint my eyes in pain. The light causes my earlier headache to arise. "Isabelle." He whispers, and I can already hear the concern in his voice.

My body's telling me to put on an act, make it look like I'm ok, but I'm just too exhausted to care. I'll be ok tomorrow, I just need today and then I'll be fine.

I open my eyes, scared of the image my brain might create if I keep them closed for too long. My dad sits on the side of the bed next to me, and feel's my forehead. Maybe he's hoping that I'm sick, and it's not what we both know is going on.

"Honey, you should've come and gotten us," He pauses, looking at me warily, Then moves my hair out of my face and sighs. "Was it a nightmare?" I nod my head, not exactly trusting my voice at the moment.

"Let me call in work, I'll take off—"

"No." I say sharply. "Don't take off, I will be ok. Besides, I'd rather be alone to ride this out. I'll be ok tomorrow." His eyes fill with even more concern. "Luna's at Leo's house, and I really don't think you should be alone right now."

"Please dad, this is what I need." He pauses again, and sighs even louder. "Ok, fine. But you need to text me when you get up to eat. I know you forget when you're stressed out." I nod my head, and force a smile at him.

He leans down, and lays a kiss on my forehead, then finally relents and leaves my room. I hear my parents whispering outside, and then the front door opens and shuts. It's clear they both have left, so I finally sit up on my bed.

My body feels stiff, and my throat feels dry. I really should go and eat something, but I'm afraid I might be sick if I do. So instead, I stand up on my feet and slowly make my way downstairs.

The house is quiet, making me feel like I can finally breathe. I know deep down my dad was right. I really shouldn't be alone, especially if something triggers me again, but I don't like other people seeing me like this.

I need to keep everything together, because if I fall apart, everything will come crumbling down with me. I need to be ok, or else I'll never move past this.

I get myself some ice water and chug it in one go. I'm on my second glass when I hear a knock coming from the front door. My body freezes up, going into panic mood. It's ok Izz, it's not him. Right, he is locked up in prison right now.

I move towards the door slowly, and glance out the side window to see... Milo? What is he doing here? I unlock the door slowly, and crack it open.

He's looking off to the side, which quickly changes when he redirects his vision to me. His eyes take a look of pure concern. Crap. I smile softly at him and say, "Hi." He runs a hand through his hair. "Hi." He says back.

I look around quickly, making sure that the rest of our friends aren't here hiding somewhere. I just need to be alone. Just for one day. "What are you doing here?" I whisper.

He grips the door, and opens it wider, probably so he can walk inside. "Your dad called me. Didn't tell me why, but said that you were going through something and didn't want you to be alone." My eyes widen, and a slight blush consumes my face.

Of course he told Milo to come watch me. Like I need some baby sitter. "Well, I am ok. So thanks. You can go." I start shutting the door, but he pushes back, and opens it even wider.

"I'm staying here, Izz." I huff out an annoyed breath, and shake my head. "Look, whatever my dad told you, he was being dramatic about it. Really, I'm fine." I give him my best smile, hoping he'll believe it.

Just one day. One day.

"You don't look ok, Izz. What's wrong?" I shake my head, and decide that letting him in is easier than telling him what happened.

He walks in, and looks down at me. "How are you not burning up in that?" I shrug, and walk back to the kitchen where I finish another glass of water.

I turn to fill it again, when I feel Milo grip my wrist lightly and turn me around. I gasp, and shake him off, backing up into the fridge. Not now, please not now.

"No hands, got it." He nods, and takes a step back. My breathing even's out quickly, prompting me to reach a relieved hand up and rub my face. When I'm done, I look over at him. He looks freaked out. Oh god, I scared him.

"Sorry." I whisper. "Don't apologize. I just want to understand what's going on." He sounds broken, almost as broken as I feel. "You don't Milo. You really don't." Telling Luna everything that happened was easy. She's my sister, and I knew that no matter what I would survive her reaction.

But if I tell Milo, and he doesn't like me anymore. He finds me just as repulsive as I once found myself. I don't think I could handle it. If Milo left me, I think I would truly be broken. I can't handle him looking at me any other way then he already does.

"I don't know what you've been through, and it was obviously some messed up shit, but I want you to know that I'm here. If you need to talk about it. Sometimes it feels better to talk about it." He shrugs, and turns away, walking over to the pantry.

His words don't really register in my brain until a few seconds later. I shake my head and look at what he's doing. "What are you doing?" He starts grabbing random things that I didn't even know we owned.

"Making you food?" He looks back at me with a quirked brow. "I'm really not hungry right now." I sigh, a little bit of annoyance seeping through my words. "Well, your dad said you need to eat, and I agree. So..." He places the items on the counter, and gives me a pointed look.

I roll my eyes, and cross my arms over my chest. "Fine, what are you making?" He grins, and looks at the things he grabbed. "An omelet? I make good ones." I sigh out in defeat and nod my head. Egg's do sound good right now. "Sure, whatever. Go for it." He laughs softly to himself, while he grabs the main, and last ingredient from the fridge.

I take this as my cue to leave, and walk around the island, so sit down on the stool. I prop my elbows on the table, and rest my face in my hands. Maybe I didn't actually want to be alone. Having Milo here isn't half as bad as I thought.

"Is there anything you absolutely do not want on it?" I shake my head, and look at the stuff he's grabbed. It all seems relatively ok to me.

I watch him cook, zoning out from the quietness. I'm afraid if I look away from Milo, I might get another flashback, or have a panic attack.

He must feel me staring at his back, because he glances behind him, and sees me looking at him. I don't look away though, I just keep staring. Something in my face must show what I'm feeling, because he shakes his head and continues to work.

I must zone out harder than I thought, because Milo is placing the plate down in front of me in seconds, and I'm flinching at the loud noise. He sits beside me, and hands me a fork, while he starts eating his own food. Geez, my mind is so wacked right now.

Looking down at the food, a wave of fatigue and disgust came over me. You're better than him. Don't let him take anything else away from you. As much as I try to fight the images of his hands, the feel of his breath on my neck, it doesn't go away. I shiver, and stare at the food.

"Hey, come on. Don't do that." I look over at Milo in confusion. "What?" He stares back and forth at my eyes, not faltering at all. "Stay out of here." He taps lightly on his temple, showing me what he means. "I don't mean to," I take a deep breath, and let out an even shakier one. "This day just isn't good." I shrug, and finally pick up my fork.

Taking my first bite, I instantly taste the goodness of his food. Then nausea overwhelms me. I push it down, and take another bite. I look over at Milo, and set my fork down. Pushing the heels of my hands into my eyes until I see white, fuzzy static.

I feel Milo's hands grip my wrist gently. So different from his. So different that it doesn't send my body into a panic like it normally would. He pries my hands off of my face and pulls them down to the table. "Did you get any sleep last night?" I let the bile settle before speaking.

"I—" What am I supposed to say? I slept until I was woken up by my rapist in my dreams? I shiver again. He's locked up Isabelle. Calm down. "A little." I shrug. He sighs, and looks at my plate. "Are you done?" He inclined his head towards the food that's barely touched.

A wave of guilt washes over me for not eating it. I shake my head and pick up the fork. Eating a bite a little too big for my mouth, and practically swallowing whole. Milo chuckles softly, and takes the fork from me. "Don't force it down Isabelle. If you're full, that's fine. You can have lunch later." The thought of eating again sends my head spiraling, but I shove it away.

Maybe things will be different later.

"Thanks. It was good." I whisper, he wraps my plate up, and lays it in the fridge, then puts his own dishes in the sink.

He leans over the counter, and smiles at me. "Ya know, if you get changed so you're not burning up, we can go outside. Sun's good for you, it's supposed to make people happy." I snort, and shake my head. "Sun?" He nods quickly

"Vitamin D." He says, as if that explains everything. I huff out a laugh and shake my head. "It's worth a shot." He says again, I sigh, and stand up. "Ok, Give me a second." He nods with a small smile on his face, and I head upstairs.

Looking in my closet, all I see are exposing clothes. I try on shorts, but my conscious screams back at me. Definitely not wearing a dress. I change my thick sweatpants to thin leggings, but keep my oversized sweatshirt on.

I leave my hair down, having it wavy from laying on it while it dried. I stare at myself in the bathroom mirror, seeing my dark eye bags, and rosy cheeks. Probably from literally burning in this outfit. I sigh, and shake my head, making my way down stairs.

Reaching the bottom, I see Milo on the couch looking at his phone intently. His eyebrows scrunched together. I clear my throat, letting him know that I'm here, and rolling on the balls on my feet.

He looks up, glances at my clothes, and shakes his head. "Izz, you're going to overheat in that." I shrug, and rub my eyes. He stands up from his spot on the couch and starts walking towards the backyard.

I freeze when I see our friends all hanging out. What the heck? When did they even get here? "Milo. I don't wanna hang out with people today...I can't." I pause and try to straighten my hair to at least look a little presentable.

I can't let my friends see me like this. God, what would they think? "Hey," he tilts my chin upward so I'm staring at his eyes. "No ones gonna judge you. You're having a bad day. We all do. What'd I say about this." This time he taps the side of my head.

"Stay out of it." I whisper. He smiles and nods in pride. "Exactly. Smile sunshine," He winks, "Can't be night forever." As hard as I try to stop it, his statement drags the smile right out of me. Tingles shooting through my body, giving me a jolt of happiness that I wish I could keep forever.

I don't get to say anything , because he's walking away before I can collect my thoughts.

'Smile sunshine, can't be night forever.'

———

Milo was right. I think the sun does make people happy. Well, it's not like my moods completely changed, but at least I'm not thinking about him anymore. It might also have to do with my friends being here.

Noah may be a little annoying with how much he doesn't stop talking, but at least he's keeping me on top. Out of my head, as Milo would say.

God, what's gotten into me? All I can think about is him. It doesn't help that all three men are working on the tree house. Yeah, they're all helping out, trying to get it done while I sit here and process everything.

It's strange, because I feel so alone all the time. Like I have no one, when in reality, I have a whole freaking family by my side, waiting for the moment to pick me up when I fall. Maybe I need to stop thinking about what I don't have, and start remembering what I do, what I should be thankful for.

"You know that's bad for your teeth." Henry says, drawing me back to their conversation. "Suck my—" Milo's hand comes down over Noah's mouth, covering the rest of whatever Noah was about to say. When he finally lets go, Noah grabs a chunk of ice and puts it in his mouth, then grabs Henry and chews it in his ear.

"Don't you just love them." Violet sighs, lifting her sunglasses from her face. We've been tanning. Ok, Lottie and Violet have been tanning, while I sit here, and burn to pieces under my clothes. I want to change, I really do, but I don't think I can handle staring at myself just yet.

I smile at them, hating that I know it doesn't quite reach my eyes. "You should really get into a bathing suit, and absorb the sun." Lottie says. I smile wider, and shake my head slightly. "Want me to get more lemonade?" They both nod, staring at the sky through their sunglasses.

I dart through the door, and sigh when I get to the kitchen island. Sweat dripped down my neck, catched at the creases of my elbows, my knees.

I take the seat at the counter, and lean my head against the cool marble top. Maybe I should just suck it up and put on a short sleeve shirt. "I told you." A strangled scream comes out of my throat, and I shoot up to see Milo standing at the door, in all his tattoo glory, with his hands on his hips.

"Huh?" I clear my throat, and stare at him in confusion. He stares at me for a few seconds, a concerned look taking over his features, then shakes his head.

"Come on. I'm not letting you wear that anymore." My face hardens, and I purse my lips. "Excuse you." My voice deepens only slightly, while I stare at him with irritation. He smiles, and laughs. "What?" I hissed quietly. "I'm not arguing with you. Nor am I letting you burn to death like that." My eyes narrowed unintentionally.

"I'm not–" He steps closer to me, then closer and– "No." I jump up from my seat, only for him to crouch downwards and throw me over his shoulder. "Put me down, Milo, or so help me–" I screech, then pause when I feel his bare, heated skin against me.

"Ew, oh my gosh you're sweaty!" I hear him laugh, and feel his chest rumble against my legs. I look upwards with a groan, only to see our whole friend group staring at me, laughing through the smooshed glass door.

My face flames, and I–sweaty skin forgotten–drop my head against his back with a mix of a groan and a whine. "Milo." He laughs again, only fueling my embarrassment, and anger.

He goes up the stairs two at a time, pausing when he reaches my bedroom door. Then, surprisingly, he lowers me slowly to the ground. Large hands supporting my hips until he knows I'm stable, then withdrawing slowly.

I cross my arms like a toddler that's getting in trouble, and stare upward at him as if he's not practically a head taller than me.

"Well, go on." I roll my eyes, and ignore the urge to wipe the sweaty strands of hair from my face. "I'm not your pet, or someone you can just command to do whatever you want." He sighs, and looks me over again. Then, with a softer voice, says. "Can you please go change? I don't like seeing you like this."

"Like what?"

"In pain. I don't like seeing you suffer." The way he's looking at me, with pure honesty, compels me to relent and finally go change. "I'm doing this for me." I exclaim, making sure he knows I most definitely did not cave because of him. A slow grin crawls up his cheek. "Sure, ok."

I can't help but look at the beautifully painted moon and sun intertwined by flowers over his heart. It's red, giving me the notion that it's new. As I change into an oversized t-shirt, and shorts, I think of the tattoo nonstop.

The sun, and the moon had beautiful faces, eyes closed with the moon kissing the sun's forehead. Such a simple tattoo, yet I have a nagging feeling that it means so much more than that.

9 781805 107705